Paradise Palms

Red Menace Mob

Paul Haddad

Black Rose Writing | Texas

The author grants the final approval for this literary material.

First printing

This is a work of fiction. Names, characters, businesses, places, events, and incidents are either the products of the author's imagination or used in a fictitious manner. Any resemblance to actual persons, living or dead, or actual events is purely coincidental.

ISBN: 978-1-68433-720-0
PUBLISHED BY BLACK ROSE WRITING
www.blackrosewriting.com

Printed in the United States of America
Suggested Retail Price (SRP) $19.95

Paradise Palms is printed in Garamond

Cover photo: "110 Freeway exit from US 101 (1950s)" by Eric Fischer, licensed under CC BY 2.0

*As a planet-friendly publisher, Black Rose Writing does its best to eliminate unnecessary waste to reduce paper usage and energy costs, while never compromising the reading experience. As a result, the final word count vs. page count may not meet common expectations.

To my father, Jack

Paradise Palms

Red Menace Mob

I

SOMETHING IN THE AIR

CHAPTER 1

Marta Shapiro would have approved. That much, Max is sure about.

Hell, he had picked the damn thing out himself. Not as cheap as the Abraham (plain pine) nor as excessive as the Galilee (oiled black walnut), the mahogany-glazed poplar Solomon casket "represents a happy confluence of funereal elegance and fiscal pragmatism in the humble Jewish tradition." Says so right on the yellow description tag, still visible on the base molding. Now, with his wife mere minutes from being lowered into the earth, Max imagines her spirit spending eternity in dignified repose instead of condemning him from the grave for one final dopey decision in their forty-seven-year marriage.

A portly rabbi with a triangular beard and hexagon specs gently undulates in solemn prayer. Behind him, two gravediggers in coveralls hunch over shovels. A steady drizzle has started, blotting the coffin with dime-sized droplets.

"Even God weeps," says the rabbi, gazing skyward with a shrewd smile.

The morning began as any other crisp fall day in Los Angeles. But as the service progressed, tufts of gray clouds coalesced into a zeppelin-shaped mass over Mt. Lee, where a radio tower seemed to split open the misty dirigible, spilling its rainy contents on Mount Sinai Cemetery in the Hollywood Hills at just this very moment.

Umbrellas fan open among the dozens of mourners. From his front aisle folding chair, Max gazes impassively at his wife's tomb. His face is the texture of chewed taffy, the residue of a hardscrabble childhood in Chicago's South Side, where fists spoke louder than words. Even now, pushing seventy, Max commands an Everest-sized presence that towers above his stooped frame.

Next to him, a buxom redhead with ruby-red lipstick has opened her funeral program to create a shield over Max's head, bald but for a frayed nylon yarmulke. Her other hand alternately squeezes his veiny wrist and dabs her eyes with a handkerchief. Her name is Abigail Schlebercoff, though only her mother calls her that. The world knows her as Kitty Kay, Max's twenty-nine-year-old companion.

"Crocodile tears." David Shapiro whispers the words into Leo's ear, cocking his head to his immediate left to indicate Kitty. Leo leans forward, squinting over wire-rim glasses. He notices Kitty dropping her hanky into a green-scale leather clutch.

"Goes with her alligator purse," he says.

David grins, the two bonding over their shared contempt. No one ever believes them when the thirty-four-year-old siblings inform strangers they're fraternal twins. Square-jawed and dark-haired, David bears a passing resemblance to Montgomery Clift – before his accident – with expressive eyes that somehow manage to be alert, brooding and soulful all at once. Leo is lazy-eyed with thinning hair and sloped shoulders, perpetually sickly-looking. Family lore attributes his condition to being stuck in the womb with minimal oxygen after David came bounding out.

The rabbi drones on, reading from Psalm 91. "Whoever dwells in the shelter of the Most High will rest in the shadow of the Almighty…"

David crooks his wristwatch and glances over his shoulder, annoyed, like someone waiting for a tardy bus. And then, as if on cue, two security guards in the back row block a visitor from entering the assemblage.

The intruder is a swarthy man in his late twenties. He is attired in a leather jacket, white tee and cuffed blue jeans. The guards mistake him for a cemetery employee, perhaps one of the gravediggers.

"We got it covered, mac," one of them says. "Thanks."

The man whips off his sunglasses, revealing a C-shaped scar that runs from the top of his forehead through his left eyebrow. "I'm a *Shapiro*," he hisses, stamping out his cigarette. "That's my *mom* they're burying."

The guards clear a path. "Our apologies. We thought you were…"

"Gimme one of 'em beanie caps."

He grabs a black yarmulke from a folding table. By now, most guests have turned around to witness the commotion, none too surprised. Rudolph Shapiro. *Rudy*. Who else would make such a raucous entrance?

Rudy nods at the grievers and flashes his pearly whites. He slips the yarmulke over his greasy pompadour and grabs a program, sliding it into his jacket's inner-pocket over a Santa Anita Racing Form.

As Rudy walks down the aisle, he betrays a slight limp, as if one leg is longer than the other. He finds an empty seat next to Aaron Shapiro. At thirty-two, the striking Aaron possesses the tossed-off élan of a male cigarette model. He bends toward Rudy, never breaking eye contact with the rabbi.

"Nice of you to join us," he whispers. "Another two minutes and Mom would be six-feet under."

The diggers stand on either side of the coffin as the rabbi wraps up the service: "The Everlasting is her heritage, and she shall rest peacefully at her lying place. And let us say… amen."

"Amen," comes the group reply.

The rabbi bows his head. The diggers crank the shaft that will drop Marta into the abyss. A loud howl pierces the clanking chains.

It's Kitty, blubbering into Max's shoulder.

• • •

The reception is on the other side of the hill. Fifties-model sedans and station wagons stream into the turncourt of a single-story California Mission-style hotel flanked by palm trees. In the distance, the gray clouds that shrouded Mt. Lee have parted, bathing the Hollywood Sign in brilliant sunshine. Framed against this world icon, the hostelry should make for a picture-perfect postcard with "Wish You Were Here" salutations. But the hotel's best days are clearly behind it. Neglect is everywhere, evidenced by broken red-clay shingles, chipped adobe stucco and grubby landscape. The palms' fronds droop forlornly, their spindly black-specked trunks resembling the legs of old men with age spots.

As the guests file through the front doors, they pass a squat wooden sign reading "Paradise Palms," with a "Vacancy" placard permanently affixed below it. Not that anyone would notice. Much of the sign has been devoured by the hungry violet vines of an untamed bougainvillea.

The interior of the hotel features a checkout counter and spacious lobby. Mismatched couches cluster around a Zenith television set. The only visible employee is desk manager Darlene Flanagan, a raven-maned thirty-two-year-old with skin the color of vanilla ice cream. With her cool Bettie Page vibe, Darlene is perhaps one of only four gals in all of L.A. to sport a tattoo — a flaming heart wrapped in barbed wire on her right shoulder. But the Shapiros also admire her implacable manner, the adroit way she makes lodgers feel like VIPs while simultaneously ensuring that the hotel always comes out ahead.

The majority of the procession turns to the right, past two easels. The first one holds a sign advertising The Easy Bar & Restaurant. Over it, Darlene has taped a handwritten note: "Closed for private event." The other easel displays a large sepia-toned photograph of a plump, plain lady with wavy white hair. She looks off-camera, unsmiling, an off-key note to the fuzzy halo that frames her. Burned into the bottom of the photo, bold typeface announces: "MARTA D. SHAPIRO, 1889-1957."

A shriveled old lady in a black floral dress and veiled hat pauses at Marta's image and scowls. Rochelle Shapiro, Max's older sister, does not approve.

"What was Max thinking?" she huffs to a youthful, dark-skinned man charging past her with a box of takeout. "She always hated that picture."

"Yes, ma'am," grunts the man. Sharply dressed in a red vest and black bow tie, Francisco "Franny" Gomez Jr. doesn't have a resting state – he is a human wave of perpetual motion who somehow never has a hair out of place, part of the overworked Cuban father-son tandem that runs The Easy. Having attended the funeral, Franny and Francisco were unable to prepare lunch for the party. On David's advice, they catered from nearby Don the Beachcomber, its name blazoned on bags with Polynesian flair.

Franny leans back-first into the swing door of The Easy, propping it open to allow Rochelle to trundle into the restaurant.

"Hold up, hijo!" hollers Francisco. Matching his son in dress and handsome elegance, he dashes through the portal with a second box from Don's. Franny pirouettes into the dining room, the door flapping shut behind them.

Inside, the Gomezes spread the feast over a long serving table. Big band swing chugs out of a jukebox as family and friends mill about the eatery, a shopworn yet cozy room of dark corners and linen tablecloths that have yellowed over time. Three adorable children – two girls and a boy – climb into a burgundy-leather booth. Peggy, their eye-catchingly attractive but harried mother, clomps over to them in stiletto heels and sets down three paper plates of Chow Dun, a Don the Beachcomber specialty comprised of scrambled eggs and crab meat. The kids all make faces.

"Eeeeew!" howls Jolene, the eldest at nine years old.

Peggy fixes her hands on her hips. "What's wrong?"

"It looks like scrambled brains!"

The kids squeal in mock horror. Peggy angrily curls her lips.

David, Leo and Aaron drift through the room, accepting condolences, sharing anecdotes, making sure everyone's glasses are never empty.

David's eagle eye catches his father and Kitty by the bar, where Rudy is shaking up Smirnoff vodka martinis. Franny floats by with a tray of bacon-wrapped concoctions. Kitty stabs one with a toothpick and feeds it to Max. After chomping down, he grabs the toothpick from her red-clawed fingertips and uses it to pick his teeth. Kitty rocks back with forced laughter. She kisses his fleshy jowl, leaving a smudge of lipstick.

Rudy hands martinis to Kitty and his father, saving one for himself. They toast. As Kitty turns to chat with Rudy, David makes for the bar and inserts himself between Kitty and Max.

"Does she have to be here?" David asks under his breath. He pulls out his pocket square to wipe his father's cheek. Max slaps at him as if swatting a mosquito.

"Do I approve your lady friends?" he grouses.

"I was really hoping we could all spend some time after Mom's funeral together. As a family."

Max works the toothpick around his mouth. "Your mother, God rest her soul, blessed my social affairs. All those years she was sick…"

"C'mon, don't start that…"

"'Go find someone who makes you happy,' she says. 'Don't be a martyr. Live your life!'"

"*My* girlfriends aren't trying to get their hooks in this hotel, Pop!"

Max removes his gnarled toothpick and flicks it toward David. It glances off his tie and falls to the floor. David, alternately shocked and chastened, picks it up and disposes of it in his back pocket.

"Sorry," he mumbles.

"Shame on you." Max grabs Kitty by the elbow and shoves off.

• • •

Leo, eyes closed, rubs his fingers over his thinning pate and exhales. He is parked at a urinal in the men's room, enjoying a few moments of private relief. Behind him, he hears the door creak open, followed by the loud unbuckling of pants.

Rudy slides into the adjacent urinal, the force of his piss-spray rivaling that of a racehorse.

"Leo Leo, my lion bruthuh," slurs Rudy, wearing a heavy-lidded grin. "I could really use some scratch. Spot me a fifty?"

Leo looks at him. "Why?"

Rudy rolls his head, cracking his neck. "Entertainment expenses. Show some cats a good time, get 'em interested in the Palms. You yourself said – "

"No, I mean, why *now*?"

Rudy focuses on Leo's face, blinking hard, as if trying to solve a word jumble.

"Because if he leaves now, he can still make the seventh race at Santa Anita." It's David, just entering the john.

Rudy twists his torso around and sheepishly smiles. "Guilty as charged!" he declares, raising his free hand.

David shakes his head, his voice acidic. "You're pathetic. You show up late. Leave early. Party never ends, eh, Rudy?" As Rudy steps away from the urinal, David takes his place, still hectoring. "Show some respect to your dead mother. To Pop. Grieve with your friends and family, for Chrissake, like normal people do. Or at least fake it for a few more hours."

Rudy sparks up a cigarette, blowing the smoke in David's direction.

"You'd rather me hanging around here, getting hammered at the bar?" he asks coolly.

Leo, washing up at the sink, catches David in the mirror – the kid has a point. David turns back to the urinal.

"Give him the money," he sighs to the wall.

Leo pulls a billfold from his pocket, peels off a fifty. Rudy snatches it and beats a quick retreat before David can change his mind.

•   •   •

Back in the dining room, Max is doing magic tricks with Peggy's children – the old nickel-out-of-your-ear and got-your-nose shtick. The younger two react with wide-eyed wonder while Jolene offers a jaded smile. Aaron comes up behind Max, winking and grinning at the children. He leans into Max's ear.

"Pop, we gotta talk," he whispers.

"If it's about business, I already told your brother to get lost."

"I don't mean now. But soon. Let me schedule some time with Darlene, get it on the books."

Max doesn't react.

"*There* you are." It's Peggy, oozing annoyance at Aaron, and it's clear now that she and the children make up his family unit. "There's nothing here for the kids to eat."

Aaron turns to face her, offended at the suggestion – after all, they dropped a fortune on takeout. "There's rumaki from Don's. It's delicious."

"It's chicken livers wrapped in pig meat. Have Francisco fix them hot dogs."

Aaron watches her march away. When he turns around, Max has already returned to the bar. Francisco hands him a tumbler of bourbon and a tablespoon, then emits a short, sharp whistle as he waves a towel in the air. From across the room, Franny nods to his dad and unplugs the jukebox from the wall, Ella Fitzgerald's sonorous voice slowing to a warbling hush.

"Everyone, can I get your attention please?" Max booms, clinking his tumbler.

The conversation dims, necks craning in his direction.

Max wags his head in disbelief. "Twenty-seven years ago…" His voice trails off in a phlegmy wisp. After an uncomfortably long pause, he takes a belt of bourbon, which seems to revive him.

"Twenty-seven years ago, I was managing the flower shop at the Hollywood Hotel. I thought I was on top of the world. Leave it to Marta to tell me what a failure I was!"

The room chuckles, except for his sons – unsure where he's going with this.

"But you know what? She was right." Max's eyes, lost in gauzy remembrance, find David, Aaron and Leo. "You guys were just little squirts back then. What did I know? The stock market had just crashed. But I had a job!"

Knowing nods from the older folks.

Max continues gazing at his sons. "But your mother… she was already looking ahead. Told me about another hotel down the street. The Mission Court Inn. We walk on over. You talk about a dump!"

More laughter.

"I says, 'Why the hell would I leave my cushy job to work here?' And she says, 'I don't want you to *work* at this dump. I want you to *buy* it.'"

Murmurs of amused assent. Yup. Marta.

"The place was in foreclosure. We took out a loan. Won the auction! Next thing I know, I'm schlepping the whole damn family into rooms one and two. But Marta wasn't done. It was her idea to change the name to Paradise Palms and pretty it up. And turn this old speakeasy into the classy joint that it is."

He pauses to look around the room, eyes glistening.

"Me – an owner? Nah. Just a lucky sonofabitch who was too scared to stand up to his wife."

A heavy reverence hangs in the room. Max stares into his drink, as if the enormity of Marta's absence is just now hitting him. He exhales. Smiles. Raises his glass into the air. The others follow.

"Here's to the woman who made all this possi—"

He's interrupted by the sudden *pooosh* of the restaurant's door swinging open. It's Darlene. She enters with a stricken look, as if she's seen a ghost. Just as quickly, she realizes she's ruined her boss's sacred moment.

"I'm—I'm sorry, Mr. Shapiro," she says in a halting, sultry register, backing out of the room. "I can come back later."

Max is unperturbed. "What is it?"

"I don't know. It's some... *thing*. In space. *Outer* space." Her eyes find Aaron, Leo and David. "It's the Russians."

The entire timbre of the room changes. Guests turn to each other with nervous gasps and "oh my God" interjections. Max swills the last of his drink, then scuttles out the door. For a moment, no one moves. But when it's obvious he's not coming back, Darlene and a parade of guests trail him into the lobby.

Max squats in front of the Zenith, its rounded screen encased in a wooden cabinet the size of an icebox. As he adjusts the rabbit ears, the ghostly black-and-white image of Chet Huntley, NBC News's distinguished anchor, flickers into focus from a New York studio. The guests settle into seats. Others are too on-edge to sit during a possible national emergency. Darlene increases the volume on the Space Command remote control.

Huntley reads copy in a somber baritone, glasses perched on the edge of his nose. Behind him is a graphic of a metal sphere with protruding antennae and the familiar hammer-and-sickle Russian emblem, along with the word "SPUTNIK."

"And so to recap," Huntley says, "at ten twenty-nine p.m., local Moscow time, on this fourth day of October, nineteen-fifty-seven, the Soviet Union launched the world's first artificial moon, designed to orbit the Earth at eighteen thousand miles an hour. The U.S. Defense Department predicts it will take only ninety-six minutes to complete one orbit, with a trajectory that will send it over our United States several times a day."

Max staggers backwards, collapsing into a loveseat. "God help us…"

"What do they want with it?" Kitty cries, squeezing next to him.

David seizes on the moment to assuage everyone's fears. "It's for science. Microwaves and weather mapping. We've been developing one ourselves."

But no one's buying it. All eyes are glued to the screen, filtering in only dread and doom. Aaron and Peggy's children scan the grown-ups' scared faces. Guests begin to chatter. Conspiracy theories float through the air, colliding in chaotic trajectories.

"Clearly they wanna spy on us," says Dirk Havenhurst, a frail long-term guest with a thin mustache and hand-carved walking staff. "Know where to target our missile bases."

"They said this is how World War Three would begin," says a bald, pudgy man named Art Mankowitz, another regular.

Peggy wraps her brood in her arms. "Aaron, the children!"

"Everyone, shut up!" Max roars. "Darlene, turn it up!"

Darlene boosts the volume.

Huntley drones on: "The so-called satellite transmits a radio code every three-tenths of a second. No one knows what these beeps signify, if anything, only that their frequency is somewhere between twenty and forty megahertz…"

Out of nowhere, an air raid siren begins to sound outside. Its earsplitting wail sends the room into a tizzy. The children are outright sobbing now. Even David looks shaken.

"Called it," Dirk utters matter-of-factly.

"Everyone duck and cover!" bleats Art. He grabs a sofa cushion and hits the floor, face-down. He bends the cushion over his fat neck, cowering beneath it.

A second, more distant siren blares under the first one. They're going off all over the city now. David checks his watch, then the wall clock. 3 p.m. On the dot. He raises his voice above the delirium. "Everyone, calm down! It's just the usual test, first Friday of every month!"

"But what if this one's *real*?" Art cries, his voice muffled under the cushion.

"Yeah," another lodger says. "What if it's just a coincidence they're testing sirens right at the same time that Sputnik thing is dropping bombs on us?"

David opens his mouth to respond but no words come out. Even if that Sputnik thing doesn't pose a threat, he can't deny that something has changed. Something from which the world's two superpowers will never return in an endless game of one-upmanship. The fact that the Soviet Union got to space first unsettles David, not out of any sense of nationalistic envy, but because it underscores the fallibility of the natural order of things. If the Communists can launch a satellite, what other existential threat is out there? From which random place will it come? And when will it hit *them*?

Suddenly, a wiry madman with a patchy goatee and matted hair explodes into the lobby, wild-eyed and flailing his scab-ridden arms. His right hand clutches a pistol. He is stark naked.

"It's happening!" he shrieks. "It's finally happening!"

The guests scream and dive for the floor, covering their heads like Art.

The lunatic leaps onto a sofa and points his gun upward. He tilts his ear toward the ceiling, as if receiving auditory signals through the sirens. "Radio Khrushchev is calling. The Presidium jacked my wavelength. I am a proletariat of intellectual labor. We are all grave-diggers of the bourgeoisie!"

He fires off a round into the overhead light fixture. Shards of glass rain down on the guests, who slither for shelter under chairs and tables.

"Rise up, fellow proletarians! The revolution has begun!!!"

Whuuump! The shooter is blindsided by David and Aaron, rushing him with the force of linebackers. He yelps like a wounded puppy as they slam his nude body onto the ground, his gun skidding across the floor.

CHAPTER 2

Aaron Shapiro cruises down the Miracle Mile in his pride and joy – a spotless white '57 Chevy Bel Air with a fire-engine red leather interior. It's nighttime but the top is down. Aaron likes the rush of air against his face, whiffs of night-blooming jasmine perfuming smog-filled promises of civic progress. A song comes on the radio, a new number from Buddy Holly and the Crickets called "That'll Be the Day." Aaron cranks it. He dangles his left arm out the window frame and drums his fist against the hardbody. Even the normally staid David can't resist its rockabilly rhythm, bopping his head in the passenger seat. Through the rearview mirror, Aaron peeks at Leo in the backseat. He is staring out the window, lost in silent thought.

"What's the matter, Leo?" Aaron taunts. "You should like this guy. Four-eyes just like you!"

Leo returns Aaron's gaze. With his best deadpan expression, he wiggles the left arm of his glasses, making his specs bounce up and down on his nose. Aaron chuckles. Leo blithely looks off again.

The Bel Air passes the Ambassador Hotel's World Famous Cocoanut Grove, where Nat King Cole is tonight's featured performer. More luxury hotels blur by, their colorful neon signs fleeting electric rainbows across the windshield. The Mayfair. The Asbury. The Arcady. Park Wilshire. The Town House. The Gaylord.

Aaron hugs his mahogany and chrome steering wheel and lights a cigarette. He makes a sweeping gesture from side to side, smoke trailing his hand.

"Look at this… everywhere. What do you see?"

"Wealth we can only imagine," cracks Leo.

"I see neon," says David.

"Bingo." Aaron slows the car so his brothers can get a better look. "Most of these buildings are thirty, forty years old. In ten years, they'll all be torn down or converted to apartments."

David looks at him. "So what're you, comparing the Palms to these palaces?"

Aaron shrugs. "Wilshire is a dying destination. Everything's moving west. All that's left are neon signs selling ghost glamour."

The brothers ruminate on Aaron's appraisal. Aaron never had the business sense of David or a proclivity for numbers like Leo. His strengths were more qualitative. A preternatural sense of people's needs, how to spot trends, a flair for timing.

As a teenager, Aaron's first job outside of hotel duties was designing World War II bond campaigns for the U.S. government. He had taken an art class at Hollywood High School, where students were given an assignment to draft mock war bond posters. The instructor was so taken by his work, he arranged for Aaron to meet with the local war bond commission. They were equally impressed and put him on payroll. Even more exciting for Aaron was the day he got to shake hands with Bob Hope, perennial hawker of wartime causes.

Collaborating with a resident artist at Paradise Palms, Aaron created a series of posters that pulled at the heartstrings of everyday Americans. One of them showed a pigtailed little girl squatting next to her angelic-looking mother to fill a scrapbook with U.S. war stamps. Next to them, Daddy's olive army helmet rested on the ground. Was he dead, or simply fighting overseas? It didn't matter; the depiction of an absentee father is what did. Across the bottom were the words: "The smallest of help can lead to our greatest triumph – Buy U.S. War Bonds."

With a degree in art from UCLA, Aaron grew frustrated by intermittent design jobs. The starving artist routine wasn't for him and his fiancée Peggy. He started buying up small properties on the fringes of the San Fernando Valley. His older brothers mocked him for throwing money away on weedy backwater plots, but it was Aaron who got the last laugh. Lured by easy government financing, returning G.I.'s from Europe, the Pacific and Korea flocked to L.A.'s newest suburbia to reap their just rewards of sparkling swimming pools, backyard barbecues and detached two-car garages. To their credit, David and Leo were quick to partner with Aaron on future investments, though Aaron still maintains his own portfolio of properties. Rudy may be the unpredictable joker card, but Aaron, David and Leo are that rare suit of siblings who are also tight friends, as close in business as they are in blood. Their partnership is forged out of mutual respect, an understanding that the sum of their efforts exceeds their individual parts. By 1955, the trio solidified their commitment by setting up a shingle at the Palms – Shapiro Bros. Properties. If they thought the *present* looked bright, David liked to say, the future was a fucking supernova.

But then Marta got sick. Over the next two years, the boys got sucked into helping their rudderless father not just operate the Palms, but keep it solvent. Much as they'd like to pull back from the hospitality business, the hotel sits on primo Hollywood property. Keeping it in the family remains their biggest priority.

As the Bel Air rolls through Beverly Hills, Aaron decelerates so his brothers can take in the Beverly Hilton Hotel, a gleaming white monolith whose sleek modernity starkly contrasts the puce Beaux Arts buildings in the rearview mirror.

"Conrad Hilton…" Aaron waggles his head in admiration. "Now there's a goy who got two things right in his life. Marrying Zsa Zsa Gabor. And opening this beaut just a couple years back."

Leo is unmoved. "Looks like a beached cruise ship."

"Welton Becket," David chimes in. "Same schnook who designed that Capitol Records monstrosity."

"It's what's inside that counts," Aaron replies, a tinge of irritation over having to explain the obvious. "Five hundred eighty-two rooms. Five hundred eighty-two televisions."

"A TV in every room?" David asks, genuinely impressed.

"Along with air conditioning, private patios… even blow dryers in the johns."

"And a mint on every pillow?" Leo again.

Aaron drives on, merging back into traffic. "Go 'head. Laugh. But even with all those rooms, the Hilton is turning people away." Aaron flings a glance at Leo. "And *Pop's* place? Twenty-four rooms, twelve of them empty. Christ, even my nine-year-old could do the math on that shitty occupancy rate."

The brothers' silence speaks for them. The Palms is in trouble, and they take it personally. When the hell did it all go so wrong?

•   •   •

It opened in 1926 as the Mission Court Inn, an alluring destination during a simpler era. The original owner, a wealthy bachelor named Theodore Kester Baldwick, had grown up in the San Joaquin Valley. His fondest memories were staying in California Mission-style motels whenever his family passed through Fresno on the way to Lake Tahoe. Years later, Baldwick recalled those motels when he built one of his own at the intersection of Selma Avenue and McCadden Place. The site's proximity to the legendary Hollywood Hotel was hardly coincidental. The businessman rightly predicted that cowtowners visiting Tinseltown would patronize the Mission Court once they realized they couldn't afford its rarified neighbor. To build his twenty-four room inn, he commissioned the architectural firm F & F Stanislaus – the same folks behind the Mission-style motels of his youth and their first job in Southern California.

Alas, T.K. Baldwick's good fortune was short-lived. The Wall Street Crash of 1929 wiped out his stock assets, rendering him cash poor. T.K. was already highly leveraged before the crash, having just closed escrow on property along the Long Beach boardwalk. As tourism dried up, Baldwick slashed his room rates, which lowered vacancies but left him short on mortgage payments. In a final desperate bid, he converted the Mission Court's coffee grill into a speakeasy. LAPD vice shut it down, prompting T.K. to fritter away more money on an unscrupulous defense attorney.

By the fall of 1930, Baldwick's holdings were in foreclosure. On October 29 – one year to the day of the market's crash – a flower shop manager named Max Shapiro and his wife Marta purchased the Mission Court Inn at a bank auction. In a cruel irony, Max's shop was located in the Hollywood Hotel. The old Victorian bastion had weathered the Depression fairly well, thanks to a robust stable of live-in celebrities like Jean Acker, John Gilbert and Norma Shearer.

The Shapiros never did know what happened to T.K. Baldwick after he lost the Mission Court Inn. Rumors were that he slunk back to Fresno to work at his uncle's filling station. Then, one day in 1938, a letter arrived from a frequent hotel guest who was visiting family in San Francisco. On her drive north, she had popped into a Fresno diner and bought a newspaper. Her letter said: "Dear Max, wasn't this the man who owned your hotel?" She attached an article from *The Fresno Bee*. Baldwick's entire life was reduced to a blunt, cold headline:

Fresno Resident Theodore Kester Baldwick, 41, Found Dead in Bathroom, Single Gunshot to Head. Coroner Rules Death by Suicide

Since the structure was only four years old when they assumed ownership, Max and Marta didn't sink much capital into their new venture. Only later did they learn that Baldwick – or was it F & F Stanislaus? – did everything on the cheap. Like a car reaching its warranty, everything seemed to break down at once at the ten-year mark – burst pipes, frayed wires, leaky roofs, rodent invasions. Max threatened to unload the "schlocky money suck" once and for all. But Marta convinced him to stay the course. Sure enough, business picked up after the Second World War as prosperity returned to American shores and the advent of live television ushered in a Hollywood renaissance.

Aaron was the first to warn about the double-edged sword of progress. He could see the landscape changing throughout the car culture '50s. Young people with disposable income didn't want to stay in kitschy Mission motels or eat in homestyle beaneries like their parents did. They preferred Googie-style drive-ins with greasy burgers and midcentury hotels with swimming pools and bars. Unless it changed with the times, Aaron warned, Paradise Palms would become obsolete.

Max resisted. Business was good, he argued, and the Palms was starting to turn a profit. So the brothers leaned on their mother. In public, Marta deferred to Max, but privately everyone knew she possessed superior business acumen. She agreed to the boys' recommended renovations, as long as they were incremental. To ease her mind, Leo assured her he would not take on any new loans until the old ones were paid off, though this oath didn't last.

David was tasked with overseeing the improvements. The first was to convert the old speakeasy space – relegated to storage and a basic kitchen – into a proper bar and restaurant. In a nod to its former life, the family named it The Easy. Rudy took to the fully stocked bar like a shark to blood, installing himself as its head bartender. Marta ran the kitchen along with Francisco, a newly arrived Cuban immigrant who moved his family to the States after rumblings of a revolution.

The other big change was to convert much of the courtyard into a swimming pool. From day one, this proved a nightmare. Leo could not believe how many city permits were required to simply break ground. Once they did, they churned through three construction companies, each more corrupt than the previous. By the time the 15-by-30-foot pool was finished twenty months later, the final tally was double the original estimate.

Still, its completion was reason to celebrate. The Shapiros threw a nighttime pool party for their guests. In a private aside, Max conceded to David – unofficially the hotel's property manager – that he had done good. The pool looked like it belonged there all along, certainly better than the sandy crabgrass it replaced. Max remarked how its rectangular blue water was nicely bordered by the hotel's four wings – "like a picture frame." As its shimmering surface reflected intersecting klieg lights from a premiere at Grauman's Chinese Theatre, the courtyard now seemed a magical manifestation of the California dream.

Their quiet moment was interrupted by a shitfaced friend of Rudy's screeching "Cannonball!" Launching himself from the west-wing rooftop, he aimed to clear the concrete deck and plunge into the deep end.

He missed it by five feet.

Paramedics treated him for two broken ankles and lacerations to his hands and face. The accident put the skids on the soiree, and everyone retired to their rooms. Max was the first to bail the scene, leaving David to handle the mess. His abrupt departure reinforced what David had already suspected.

The fate of Paradise Palms was resting more and more in his hands.

CHAPTER 3

David soldiers past the birds of paradise lining the walkway between the lobby and swimming pool. He's dressed in a casual charcoal suit with an open-collared shirt and slip-on oxfords, a look that says, "Important but not pretentious." He whistles tunelessly, chin jutted upward. He had read in *Reader's Digest* that whistling is a natural repellant to stress. That, and good posture. He is going to need both this morning.

A cleaning cart sits just off the path. Two African American maids in freshly starched white uniforms – one about fifty, the other in her twenties – organize supplies as they prepare to clean rooms.

"Yolanda... Flori..." David gives them a little wave as he passes. The women smile back placidly.

As David resumes his warbling jaunt, the pool comes into view – or what remains of it. Dead leaves drift aimlessly on its green, gnat-infested waters. "The Swamp," David calls it. "An insult to swamps," Leo always retorts. The pool's wretched condition is the product of a chicken-and-egg argument among family members. Why throw away good money to keep it clean and heated when hardly anyone uses it anymore? On the other hand, why would anyone brave its brackish water, which looks like it could harbor the Creature from the Black Lagoon?

Nonetheless, knee-jerk pride compels David to fish out an empty carton of Viceroys floating by the pool's edge. He notices a scrawny goateed guest sunning himself on a chaise longue, with little opaque goggles to block out the sun. A ball-point pen and open spiral-bound notepad rest on his swim trunks. The pages are blank.

"Doing okay, Elron?" David asks.

Elron Jakes jerks upright, goggles tumbling off his face. He squints at David and paws his brow. He's the same naked gunman who stormed the lobby.

"Hi David," he croaks. "Didn't see you standing there."

"You don't remember, do you?"

Elron squints harder, shielding his eyes with his jittery right arm. "Remember...?"

"Last night. You were in rare form." David chuckles. "If you want your pellet gun, Darlene's got it locked up."

David spots fresh track marks on the underside of Elron's arm.

"Y'know, you really should visit that methadone clinic on Wilcox. I told you, we'll pay for it. You're one of our longest tenants." David smiles warmly. "We'd like you to continue to be."

David moves on, not waiting for a reply. He's suggested it so many times, it's become a game between the two. He crosses over to the north wing, whistling past six rooms in descending order – Room 6, Room 5, Room 4 – stopping at the door labeled "1." David closes his eyes and exhales deeply. He raps three times on the door, then opens it anyway with a key.

The room is dim and dank, with visible dust particles in the air. In their twenty-seven years of hotel ownership, Max and Marta never once bought a house. Instead they simply shuttled their growing family between an apartment off Franklin Avenue and the Palms' Rooms 1 and 2, linking them with a connecting door.

To Max, Room 1 is, simply, home.

Stepping inside, David instinctively crinkles his nose. He used to love the blend of odors – acrid cigar smoke and tangy Aqua Velva aftershave competing with the sweetly pungent scent of his mom's perfume. It was a sensorial effect that distilled his parents to their very essence, and it made David feel safe. Now when he scrunches his nose, it's out of repulsion. Somewhere along the line, the room took on a strangely sour smell, like a dog bathed in chicken soup. David pegged it around the time his father took over this room, after his cancer-ridden mother was exiled to Room 2 and, eventually, to a unit in the south wing. Throw in the lack of oxygen caused by shuttered windows and David tries to keep his visits under ten minutes; any longer, he starts to feel nauseous.

The room is anchored by two queen beds opposite a wooden bookcase, its shelves stuffed with detective tomes, boxes of Havanas, and random trinkets gifted by guests. Slung over the top with string is a pair of red boxing gloves.

The right glove is signed by Jewish heavyweight champ Max Baer and dangles over a framed photo of Marta. Max's bureau rests against the far wall. Its half-open drawers belch out articles of clothing, suggesting a recent fit of fashion uncertainty. Skipping past the bathroom doorway, the remainder of the wall is obscured by a wet bar and Max's small desk, currently occupied by assorted pamphlets and a stack of fedoras. Under the desk, a naughty novelty trash bin overflows with old racing forms and oily takeout boxes.

The other walls are lined with photographs, mostly Max posing with B-Listers and starlets from the '30s and '40s during the Palms' salad days. Framed between the two beds, a thirtysomething Max proudly leans in the doorway of his floral shop at the Hollywood Hotel. Behind him are Aaron and the twins, mere toddlers, barefoot and quizzical as they stare into the camera's lens. Rudy is presumably not born yet or, if he were, with Marta.

David finds Leo and Aaron already seated on the bed by the door. Leo has a pencil in his ear, a stack of spreadsheets on his lap. The brothers exchange sympathetic nods.

Max, freshly showered, shuffles out of the bathroom in billowy boxer shorts and black socks held up by garters. He pauses to sip from a glass of bourbon.

"Big date tonight, Pop?" David asks.

Max flinches – he hadn't seen David enter. He turns to the bureau. "I'm taking Kitty to Musso and Frank's."

"What's the occasion?"

Max looks at David confusedly. "There has to be an occasion?"

A white dress shirt hangs out of the bureau's middle drawer. Max slips it on and starts to button it.

David can't help himself. "Pop, a steak there runs ten bucks. She orders up the menu then eats like a bird. And how many vodka martinis – "

"Jesus Christ!" Max erupts. "Can we get through one conversation without you all bad-mouthing the poor girl?"

Aaron jumps in, smooth and measured. "Pop, we're just thinking about the hotel. If we can't fill these rooms, we can't pay the bank. And if that happens…"

"You don't wanna end up like the *Hollywood*, do you?" David clucks. It was a calculated response, with special emphasis on "Hollywood" as an understood shorthand for the Hollywood Hotel.

Max puckers as if struck by a pang of gas. He still has an emotional attachment to the old place, and David knows the pathway to his sentimental heart.

"Been by there recently?" David shakes his head ruefully. "Giant hole in the ground. They're putting up a twelve-story office building. Who'd have thought?"

"Word on the street is Garden of Allah is next," Aaron adds.

Max harrumphs. "No surprise there. That place has long been a halfway house for drunk writers and Hollywood has-beens."

The brothers look at each other. Sounds familiar.

Max lifts a pair of slacks off his rumpled bed and comes around the nightstand, which holds enough pharmaceuticals to keep Schwab's in business for years to come.

David clears his throat. "Pop, remember when we talked about getting a new sign out front?"

Max appears not to hear him. He's busy steadying himself against the nightstand as he tugs on his pant leg.

"When Mom was alive, we talked about more upgrades. Starting with the sign. Something… bigger. More modern. Anyway, we've given it some more thought." David's eyes dart to his brothers. "And we think the way to go is neon."

He awaits his father's condemnation. But Max is quiet. He crosses to the bathroom mirror, flicks on the vanity sconce, and aligns the straps of a necktie over his turned-up shirt collar.

"Won't be cheap, but proven effective," Leo hollers. "Good return on investment. Hell, it's all the rage in Vegas. You yourself said how neon is transforming that city."

Max finally speaks. "I'm one step ahead of you."

"What?"

"Your mother and I… we were working on that before she died."

The brothers trade concerned looks.

"You — you were?" stammers David.

"Sure." Max studies his reflection, adjusting his tie. "Believe it or not, you're not the only Einstein in this family."

David stands up and approaches Max. "That's wonderful. Leo can start calling — "

"Don't bother," Max interrupts, knotting a half-Windsor. "I know just the guy."

David pinches his eyes. *Breathe.*

"Pop, we know you and Mom were used to doing things a certain way," Leo says. "We respect that. But maybe we could consider multiple bids, get some references. Do it right. Not make the same mistakes we made with the pool."

"I know some sign experts who could come up with some fresh ideas," Aaron offers.

"Aaron's right, Pop," David exults. "He's all over this."

Max puts up a dismissive hand, a traffic cop ordering everyone to stop. "Red will arrange everything. He has connections in Vegas where they make these things."

There follows a fraught silence. Then, Aaron, in an exasperated tone: "Red Gordo… that construction business consultant, or whatever he calls himself?"

David's eyes flicker in a slow burn. "*Shit*, Pop, that putz stiffed us on the pool, remember? We put his cronies up for three nights and didn't see a dime! And they blew a hole in our alcohol budget."

Max struggles with his collar. "He doesn't deal in hard currency."

"No? Then what does he deal in?"

"Favors." He turns to David. "Gimme a hand here, will ya? Your mother usually did this…"

David wants to continue the argument – Max always had a soft spot for that meathead Red and he could never figure out why. Instead, he dutifully stands behind his father, who raises his jawline to allow his son room to maneuver. Using the mirror as a guide, David reaches under Max's turkey neck and clasps the top button. He then creases the collar over the tie strap so it's no longer peeking out the back. Perfect.

"Red knows they owe us," Max continues. "He'll do it free of charge. You boys wanna work with him on designs, that's on you. I'll set up a meeting. He'll arrange the labor, get the best fellas on it. Just don't tick the guy off, huh?"

"Why?" David asks suspiciously.

"Whaddaya mean, '*why*?' He's cutting us a break, is why, so don't go giving him the third degree." Max walks over to his desk and jabs his finger at the pamphlets. "The money we save can go toward room fortification."

More looks between the brothers. *Wait – what?*

As Max sits on the bed to slip on his loafers, David picks up a couple of brochures. He brings them to the other bed, where the boys huddle around to check them out. The cover art is classic 1950s alarmist propaganda. One of them says: "Protect Yourself from Radioactive Fallout." A drawing shows a city being obliterated by an atomic bomb mushroom cloud. The other says: "What About You and Civil Defense?" It includes a smiling, pipe-smoking father presiding over his perfect wife, son and daughter, all rendered in floating heads. A triangular "CD" ensign appears on both.

David flips through the materials. "Radiation shields...?"

"I wanna line the rooms with 'em," Max explains. "In the walls, above the ceiling. They come in lead sheets."

David looks up, blinking.

"Look around, son. The world is changing. L.A.'s a target, and Hollywood's the bullseye. I wanna protect our investment. Our survival tomorrow depends on – "

" – our preparedness today." David and Max utter the last few words in unison, which throws Max.

"Just like it says here," David says glibly, pointing to the preparedness phrase in a pamphlet. He flings the booklets on the bed with disdain.

Leo pulls the pencil from his ear and flips to their price lists.

Max is undeterred. "People wanna feel safe. If they knew the Palms shelters 'em from gamma rays on account of a nuclear holocaust, that gives us an edge over our competitors."

Leo scribbles on the pamphlets, his owl-like head swiveling back and forth to his spreadsheet as he cross-checks figures. "Just off the top of my head, for the amount of money we'd spend on this, we could put a TV and an A.C. in every room."

Max stares at Leo, bemused. "Who said anything about TVs? We already got one. It's in the lobby if anyone wants to come watch. And what good's an air conditioner? So we have three hot weeks in August. That's what the pool is for."

Leo peers over his glasses. "The Swamp?"

David and Aaron are pictures of frustration. Max returns to the mirror to splash on cologne. He runs a comb through his nineteen strands of hair, topping it off with a checkered fedora, angling it just so.

"I'll get Rudy to measure the walls and ceilings," David says numbly. "Price it out, see what we're dealing with."

"Atta boy." Max heads to the john to take a leak. "Don't worry about my room," he calls from around the corner. "I'm almost seventy. If my time is up, so be it!" He emits a hacking chuckle. "Also leave room two alone. I don't want all the clanking and meshugas. Just do rooms three through twenty-four."

Aaron mouths "What the fuck?" to Leo and David. They shrug.

Leo folds the brochures to their original states. As he does, he notices something on the back of the second pamphlet – a handwritten message in red ink. In obvious girlie writing, someone has scrawled: "Sweetie – WE NEED THIS!!!" Next to the note is a little happy face.

As they hear Max peeing, Leo motions for his brothers to take a look. Aaron and David hunch over and read the memo. David stands up stiffly, his jaw clenched in silent fury.

"We gotta get that gold-digging bitch out of Pop's pants."

CHAPTER 4

David and Aaron meander through a forest of giant neon signs propped up in the dirt at a Valley scrapyard. A dust devil whirls past them, forcing the brothers to blink their eyes. Their tour guide is thirty-five-year-old Vance "Red" Gordo, an apish man in a white tank top with suspenders holding up his pleated pants. He has a flat, crooked nose and a V-shaped face that bottoms out into a sphincter-like mouth. His hairline sits disturbingly low on his forehead, nearly touching his unibrow, and his greased-back strands are not red but jet-black, making David wonder if his sobriquet is some sort of inside joke. He's shadowed by his pet dog Sally, a one-eyed pit bull with rippling muscles and scarred skin who looks like she eats nails for dinner.

Gordo leads the brothers down a path with more neon signs in various states of decay. They come in all shapes, colors and sizes, trumpeting hotels, motels, restaurants, bars, burlesque clubs and nightclubs, rusted-out fossils from a more glamorous epoch.

"Look at that, superstars. You're in luck." Red's voice is pinched and trebly, like an AM radio without a bass setting. "We just got in two palm trees from The Oasis, little place on Fremont that went belly-up before it even opened."

He steps aside so David and Aaron can take in a massive metal sign leaning against a burnt-out car. Painted-on palm trees are outlined in neon tubing. Welded to the top is a metal extension, telescoping the trees another five feet beyond the sign. To the right of the palms, golden neon spells out "The Oasis."

"'Nother week, we woulda shipped this off to an associate in Miami."

David tilts his head and crouches, appraising the sign from various angles. He turns to Aaron. "What do you think?"

Aaron hunches his shoulders in an exaggerated shrug, as if still formulating an opinion about this whole two-bit operation. "The palm trees could work. But 'The Oasis' part…"

"We'll pop that out, obviously," Red says. "Fact, I got the words 'Palm Beach' around here somewhere. Y'know, mix-n-match."

He draws his spherical lips together and whistles. Two young flunkies — squat, flinty-eyed guys with bodies like badgers — come around a row of steel oil drums, grunting and pushing another sign into the open.

Red introduces them. "My apprentices… Snig and Felix."

This sign is more weathered than the other. It says "Palm Beach Supper Club" in white neon. Positioned side-by-side with the other sign, the words "Palm Beach" look large enough to replace "The Oasis."

Gordo's sausage-like fingers flex above the "Palm Beach" letters. "I was thinking, lose the word 'Beach,' keep the 'Palm,' and add an 'S' so it says 'Palms.' We'll throw that in, no cost."

"Throw what in?" David asks.

"The 'S.'"

David looks to Aaron for help.

"What about 'Paradise'?" Aaron asks, arms folded over his chest.

"Come now?" Red says.

"Our hotel is Paradise Palms. We still need a 'Paradise.'"

Gordo looks at his grunts. They shake their heads. "Sorry, don't got nothing like that here."

"No, I mean… we need you to *create* that," Aaron says, barely containing his scorn. "Make it match 'Palms' so it's all the same typeface."

Gordo stares at Aaron and David, then breaks into a patronizing chortle when he sees they're not joking. "Whattaya think we are, 'Signs Incorporated'?"

Aaron starts to walk away.

"There must have been a misunderstanding," David says. "Our father said you could hook us up."

"And I will," Red says. "With what we got in the yard. But Red ain't got 'Paradise.' You want I should arrange something, that'll be extra."

"How much extra?"

Red throws up his hands. "Not my department. I'm just the facilitator."

"Let's go," Aaron snipes at David.

David doesn't budge. "Can you... facilitate... a discussion with someone who knows?"

Red nods. "I could facilitate that."

There's a long silence as everyone watches Sally roll over and wiggle her back against the dusty dirt, her pink, bear-trap jaw opening wide as if laughing.

"So, uh, I guess we'll get back to Max about all this," David says curtly. "We'll be in touch."

The brothers escort themselves toward Aaron's Bel Air, parked in a clearing near the razor-wired front entry.

"He's a good man!" Red shouts at their backs.

They turn around.

"Max." He tightens his bungus mouth, his head oscillating like a fan. "I was really sorry to hear about Marta."

"Thanks," David says. "Mom ran a tight ship. Pop seems a little lost without her."

"I can see why. She wanted to keep it all in the family. But your old man... we have a history, y'know. He reached out to me. Smart move."

David and Aaron steal glances.

"Your hotel is dated. Hard to go it alone in this climate. That was one thing your mother never understood." Red snorts. "But then, what do women know from business, right?"

The brothers respond with stiff grins.

"I'm sure we'll be seeing a lot more of each other," Gordo says, his tone both reassuring and threatening.

He and his toadies disappear behind the wall of rusty drums. Sally rolls back onto her feet and follows.

David turns to his brother. "I don't like the looks of all this."

"It's a junkyard," Aaron shrugs. "It's not supposed to look pretty."

A cloud of dust whips across David's squinting face. "I mean him. *Her.* Red and Kitty. Pop's getting played." He spits a wad of dusty saliva in the dirt. "If we don't take control of this situation, we're not just gonna lose Pop. We're gonna lose the whole goddamn hotel."

• • •

Rudy is perched atop a freestanding ladder, securing a light fixture into the ceiling of the Paradise Palms lobby. It's a flying-saucer model, a replacement for the one shot to hell by Elron's pellet gun. Leo holds the base of the ladder in place.

Dirk, Art and several other guests are gathered around the Zenith television. It's tuned to CBS's *Nightly News*, which is carrying a live press conference by President Dwight Eisenhower. An on-screen chyron says "Sputnik: First 5 Days." The president reads from a prepared statement: "I consider our country's satellite program to be well-designed and properly scheduled. It has never been conducted as a race with other nations...."

Rudy peeks at the screen. "Wish the Reds would just attack us already. I can't take no more suspense."

The doors to The Easy swing open. Out come Aaron and David, who clutches a doggie bag.

"Aaron and I are heading home," David says to Darlene, working the desk. "We'll see you tomorrow."

"Have a good night, gentlemen," she says.

As David and Aaron reach the front door, their path is blocked by an incoming guest. She's a pretty African American girl, eighteen years old, neatly dressed in a quilted fuzzy blouse and flowered skirt, her tightly curled hair in an up-do. She pushes past the brothers with a self-assured gait as if they're not even there. They look at each other and follow into the lobby.

Darlene addresses the visitor before she even approaches the front desk. "Excuse me, may I help you?"

"How much is a room?" says the girl.

The guests turn around at the sound of this young female voice. Darlene sees that everyone is watching, including all four Shapiro brothers.

"I'm sorry," she tells the girl, "but we're booked at the moment."

"But your sign says 'Vacancy.'"

"Yeah, that's... old." Darlene appears conflicted, her words telling the visitor one thing, her tortured expression signaling something else. Yolanda, the older Black maid, is returning room keys on a hook behind Darlene.

"Sugar, you wanna get yourself a room on Crenshaw or Central," Yolanda advises the teen. "There's nothing for you here."

"I'll pay you twenty dollars," the girl tells Darlene, ignoring Yolanda.

"I really *am* sorry," Darlene says forcefully, "but — "

"Let her stay."

It's Max, strolling out of The Easy, whittling his teeth with a toothpick.

"Give her room twenty-four," he utters matter-of-factly. He turns to the girl. "It's on the house. Be out by eleven a.m."

Across the lobby, jaws drop open in disbelief. This is way out of character for Max, a known tightwad who never allows strangers to stay for free, let alone a Black one.

"Gotta be trashed," Dirk whispers to Art.

The girl looks at Max and nods solemnly. He grunts and exits through the lobby's rear door.

CHAPTER 5

Entrenched at their stations behind the front desk, Leo tallies up hotel expenses on a mechanical calculator while a bored Darlene thumbs through *Harper's Bazaar*. Snig and Felix are visible through the lobby window, sledgehammering the old "Paradise Palms" sign into oblivion. Red Gordo supervises their demolition, barking out empty commands, fists on hips as an unleashed Sally whizzes on a bed of droopy geraniums.

Back in the lobby, a young, fresh-faced couple approach the check-in counter. The husband lugs two hard-body suitcases. His cute, petite wife drinks in the splendor of the nondescript lobby, mouth agape, as if she's just stepped into the Sistine Chapel.

"May I help you?" asks Darlene.

"I hope so," the man says, straightening up. "My name is Norman Peters. My wife June and I are looking for a room. That is, if you have one."

Darlene's eyes glide past the rows of empty lines in her ledger. "Well... this is your lucky day," she says, trading sideways smiles with Leo. "We just had a last-minute cancellation."

June squeals and does a little bunny-hop like a game-show contestant.

"First time in Hollywood?" Darlene inquires.

June covers her mouth. "Oh my God, is it that obvious?"

"We're from Calgary," Norman explains, flushing. "On our honeymoon."

Leo reaches over the counter to shake their hands, his tone warm and sincere. "As my people say, *Mazel Tov!*"

"Thank you," June says.

"Darlene, have Flori send a bottle of California Bordeaux to their room."

"That's very kind of you," Norman says.

As Norman checks in, June continues scoping out the lobby. She notices the sign for The Easy, closed until Happy Hour. "So... do you have many movie stars coming through here?"

"Oh, all the time," Darlene says without missing a beat.

"Like who?"

Darlene and Leo share knowing looks again. "Well, one of the reasons they like it here is the privacy. That's why you don't see any paparazzi outside. We make it a practice not to publicize."

June's face drains of all vitality.

"Makes sense to me," Norman says absently as he signs his name.

Reading June's disappointment, Darlene follows up with a loud, conspiratorial whisper. "But just between you and me, Rock Hudson dropped by last week after a film shoot. Had to put him up in a room, he got so pickled at our bar."

June resumes her game-show persona, squealing with delight. "Oh my God, was he a dreamboat?"

"Total."

Darlene takes the signed sheet from Norman and hands the couple their room key. As they depart through the back door that leads to the courtyard, June lowers her voice to Norman: "I *told* you we should stay here! It's always the rundown-looking places where they hide out!"

Darlene returns to her magazine with a smile, but Leo is piqued by a new development out front. His father has appeared on the scene with Kitty. Red and Kitty exchange pecks on the cheek – Red giving her a sly pat on the ass – while Max stands back to admire the teardown work. Also present are a dorky fellow in a Hawaiian shirt and a curvy platinum blonde with gobs of makeup covering her crater face. Leo has never seen them before.

Gordo takes an instant shine to this unlikely couple, greeting them with smarmy charm. He cocks his head for them to follow him. With Sally in tow, the threesome disappears from Leo's view around the side of the hotel, leaving Max out front with Kitty, Snig and Felix.

"Who the hell were that couple?" asks Leo, craning over the counter.

"Beats me," Darlene shrugs, eyes glued to her glossy.

"Why didn't we check them in?"

"Friends of Gordo. They use room two whenever they want. Different people all the time." She catches Leo's befuddled scowl out of the corner of her eye. "Your father okayed it. Been going on for months."

"I don't understand."

She snaps a page in her *Bazaar*. "With all respect, Mr. Shapiro, you and your brothers weren't around much before your mother died. There's a lot you don't understand."

Leo pops off his stool and cups his eyes over a window by the back door. Gordo and his two guests have reemerged. He leads them down the pathway alongside the pool. As they pass by Room 5, a flabby man flips back his curtain to take a peek. It's Art, caught in a half-clown state, a moat of incomplete whiteface encircling his trembling cherry-red lips. His shoulders, thick as beef slabs, undulate as if to suggest an act of self-pleasure.

Red stops at Room 2. He digs into his trouser pocket and, somehow, extracts a room key and opens the door. Like a car salesman luring customers into his showroom, he extends his arm across the threshold, his little lips parting into a buck-toothed hamster grin. The girl ducks into the room first. The man, skittish and glancing over his shoulder, slips in behind her. Red gives him a vigorous slap on the back and shuts them inside.

•   •   •

"A prostitution ring? *Pop?*"

Aaron's incredulous voice bleeds out of a phone handset, resting sideways on the desk in Room 3. The drawn curtain casts the room in darkness, save for a lone desk lamp illuminating David's and Leo's faces as they huddle around the phone.

David leans into the mouthpiece. "Aaron, I shit you not. Leo saw Gordo set the whole transaction up. He saw the hooker and her john enter room two."

"Mom's old room." Leo shakes his head. "Probably kvetching in her grave."

Aaron exhales a long, tired breath. "So Gordo's a pimp. Doesn't surprise me. That doesn't mean Pop's involved."

"Pop was *with* Red out front," Leo says. "How else would that weasel get a room key unless the old man was in on it? Darlene even confirmed the set-up."

David rakes his fingers through his tangle of hair. "It's starting to make sense now. Pop gets a kickback…."

31

"Probably how he's been covering the mortgage despite all our vacancies."

Aaron concedes their points. "Red did imply he and Pop had certain 'arrangements.'"

The brothers wallow in a thick silence, their brains needing time to catch up to the realization that their father is not the person they thought he is – or rather, that he really *is*. Even with Marta's taming influence, you couldn't take the street fighter out of Max Shapiro, a man most comfortable in the margins of society. Someone who rubs elbows with mobsters. Plays the ponies. Has a weakness for dames. But these were things they *knew*. What else was he withholding from his adult children, either out of controlling obstinacy or as a means to protect them – or both? And yet his boys forgive him his sins out of love and respect.

But trafficking in the sex trade?

On the other end of the line, Aaron paces the redwood deck of his Brentwood home, clutching a red phone with a long cord. As he swishes the ice in his Tom Collins, he soaks in the view of his neighbors' leafy backyards against a tableau of pink-and-blue-tinged clouds strewn across the dusky firmament like wisps of cotton candy.

"What about the Negro girl?" he asks. "How does she figure into all this?"

"Rae?" David says. "I don't know what the story is with her. Been here three days now. Every time I ask Pop about it, he says – "

"'My business is my business,'" Aaron parrots in unison with David.

Leo chortles. "Typical."

Aaron's gaze drifts to the house below his. His male neighbor, a tall, sandy-haired professional, has padded out onto his back patio in Speedo squarecut bottoms. Peeling off his T-shirt – sinewy muscles flexing over his ribs – he makes a perfect, splashless dive into the deep end of his kidney-shaped pool. Aaron shifts away from an obstructing tree branch to watch him glide beneath the surface, fluid as a seal.

"Anyway," David says, "Leo and I are thinking of moving in. Y'know, keep an eye on things for a while."

Aaron doesn't answer, lost in the nautical aerobics of his neighbor.

"Aaron, you there?"

"Yeah," he says. "I just can't believe it. You're gonna move into that rap trap? Like Pop?"

Aaron's four-year-old, Nancy, dawdles outside clutching a Mickey Mouse balloon. He turns his back on her and speed-walks to the far end of the veranda.

"What choice do we have?" David says. "We've all been so goddamn busy with our own lives. This rat trap is our future. If we don't act now, there'll be nothing left for us. It'll all be controlled by Kitty or Red or some other moocher digging their meat hooks in Pop."

Suddenly, Nancy lets out an ear-piercing shriek. Aaron turns and watches her balloon fluttering into the twilight sky. "*Daaaaaa-deeeeeeee!*" she wails, running toward him with helpless, flailing arms. Aaron fends her off with gentle knee thrusts.

"Honey, Daddy's working," he implores. "Go inside to Mommy." Then, turning back to the phone, "Sorry, this is just a lot to absorb. We just got home from Disneyland and my head is still spinning from the Tea Cups."

David chuckles. "Hey, no one's expecting you to move out of your dream home in Brentwood. Leo and I are still bachelors…"

"Still leaving the toilet seat up and eating over the sink," Leo quips.

David laughs somewhat wistfully. "It'll be just like old times, the two of us sharing a room here."

Aaron turns back to his neighbor. He's finished his dip and is now toweling off on the patio.

"Thanks, guys," Aaron says. "I'm awfully appreciative. You know I'm here to help however I can." He takes a stab at a little wit himself. "Who knew the old geezer was such a perv, huh?"

He's met by an unsatisfying long gap before David gravely sighs, "Lotta secrets in this family."

"Our love to Peggy and the kids," Leo says.

Aaron hears a click and then dial tone. Nancy has pinned herself to her father's leg, whimpering into his thigh. Aaron drains the rest of his drink and peers over the railing one last time.

The neighbor has gone back inside, a trail of wet footprints leading to the sliding door.

•   •   •

Back in Room 3 of the Paradise Palms, David peels back the drapes to monitor an impromptu shindig that has gathered by the swimming pool. The onset of evening has dropped a gray curtain over the distant Hollywood Sign. Gordo, bulging out of a white tank top, tilts a bottle of nectarine brandy into cocktail glasses held out by Norman and June, perched on a chaise longue.

"Lemme freshen that up for you," Red winks at June, her glass still three-quarters full.

Reclining on a lounge next to the honeymooners are Kitty and Max. Kitty swills straight from her own bottle of Smirnoff, her alabaster-white knees exposed under the gathered hem of a red polka-dot dress. Max's chin rests on his chest in an apparent alcohol-induced blackout, impervious to the portable radio blasting rhythm and blues. Sally is curled up on the dying grass, gnawing on a fallen palm frond.

In the distance, the curtain of Room 3 flaps back as David disappears from view.

"You look like you know a lot of movie stars, Mr. Gordo," June gushes, a slight slur in her voice.

"Please, call me Vance. Matter of fact, I was once the head bouncer at Slapsy Maxie's," he boasts. "I saw 'em all come through there. Dean Martin, Martha Raye, Eddie Cantor... he was real swell."

June squints at Red, trying to cobble together a clear thought. "Slapsy's... that's the place Mickey Cohen owned, right?"

Gordo snickers. "That's just a rumor. He was only a customer when I was there."

"No, I read he owned it." June is certain now. "He was shot out front."

"No, ma'am, you're thinking of Sherry's on Sunset."

"Did you work there, too?"

Red's sphincter-mouth contracts to such a degree, it almost disappears into his face. "You sure know a lot about Hollywood. Maybe you should become a movie star."

"I keep telling her that!" Norman exclaims. "That's another reason we're here, actually. To test the waters – "

"Norm!" June protests.

"What? He might as well know. Maybe Vance has some connections."

Red folds his arms over his simian chest and grins at June, as if to say, Go on...

June gulps some brandy and winces. "Well, if you *must* know... I played Crystal Allen in *The Opposite Sex* at the local playhouse."

Kitty's eyebrows nearly spring off her head.

Norman, still focused on June: "She's being humble. She got rave reviews in the *Calgary Courier*."

"*I* was up for Crystal for the *movie* version!" Kitty interjects.

"Get out!" June squeals. "You mean the role that went to Joan Collins?!"

June's innocent comment brings the conversation to a dead halt. Kitty forces a smile, then drops her head, deflated at the memory. Gordo walks behind her, massaging the nape of her neck while Max continues to snooze.

"Kitty was a specialty dancer in all them MGM musicals. But now that they're... phasing out... she's making the transitionals to bigger parts."

"Ann Miller borrowed my shoes once on *Kiss Me, Kate*," Kitty says pointlessly, staring at her bare feet. "We wear the same size – eight-and-a-half."

June blinks heavily at her, her head lolling back and forth.

Norman clears his throat and addresses Vance. "Say, uh... you wouldn't happen to know a photographer who could do good head shots, would ya?"

"For your wife?"

"You bet."

Gordo strolls over to June. His hulking presence makes her look like a little girl. She gazes up at him with eager eyes. He clasps her delicate chin between his stubby thumb and forefinger, tilting it toward the light from a lamppost.

"You wanna find a guy who knows how to play with light. Someone with a firm hand to accentuize your jawline..." Red subtly lowers his palm until it's lodged against her windpipe.

"... the delicate lines of your chin..."

He slowly starts to constrict her flesh.

"... your neck..."

As her bottom lip drops open to breathe, he presses his hand firmly under her jaw, jamming her mouth shut. Her eyes bug out in fear.

Red, practically cooing: "Shadows are everything..." With his palm cupped against her neck, his fat fingers squeeze her cheeks together, pushing her lips out like a fish's. He yanks her head left... right... left...

"Just an inch or two the wrong way, it could kill your career before it even begins."

Just as June raises her hands to grab his wrist, Gordo suddenly lets go — distracted by his dog defecating by the walkway.

"Sally, for fuck's sake!" he roars.

June clutches her reddened neck and pitches forward, gasping for air. Norman stands up, confused and useless, trying to make sense of what the hell just happened.

Gordo notices Rae, the mysterious Black girl, crossing the courtyard in the shadows. He hollers out to her in a mellifluous tone. "Uh, miss… would you mind terribly? My doggie just had a boo-boo…" He points to a lump of fresh dog shit.

Rae ignores him.

"Hey," he barks. "I'm talking to you!"

Without breaking stride, she insolently snaps, "I'm not your slave!"

Gordo guffaws – the balls on this girl!

Kitty stands up to wag her finger at Rae. "How *dare* you speak that way to a guest!"

"Yeah, I meant no offense," Red says with syrupy innocence. "I was just wondering if you had a bag so's I could pick up after her."

"I'm no maid either!" Rae yells back.

Kitty starts to stomp over to Rae but Red blocks her with his forearm. Redirecting her anger, Kitty turns to Max, still out cold.

"Max, are you gonna stand for this?" She shakes him violently. "Max!"

Max's eyes momentarily flicker to life, then roll back in his head.

Red turns off the radio. "I think it's nighty-night time for Mr. Shapiro, Kit. Maybe you should put him down. I'll help ya."

He and Kitty grab under Max's armpits and hoist his ragged old frame out of the lounge. But propping him to his feet is futile in his half-conscious state. Something's not right – he's not acting like a man who simply had too much to drink.

All the commotion has caused David to peer out between the drapes of Room 3 again. The fluttering of the curtain alerts Red, who turns to look just as David ducks out of view.

As Gordo and Kitty drag Max away from the pool, Norman huddles over June, sobbing quietly in his arms.

• • •

Later that evening, David creeps out of his room and approaches Room 2 next door. Skulking in the shadows, he notices the drapes have been parted just enough to look directly into the dimly lit interior, almost as if by invitation.

He hears it before he sees it. Muffled, rhythmic noises. A woman's moaning. A man's grunting. Skin on skin. The unmistakable sounds of fucking.

Through the window, David spies Gordo standing at the foot of the bed, trousers pooled at his ankles. He is pumping a girl doggy-style. His white tank top rises above his hirsute butt crack, his pelvis thrusting back and forth in short, violent bursts. The woman's red polka-dot dress is hiked above her ample hips, which Gordo slaps repeatedly.

Under a tangle of red hair, the woman is revealed in profile: Kitty. Eyes clenched, mouth agape, her twisted mien residing somewhere between pleasure and pain.

Suddenly, Sally trots toward the window and locks in on David with her one eye. She starts to whimper.

Alerted by his dog, Gordo pauses his sexual conquest, then starts to pump away again, fixing his fiery, carnal eyes on the window's glare. David recedes into the dark recess of the corridor, but it's too late. He's been made.

Gordo's round lips flatten into a wide, cat-that-swallowed-the-canary grin.

CHAPTER 6

A small black-and-white television is tuned to the national news, the audio on mute. Staticky animation shows a spherical metal object circling the Earth, dotted lines projecting from its antennae to represent intermittent beeps. "Sputnik – Week 10" flashes on-screen.

The TV is mounted behind a tavern counter, but no one's watching it. Customers aren't here to take in the news. They're here to get away from it. Heavy-lidded barflies slump over cheap, stiff drinks, the stale air choked with cigarette smoke.

Across the bar in the modest dining room, David sits alone at a corner booth. He quaffs from a dimpled copper mug and checks his watch. 10:45 p.m. He picks up his beverage coaster and taps it impatiently, red-and-white letters spelling out "Boardner's, Est. 1942."

At last, breezing through the black-curtain entryway is Kitty Kay, dressed in a simple sailor dress. Even though it's nighttime, she's wearing sunglasses. She takes them off when she spots David, who rises to greet her.

"Thank you for coming," he says. "You look great."

Kitty does a little twirl. "Thank you. Your father bought this for me."

She glides into the booth first, David behind her. "What're you drinking?" he asks. "Vodka martini?"

"What're *you* drinking?"

"Moscow Mule."

"Oooo… I like the sound of that. I'll take one of those."

David flags down an ancient waiter through the smoky haze, holding up his mug. "One more of these for the lady."

"Do you come here a lot?" Kitty asks David.

"Sometimes after we close up the lobby. I like that it's only a few blocks from the hotel. People leave you alone."

Kitty cups her chin in her hand, raising a suggestive eyebrow. "So why the company tonight?"

David dismisses her flirting as a harmless personality tic, but uses it as motivation to stay focused. He takes a healthy swig from his mug and slams it down, perhaps louder than he intended.

"I don't think it's appropriate for my recently widowed father to be going with someone half his age," he says. "It's bad for business."

Kitty crosses her arms. "Couldn't you at least wait until my drink arrives before you insult me?"

"Look, we all know his days of running the Palms are numbered. But let me make one thing clear. My brothers and I intend to own the hotel forever, no matter what plans you and your greaseball boyfriend are cooking up."

Kitty looks like she wants to spit in his face.

"Now, we recognize Max likes having a pretty face around. We're happy to put you on payroll if you'll leave him alone. Your title will be 'Hospitality Consultant' and you'll draw a salary. Say, a hundred dollars a week?"

Kitty pulls a cigarette from her purse. David reaches for a matchbook, but she lights it before he has a chance to be a gentleman. She takes a long drag and replies in cool, measured tones. "I don't know what kind of woman you take me for. I love Max. I'm very loyal to – "

David closes his eyes and puts up his hand – *can it.*

"Look, it's no secret me and your father met through Vance," Kitty says. "I was working for Vance's company. I left them two years ago and he and I have remained... friends."

"*Friends.*"

"Swear on my dead daddy's grave."

David issues a trenchant smile. "The same daddy who abandoned you when you were eight?"

Kitty scowls. She fumbles for an ashtray.

"Why did you tell Pop you wanna cover the rooms in lead panels?"

"For protection. What else?"

"Bullshit. Leo showed me a work order estimate from a Del Vista Haberdashery for twenty-two thousand dollars. What's a men's clothing store have to do with sheet metals?"

Kitty half-shrugs. "You'd have to ask Vance. The company he works for owns a lot of enterprises. Probably just for tax purposes, a way to spread money around."

"It's a front, is what it is. For what, I don't know. Tell Red we're cancelling the order. We're doing our own upgrades through a legitimate party."

Kitty's face contorts to seething outrage.

"And I don't want Red hanging around the hotel," David continues. "As of tomorrow, he's no longer welcome. He shows up, we call the cops for trespassing."

"Well... aren't *you* the big boy," Kitty hisses. "Sorry, but we take our orders directly from Max."

"Max is being played by two con artists. He's not in a position to know what's best for him or the hotel. Just like he didn't know someone slipped a mickey into his drink last night so you and 'Vance' could fuck like hyenas while he was out cold in the next room."

Just then, the waiter swoops by with a Moscow Mule. "Theeeere you go, ma'am," he chirps, placing a copper mug in front of a shellshocked Kitty.

David turns to him. "How much I owe, Howie?"

"Dollar-fifty."

"Here's five." David tosses the bill on the man's tray. "Thank you, we're done here."

Howie bows and heads back to the bar.

As Kitty stares icily at her drink, David leans back, pleased with himself. "Go 'head. Drink up. I can wait."

"Don't want it."

"Suit yourself." He rises and slips on his overcoat. "Walk you back to the Palms?"

She doesn't answer.

He raises his voice as if addressing a deaf person. "I *said*, 'Walk you back to – '"

"I'm headed to my apartment. I'll call a cab."

"We'll get one together."

"No. You go."

David sees she needs time to be alone. He places a hand on her shoulder and bends toward her ear. "This is just about running a clean operation. The Shapiros don't run crooked."

Kitty slowly lifts her head, hurling her words like a ninja throwing-knife. "That's what you fucking think."

David allows her retort to glance off him, though his face betrays a flash of concern. Regaining his composure, he flashes a pat smile and brushes past the black curtains.

Stepping onto the sidewalk, David finishes buttoning his coat. It's a brisk December night. The bar's buzzing green-and-red neon sign provides the only illumination on an otherwise dark side street off Hollywood Boulevard.

David steers away from the boulevard, turning right on Selma toward Paradise Palms. He starts to whistle. He's the only pedestrian out tonight, save for a shadowy figure across the street. David catches him in his periphery: A man in a long coat and wide-brimmed hat, leaning against the doorway of a bungalow at the Crossroads of the World plaza.

Not taking any chances, David hustles north on Las Palmas Avenue toward the bright lights of Hollywood Boulevard. Halfway up the sidewalk, a second man approaches from the other direction. His hobbling gait and thuggish build can only signal trouble.

David spins around, only to find the first man now closing in on him. He's trapped. Fight or flight.

He chooses flight, bolting down an alley that juts off the sidewalk. It takes him to the backside of the Egyptian Theatre. He hears the quick angry patter of boots hard on his heels.

The alley dead ends, but David finds a walkway. He cuts down it. It leads to a long red carpet that ends at the Egyptian's shuttered box office. David peeks over his shoulder. Sees the elongated shadows of his pursuers playing off the murals of the forecourt. In his distracted state, his feet clip a fold in the carpet. He goes down.

They're on him before he can get up.

Prone on the ground, he covers his head with his hands and absorbs a flurry of kicks against his ribs. The men grunt in exertion as a male voice rings out nearby: "I'm calling the cops!"

David slits his eyes just enough to peek at the men's shuffling boots against a miniature Sphinx and a tableau of falcon pharaohs. The men step over him, but not before one of them gives him a parting gift – a swift *thwack* in the back of his skull.

David sits up, woozily, emitting a long groan. A warm viscous fluid is oozing from the back of his head. He runs his fingers through his hair and pulls them back. They're coated in blood.

"You okay, mister?" A baby-faced security guard breathlessly appears at his feet.

"Red." David repeats the word out loud. "*Red.*" Improbably, he starts to giggle. Even though Gordo had others do his dirty work tonight, he knows now why they call him "Red."

The security guard takes a step back, alarmed by David's weird behavior.

Just as quickly, Max's voice cuts through his ringing ears. *"Just don't tick the guy off, huh?"*

What the *fuck* does his father know that he doesn't?

•   •   •

Like a lot of men from his generation, Max didn't discuss his upbringing with his sons very much. Most of what they knew about their father, they gleaned from either Marta or Aunts Rochelle and Lydia – Max's sisters. As the youngest child and only boy, Max was doted on by his sisters and mother Gladys. The three siblings rarely saw Papa, who cycled between odd jobs at odd hours. For a while, Carl Shapiro worked the graveyard shift for the Sanitation District of Chicago. Another time, he disappeared an entire summer as a door-to-door salesman throughout the Midwest, shilling hand-pumped carpet sweepers, an early version of the vacuum cleaner.

As a result of Carl's sporadic absences, Max's impressions of him read like an incomplete scrapbook, a collage of images with long stretches of blank pages. One of his earliest memories was of Papa cooing in his ear as they rode a gondola along the "Canals of Venice" at the Chicago World's Fair. Max couldn't have been more than three or four. He recalled Carl's brush-like mustache tickling his cheek whenever he bent over to kiss him, his slanty fuzzy-caterpillar eyebrows, the noxious odor of moth balls emanating from his wool suit.

When Max was nine, Papa disappeared again for a long stretch. Returning six months later, he looked like he had aged twenty years – a decrepit, hunched-over shadow of his former self.

"War cooties." That's what the kids in the neighborhood called his father's state. It was only later that Max found out the real diagnosis: typhoid fever. Carl had contracted the disease in Cuba as a noncombatant volunteer in the Fifth Army Corps during the Spanish American War. Max hated going into Papa's darkened bedroom where he wasted away his days. It smelled like piss and vomit mixed with Vicks VapoRub. The bacterium had wormed its way into his neuromuscular system, short-circuiting his brain and nervous system. He became paranoid. Delusional. He thought his family were Spanish spies. More than once, Gladys woke to find Carl pummeling her ribs with his weak fists, forcing her to sleep on the sofa.

But his family still loved him. Gladys in particular liked to boast to other wives that her husband was awarded a military medal, even if it was just for General Service, the army equivalent of a participation award. He had finally risen above his station as a lifetime menial laborer. Was he not a crippled veteran worthy of our pity and honor?

One morning, as Max helped feed his father oatmeal, he searched in vain for flickers of recognition in his hollowed-out eyes. But he saw only blankness, like a doll's eyes. It scared the hell out of Max. And then it hit him. While Papa's body might still be alive, he had died in the war after all.

Max's acceptance of his father turned to resentment. Other friends' dads were providers. His own was a burden at worst, a disappointment at best. He resolved to be stronger and wealthier than Carl ever was. Inspired by the Strongman in Barnum & Bailey's Circus, Max started popping vitamins and lifting weights. At thirteen, he got a job selling the *Chicago Tribune* before and after school. It forced him out into the world, where he met other prospective employers. One of his deliveries was to Windy City Blossoms in South Commons, which advertised for a flower delivery boy. Max pried the sign off the window and brought it inside. "I don't care what the pay is," he told the proprietor, Leonard Elbowitz. "I'll take it." Lenny admired the kid's chutzpah. He was hired on the spot.

The flower shop was a dark, cramped space with cold brick walls, a pointed contrast to the room's ambrosial floral fragrances. Bunched against the walls were water-filled pails of long-stem roses, along with whatever other perennials Lenny could acquire from the wholesaler. A narrow pathway led to the back counter, where bouquets were prepared by an elfin, English-challenged immigrant named Otto. Behind the counter was a steel door. The only other time Max had seen one was at the First National Bank. Every so often the door squeaked open and "back men" who worked in the warehouse shambled out.

They were always men, which Max found odd for a flower store. Some reloaded the pails with freshly cut arrivals, others marched purposefully out the front door clutching briefcases. They rarely spoke to Max, and when they communicated with Lenny, it was always in Yiddish with hushed tones and grim faces. Max never questioned Lenny about any of it. The warehouse wasn't his business. Everything he needed for deliveries was handled out front.

Holding down two jobs, Max's confidence grew. He remembered the puff of pride he felt handing over hard cash to his mother to supplement the laundry she took in and Carl's disability checks. For the first time in his life, he had *spending money*. He treated himself to a second pair of shoes. When winter hit, he bought Rochelle and Lydia knit caps he had noticed them admiring in the window at the five-and-dime on Michigan Avenue.

This was also when Max's romantic vein took hold. He took his cue from his flower store boss. Curiously, Leonard Elbowitz was no great shakes. His face was a caricature in profile, with a cartoonishly pronounced Adam's apple that only drew more attention to his weak chin – an unfair anatomical swap-job. At six-foot-two, he was all angles and straight lines, lending him the nickname Elbows. But that angular frame looked great in a suit, and Elbows always dressed to impress. Depending on the outfit, he rotated between different patterned fedoras, each pitched forward at just the right angle to cover his receding hairline and prevent the shade of the brim from concealing his soft hazel-brown eyes. After Max bought *his* first fedora at a thrift shop, Elbows playfully smacked it off his head. "No girl's gonna go near you with that rat's nest on your noggin," he teased his young charge. "C'mon, kid, let's get you some real threads."

That afternoon, Elbows took Max to the finest department stores in the Loop – Marshall Field's, Mandel Brothers, Schlesinger & Mayer. Lenny sprung for three suits, three matching fedoras, and a set of argyle socks. Max watched him peel off rolls of bills with a nonchalance akin to handing out candy to orphans. The saleslady at the last store let Max walk out in the suit they just purchased. It was similar in style to the one Elbows was wearing. "Like a miniature version of your father," she remarked, beaming at the two.

Max felt eight feet tall.

Properly attired, Max received a life-changing lesson on courtship from the stork-like Lenny, who was never at a loss for female companionship. The key to a girl's heart, he counseled Max, was to make her feel like she – and she alone – is the most special person on Earth. Elbows didn't see it as a put-on; he truly believed everyone *is* special in their own unique way, but few of us take the time to notice it in others. Sizing up a prospective broad, Elbows always asked himself, what's the one thing about her that makes her different? It could be the way she fiddles with her earlobe when she listens, her love of stray dogs, the dimples that appear when she smiles – *anything* – just as long as it's about her essence and not something superficial, like, say, her necklace or choice of footwear. She'll appreciate your attention to detail. She'll think, here is a man who notices me for who I am.

When he was fourteen, Max had occasion to try out Elbows' approach. She was a slight, sweet girl with thin lips and a wavy auburn bob. She appeared to be the daughter of Freddie Schenk, the gregarious man who ran Schenk's Pretzel Stand a few blocks from the flower shop. Max swung by the little wooden cart almost every summer afternoon for a hot salted pretzel. The girl was always seated next to the stand on an upside-down white bucket, her face buried in sweeping Victorian novels. She almost never looked up when Max purchased his pretzels. The few times she did, Max's knees buckled and his throat clenched up and he would slink away, cursing his cowardice.

Back at the shop, Max explained his predicament to Elbows. How could he compliment a girl with whom he's too timid to even strike up a conversation? Of course, Lenny had an answer for that too. One need not appeal to another's specialness through words. A small, simple gesture of romance could suffice. Max racked his brain to contemplate his next move. Elbows smiled and told him, "I'm sure you'll figure it out soon enough." It didn't take Max long to realize he was sitting on a goldmine.

His courtship commenced with a single long-stem red rose.

With Lenny's blessing, Max procured it from the flower shop early one Monday morning. He proceeded to walk it down to Schenk's Pretzel Stand, which didn't open until 10 a.m. and, when not in use, was cloaked in a giant burlap hood secured to its legs. Untying one of the knots, Max lifted a flap and methodically placed the rose in a diagonal manner on the pay counter. He then gently lowered the burlap so as not to damage the flower's petals, retying the strand. It would be the first thing the girl and her father would see when they lifted the cover at the start of business.

Max continued his anonymous overtures throughout the week, a different flower every morning. A single tulip on Tuesday. A single aster on Wednesday. A single hydrangea on Thursday. A single black-eyed Susan on Friday. All the while he avoided patronizing the pretzel stand, not wanting to give himself away. Not yet. Monday would be the day.

That weekend, Max noticed Elbows was uncharacteristically crotchety in the shop. When Max tried to solicit his advice on how to play his "reveal," Lenny told him to quit bugging him with such trivial matters. The time had come for Max to stand on his own two feet. Max was hurt. He thought they were a team.

After his shift ended on Sunday, Max told Lenny he'd see him tomorrow — the same day he'd introduce himself to his prospective sweetheart.

"Don't bother coming in tomorrow, kid," Elbows said coldly.

Now Max was confused. Was the shop going to be closed? Or was he being fired? Just then, the steel door clanked open. A heated quarrel ensued in Yiddish between the employees and Lenny. The bellicose men motioned toward Max, yelled some more at Elbows. Max didn't understand them, but he understood enough. He was not welcome there anymore. He left the shop and plodded home, never getting an explanation from Elbows.

The next morning, Max had gotten over his disappointment and sprung out of bed with renewed vigor. Returning from his paper rounds, he slipped on his least-dirty suit and fedora and headed down to the sidewalk. Instead of taking the streetcar, he opted to walk the five miles from his apartment to the pretzel stand, giving him a couple hours to expend nervous energy and rehearse his opening line and conversation points. The truth was, he would've walked to the ends of Earth to meet her.

Max reached Schenk's at twenty to ten, loitering until 10:02 a.m. That's when Freddie showed up to pull off the burlap. But he was alone. Where was his daughter?

The next few hours were excruciating. Max aimlessly paced Michigan Avenue, monitoring the stand from behind passersby. For weeks, the girl had shown up to read books on her upside-down bucket. Maybe it was a sign that it wasn't meant to be. *No!* He could hear Elbows' admonishments to be a man. He would have to approach her father and unveil his whole clunky scheme, whose payoff was now vaporizing like steam off hot wet pavement.

Max waited until Freddie finished with a customer. Pushing through the current of foot traffic, he approached the stand, gazing downward, hat in hand. And, then, miracle of miracles! When he looked up, Freddie was being relieved by his daughter so that her father could dash across the street for a hot dog.

It was just him and the girl, one-on-one. Max fought the urge to flee. He had precious seconds to lay it on her.

Now. The time was *now*.

"The curvature of your upper lip is a most wondrous thing."

Even decades later, Marta laughed heartily when recalling Max's oblique pick-up line.

But at the time, all Marta could do was cock her head in confusion like the RCA dog in a gramophone ad. She had recognized this self-possessed young man from his repeated visits. But he had never given her two hoots, and thus, had never entered her mind as the secret Romeo behind the floral endowments.

"Thank you?" Marta answered, more as a question. She squinted. "Is that from a play or something? Sounds like Blake."

Max was crestfallen. Here he was, crafting a deeply personal observation just for her, and she thought he was plagiarizing. It threw him off his game, and he forgot to follow up.

"Would you like a pretzel?" Marta asked, breaking the silence.

"Sure. My name is Max. Max Shapiro," he finally said, straightening his back. "And I meant what I said."

Marta looked him up and down, admiring his stylish ways. "You're the one who's been leaving me flowers." She smiled warmly, the corners of her wondrous upper lip curling to reveal a row of pretty teeth. "That was sweet."

As they locked eyes, Marta felt a suspension of time in which the noises of the city abruptly receded, like someone shutting off a waterfall, the handsome image before her crystallizing into stark relief. In her tunnel-vision state, Marta had forgotten to fetch his pretzel. Now it was her turn to lose her train of thought.

If staring at her future husband assured Marta that she would always remember this moment, what followed memorialized it.

Several blocks away, a fusillade of clapping noises echoed off the edifices of downtown, like kids setting off firecrackers. *Pap-pap-pap. Pap-pap. Pap-pap-pap-pap.* Marta and Max snapped their heads left to right, trying to pinpoint the source.

The pops were followed by the scream of sirens. Police cars rumbled past the stand, heading south on Michigan.

Marta turned to look at Max. His face was ashen.

"What is it?" she asked.

Max's eyes brimmed with tears. Without so much as a goodbye, he spun on his heels and tore down the sidewalk, toward the chaos.

Toward Windy City Blossoms.

Marta figured that was the last she'd see of this strange boy, who never even got her name or shook her hand. She was struck by a singular odd thought that summoned an unexpected sense of longing: Pity I'll never know his touch.

CHAPTER 7

"Boy, do I need a drink." Art Mankowitz clomps into The Easy in floppy clown shoes and a baggy, polka-dotted jumpsuit. "Franny, the usual!"

"Of course, Mr. Mankowitz." Franny scampers into the kitchen with a tray of dirty glasses.

Art collapses into a booth and tugs off his footwear. Scrubbed-off whiteface lines his temples and sagging jawline. Errant wisps of hair – what few he has left – press against his dome from an orange fright wig, which he flings onto the seat.

The dining room is sparsely filled with the usual cast of characters. Dirk peruses the *Daily Variety* between sips of a Bloody Mary while Elron regales a doe-eyed betty with his Hollywood misadventures as a "can't miss" actor. Leo pores over receipts on the bar counter, nursing a glass of milk. Squinting over his specs, he asks Art, "How was the birthday party?"

Franny returns with a large salad for Dirk, a scotch for Art. "Everything was peachy till I got to the balloon animals," Art asserts, taking a satisfying sip. "The mom accused me of making a penis and kicked me out!"

"What were you trying to make?" Leo asks. "A dachshund?"

"A penis."

The room breaks out in dirty laughter – all except Dirk. Chewing on his first bite of salad, he works the lettuce around his mouth and furrows his brow as if discovering a hair ball. He drops his fork with dramatic flourish.

"What the hell's eating him?" Art says, drawn by the fork's *clank*.

Dirk peers down at his plate, slack-jawed. All heads are now turned in his direction.

Leo drops his pencil. "Dirk?"

Dirk slides out of his booth and decamps for the kitchen.

"Shit," Leo says, taking off after him, Franny on his tail.

Dirk swings through the doors and ambushes the food prep station, where Francisco is chopping onions. Seeing the excitable Dirk come toward him, he steps away from his stall, butcher's knife between them. Leo and Franny linger at the doorway, ready to pounce if need be.

Dirk lifts his walking staff and shakes it at Francisco. "What did you do to the Shrimp Louie?!"

"W-what do you mean?"

"It hasn't tasted this good since Marta died. *She* was the only one who did it right. You always use too much mayo and not enough lemon zest."

Francisco lowers the knife, visibly relieved. "Heh. Must've just gotten lucky."

Dirk's not buying it. He thrusts his stick at Rae, who watches the stand-off from her post at the sink. An epiphany dawns on Dirk's face.

"It was… *yoooouuu*," he says slowly to the part-time dishwasher. He turns to Leo. "*She* did it. She brought it back to the way it was."

Rae returns to her dishes. For a long moment, no one says or does anything. Finally, Francisco places his knife on the counter and walks over to Rae. He gently spins her around to face the others – a united front.

Leo looks confused. "Rae? Are you… cooking?"

Francisco slings an avuncular arm over her shoulder. Rae gazes at the floor, toying with her apron strings, embarrassed by all the fuss.

"I needed help," Francisco maintains. "We never replaced your mother, y'know. I kept telling you" – he looks at Franny – "me and Franny, we can't do everything. I was overwhelmed!"

Leo, ignoring his cook's protestations, says to Rae, "You're not even earning anything close to cook's wages…"

"It's okay." She looks at Francisco. "I wanted to prove myself first."

"Last few weeks, I've had more customers than usual complimenting my dishes," Francisco says. "But it's been all her."

"Not so sure I'd want to admit to something like that…" quips Dirk to no one in particular.

"You should try her desserts," Francisco raves. "Word is out among the guests. We can barely keep up with the to-go orders."

Leo scans the kitchen's takeout counter. His eyes feast on an array of culinary treats that have heretofore never passed through these kitchen doors — blueberry muffins, peanut-butter cookies, lemon squares and sweet potato pie.

"Where'd you learn to make all this?" asks Leo.

"McDaniel's Residentiary," Rae says.

"What is that, like, a group home?"

"Yes, sir. I learned to cook for sixty-five kids. Ran the whole kitchen by the time I left."

"Why'd you leave?"

Rae shrugs. "Turned eighteen. I had no choice."

Leo bobs his head, lost in thought. "*If* we hire you as a full-time cook, you'd practically be living in the kitchen. But understand" — he winces in embarrassment — "living at the hotel… that would be problematic."

Francisco gives Rae a squeeze. "She's not looking to move in. She's got a place at Nickerson Gardens."

Rae offers Leo a tight-lipped smile. Leo forces one back, still trying to process it all. Once again, Dirk breaks the silence.

"Well, hell… someone hire this young lady, because if you don't, I'll make her *my* personal chef."

• • •

Aaron swings his Bel Air into the Paradise Palms' turncourt, parking next to a ratty Ford pickup with construction supplies. Hopping out of his car, he steps down the driveway to appraise the hotel's new sign. It stands fifteen feet high along the sidewalk, a beacon for through-traffic. Neon palm trees jut out from its rectangular field, with "Paradise" and "Palms" in glass tubing. It's far from perfect — the two words have mismatched typefaces, and soldering scars are visible where Gordo's crew patched the sheet metal together — but it's a vast improvement over the old wooden sign smothered by the bougainvillea. In some ways, the Frankenstein job lends the whole thing a whimsical off-kilter vibe that befits the times.

Aaron finds David overseeing two Mexican laborers wrapping up the installation. The back of David's head is swathed in gauze and medical tape. He stands with his arms interlocked, looking fatigued and wan. There's no sign of Red.

"How're you feeling?" Aaron asks.

"I'll live." Annoyed by the question. "I told you, they were just trying to scare me."

"Cops turn up anything?"

David snorts – c'mon, seriously?

He steps toward the workers, who are smoothing out wet concrete. "Shouldn't you boys be using an edger for that? You're gonna splatter concrete on the ironwork."

The laborers regard David with blank expressions, not understanding a lick of English.

Aaron escorts his brother toward his car. "You should take it easy. Let me take charge of things for a while so you can rest. Peggy will understand."

"I'm not resting until I know Kitty and Gordo are totally out of the picture."

Out of nowhere, a caravan of cars blaring rock music cruises down Selma Avenue, the drivers jamming the hotel's driveway and front curb. Boisterous young men and women spill out of tricked-out rides and swarm the lobby doors, buzzing past Aaron and David.

"Looking bueno, muchachos!" It's Rudy, calling out to the workmen as he slams the door to his street-parked Thunderbird. "Looking *muy* bueno."

Rudy catches David's eye, then quickly looks away. David stops him as he limps by.

"What the hell's all this?"

"Buddies from the track. They were looking for a place to celebrate New Year's Eve, so I invited them here."

Aaron, backing up David: "Our hotel is not a crash pad for your carousing pals."

"Really." Rudy digs into his pocket and pulls out a thick wad of money. "Even if they pay us up front?" He flashes the bills like a deck of cards – a blur of twenties. "I charged 'em forty bucks a head. Eleven vacant rooms, twenty customers… came out to eight hundred dollars. Figure they'll spend at least another three hundred on food and booze."

Aaron's eyes light up.

"You did this?" David asks suspiciously.

Rudy dons a self-satisfied grin, eager for his big bro's approval.

"How did you manage to get them all interested?"

"Easy…" Rudy goes to his car and pops the trunk, producing a case of jangling champagne bottles. "I told 'em they'd each get their own bottle of Remy Martin – on the house."

"How much did *that* run us?" Aaron asks.

Rudy plunks the case down on the sidewalk. He makes a circle with his thumb and index finger. "Zilcho."

David still looks dubious.

"Don't worry," Rudy crows, "I got it covered."

"Take it back."

"What?" Rudy extracts a bottle from the case. "Do you realize the street value of – ?"

"Goddamn it, Rudy, don't you get it? Everything on the level from now on. If you can't provide a receipt, it's not legit and *we don't want it*."

Two tittering girls blow past the brothers on their way to the front door. "Are you coming?" one of them asks Rudy.

Rudy flashes a thumbs-up. He turns to David and Aaron. "Look, if I take this shit back, these cats are gonna cut out and I'll hafta return their money. You really wanna turn away eleven hundred bucks?"

David watches the girls join the herd of shiftless spendthrifts stampeding into The Easy. He gives a tired sigh and steps away from his brothers. He doesn't say anything to Rudy, but he doesn't need to. His slumped shoulders say it all.

Rudy smiles.

• • •

That night, a placard invites guests to welcome in 1958 with special "Atomic Cocktails!" The doors to The Easy are propped open to accommodate boozy celebrants flitting between the bar and lobby as Juan Garcia Esquivel space-age pop rattles out of the jukebox. Yolanda and Flori bus glasses and hors d'oeuvre plates, racking up overtime, navigating the sweaty crush of guests. Darlene attempts to reattach a string of sparkly cosmic décor over The Easy's doorway but keeps getting goosed by mischievous men. The Paradise Palms is *happening* – even if for just a few fleeting hours.

Inside The Easy, David, Aaron and Leo kibitz with friends, extended family, and long-term tenants. The diminutive Franny wades past them with a tray of drinks arched over his head. One of Rudy's track buds lifts two martinis off the tray, handing one to his gal. As they toast, the man stares sideways at their beverages. The toothpicks spearing their submerged olives hold a *second* olive on top, from which two broken-off toothpicks jut out like antennae.

"What the hell…?" he shouts above the music.

"Sputnik Martini," she explains. "It's all the rage."

The man rocks back in delight. "What ever happened to that contraption, anyway?"

"It's losing orbit. They say it's gonna plummet to Earth any day now."

Her date scoffs. "If Ike had any balls, he'd shoot the damn thing out of the sky." He plucks the "satellite-olive" off his toothpick and flings it into an ashtray.

The din dies down momentarily when Max Shapiro enters The Easy. He's dressed in his sharpest get-up – fat, drunk and happy from another pricey night out with his favorite dish on his arm. Kitty makes sure the Shapiro boys spot her, then fixes David with her best "fuck you" sneer.

Darlene helps Kitty out of her fur coat and notices a glistening white gold ring on her left ring finger. Kitty holds it out so Darlene can admire it.

Max finds his sons at the bar. "Sign out front looks great," he says, flagging Francisco down. "Told you that Gordo was alright. Why the hell isn't it turned on?"

"We blew a fuse," Aaron says. "David's got Rudy on it."

David motions to Kitty. "You proposed to her, Pop?"

Max turns and sees his squeeze flaunting her ring to guests. "Truthfully? She proposed to *this* ole bag o' bones. Can you believe it?" He wags his head. "They call it a 'promise ring' or some such shit. Doesn't mean anything. Makes her feel good."

Francisco hands Max a glass of bubbly. The Shapiro patriarch can't help noticing his sons' dour faces. "Smiles, boys. Smiles. It's New Year's Eve. Live a little!"

He disappears into the crowd.

Leo shakes his head in disbelief. "Leave it to Kitty to work the old man for three rings instead of the customary two."

"We gotta tell him about her and Gordo," Aaron says. "It'll break his heart, but we *gotta* tell him."

David keeps his gaze trained on Kitty, jaw clenched. "Leo, you have the number handy for our estate lawyer? Spiegelman?"

"Yeah."

"Let's call him tomorrow."

"Tomorrow's New Year's Day. He won't be in the office."

"Look up his home number. Call him there." He looks at Leo. "This can't wait."

Leo starts to protest and looks to Aaron for help. But Aaron is staring at the floor. "Okay," he groans, sipping his glass of milk.

• • •

As the clock descends toward midnight, guests cluster around the lobby television in festive hats and masks. The Zenith is tuned to Lawrence Welk and his "champagne music" orchestra counting down to New Years from the Hollywood Palladium. Kitty, clutching a vodka tonic, nestles next to Max in his beloved loveseat. Aaron, David and Leo roam behind various sofas, ceding prime seats to older folks like Dirk and their aunt and uncle. Rudy bops around the back wall with his racetrack chums, each with his own Remy Martin.

Francisco and Franny make sure the Palms' VIPs have full libations. Flori and Yolanda have gone home for the night, but Rae has stuck around to clean up. As she crosses in front of the TV, Max reaches out with fumbling hands and wrangles her arm.

"What the hell you still doing here?" he mutters.

"Just helping out."

"You should be home. Why'ya working? I gave you enough money to cover three months' rent!"

"I can't live on part-time dishwashing." She glances at Leo. "Leo and David were gonna talk to you about a full-time cook job…"

All heads swivel toward Max and Rae, their interaction far more interesting than Mr. Welk.

Max rises unsteadily from his seat, his paper hat askance. "Is she running the kitchen?" he bellows at his boys. "*My* kitchen? Where your mother used to cook?"

"She's good, Pop," Leo says firmly. "Trial run for two weeks. That's all it is."

"Try her Shrimp Louie, Max!" It's Dirk, three sheets and wearing a Zorro mask. "I know it's sacrilege but dare I say, it's better than Marta's!"

A scandalous buzz ripples through the room.

Max lets go of Rae's arm. He leans into her ear but continues to broadcast his thoughts in a too-loud tone of anger and hurt – a drunk man betrayed.

"Whattaya trying to do? *Eighteen* years, I supported you. Did the responsible thing. *Paid* for my mistake. Now you wanna rub my nose in it by being around here every day?"

The year 1957 has seen thirty-four nuclear bomb detonations in the U.S. But in its waning seconds, in the lobby of the Paradise Palms, number thirty-five just went off.

"Jesus, Mary and Joseph…" Franny utters, a bottle of Moët slipping out of his hands and shattering on the floor.

Rae, absorbing the guests' penetrating stares, squares her shoulders to meet Max's gaze. Her voice is strong and steady. "I just want to work. And I'm willing to work for you. Just like my brothers." She glances at David, Aaron and Leo, then corrects herself. "*Half*-brothers."

The brothers exchange gobsmacked looks – each speechless except for Rudy.

"Wait a minute… I got a fuckin' Black sister?" He slaps his knee and releases a hooting, high-pitch laugh.

As the guests begin to process all this explosive news, their attention is diverted by Welk's countdown as his band ramps up "Auld Lang Syne."

"Fifty-three… fifty-two… fifty-one…!"

Rae continues staring at Max, but instead of responding he simply turns to his sons. "Never hire a key position without my say-so again. I still run this joint. I'll fire the whole mess of you if I have to."

He collapses back into his seat. Kitty, unsure how to react to the sudden bombshells, resorts to snuggling closer to him. He elbows her away.

Francisco rushes over to Max to deliver a fresh flute of sparkling wine. Max takes it, distracted, watching Rae resume her clean-up duties. He pulls Francisco back down by his lapel.

"Fran," he growls. "Give her a goddamn drink, would ya?"

Francisco nods, pleased. He approaches Rae with his tray, offering her the last glass of good champagne. She accepts the drink but is confused. She looks over at her father. Lips pursed in consternation, he tilts his glass forward in a mid-air toast.

With a tentative smile, she toasts him back.

Outside, the new Paradise Palms letters are aglow in colorful neon, the protruding palm trees sizzling green and brown. Revelers are framed through the lobby windows in a haze of overflowing champagne bottles and shrieks of "Happy New Year!"

Just at that moment, high above the sign, a concussive burst of sparks lights up the Hollywood sky, raining down a smoky streak of fire and ash behind the hotel, like a disintegrating celestial orb plummeting to earth.

II

DAVID FUCKING SHAPIRO

CHAPTER 8

David feels the harsh knock of sunlight against his eyelids in that distinct way only January can deliver. There is something annoying about the L.A. sun this time of year. Maybe it's because it crests lower in the sky during the winter equinox, creating a more direct glare. Or the way its insistent beams penetrate the crisp air. Whatever the case, this morning feels like someone trying to pry his eyes open with a blast of energized photons.

"Mr. Shapiro?" A woman's voice – snappish, demanding. "David!"

David blinks his eyes open, acclimating to the radiation-level sunniness. Seeing his discomfort, the woman adjusts her body to block the sunlight. It is only then that David can make out the backlit silhouette by the window of Room 3.

"Darlene?" He stirs from his bed by the window, then squints over at the other bed, where Leo had sacked out the night before. It's empty.

David starts to sit up, his head heavy, as if someone replaced it with a medicine ball. Empty Moët bottles on his nightstand remind him why.

"Christ," he moans. "What time is it?"

"Two in the afternoon," Darlene says.

David kicks off his rumpled covers, clad only in boxer briefs. Darlene has never seen him in such a vulnerable state, and it makes his cheeks burn. For a split second, he wonders if the two of them ended up together last night. But then he remembers stumbling to his crash pad alone.

"Why—why are you here?" he says vexingly. "Is it Pop? It's my dad, isn't it?"

"Yolanda got me. And no, it's not Max. We knocked but you wouldn't wake up, so…"

David notices the slightly ajar door behind her. Through the crack, he sees Yolanda with her back turned, clutching a ring of keys. He starts to slide out of bed, then hesitates, waiting for Darlene to look away. She doesn't.

"Yolanda was worried that – " Darlene starts.

"Hey, if this is about her cleaning my room, I'm sorry I slept in. But it *is* New Year's Day."

"It's not that." Darlene comes around the bed and hands him his pants off the floor. She watches him shimmy into them. "She and Flori were doing their rounds this morning. And when she got to some of the guest rooms, she… well – "

"What guest rooms?" David asks, before answering himself. "*Rudy's* friends?"

Darlene shifts her gaze toward the door.

David finds his shirt on the nightstand and starts to button it. He smirks. "Let me guess… an overdose? Cocaine party? Wild orgy?"

"Better you should see for yourself."

David doesn't like the sound of that. He steps into his slippers and follows her out into the empty courtyard – save for Yolanda and Elron, sunning himself by the pool.

Darlene charts a path to the east wing, where Rudy's gang spent the night. Walking behind her, David allows his eyes to drift to her backside. She's outfitted in simple jeans and a black halter top, her hair pulled back into a rare ponytail that sashays across her bare shoulders, which has the effect of playing peekaboo with the flaming heart tattooed on her right flank. Waking up to her in his state of undress unexpectedly aroused David. Anxious and hungover, his brain still finds room for impious thoughts. Gawd, the things I'd like to do to her, he thinks.

They are twenty yards from Rooms 7 through 12 when David notices the doors are flung open. As he gets a closer look, his heart drops. The rooms are trashed – windows cracked, curtains ripped off hinges, gaping holes in walls. Room 10 looks like it hosted a bonfire. The rooms reek of ash and booze, the floors littered with empty champagne bottles, beer cans, and spent condoms.

Darlene sees the horror on David's face and instinctively grabs his arm. "I'm sorry," she says somberly.

David pushes past her into Room 10 to inspect the fire damage. He flicks the wall switch but no lights come on. He looks up at the ceiling fixture, melted and covered in soot.

"It's broken," she says.

David catches his reflection in the cracked dresser mirror. The image staring back is distorted, dark, disheveled – truly alarming. How did this happen to him? To David *fucking* Shapiro?

"Where's Rudy?" he asks quietly.

Darlene comes up behind him and gently drapes her arms over his broad shoulders, pressing against his back. "Don't," she whispers.

Her reaction surprises David. He clenches his eyes. "Where is he?"

She sighs. He can feel her warm breath on the back of his neck. He could never tell with girls. They play games, and Darlene plays her cards as close to the vest as anyone. Not that he hasn't tried. But every time he's tested the waters with harmless innuendo – always in social situations, never on the job – the most he's gotten out of her is a roll of the eyes or a wry retort.

And then it hits him. She's just trying to disarm him. Restrain him so he won't kill his brother. Kill Rudy. Motherfucking Rudy. *Always Rudy.*

In the distance, he hears the gimp laughing, that goddamn high-pitched hoot. It stabs his ear canals like a rotary mower blade. The hooting gets louder, coming toward him. He hears a second party, also laughing. Giggling. Some chick. Goodbyes are exchanged. Her voice, receding.

David looks outside, past the doorway. Rudy is shuffling past Room 10, hands in pockets, carefree as a butterfly.

"Don't," Darlene repeats, her hands squeezing tighter over David's chest.

David pries her loose and stalks out the door. Rudy sees his brother coming for him.

"Pretty wild, right?" Rudy says, rubbing the scar on his brow. "Don't worry about it, bruthuh. We'll put in a vandalism claim. Insurance will take care of every—"

David upthrusts Rudy's collar so hard, his shirt veils his entire face, exposing his belly and locking his arms above his head.

Rudy titters. "Whoa, who turned out the lights?"

David sinks a fist into Rudy's abdomen. Rudy makes a low groaning sound, like a bear being shot by a tranquilizer gun, and accordions onto the walkway. David drops onto Rudy's thighs, raining blows over his face and torso. Shackled by his contorted shirt, Rudy is blind and defenseless. David remains eerily silent, leaving only the thick sounds of knuckles-on-flesh and Rudy's muffled squeaks to fill the vacuum.

All that's missing is Marta's voice, sharply scolding David before tugging him by his ear off his poor baby brother.

•   •   •

Perhaps things would've turned out differently if David hadn't asked for a Buster Brown sundae.

Back when all four boys were living with their parents under one roof, the brothers were constantly at each other's throats. Part of it was just boys being boys. But Max's middling salary as the manager of a flower shop at the Hollywood Hotel meant they could only afford a cramped two-bedroom apartment off Franklin Avenue. Even after buying the Palms shortly after Rudy's birth, the Shapiros held onto the shacky dwelling, the hotel an unfit place to raise a family. When the larger, three-bedroom unit in their duplex opened up, the boys clamored for a move. But Max's free-spending ways and the stress of managing hotel costs during the Depression made it a non-starter. The family would occupy the duplex until all the boys moved out.

While Max and Marta shared one bedroom, the brothers squabbled over who slept in the second one. Marta wasn't keen on Rudy, as the youngest, sleeping alone in the living room. What if he toddled out the front door in the middle of the night? As the recognized alpha among his siblings, David became his brother's keeper, relegated to the living room sofa while Rudy slept on a cot. He was deeply resentful and took it out on Rudy, who regularly burst into his parents' bedroom in a flood of tears.

Just before the twins' senior year, Max and Marta agreed to let David and Leo overnight in Room 2 of the Palms during summer break and on weekends. The hotel was an easy four-block walk from the apartment, and the arrangement freed up the other bedroom for Aaron and Rudy. Other than late nights out when Max never came home – he claimed to crash in Room 1, but David and Leo rarely saw him there – a semblance of peace visited the family. David's absences from the house improved his relationship with Rudy, who was becoming more independent anyway. The late '30s and early '40s were a vibrant time in Hollywood and the Shapiros lived one block from its namesake boulevard – the West Coast's own Great White Way. A preteen Rudy liked to sneak into cinema houses, where he pilfered knock-off props from elaborate movie lobby displays. He then convinced his movie-mad pals they were actual props that he picked up at estate sales. Western items were especially popular. He once made a five-dollar sale on a bandana he swiped off a cowboy mannequin, claiming it was worn by Roy Rogers in *Young Bill Hickok*. He stole gum, candy and toys from various five-and-dimes, selling them on the schoolyard for twice their list prices. Kids gladly paid for the convenience. With the money from his rackets, Rudy took up small-time gambling, stalking Le Conte Junior High to hustle marbles and cards with cigarette-smoking seventh graders after school.

One night after dinner, Rudy casually announced that his fourth-grade class was planning a picnic in Griffith Park to celebrate Arbor Day. Rudy needed three dozen lemons so the students could all make lemonade. After launching into a Yiddish-laced tirade about Rudy's belated request, Marta ordered David – the only brother with a car and a license – to go buy lemons for his brother. With that, she left to attend a Woman's Club of Hollywood meeting down the street.

David looked over at Rudy and stewed. Once again, his kid brother's irresponsibility had become his problem. He figured he might as well get something out of the deal.

"I'll get you the lemons if you get me some ice cream," he chimed to Rudy, clapping his hands in a transactional manner.

"I would," Rudy shrugged, "but we don't got none in the ice box."

"I mean C. C. Brown's. I want you to walk down to C.C.'s and get me a Buster Brown banana split with extra hot fudge to-go."

"Can I get one for myself?"

"Of course!"

Pleased, David grabbed his car keys. "I'm headed to Ranch Market. It's the other way, otherwise I'd give you a lift."

Rudy just sat there, staring back at David by the door.

"What is it?" David asked.

"Aren't you gonna give me money?"

"Mr. Moneybags is asking *me* for money?" David laughed. "I know how you make out with your carousing pals. Besides, who's doing *who* a favor here?" He disappeared down the walk.

Rudy promptly reached under the table and pulled a dollar out of his shoe, then skipped out the door.

C. C. Brown's ice cream parlor was only two blocks away. Even by 1940 standards, it was considered "old-timey." Chairs and tables had curlicue metalwork, and the high-backed booths of black walnut and mahogany made you feel underdressed in anything but formal wear. Their biggest claim to fame was as the inventors of the hot fudge sundae. Day and night, the irresistible aroma of homemade fudge bubbling in kettles wafted down Hollywood Boulevard. Passersby were powerless to resist.

By the time Rudy arrived, the place was bustling with chatty moviegoers who had just left the Chinese. Rudy fought his way to the counter. The harried scooper with a peachy complexion – name tag: Myrna – recognized him and took his order: Two Buster Browns to-go. Extra hot fudge sauce. And could she hold the peanuts on one of them?

Rudy uncrumpled his bill at the cash register, waiting for his change from Dorothy, the elderly cashier with the hairy mole on her cheek. He never liked her – her mole made him nervous. To his right, a pack of college-aged kids bumped into Rudy, pushing him off his feet. Rudy shoved them back but they wouldn't budge. Then, something clicked in him – an opportunity. Could he help it if opportunities just found him? If they flashed themselves before his eyes like blinking red lights?

The person nearest him was a tall collegiate with an overcoat that grazed a basket by the register. It was filled with lapel pins – "C.C. Brown's – the *Original* Hot Fudge Sundae!" – selling for "5 ¢ents." Almost by instinct, Rudy casually slid his arm under the man's coat flap and rested it by the basket. His spidery little fingers crawled into the sea of pins, scooping out half a dozen. Still shielded by the coat, Rudy pulled his arm back and safely deposited the pins in his right pocket.

"Whatcha doing, hon?" said Dorothy.

Rudy's face went white. Then, as if coming out of a trance, he noticed the cashier was holding out his change.

"You want I should keep this or what?" she said with a cheeky smile that further thrust her mole toward him.

"Thank you," he mumbled, taking his money.

She placed two white cartons of banana splits onto his outstretched arms. Rudy was pretty sure he could feel her eyes lingering on him as he scurried toward the exit. A winsome couple entering the parlor held the door open for him.

As he started down the sidewalk, Rudy glanced one last time through the front window. He saw Myrna whispering to the old lady. He picked up his pace.

Dorothy's voice resonated behind him on the sidewalk. "Young man. Young man! *Wait*."

Rudy didn't wait. He ran. Ran as fast as he could across the street, not bothering to check traffic. Not noticing the Pacific Red Car rumbling down the center median. By the time he did, he had a nanosecond to react. He made a mad leap for the other side, banana splits exploding off the trolley's windshield. The brakes squeaked and squealed, sparks flying, steel on steel – but it was too late. The train's bumper crushed Rudy's left hip, launching him ten feet forward like a rag doll. His mangled body came to rest on a manhole cover amidst the screams of onlookers.

Back on the sidewalk, everyone from C.C. Brown's rushed outside to witness the horrible aftermath. Rudy's bloodied forehead looked like a cracked-open watermelon, his teeth strewn about like white seeds. Myrna collapsed in Dorothy's arms at the sight of him. The old lady seemed to be in a state of shock herself.

"I was just gonna tell him we accidentally sprinkled peanuts on the second one," she told Myrna, her voice cracking.

• • •

Doctors at Queen of Angels Hospital told Max and Marta to prepare for the fact that their son might die, or, at best, never walk again. The streetcar's impact had fractured vertebrae in his neck and damaged the sixth cervical section of his spine. Just as concerning was the skull fracture from landing on his head. Surgeons ran into problems draining brain fluid. During one dire point, the hospital informed the Shapiros that a priest was on standby to administer last rites. Max told them to keep the Catholic cocksucker away from his son.

Turns out the Shapiros didn't need a man of the cloth to pray for miracles – it happened anyway. After six weeks, Rudy regained some feeling in his hands and feet. After three months, he could feel his arms and legs. As the swelling went down in his spine, it released pressure on his sixth cervical, and new, clearer X-Rays revealed that the vertebrae were merely bruised – not broken. Still, it would take months before he could walk again. He was discharged from the hospital in a wheelchair to begin his long recovery at home. "Kid has a horseshoe up his ass," Max marveled.

For the next year, Rudy slept in a gargantuan mechanical hospital bed. Too big to fit in the bedroom, it dwarfed the living room, making it impossible for anyone to get comfortable or have guests over. The Shapiros couldn't afford a full-time caregiver – house calls by physical therapists were sucking them dry – so Rudy's siblings were expected to help with his needs. And Rudy had a lot of needs. As usual, David did the bulk of the heavy lifting, hefting his naked body to and from the bathtub. With each passing week, Rudy became more needy, more emotional, more belligerent. Max was convinced his son's head trauma fundamentally changed him. He had seen his own father become a different person after contracting "war cooties." There might have been something to this, although David was convinced that his conniving little brother was not above exploiting his situation to garner more attention. Hell, he was probably trying to get back at David – wasn't he the one who sent him for ice cream? – although the discovery of six C.C. Brown's lapel pins in Rudy's pocket did make David wonder if there was more to this story than meets the eye.

At last, David saw his escape hatch when he was accepted into Pepperdine's business school for the fall of 1941. But Marta couldn't imagine not having him around to help care for Rudy and guilted him into delaying his start date until the next semester.

It was a decision David would come to regret for the rest of his life.

In December of that year, the United States entered World War II after the bombing of Pearl Harbor. David got swept up in war fever, and any plans of attending college in January were dashed. He was hastily assigned to the San Antonio Aviation Cadet Center (SAACC), where the thrown-together quarters were so miserable, trainees referred to it as Sad Sack, a permutation of its acronym. The best part of the camp was pre-flight training. David imagined himself buzzing his B-24 low over Japanese targets. But Army officials killed his dream when an eye examination revealed David had "below-average depth perception." They assigned him to the bombardier unit.

Each day started at the crack of dawn. Cadets lined up outside their barracks – often in ankle-deep mud from pouring rain – and hoisted 100-pound deactivated bombs in the air to keep their muscles toned. Without fail, pilots-in-training razzed the bombardier students during their morning jogs. David hated them as much as he hated himself. Even at Sad Sack, he was second class.

Still, he was *David fucking Shapiro*. And if he was going to be a bombardier, maybe he would be called upon to firebomb Tokyo. But even here, his dreams betrayed him. David's circular error – a bomb's average distance from its intended target – was in the bottom-third of his class. One by one, he watched friends get deployed overseas while he was left behind.

Realizing he was not pilot or bombardier material, Army officials shipped him off to a new base called Dugway Proving Ground, a god-forsaken outpost in a remote corner of Utah. There he was trained to test biological and chemical weapons. The work was monotonous and dangerous. Human guinea-pig recruits were outfitted in "protective" clothing, then doused with chemical-laden sprays and flamethrowers to see how they held up. At the end of each day, David mopped up toxic slop in his coveralls, and he would hear the roar of fighter planes from nearby Hill Air Force Base. Looking up, he could see their jet streams carving glorious ribbons in the twilight sky.

After three years of military service, David was unceremoniously discharged. His veins pulsated with rage and shame. Though Grandfather Carl had returned a broken man from the Spanish American War, at least he had seen action, *real* action. Absent a hero's welcome, David fell back into an unremarkable existence. He was demoralized and directionless, grinding through shit jobs at the Palms just as he had at Dugway.

With Aaron and Leo away at college, David was cohabiting with the person he least wanted to see – Rudy, now in ninth grade and back to his normal incorrigible self. Even here David was an afterthought. Rudy was Marta's miracle child, a lying, stealing, manipulative mama's boy who could do no wrong. But to David, he was a living reminder that the gods of fate were conspiring against him. All his life, he had strived to do the right thing under the heavy mantle of "big brother." And yet the gods had gleefully punished him and smiled upon the huckster. Maybe, he often thought, he was going about it all wrong.

Maybe the only way to curry their favor would be to surrender to his worst impulses.

CHAPTER 9

Max jams a corned-beef-on-rye into his maw and chases each bite with a gulp of beer. Sharing the table are David, Aaron and Leo, picking at a plate of cheese and pickles over bottles of beer, with a milk for Leo. It's closing time at The Easy. The dining room doors are locked, the lights dimmed. The kitchen door is lodged open, allowing Franny to drift in and out with a rag and a mop bucket. Everyone looks a little weary, still nursing hangovers from last night's New Year's fete.

Max waits until Franny is back in the kitchen, then hunches over the table. "What happened last night stays within the family," he says in a gravelly whisper. "Understood?"

"Sure, Pop," Leo chirps, eyeing his brothers. "Our business is our business."

David smirks. "Little late for that, isn't it, Pop?"

"Whattaya mean?" says Max.

"The whole room heard and saw everything. Aunt Rochelle, Uncle Philip... all the regulars..."

"Ah, they're practically family anyway."

David notices Rae trudging past the kitchen doorway in her culinary whites, cradling a stack of plates. She starts to shelve them in a cabinet.

"You gonna tell us the story behind her?" David asks Max.

"What's to tell?" he grunts between bites.

"Like, which cleaning lady it was?"

Max stops chewing and drops his sandwich, as if he just lost his appetite. He glowers at David.

"C'mon," David entreats, "you're not gonna tell us who our sister's mother is?"

"Half-sister," Leo corrects.

"Even your own mother didn't know about any of this," Max grumbles, as if to justify his secrecy.

David folds his arms. "Yeah? Well, she's dead now."

"Show some respect!"

"How 'bout you show some respect to the living, Pop? If you really care about us, why do you keep shutting us out...?"

David stops when he sees Rudy slink out of the kitchen – straight to the bar for a scotch and soda. Max turns to acknowledge the gimp, then does a double-take when he sees his face. He has a split lip and swollen, bruised cheeks.

"Jesus Christ," Max exclaims, "what the hell happened to you?"

Rudy totters around the bar. "A girl got fresh with me," he says, locking eyes with David.

Max cackles. "Some girl."

"Yeah" – still looking at David – "a real bitch." He ducks back into the kitchen.

Max shakes his head and grins at his sons, who aren't joining in the jollity. He clears his throat and scowls at his glass of beer.

"It was Penny," he says gravely. "Penny Lynn."

The boys look at each other, racking their brains. David is the first to react. "Jesus Christ, Pop."

Aaron shrugs. "I liked her. Nice laugh. I remember she was always kind to us."

"Gave us lollipops," Leo adds.

"She had a sweet tooth," Max concedes, his eyes taking on a faraway look. "And yes, she was kind."

There's a long, awkward silence.

"Was it... was it one time?" David probes, "or did you two have a regular thing...?"

Max keeps staring into the depths of his suds – either not hearing the question or simply ignoring him.

"What ever happened to her anyway?" Leo asks. "Never missed a day for, what, two years, and then one day – *poof!* No goodbyes or noth—"

David and Aaron look at him.

"Oh... right..."

Max vigorously grabs his sandwich again as if to reseize the conversation. "*Obviously* I couldn't have her working here once we knew. She moved back in with her family. They cared for her until she had" – he avoids saying her name – "the girl."

"Rae said something about growing up in a group home in Val Verde," Leo says. "You were… supporting her this whole time?"

"Who else?" Max scoffs. "Santy Claus?"

"Why couldn't she live with Penny and her family? And you just send them money on the side?"

Max pounds his fist against his chest to clear a gas bubble. "I got a better question. Where the hell's Francisco been picking up the corned beef? It's grislier than a witch's snatch. Find out, would ya? Think it may be time to change wholesalers."

He pushes himself away from the table. The squeak of his chair alerts Franny, who scrambles over to give him room to stand up.

"I need one of you to help her move out of the home," Max says, flicking a toothpick into his mouth. "They still have the rest of her stuff. She wants to move it into her apartment."

"You can't take her yourself?" Aaron asks.

"It's an hour drive up there… it's a rough go through Newhall Pass. Caddy's prone to overheat." He sighs heavily. "I'm too old for this shit."

David, realizing: "You've been there…"

"Few times."

David looks at Leo and Aaron, all of them registering surprise. He turns back to his father. "We'll figure it out, Pop. One of us will drive and we can handle her luggage. But probably best if you come along. I don't like how it might look if only one of us were with her."

Max considers this. He pats David's head like a puppy. "You're good boys."

The brothers watch him leave through the kitchen, brushing past Rae as if she isn't even there.

"We should talk to her," David says, watching Rae scoot around the kitchen.

"And say what?" Aaron says.

"I don't know. Something beyond 'hello… how's it going.'" David turns to Leo. "You know her more than us. What's she like?"

Leo thrusts out his bottom lip. "Quiet. Assertive, obviously. There's a lot going on in that head of hers. She strikes me as very smart."

"Naturally," Aaron smirks, "she's a Shapiro."

"I think it makes the most sense for me to drive her and Pop. There's a comfort level between us."

David and Aaron bob their heads in agreement.

"In fact," Leo ventures, "the more I think about it, it's ridiculous she's staying at a place twenty miles away. Takes her four buses to get here."

"What are you suggesting?" Aaron asks warily.

"We have plenty of vacancies. She should move in."

Aaron puffs out his cheeks. "I don't know, Leo…"

"You just said a minute ago, she's family."

"Yeah, but… you heard Pop. People will ask questions…"

"Let 'em ask."

"Look, *we* don't care," David tells Leo. "But I think what Aaron's trying to say is… or what Pop is…" He stalls. "It could be bad for business."

Leo's neck stiffens. "Then maybe we shouldn't be in this business. We keep talking about what's best for us. What's best for Pop. What about what's best for *her?* All her life, he stashed her away like… a forgotten leper. Now we're doing the same."

Leo's unexpected passion moves David. As he marinates on his brother's point, Franny swoops by their booth on his way back to the kitchen. "Sorry, fellas," he says, "but I'm gonna close up. I can wait, though…"

"Huh?" David notices him reaching across the table for his empty beer bottle. "That won't be necessary, Franny. We were just leaving."

Franny smiles serenely. He reaches for Aaron's bottle, which Aaron is still clutching. The men's hands graze one another's, causing Aaron to jerk his hand back as if touching a hot stove. David and Leo look at him.

"So sorry," Franny says to Aaron, "I thought you were done."

"Take it," Aaron says gruffly, looking away.

David rubs the bandage on the back of his head, mulling the Rae issue while Franny silently wipes down their table. Aaron peeks at Franny out of the corner of his eye. He can feel the kid's dark eyes sweeping over him.

Franny straightens up. "Goodnight, gentlemen."

"'Night, Franny," David and Leo reply in unison.

Franny disappears into the kitchen, closing the door behind him.

David turns to Aaron. "What do you think?"

Aaron flushes. "About what?"

"What Leo was just saying?"

Aaron searches David's face for clues. For the life of him, he can't remember what they were talking about.

"I think old four-eyes's got a point. We're bleeding money." David shakes his head, as if ashamed of himself. "We should be *taking* guests like Rae, not turning them away. Times are changing and we're always pushing Pop to change with 'em."

"He's never gonna change," Leo grouses.

"Then we change without him. The old man's a dinosaur. I'm not gonna let this hotel go extinct too."

CHAPTER 10

As David's eyes navigate the Paradise Palms basement, he can't help but smile. So much of his youth was spent in here. It was his secret hide-and-seek place, a refuge from annoying brothers and mean adults. He liked to make-believe it was his "office." A kindly janitor named Julio had set up a little stool and table for him. He would come down with his connect-the-dots and *Amazing Mazes!* books, conducting busy work like the grown-ups at the front desk did. As he "worked," Julio would sneak treats from the kitchen – cinnamon raison toast with butter, or a tray of sugar cookies freshly baked by Marta – and the two of them would greedily savor them together, comfortable in their silence.

When he was feeling especially insecure, David would perch on the steps in the pitch black and imagine he was being held prisoner in the dungeon of a medieval castle under the threat of torture. How long could he endure the darkness before succumbing to his captors' demands? In another test of his mental toughness, he liked to see how long he could stand it while imagining black widows dangling off the ceiling or rats scurrying at his feet. He usually lasted no more than thirty seconds before his imagination got the best of him and he fumbled for the light switch in a rush of panic.

His fears weren't completely unfounded. When he was little, he was ecstatic that someone – he surmised it was the Easter Bunny – left a trail of chocolate-covered raisins on the basement floor. When he went to pick them up, Julio appeared out of nowhere to slap his hand away. "*Ratas,*" he warned him with a wag of his finger. With a flashlight and a ladder, Julio showed David that rodents were entering from an open ventilation duct that hugged the ceiling. It led out the side of the hotel at ground level. Rather than set traps that would endanger the boy, Julio simply installed rat-proof steel mesh on the pipe's exterior hood. Legend had it that the ceiling conduit was installed during Prohibition.

Bartenders in the upstairs speakeasy dispensed of beer through the pipe, whose hose connected to a truck parked on the side street with a keg in its hold.

Today the basement seems much smaller than David remembers it. Now it's mostly dusty shelves of canned food, bags of flour, and improperly stored, neglected wine bottles. He wonders how a room so dull and utilitarian could have ever held such a magical spell over him.

The squeak of the basement door snaps him out of his reverie. He looks up to find Rudy tramping loudly down the wooden staircase.

"You wanted to see me?" Rudy says with a note of caution.

David greets him with an overly solicitous smile. "I heard Pop had you measuring the cellar for radiation shields." He shakes his head. "Crazy bastard. Guess doing the rooms isn't enough for him."

Rudy's eyes skim the basement. "He wants to turn this into a fallout shelter using Civil Defense specs."

David nods vacantly, distracted by his handiwork on Rudy's puffy face.

"Novaya Zemlya," Rudy says.

"What?"

"Novaya Zemlya. It's an island near the North Pole. The Russians have been testing A-bombs there that make Hiroshima's look like a popgun."

David clears his throat. "Right. Well, be that as it may... we're not gonna worry about Russians here at the Palms. I've ordered Leo not to authorize any expenses toward bomb-proofing. We'd rather spend the money on spiffing the joint up."

Rudy arches his eyebrows. "Does Pop know...?"

"I'll handle Pop." David can't stop staring at his kid brother's face, which has taken on a vaguely greenish hue in the fluorescent light.

Rudy throws up his hands as if to say, Is that it?

As he turns to leave, David calls out, "Hey, uh... looking better. Though I can't do anything about your naturally ugly puss."

Rudy turns to face him, eyes rolling.

David's fingers twiddle in the air, as if trying to communicate with someone who doesn't speak his language. "Anyway... my apologies."

Rudy smirks and strokes his brow-scar. He murmurs something under his breath.

"What?" David says.

"THAT'S...WHAT...YOU...AL...WAYS...SAY," Rudy repeats, overly enunciating each syllable. "Never 'I'm sorry.' Always 'My apologies.'"

"What's wrong with that?"

Rudy emits a sarcastic hoot. "Nothin'. 'Apologies' accepted."

David can feel the room getting smaller. He has a racking urge to race up the steps, but his path to the door is blocked by Rudy, who suddenly doesn't appear eager to leave.

"Listen, since we're being all lovey-dovey," Rudy taunts, "I have a proposition I was gonna take to Pop..."

"'Cause you knew I'd hate it?"

"'Cause I know he'd *like* it."

Rudy reaches in his back pocket and pulls out a newspaper clipping. As he opens it up, David can see it's a torn-out page from last week's *Los Angeles Times'* sports section – January 3, 1958. A headline blares "Dodgers L.A.-Bound: Team Looks Forward to Celebrity Status."

David is nonplussed. "The Brooklyn Dodgers are moving out here. That's old news. What, you wanna go in on season tickets?"

Rudy snorts. "And pay full face price? What kinda sucker you take me for?" Rudy thrusts the paper into David's hands. "No, bruthuh, read the bottom half."

David reads aloud: "'I can't wait to see some Hollywood stars,' said Dodgers' first baseman Gil Hodges, an All-Star himself. One Dodger who is no stranger to the Hollywood lifestyle is L.A. native Duke Snider. The striking slugger has appeared on TV's *Father Knows Best*, and envisions himself continuing in entertainment once he hangs up his spikes.'"

In his excitement, Rudy snatches the paper back and reads the next paragraph. "'But before they get all starry-eyed, the players' first order of business upon arriving in their adopted hometown will be to find temporary lodging while they look for homes. And the City of Angels has no shortage of desirable – '" Rudy looks at his brother. "And so on and so forth. I also read they got some kid from the Valley named Drysdale who mentioned all the Hollywood clubs he can't wait to get back to."

"And so you think they should stay *here*..."

"It's right there in black-and-white!" Rudy jams his finger onto key phrases in the article. "'Temporary lodging... Wanna be where the action is....' We're *both* those things."

David can't decide if it's the best or worst idea Rudy's ever had. As is often the case, the line separating one from the other is often a tenuous one.

"Hear me out," Rudy says, splaying his hands in front of him like a land prospector. "In three weeks, the team will be going to Vero Beach, Florida for spring training. Real shithole, from what I hear… middle of nowhere. Nothing to do but get drunk. I fly down there and, y'know, meet the players at the local bars. Chat 'em up, all casual-like. Buy a couple rounds. Mention my family just happens to have some 'temporary lodging' right in the heart of Hollywood, only twenty minutes from the Coliseum – that's where they're gonna play their home games. I slip 'em my business card, and – "

"How much you need?"

"What?"

"I'm saying yes, Rudy. How much to cover travel and expenses?"

Rudy stammers. "I hadn't really thought of it. I figured you'd say no, so I uh –" He recomposes himself. "Four hundred bucks for the week."

David turns his head and squints, as if trying to get a read on some invisible bullshit meter. Finally he says, "It's worth a shot. I'll tell Leo to find you the cash."

Rudy punches the air victoriously. "*Thank* you. You won't regret this."

David hastens past him and ascends the stairs. "I hope not, because we can't afford any more fuck-ups. *Literally* can't afford 'em." He stops and addresses his brother from his upper perch. "You screw the pooch on this one, Rudy, and we're finished."

Rudy recoils. Finished? Who's finished? Finished with what?

David leaves him with a slavish smile. "Good luck!" he brays on his way out the door.

Rudy stands alone in the room, his face seeming to melt in the sickly light. "Always did have my back, didn't ya?" he hollers.

• • •

David's path out of the basement takes him through the kitchen. He nods at Francisco, Franny, Rae and a part-time line cook – the Hispanic man with vitiligo whose name he could never remember – as they prepare the night's meals. Through the dining room and into the lobby, he finds Darlene alone at the front desk, thumbing through another magazine.

"Would it kill you to pick up *War and Peace* now and then?" he asks.

Darlene looks up. Sees his playful grin. "I prefer fiction," she says drolly.

David chuckles. "I can't take any more of the hash they're slinging up in the kitchen. Join me for a bite?"

Darlene crooks her head back on her shoulders. "You know my shift goes till ten."

"I'll wait."

They end up at a comfortable diner off the boulevard called the Tick Tock, its walls festooned with dozens of working cuckoo clocks. Darlene sips a vanilla milk shake and pulls chunks off gooey dough off an orange cinnamon roll. David lingers over a Salisbury steak and water.

David points to her sugar-fest with his fork. "That all you're gonna have?"

She shrugs. "I'm consuming more calories than you are."

"Yeah, but it's the wrong kind of calories."

She licks frosting off her fingers. "My favorite kind."

David feels himself unexpectedly blushing. He concentrates on cutting his steak, avoiding eye contact. "Listen, you probably noticed my brothers and I are trying to take a more active role in the hotel since Marta died. We're worried about Pop."

"Understandably."

"Red Gordo is trying to muscle in on our operations. We don't exactly know his endgame, but we wanna stop it." He looks up at her. She has tilted her shake back and is waggling her straw to get to the ice cream on the bottom. "Working check-in, you're kind of on the frontlines. You'd certainly know more about his comings and goings than I would."

She is drinking straight from the glass now, the last blob of ice cream sliding down her throat.

"How much is he paying you?"

This gets her attention. She wipes vanilla ice cream from her red lips with the back of her hand and scowls, as if not understanding the question. "Gordo?"

"He pays you to keep room two open for his prostitution clients, doesn't he?"

Darlene makes a sour expression.

"Look, I'm not mad at you," David says. "I know we don't pay you enough as it is, so I don't blame you for – "

"So is that what this is? A cross-examination disguised as a date so you could pump me for dirt on Red?"

David realizes he's made a tactical error. He has conditioned himself to believe no one could ever have genuine feelings of affection for him and always assumes an ulterior motive when someone does.

"Your family has been very good to me. I would never take one cent of that scumbag's money and I'm offended you think I would."

David audibly chastises himself. "Sonofabitch," he mutters, pinching his eyes.

"He pays your father. I don't know how much, but I know he gets a cut. I know because I've seen it." She pauses to wipe away a rageful tear. "Yes, I give Red the room key. But only under orders from Max."

David covers her hand with his. "I know you're on our side," he says softly. "My apologies. I – " He looks down at their hands for a beat, then back at her, his eyes soft and sincere. "I'm sorry."

She clasps their hands together and squeezes tightly.

"Will you help me?" he pleads.

After their meal, the pair step onto the sidewalk along Cahuenga Boulevard. It's midnight. The normal hustle and bustle of Hollywood has given way to an unsettling quiet, save for a ranting homeless vet standing outside the Tick Tock. David slips a dollar into his cup, set on a newspaper stand.

Darlene points north. "I'm two blocks from here."

"I'll walk you."

Darlene lights up a cigarette as they stroll in silence. At the intersection of Wilcox and Yucca, two obvious hookers – one Black, one white – patrol on opposite corners like sentries of sin. Darlene heads west.

"Never knew you lived on Yucca," David observes.

"We call it 'Yucky.'"

"We?"

"My roommate and I." Then, unprompted: "She's at her boyfriend's tonight."

Her building is a two-story stucco structure, the words Yucca Knolls affixed in rusty cursive above the glass entryway. A streetlight out front flickers intermittently. Darlene unlatches the front door and the two of them pad down a long hallway with teal walls and stained flesh-colored carpeting.

Entering her upstairs apartment, Darlene leads David into her small bedroom. She cautions him against bumping into an ironing board partially blocking the door. Her room is messier than David imagined for such a well-put-together girl. The floor is strewn with heaps of black hosiery, lace bras and other undergarments David can't quite identify but recognizes from blushing past the windows of Frederick's of Hollywood. Sleeveless LPs and 45s clutter her dresser. Darlene drops the needle on her turntable. The smooth strains of Sam Cooke's "You Send Me" caress David's ears like sonic velvet.

Darlene leaves to use the bathroom. David perches on her unmade double bed with its leopard-skin spread. He notices a red satin sham between the two pillows. It displays a drawing of a kitten poking its head and front legs through a tangle of yarn, with a caption reading "Ain't I Paw-ful?" David smiles.

Darlene returns to the bedroom with a mirrored medicine box. She sits next to her guest and opens the lid. Inside are a lighter, rolling papers, a small baggie of grass and pre-rolled joints. She pulls out two of them.

"Would you believe I've never had one of those before?" David says.

"You don't 'have' them," she giggles. "And yes, I guess I would believe it." She returns one of the joints to the box. "Maybe we should just share one for now."

The pot hits him almost instantaneously. He knows this because he soon finds himself resting on her bed in his boxer briefs – floating, really – a feeling akin to relaxing in a warm bath, only better, because his bones are melting into his body, which has taken on the texture of broth. When he thinks about this image too much, he starts to freak out, but after a few more hits he closes his eyes and surrenders to the idea that his skin is the only thing holding in his soupy innards.

It is in this relaxed state that Darlene takes over. Lying next to him in her black bra and underwear, she rolls on top of him and mounts his groin, her inky hair tickling his face. David drinks in its essence, its earthy-sweet fragrance of shampoo and patchouli. Like newly-hatched turtles lusting for the ocean, his hands find the waistband of her panties and start to slide them off her gyrating hips. Darlene swings her hands down and stops him, grasping his arms like ski poles and arcing them up and over his head so that his knuckles bang against the metal headboard.

"Whoa!" he blurts, opening his eyes.

"Shhh." She runs her thumbs over his eyelids and gently forces them shut again. "Do you trust me?" she whispers into his ear. Her breath is hot like steam.

"I… trust you," he says slowly.

"How much?"

He wants to say "Implicitly" but the word sounds weird when he says it in his head, so he says nothing.

Out of nowhere, Darlene extracts a purple satin eye mask. She pulls the elastic over David's crown and fixes the mask over his eyes. She waits a beat for his protest. It never comes. Next she fastens a pair of lace satin cuffs around his wrists. David keeps his arms extended above his head, allowing her to tie the cuffs to the headboard.

Her partner properly submitted, Darlene strips them of their clothing.

As her lips close over his penis, a startingly sober thought punctures David's rapture. He has a vague sense of having wasted his life until now, and it causes him a momentary fit of panic on the verge of a full-on crying jag. He can feel his stomach heaving and wants to undo the cuffs and reach out and hold and *be held*. But her feathery fingers have a soothing effect on his body, bringing him back to safety. By the time her breasts brush softly against his cheeks, he realizes he has entered her, and he knows his world will never be the same again.

• • •

Darlene lies belly-down on the sheets gazing at David. Propped up on his elbow, he runs his fingers along the curvature of her buttocks and the arch of her back, forming goosebumps on her skin, so soft and pale as to be almost translucent. His fingers trace the flaming heart tattoo on her right shoulder.

"I'm sure there's a good story behind this," he ventures.

Darlene rolls onto her back with a sideways smile. "Not everything is a good story."

She pushes off the bed. David sits up and watches her naked form cross the room and flip the record over. She returns to the bed and picks up a carton of Lucky Strikes from her nightstand.

"I've been thinking about how you wanna know Gordo's endgame," she says, dragging on a cigarette. "There's a lot of hysteria in the air these days. It's obvious he and Kitty are duping your father into spending money he doesn't have on all those radiation shields." She nestles next to David's naked body. He kisses her shoulder.

"Red wants him to run the hotel into the ground," he speculates. "That way he can swoop in and buy it out from under him in a distress sale. And if that doesn't work, he's sending Kitty in as a Trojan Horse. My father's losing his marbles. If they get hitched, we're all fucked."

He reaches around her and plucks the lipstick-stained cigarette from her fingers – as surprised as she is that he's taking a puff. "The question is – why?" He hands the cigarette back and puckers, waving the smoke away. "Hollywood's going to seed. I just don't see a simpleton like Gordo having a long-term vision for our place."

She ashes the cigarette out. "Maybe that's the problem. You're thinking long-term."

"What do you mean?"

"A lot of hotels off the boulevard are rented out by the hour now. Supply and demand. You've seen the street-walkers."

"Yeah, like mushrooms. Popping up overnight."

She rests her head on his chest, feeling his heart. "You know how much money you can make turning over rooms multiple times a day? Especially a place like yours sitting in a prime location?"

She's right, he concedes. How could he not see what was right in front of him?

"He's already started it," she continues. "Room two was 'whore central' for months. A kind of test case."

"And yet he was cutting my dad in on the action…"

"Gordo's not an idiot. By giving him money, he'd come across like a friend who could enrich both their pockets."

Darlene stares at him. He notices for the first time that her iridescent blue eyes have little brown dots swimming in their irises. And they are casting anxiety.

"What is it?" he asks.

"There's just no way Gordo came up with this scheme by himself. There's someone above him."

"I've been trying to figure that out myself. He calls himself a 'facilitator.' But for who?"

She lays her head back on his chest. "Mickey…?"

David laughs so hard, the entire bed shakes. "Mickey Mouse, eh? I could see that, he's everywhere these days."

Darlene looks back at him. Serious as a cardiac. "Mickey Cohen."

David groans.

"One of his rackets is prostitution," she says. "It may not be him directly, but *someone's* giving orders to Gordo."

"Let's not flatter ourselves. We're small potatoes. What would Mickey's empire be doing bothering with us?"

Darlene leans into him, kissing his forehead and stroking his hair. "Who *else* would have enough money and influence to hire goons to bust your ribs – and get away with it?"

He tilts his head to get a good look at her. "How'd you get so smart?"

"I'm not smart. I only appear that way next to dummies."

CHAPTER 11

Leo finds the drive to Val Verde even more arduous than Max had advertised – there's no way the old man could've driven Rae up here in his current state. Just north of Sierra Highway, the cutoff road is washed out from flooding, forcing Leo to turn his Mercury M74 back around and look for a detour. Now he's truly lost, testing the outer limits of Los Angeles, a backwater country dotted with horse ranches, roadside shacks, and narrow mountain passes dusted with winter snow. Adding to Leo's discomfiture, Max keeps cranking the volume on the radio to ear-splitting levels, making it hard to think. Through it all, Rae sits in the backseat absorbed in a paperback she brought along, *My Mother's Castle*, by some French author.

After getting directions at a filling station, Leo encounters a whole grid of streets not on the map, part of a subdivision going up in Saugus. Realtor billboards line the road, advertising cheap lots and model homes. "Sears Coming Here!" brags the sign fronting the skeleton of a future shopping center.

Fifteen minutes later, Leo finally rolls into Val Verde, a community near the Santa Clara River. He's shocked to find such a mature town out here, as if a tornado had lifted the whole thing up and plopped it down on the edge of the county. Unlike suburban Saugus, Val Verde feels like a real, lived-in place with a deep history. Its business district includes Baptist churches, hardware stores, pharmacies, social halls, schools and parks with sports fields – a small-town America snapshot with one key exception: everyone is Black. Conversely, Leo himself draws curious stares as he cruises by in his Mercury.

"There!" Max points toward a lush valley at the end of town, where windmills and a water tank poke through towering oak trees. Leo notices Rae leaning forward in her backseat.

He swings into a dirt parking lot holding a smattering of cars and a yellow school bus. A beige clapboard house with multiple hummingbird feeders is bookended by two cinder-block dorms. Between the structures, boys' and girls' garments hang off clotheslines, billowing in the dusty breeze.

Furnace-hot heat blasts Leo's party as they exit the car. They're greeted by a gray cat with matted fur wending through Rae's legs as they amble to the front porch.

Rae reaches down to pat its head. "Hi, Misty," she says, smiling for the first time today. The cat purrs loudly.

Rae rings a doorbell encircled by a painted rainbow. After ten seconds, the door is opened by an African American woman about forty years old. Bucking styles of the day, her salt-and-pepper Afro bounces over her open, friendly face. She wears a multi-colored cotton dress and sandals in full-on Earth Mother mode. Everyone knows her simply as Glynda.

"Rae Lynn!" she cries. Her radiant smile creates little dimples in her cheeks and turns her eyes into mini-crescent moons.

Rae lights up. "Heeeeey!"

Glynda hugs Rae so hard, she lifts her off the ground. Putting her back down, she squeezes Rae's cheeks with both hands, causing her bracelets to noisily clank down to her elbows.

"You look good, sweetie. We all miss you."

"I miss you too," Rae says, eyes welling.

Glynda turns and sees Max. She nods at him – friendly, but less effusive. "Mr. Shapiro, long time. Always good to see you."

"How are you, Glynda?" he says, shaking her hand.

"Can't complain, and if I did, who would listen?" She spots a second man trying to blend in with a pillar. "And you must be Leo hiding back there."

Leo grins and steps forward. "Indeed I am. But how did you – ?"

"Rae tells me everything in her letters." She looks at Rae, then back at Leo. "Tells me you're a good man. Helped set her up in her new life, God bless." She guides them all inside. "Come on in. You're all probably hungry after your long drive."

"Starving!" Max proclaims.

"Well, that's good, because we're about to serve lunch in the commissary. It's meat loaf, yams and green beans today." Then, turning to Rae, "Though to be honest, we haven't found anyone yet who can fill your shoes in the kitchen."

Glynda has Max sign the Visitor Log in the vestibule, where a giant embroidered quilt reads "McDaniel's Residentiary – Home Is Where the Heart Is."

Leo wanders into the adjoining front room, a receiving area for incoming children. The walls are decorated with hand-painted flowers and framed photographs that chart McDaniel's throughout the years. Leo squints through his glasses and inspects one of them. It shows a group of beaming African American kids of all ages gathering around a moon-faced woman in the parking lot. A caption says "McDaniel's Dedication 1947." Leo can't help thinking that he's seen the lady before.

"Look familiar?" Glynda says, suddenly standing next to him and reading his mind.

"I can't quite place her…"

"Ever see *Gone with the Wind*?"

"Of course."

Glynda bobs her head. "You can place her."

She moves onto another photograph. Leo follows her. "This place was built by Hattie McDaniel?" he asks excitedly.

"It was actually founded in the thirties but could only hold a dozen children. By the time she came in, it was falling apart. County wanted to close it. Said there was no money to upgrade." She points to a weathered photo of the house they're in now. Next to it is a later image of the same house, now flanked by additions. "Mrs. McDaniel fixed it up and built the dorms, which increased our capacity five-fold. Also put in the garden and windmills. We can go offline if we have to."

"Wow."

"Pull your car round back and I'll show you. We got Rae's stuff in the barn anyway. It'll be easier to load."

Returning to the parking lot, Leo steers his car down a dirt driveway that leads to the redwood barn. A maintenance worker props open the doors, revealing a suitcase and large battered footlocker. Leo helps the worker lift it. Glynda and Rae come outside to join the two men.

Leo's slight, stooped body struggles to hold up his end of the chest. "Whattaya got in here, Rae?" he grunts. "Bowling balls?"

Glynda tsks and attempts to commandeer the footlocker from Leo. "Let me show you how it's done."

"No, this is a man's work." He nudges her aside on his way to the open trunk.

"Oh really?" Glynda puts her hands on her hips. "So what's a woman's work?"

Leo closes the trunk on Rae's belongings. He wipes his brow and looks at Glynda, who's clearly offended.

"I didn't mean it like that," he says apologetically. "Guess I was just trying to be chivalrous…"

Glynda lets him sweat a little bit more – then bursts out laughing. Even Rae finds her mock indignation amusing.

"Let's get Sir Leo some lemonade," Glynda jests to Rae, "before he passes out from gallantry."

Leo follows them to the one-acre backyard, or as Glynda calls it, the "life force of McDaniel's." Everything about it seems designed for maximum tranquility. A small spring-fed stream meanders through a well-kept garden with lots of benches. A tire swing hangs from a shade-bearing willow while citrus trees offer up a bounty of fruit. There are other little touches – birdhouses here, a stone sundial there, a chicken coop and a "wishing tree," from whose branches the children tie notes that contain their deepest desires. The water tower and windmills provide a picturesque backdrop to it all.

"It's almost like a movie set of the perfect garden," Leo observes.

"All Mrs. McDaniel," Glynda says. "She sweet-talked some MGM studio landscapers into designing it. Everyone adored her. They did it for free."

"You must've loved this," Leo says to Rae.

"Didn't love the chores," she says dryly. "But the kids realize, that's what keeps it nice."

"Speaking of which, where is everybody?"

Glynda leads him up the steps to an expansive covered patio. "Finishing up morning classes. Don't worry, you'll hear them before you see them."

Leo notices long picnic tables on the patio. A young girl sets the tables as several teenagers buzz through the back door holding steaming trays of meat loaf and vegetables.

"*This* is your commissary?" asks Leo.

"Al fresco dining is good for the soul," Glynda replies.

Rae recognizes the food preppers and exchanges pleasantries. Max is already seated at one of the tables, scarfing down lunch, a napkin tucked into his shirt collar.

"How is it, Pop?" Leo shouts loudly.

"Get me more lemonade, would you, son?" he says between chomps.

Before Leo can grab a pitcher of lemonade, Glynda fulfills Max's request, then asks Leo, "You hungry?"

"Not quite yet." He dabs beads of sweat off his thinning pate with a handkerchief. "I could really go for that lemonade though!"

Clutching two icy glasses, he and Glynda fall into wicker chairs overlooking the garden. Leo takes a long chug, then loudly gasps, as if coming up for air after being underwater a long time.

"How long you had asthma?" she asks him quietly.

"Me?" This woman doesn't miss a beat. "It comes and goes. It actually kept me out of the service, it was so bad once." Leo is fond of telling people this so they don't think him unpatriotic, though he conveniently leaves out the other disqualifying detail about his undescended testicle. "Nowadays it usually acts up when the smog is really bad in L.A. Didn't think there'd be smog way out here."

"Must be the dust storms. Had one blow in here yesterday."

Leo opens his mouth in a silent "ah." He continually fidgets in his chair as if he can't get comfortable.

"You sure you're okay?" Glynda asks.

Leo places his drink on the table between them. "Just a little… agita…"

"Well honey, why didn't you *say* so."

Leo is eager to shift the subject off himself. "How long have you been working here?"

"Almost twenty years."

"Husband? Kids?"

"Yeah, about sixty-five! What do I need a husband for when I got all them?" she laughs, the dimpled cheeks and crescent-moon eyes making an encore. She looks out over her Eden and turns wistful. "There was a time they called Val Verde the Black Palm Springs. We had movie premieres. Art galleries. Fashion shows. The WPA built an Olympic-sized pool you might've seen on your way in. But Black folks aren't trekking out to Val Verde much as they used to."

"How come?"

"Desegregation. Used to be only certain places we could go to in L.A. That's all changing. Why come all the way out here when you can just visit a local beach or park that used to be closed to coloreds?"

Leo thinks on that. "Ironic."

"What's that?"

"The more integrated the city becomes, the worse off it is for you."

"It's the kind of change we need. I just worry about the kids. Most of them have no parents or come from broken homes. If we lose this place, what will become of them?"

As predicted, Leo hears the cacophony of children before he sees them. Pouring in from the back door and the side yard, they stampede the patio with floorboard-shaking force, all clattering chatter and whooping laughter.

"The monsters are upon us," Glynda announces.

Max, still at the table, is caught off-guard and gets swallowed into the swirling vortex of youthful energy. Leo catches him feebly calling out Rae's name through the chaos.

"Excuse me," Glynda says to Leo, pushing off his knee as she rises out of her chair. Just like that, she flips the switch to matriarchal dominance and wills her charges into a semblance of order.

• • •

That afternoon the seating arrangements are rearranged for the drive home. Max, fatigued and wanting to catch some winks, occupies the back seat, bumping Rae to the front. He's out by the time they hit Newhall.

Leo finds a jazz station on the radio and turns it up. He lets a Charlie Parker number play out, then starts talking over the next tune, the music functioning as an audio buffer.

"My brothers and I have talked it over," he says, turning to Rae. "We don't like the idea of you living down in Watts. We want you to stay in the hotel. No charge."

She looks at him, confused, then stares out her window. Leo wonders if he's offended her in some way.

"Only if you want to, naturally," he offers.

She glances over her shoulder at Max, then at Leo. "What about…?"

"You're family, Rae. It's where you belong. At least till you've saved enough money to find a better place that's closer."

"Thank you," she says after a beat. "But can I think about it?"

"Of course."

She looks out the window again, the corners of her mouth faintly turning upward. Then: "I was there once before, y'know…"

"Where? The Palms?"

She nods. "I don't remember it. I was just a baby. The county wanted to meet my father before admitting me to McDaniel's. He couldn't drive out there for some reason, so they went to him."

Leo racks his brain for this memory. He would've been about sixteen years old when this happened. Probably either in school or at home. He and David wouldn't be temporarily moving into Room 2 until a year later.

"I'm sure he did it all in secret 'cause your mother never knew about it," Rae adds.

"And *your* mother… Penny Lynn?" Leo asks. "Had she passed by then?"

"Your father never told you?"

Leo notices her switching between "my father" and "your father," as if she can't quite reconcile how to refer to him. "He doesn't tell us much," he says.

"She was dead from complications within three hours of me being born."

"Jesus Christ…"

"Probably preventable." She pauses. "Not the best of care."

Leo looks at her. He wants to say "I'm sure our father could've admitted her to a nicer hospital." But he says nothing. A car commercial comes on the radio. Leo flicks it off.

"Do you know where she's buried?" he asks after a prolonged silence.

"Oh yeah. Evergreen."

"In L.A.…."

She bobs her head. "They had her in kind of a potter's field. Her family couldn't afford a proper tombstone or anything, so…"

"So you can't even visit your own mother's grave?"

"Oh no, I can." She sneaks another peek at Max. His head is wedged against the window, eyes closed. "Your father eventually paid for one. A nice one. Then he did it for my grandparents when they died."

Numbed by this stunning information, Leo nearly drives off the road. "That doesn't sound like him," he muses, steering the car away the shoulder. "But then,

I don't really know the man myself. He often comes around to the right thing. But when he does, he likes to hide his charity."

Rae nods in concurrence.

"Maybe I can take you down there to visit her someday soon," Leo casually suggests.

"I'd like that."

Leo looks at her, pleased.

"And yes," she adds.

"Yes?"

"I think I would like to move in."

CHAPTER 12

The call comes at 3:52 in the morning in Room 3, jolting David from a deep sleep. The phone's ring sounds extra shrill at this ungodly hour, triggering a memory of Marta whenever the Shapiro household was stirred from slumber. "Acch, don't answer it," she would kvetch. "No good can come from a phone call after midnight." She was always right.

David flips on the nightstand lamp between his bed and Leo's. Worried it could be about Max, he picks up immediately.

"Hello?"

Leo sits up and fumbles for his glasses. David mouths the word "Rudy" to him.

"Hold on, hold on," David says, swinging his feet to the floor. "*Where* are you?" Then, incredulous, "Las Vegas?!" He places the handset sideways on the nightstand. "Wait a minute so Leo can also hear."

Rudy's voice crackles out of the earpiece. "Room one-five-five. At the Riviera Hotel. And Casino," he says. His delivery is dilatory and heavy, the words overly specific. David knows from experience this means he's wasted.

"What the fuck are you doing there?" David chides, fisting his scalp. "You're supposed to be in Florida making happy with Dodger players."

"I made a little detour. And then I couldn't find my way out of it."

"What's that mean?"

Another man comes on the line, his voice deep and lispy. He sounds uneducated. "It means he got in over his head at craps and owes the house ten thousand G's."

"Who is this?" David demands. "Who's on the line? Rudy, are you there?"

There's a fumbling on the other end, some muffled chatter. Rudy repossesses the phone. "Hello? Is this David?" he asks, as if David had called him.

"Rudy. Focus. Is what he's saying true?"

"No. It wasn't all craps. Some of it was at blackjack, roulette…"

"Jesus fucking – " Leo starts, pounding his pillow.

David pinches his eyes, trying to keep it together. "What'd you stop for in Vegas in the first place?"

"I needed to make good with Gordo. He lent me money at the track, so I thought I could make a quick buck to pay him back."

David and Leo look at each other. They knew Rudy rubbed shoulders with Gordo and his gang at Santa Anita, but who would be stupid enough to be in hock to Red? They brush over that for the moment.

"How did you even run up such a huge debt there?" David sighs. "With what bread?"

"They let me play with house money."

David and Leo look at each other again – now even more dumbfounded.

"Well congratulations," David says, dripping with sarcasm, "now you got *two* hoods after you for gambling debts – Gordo and… who was that on the phone anyway?

"I dunno. Some associate of the hotel. The Riviera Hotel. Room one-five-five. Said he works for Turtle-tot or someone…"

"You mean *Turtletaub*? Sheldon Turtletaub?"

"Yeah, you know him?" Rudy sounds excited for all the wrong reasons. Snide laughter emanates from at least two men in Rudy's room. David drops his head.

"Hello…?" Rudy says. "You there, bruthuh?"

Leo jumps in. "What were you thinking? Where do you expect me to find ten thousand dollars?"

"Oh, hey Leo." Rudy muffles the mouthpiece, but the twins can hear him ask the others to give him a moment. This is followed by a gravelly voice uttering "Five minutes" and a door slamming shut.

"See, here's the rub," Rudy says once he's alone. "They said they're gonna lock me up in this room until I can secure payment. But I was thinking. If you guys could just come up with *half* of it up front, maybe they'll let me go as a show of faith…"

"How do I know this is not another shakedown for more money?" David says curtly.

"What?"

"You heard me, Rudy. How do I know you're not lying?"

"You just heard the guy on the phone."

"That could be a friend of yours putting me on."

Rudy hoots in disbelief. "I *said* I was in Vegas."

"You could be in Florida. Or Nova Scotia. Or Tim-buk-fuckin'-tu. We don't know *where* you really are."

There's a long pause on the other end of the line. When Rudy finally talks, his voice sounds thin and scared. "David. You gotta trust me. If they don't get their money, they said they're gonna cut off my pinky toe." A strangled laugh. "You want me to be even *more* of gimp than I am now?"

David and Leo look at each other, wide awake now, more awake than they've ever been. They realize at this moment that Rudy is telling the truth. It was only a matter of time before they too got ensnarled in his chicanery, and now that it's here, there's no going back. The road from this point forward will only be more bumpy, more chaotic, more unpredictably dangerous.

"I need to go," David says woodenly.

"So – so you're gonna try to arrange something?" Rudy's voice is trembling now.

"Goodbye, Rudy."

"Wait, what?! You can't leave me hanging! Go wake up Pop, I wanna talk to him!"

David grabs the handset and shouts directly into it. "Leave Pop out of this!"

Rudy's pleading voice bleeds out of the receiver.

"I said we're done!" David slams the phone down.

Facing each other on the sides of their beds, the twins strike identical poses – elbows resting on knees, hands steepled, tenebrous portraits of desperate contemplation in briefs and tank tops.

"Want me to try to take out a loan at the bank?" Leo asks wearily.

"I thought our credit's no good there anymore."

"It's not. But I can try other banks."

David crosses over to the window. He lifts the curtain and peeks into the darkened courtyard as if waiting for some nocturnal demon to come galumphing up to devour him. "I don't see the point in bailing him out. He's just gonna end up in hot water again. The cycle never ends." He sighs heavily. "Just a matter of time before he takes us all down with him."

"He's our baby brother. We can't just leave him to the wolves."

David, still staring out the window: "Maybe it's where he belongs."

●   ●   ●

Aaron leans on the door of his convertible '57 Bel Air, eating a sandwich. He's parked in front of Security Trust & Savings, an immaculate Italian Romanesque building at the corner of Hollywood and Cahuenga. It's the final stop on the brothers' daylong credit odyssey, which has taken them to a dozen lenders in the area. Leo had wanted to hit it last, figuring they'd probably offer the brothers a loan but at an astronomical rate. With high-end clientele that includes Charlie Chaplin, Cecil B. DeMille and Howard Hughes – rumors are he keeps his jewels here – the bank simply doesn't need the business of peons like the Shapiros.

Aaron spots David and Leo exiting the bank's copper-framed glass door, held open by a doorman in a red blazer. They look glum. He reaches into a paper bag and hands his siblings sandwiches as they reach the car.

"We didn't get the loan," Aaron says, trying to read their minds.

"Au contraire," Leo replies, "they'll loan us five thousand dollars…"

Aaron brightens. "Seriously? That's five thousand more than the other banks offered!"

"… if we agree to a fifty percent interest rate."

"Fifty percent?" Aaron's jaw drops. "Is that even legal? That's highway robbery!"

"It's fucking rape."

"It's getting raped on a highway after a robbery."

"Look, this is the best we're gonna do for an unsecured note," David says to Aaron, tearing open his sandwich wrapper. "We're delinquent on mortgage payments and back taxes. We haven't paid back a loan on time since '54. They had all the paperwork in front of 'em. We're not just high-risk, we're in the jet stream."

"What about a secured loan?" Aaron asks. "We'd get a better rate, right?"

"The banker suggested that," Leo says. "He said the land our hotel sits on is worth two hundred thousand dollars alone. But putting the Palms up for collateral…?"

"We told him to take a hike," David growls.

Aaron hunches his shoulders. "We *do* have our lots in the Valley. We could unload some of those."

"Those are untouchable," David insists. "That's our future."

"I thought the hotel is our future."

"Can't they all be?"

"Not at this rate," says Leo.

Aaron and Leo gobble the rest of their sandwiches in silence while David throws half of his away, griping about the stale bread. The boys climb into the cabin. As the sun drops behind the wall of buildings along the boulevard, long shadows streak across their sullen faces during the two-minute drive back to the hotel.

Pulling into the Palms' driveway, the brothers immediately sense something wrong. Darlene paces out front, having a smoke with Yolanda and Flori, who squat on the curb in their starchy uniforms. Distress is etched into their faces, and it's not like the girls to take their breaks at the same time.

David leaps over the passenger door and makes a beeline for Darlene. "What is it?"

She opens her lips to answer but can only muster a mournful gasp.

As David and Aaron rush inside, Leo stops to talk to the maids. "You two go home," he advises. He and Darlene follow the other two into the lobby.

They're greeted by Vance "Red" Gordo holding court behind the check-in counter, tanned, chipper, checkered jacket over an open-collared shirt. Seated next to him is a blonde bombshell in a tight sleeveless turtleneck filing her nails.

"There they are – the superstars!" Gordo crows. "Welcome to Paradise Palms!"

David forces himself to grin and play it cool, masking his outrage. "May I help you with something?"

Red places his hand over his heart in mock surprise, his sphincter mouth pinching into a little black hole. "May you help *me* with something?" His head swivels left and right. "I'm the one behind the counter. Looks like I'm helping *you*."

"Oh yeah? How do you figure?"

Red picks up a gooey lemon bar from a napkin on the counter. "Figure? I got a figure. Ten thousand dollars. See, that's the figure I'm out after paying off

Sheldon Turtletaub." His protruding incisors chomp down on the pastry, leaving a dusted white sugar ring on his wet lips.

David eyes the lobby. "Where's Rudy?"

Gordo chews his food with odd, rabbit-like rapidity. "He's around. Snug as a baby bird in a rug. Pinky toe still intact." Then, loudly smacking the sticky residue off each finger, "You're lucky. If ol' Red hadn't stepped in, that's not all he woulda lost. Most people who cross Turtletaub don't live to tell the tale." He stares down David for a long beat. "You're welcome."

Aaron makes a play for the house phone on the check-in counter.

"If you're calling Max, he ain't in his room. He and Kitty are out on the town. But don't worry, he approved the whole set-up."

"What set-up?" Aaron says, hanging up the phone.

"Y'know, I'm still not seeing any appreciation for what I did for your all's brother. You can't even manage a simple 'thank you'?"

"Up yours, asshole," David seethes. He comes around the front desk between Gordo and his floozy to hop on the phone for outside calls – and is immediately attacked by Red's torpedo-shaped pit bull, stirred from her slumber on the floor.

"Whoa Sally! Is that any way to treat our guests?" Red plucks her up by her scruff, making kissy noises as she snarls inches from David's face.

"I wouldn't bother with the cops," Red says as David dials. "Just gonna be a waste of your breath." He puts the dog down and tosses her his remaining lemon bar. David drags the phone away from the desk, turning his back.

"Yes, hello…?" he says eagerly into the mouthpiece. "Yes, this is David Shapiro at Paradise Palms. I'd like to report a trespasser… I said 'trespasser'… That's right. He's threatening us with… extortion." He makes eye contact with Darlene, as if to seek her reassurance. He gets back an uneasy stare. "He's trying to… hijack our business." A long beat. "Do I *know* him?" His shoulders start to sag. "Well, kind of. His name is Red. Vance Gordo. But I don't see where –"

David dangles the handset in exasperation, then bends it back to his mouth. "Hold on!" He walks it over to Red. "He wants to talk to you."

A grinning Gordo grabs the phone and kicks off the kind of convivial conversation two old friends might have. "Vance here… Detective Nash?!" He chuckles. "How's the family?… Oh, that's wonderful. Say, did your wife ever get that perfume I won at the charity auction? I had no use for that." A pause. "Wonderful. Hey, all for a good cause, I know how hard you fellas work. I bet your bedroom is smelling like a high-end Parisian cathouse." Gordo guffaws, then becomes more serious as he looks at David. "Nah, he's a good kid. Just a little steamed his old man hired me out to help around the hotel. Max sends his best, by the way." He starts to hang up. "Okay, you take care. Hugs to Gloria. Mm-bye."

Gordo returns the phone behind the desk. David sinks into a sofa, eyes glazed over, his body visibly deflating.

Darlene steps up to Red, jaw set. "Who are you working for? Is it Mickey Cohen?"

He chortles. "That old kike? You gotta be kidding. Last I heard, he runs an ice cream truck, pushing his Big Sticks onto little kids."

He flips open Darlene's check-in registry on the counter. "Let's get down to brass tacks, sweetie. I was looking at your books. You got a few longtime guests who are paying *way* under market value." He looks at the brothers and makes a sucking sound. "And your vacancy rate? I don't see how you stay in business! What's the point of your beautiful new signage if you ain't offering special services that separate you from all of 'em other dumps?"

He creeps over to David, who moves over to Darlene, feeling the need to be in her sphere.

"Heard you won't cough up the money for your old man to install them radiation seals," Gordo says. "That's too bad. These are scary times and people wanna feel safe. But that's okay. I got another plan that'll fill your rooms."

"You wanna turn the Palms into a whorehouse," David states bluntly.

"I prefer the term 'short-term adult-only occupancy.' You got a shit-ton of tourists around here. Many of 'em wanna take a load off their feet for a couple hours. You guys being right off the boulevard, and Candy here, hawking fliers on the sidewalk?" He angles his head toward his lady friend. "Seems like pro kid quo, you ask me."

"So she's the bait, huh?" David says tiredly.

"You busting on Candy? She don't just do PR, y'know. She's also my accountant. Got herself a business degree from..." He turns to Candy. "Where was it, hon?"

"The University of Advanced Finances," she answers in a girlish voice.

"There you go... UAF. And that's important, 'cause we gotta keep separate books." He points to Darlene's registry. "You run your business, we run ours. No reason we can't play nice together."

"I need a drink," Aaron announces out of the blue. David and Leo watch him march into The Easy.

"Great idea! A toast to our new partnership!"

"We're not fucking partners," David spits. "It's a temporary arrangement until you make back your ten thousand dollars."

"Well, hold on. Who said we're square after ten thousand? I got a commission coming for saving your brother's hide."

Darlene observes David balling his fists. Her hand gently drifts over his back.

"Normally, Red gets twenty percent. But you know how high I think of your old man. I told him, don't worry, we'll do ten percent, call it an even eleven G's. After that, who knows…?"

"What the hell's that supposed to mean?" David says.

"Nothin'. But from what I hear, Kitty and your pop are mad about each other. Who knows where it goes?" Red fixes David with the same fiery eyes and predatory grin he shot him when he was humping Kitty. He sticks out his beefy mitt to shake. "Whattaya say?"

David refuses his gesture, turning to head into The Easy. Darlene and Leo follow.

"What I tell ya?" Gordo carps to Candy. "No gratitude."

Candy pouts her lips.

"You'll be seeing some new personnel around here besides Candy," Red shouts at David's back. "I got some spics to help with the extra housekeeping. Those coons you got, they ain't on board with my plan. Unless that one in the kitchen wants to make a little extra – "

"Her name is Rae," David snaps, whirling around. "She's our *cook*."

"Don't I know. Makes a mean lemon bar. All the same. She got a mouth on her, that one."

Inside The Easy, David, Leo and Darlene find Aaron slumped over a drink at the bar. The restaurant is nearly empty at this late afternoon hour except for a smoky corner booth, where Gordo's apprentices – Snig and Felix – entertain two giggly girls who can't be a day over sixteen. A dozen empty beer bottles line the table. The thugs' unquenchable broad builds suggest they could just be getting started.

"Well, look who it is," Leo mutters to David. "Tweedledee and Tweedledum."

As Franny comes out to check on David's group, Snig barks at him from across the room. "Yo, Señor!" He raises a dead soldier. "Four más!"

David tugs Franny's sleeve. "Fran… they paying for those beers?"

Franny shrugs. "I think they think it's on the house."

"We're cutting 'em off. Tell 'em they gotta settle the bill. They got a problem, they can come talk to me."

Franny bites his lip and nods. He ambles over to Snig and Felix's booth, placing his empty tray on their table. The brothers watch him address the foursome with deferential body language – head bowed, hushed tones, shoulders folded in an apologetic manner.

Suddenly, Snig shoots out of his seat in defensive righteousness. Franny stands his ground, pointing out David so the men know to take it up with him. The men take it up with Franny instead, coming around the booth to confront him.

Aaron sees the situation quickly unraveling. "Guys…."

Felix kicks Franny's legs out from under him, dropping him to his knees, at which point Snig gets him in a headlock. The girls scream.

Aaron is first on the scene. "Enough! Stop it!" He attempts to pry Snig off Franny. Felix sends him reeling with an elbow to the nose.

Snig grabs a clutch of Franny's hair and jerks his head back. "You think you're too good for us, you piece of shit?" he squawks. David picks up the tray from the table and smashes it over Snig's head. The thug yelps and throws up his hands, allowing Franny to crawl away.

Felix spins around and launches a fist at David's head. He ducks.

Suddenly, a sharp whistle pierces the air. All heads turn to find Gordo in The Easy's doorway. Snig and Felix prick up like obedient Dobermans.

"Fun's over, boys," their boss says with a sly grin. "I need you on a job."

The goons lumber out the door as if nothing ever happened, leaving behind their trembling, sniveling dates. "Let me call you a cab," Darlene says, handing them tissues.

As David tends to Franny, Leo squats next to Aaron. He is slumped against the wall, blotting his bloodied nose with a handkerchief. He waves Leo off and rises to his feet, turning his concern to Franny. The kid is bent at the waist, legs folded beneath him, massaging his neck.

"You okay?" Aaron asks him.

Franny manages to raise a jittery index finger to indicate he's all right.

"Think you can lift your head up?" David asks.

Franny opens his eyes and slowly cranes his neck, blinking hard.

David turns to his brothers. "We gotta get him home."

Franny utters a meek protest.

"Leo, tell Francisco we had a little scrap out here but that everything's fine. Don't make a big deal about it. Franny will be home waiting when he gets off his shift at midnight."

Leo nods and heads to the kitchen.

"Aaron, give him a ride, would ya? You can just drop him on your way home."

Aaron hesitates. "Van Nuys is not exactly on the way to Brentwood…"

David gives him a hard stare.

"But yeah, no – of course!" Aaron turns to Franny. "Let's get you home. I'll pull my car up to the door."

CHAPTER 13

The drive to Van Nuys would normally take Aaron up Highland Avenue to the recently built Hollywood Freeway along the Cahuenga Pass. But after the trauma that just visited them, Aaron suggests a more serene route through the Hollywood Hills. Franny readily agrees. As Aaron's Bel Air climbs Mulholland Drive, both men start to feel better already, the cool mountain air a restorative salve as it rushes through the roofless cabin.

Aaron flips down the visor to check his sore nose, then flicks on the radio. "I'll make a right at Laurel Canyon," he shouts above Johnny Cash's "Next in Line." "After that, you'll have to direct me."

"Yessir," Franny yells back, relaxing against the headrest.

Aaron guides the Chevy along Mulholland's swooning curves with the deftness of a riverboat captain navigating a lazy river. Far off to the right, the San Fernando Valley unfolds as a checkboard of twinkling lights.

"Quite a view, huh?" Aaron says.

"Sure is. I've never been up here before."

"You're shitting me."

Franny turns to him and smiles. "I don't lie."

"Well then," Aaron finds himself saying, "we'll just have to take in the show."

Aaron steers the car off the roadway at the next turnout. He kills the headlights and parks in the direction of the glittering glow, creating the vertigo-inducing illusion of teetering off a cliff.

"Front row seat," Aaron boasts. He watches Franny lean forward in his seat — *their* seat, really, since it extends from door to door — taking it all in through the windshield, like someone enjoying his first roller coaster ride. Aaron reaches over and turns off the radio. Almost immediately, he wishes he hadn't. The chorus of crickets only accentuates the quiet, laying bare that it's just the two of them now with no distractions except each other.

"I used to come up here with Mrs. Shapiro – Peggy – before we got married," Aaron blurts. Again, more regret – it's as if someone else has taken over his impulses.

"I can see why," Franny replies in his customary polite way. Aaron notices their reflections in the windshield. Even in the distorted glass, Franny cuts a beautiful profile, what with his chiseled chin, angular cheekbones and dark, deep-set eyes.

Despite his best efforts, Aaron continues to prattle on about himself to fill the air, irradiated words that inadvertently shed light on his psyche. At first he just chats about hotel business, but this leads to talk about how marriage is like a business relationship, how it starts with love and becomes transactional. He talks about how children are like dogs in their obsequious acceptance of others. He talks about trying to break the patterns of his father, how Max will take secrets he and his brothers will never know to his grave. Mostly, he just talks.

"I'm sorry," he finally says. "What about you? Are you… happy at the hotel?"

"Happy?" It's something Franny never seems to have contemplated. He stares out into the void. "Yes, I suppose I am. I have a good job. Meet interesting people. I get to work with my father." He looks at Aaron. "I get to work with you."

Locking eyes with Franny, Aaron feels his heart pound against his chest wall and reverberate in his ears – so thunderous, he wonders if Franny can hear it too. He is suddenly frozen in fear, a scared little boy afraid to jump into the deep end of the pool, preferring that someone just push him in.

And then, in the tenderest of moves, Franny pushes. His left arm floats through the air as if being guided by a marionette-puppet master, then settles on the small square of upholstery between them. Aaron's right hand, clutching the bottom of the steering wheel, is tantalizingly close to Franny's. He remembers how Franny's hand felt when it grazed his own in The Easy – soft and warm and masculine all at once, exactly how he imagined it would feel like. And now Franny is waiting for him – he *is*, isn't he? – and all he needs to do is marshal the courage to lay his hand over—

"Get a room, faggots!" The bleating taunt comes from some cretin sticking his head out of a passing roadster, followed by peals of laughter. Someone hucks a beer can. It clanks off the Bel Air's trunk.

Aaron feels the blood drain out of his face. He starts the engine and jams the car in reverse. Within seconds they are back on Mulholland blacktop, racing west.

Other than Franny's occasional directions, neither speaks the rest of the way.

• • •

Later that night, in the darkness of Room 3, David perches on the windowsill to surveil the hotel's comings and goings. Gordo now "owns" the south wing, and his fuck pads are open for business. David has counted at least six shady couples coming in and out of Rooms 13 through 18 – some in as little as eight minutes. But he also keeps a watchful eye for his father. Ever since moving in with the old man, Kitty often keeps him out past midnight, no doubt contributing to his torpor and confusion. David and Leo have reason to believe that she – and Gordo by proxy – continues to sedate him to keep him in a constant discombobulated state.

Unfortunately, when the boys brought up their theory on a call with the family's estate lawyer and designated trustee, he was worthless. Relax, Robert Spiegelman told them, the trust was in good working order. With Marta now deceased, the brothers were equal heirs in the event of their father's death. If Max remarried, Kitty would have no rights to the trust. Not unless Max amended it and made her a co-trustor, like Marta was. Could he do that? Technically, yes – it *is* a revocable trust. But why, Spiegelman posited, would Max want to stiff his kids like that?

Unless, David countered, he was not of sound mind. Grifters took advantage of elderly folks all the time. Clearly, Max was being manipulated.

That's when Spiegelman laughed them off the phone while quipping they had watched too many gumshoe movies. One week later, Leo received an invoice in the mail – $58 for services rendered. Yet again, another battle the brothers would have to fight alone.

"Leo – wake up. They're back," David hollers to his brother, out cold on his bedspread.

Leo wakes with a start and grabs his glasses. David motions out the window. Max and Kitty are passing their room, about to turn in for the night.

Leo and David dash out the door. Max has just opened up Room 1, allowing Kitty to step inside first.

"Hey-ya Pop," David says casually as Max crosses the threshold. Before his father even knows what's going on, David and Leo have somehow wormed their way into his room.

"What?" Max says, disoriented. "David! Leo! When did you get in here?"

"Hi, Kitty," David says.

Whipping off her heels, Kitty hikes her stocking foot on the bed frame to unfurl her nylons. "Do you mind? What are you *doing* here?"

"We just need a minute with my father."

"It's gonna have to wait till morning."

"It can't wait."

Kitty sags onto the bed. "Well, make it snappy then. We're bushed."

"We need to see him alone," Leo adds.

Kitty shoots back up, arms akimbo. "Where do you expect me to go at this hour?"

Leo shrugs. "We hear Red has a nice warm bed."

"All of you, shut the fuck up!" Max bellows. "You're giving me a headache."

Kitty points at Max. "There! See? You see what you've done?"

David dips into his pocket. "Here's ten bucks." He shoves the money into her palm and physically closes her fingers over it. "Go watch the *Late Show* in the lobby. Fix yourself a vodka tonic from the bar. We'll be out in fifteen minutes."

Kitty starts to protest to Max, but he has already crossed over to the bureau to take off his fedora. David escorts her out the door and Leo shuts it behind her.

Max dumps an avalanche of coins on the dresser. "Whattaya gotta antagonize her like that for?"

"It's true what Leo says about Red Gordo, y'know," David says. "They're bawling on the side."

Max starts to unbutton his shirt. "You think I don't know that?" He emits a terse cackle. "I'm almost seventy years old. I get jealous of a stiff wind. Who am I to deny her a little fun, just like your mother did me, God rest her soul."

"Look, Pop, what you do in your private life is none of our business. But when it comes to the hotel, we're very concerned that Gordo – "

"Yeah... I know all about your cockamamie theories. No one's taking this place out from us." Max, now in his T-shirt and boxer shorts, runs a white hand towel under the faucet.

"He's already started. He moved in his hooker operation. Said you know about it. That you *approved* it. What *is* it with you and Gordo?"

"I had no choice!" Max barks. "You know what those monsters in Vegas almost did to your brother?" He suddenly looks very woozy, as if his outburst sapped his last bit of energy. "'Course you don't."

Max reclines on his bed and places the damp towel over his eyes. "You never looked out for the poor kid. Always in it for yourself."

Leo, coming to David's defense: "Pop, that's not fair of David."

David puts up his hand and shakes his head at Leo.

Max continues, "Look, Gordo's no mensch. But if there's one thing I learned is you gotta keep people like him on your good side. You do that and they'll help you out when you're in a pinch, just like with Rudy."

"And *fuck* you when you don't want their help?" David asks rhetorically.

Leo notices a jumble of pill vials on the nightstand near Max's head – so many of them, they cover almost the entire surface. "This place is starting to look like a regular drug store, Pop," he says off-handedly, inspecting their labels.

"Wait'll you get old, you'll see," Max croaks underneath his towel.

"Do you even know what these are all for?"

"Ask Kitty. She takes care of me."

Leo quietly scoops up a handful of vials and slips them into his pocket. David sees this and nods approvingly.

"I worry about you, m'boy," Max says hoarsely to David. "I don't know if you have the stomach to run a place like this. You're too worried about playing it straight. The system is crooked. Only way to survive is to run a little crooked yourself."

"I disagree," says David.

"You can agree or disagree, I'm just telling you the facts of life."

Leo, still nosing around the room, has now crossed over to the trash bin. It's overflowing with unopened envelopes.

"Pop, what are all these letters doing in the trash?" Leo asks. He plucks them out, starts rifling through them.

"I told you, you gotta ask Kitty. She sorts out the bills from all the crap mail." He whips the towel off his face and sits up. "What're you going through my stuff for anyway? And where *is* Kitty?"

"She went for a little walk," David says calmly.

"When?" Max blinks. "Did she come in with me?"

David and Leo trade concerned looks.

"She'll be back any second," David reassures. He comes to the bed and kisses his father on the forehead. "'Night, Pop. We'll let you get some sleep." The brothers see themselves to the door.

Once outside, David says to Leo, "Good job in there."

Leo's front trouser pockets bulge with prescription bottles. Envelopes flop out of his back pockets.

"Find anything out with the drugs?"

Leo wags his head. "They all have such long names, I don't know what most of them are for. Some don't even have labels."

"Let's show 'em to Elron. He's a regular candy man – he'll know."

"Heh. Good idea."

"What about the letters? Anything interesting?"

"As a matter of fact," Leo says, pulling an envelope out of his pants, "there just might be."

CHAPTER 14

As the newest habitué at Paradise Palms, Rae Lynn acclimated to life in Hollywood like a Labrador to water. After a lifetime in the insular, dusty purgatory that was Val Verde, she was energized by everything the urban scene had to offer. In car-centric L.A., it followed that her first taste of real freedom was behind a steering wheel.

"Buses are for losers," Rudy had advised her once as he pulled up to the hotel in a Corvette he was borrowing from "a friend." "Here, hop in and I'll show you how to drive."

He took her down to Riverside Drive along the Los Angeles River. It was a long straight road with few traffic signals, perfect for moving in one direction and letting it fly. The hardest part for Rae was learning how to shift gears, resulting in some lurching stall-outs. But once she grasped the concept of the clutch, the driving part was fairly easy. Rudy encouraged her to work toward getting her driver's license – he would lend her clunkers whenever she needed wheels until she had enough money to buy her own. Rae was humbled by Rudy's generosity but also wary of getting too comfortable with her youngest half-brother, knowing that magnetism is a charlatan's default veneer.

On the way back to the hotel, with Rudy back behind the wheel, they got pulled over by a police officer. Before even explaining why he was stopping them, the cop, a fleshy, ruddy-faced man with a blond buzzcut, asked Rudy if the young woman in his passenger seat was "his date." Rae's heart raced – she knew she wasn't guilty, but she *felt* guilty, certain that her mere presence in this hot rod must be against some sort of moral decency codes.

Rudy responded to the officer's question by grabbing Rae's hand. "She sure is," he avowed with a rascally twinkle in his eye. "Ain't she a looker?"

The cop's cheeks bloomed a deep scarlet. Disarmed, he told Rudy to mind his speed and let him go with a warning. Within weeks, Rae procured her license, fulfilling a silent promise to stop being a passenger in her own life and to drive her own destiny.

Still, most of her free time had nothing to do with automobiles. In between kitchen shifts, she liked to walk up to Hollywood Boulevard to browse fashion store windows or roam the aisles at Pickwick Bookshop, where the friendly clerk let her while away hours flipping through pulpy paperbacks. She reconnected with two former housemates, Regina and Alison, who had a flat on Ivar and worked as domestics in Hollywoodland. The trio got together for movies, always followed by malteds at C.C. Brown's, where they would gossip about the latest "graduates" from McDaniel's and what they were doing with their lives. They kept tabs on who had "crossed over" to mainstream society. This meant not just gainful employment and a place to stay, but changing one's look. Embarrassed by their staid, state-issued duds, Rae and her friends were constantly upgrading their wardrobe from their meager savings, starting with cheap accessories – a winter scarf, a cute hat, a small handbag.

• • •

One Saturday afternoon in early spring, Rae makes her first big purchase. It comes courtesy of the Broadway department store at Hollywood and Vine, where she plunks down five bucks for a discounted sleeveless frock with a rickrack collar – something Doris Day might wear. She convinces the saleslady to let her wear the dress out, then, on a whim, purchases a pair of cat-eye sunglasses as well. Slipping on her shades, she glides past the doorman into the warm sunlight and is struck by the urbane stranger reflected back in the store's mirrored windows.

By habit, she rummages through her purse for loose change to hop a Red Car back to the Palms. But then she remembers the trolley down Hollywood Boulevard has recently been ripped out, part of a citywide movement to purge its archaic streetcars. She considers taking a bus when a man yells her name. She lowers her glasses to find David jogging over from the other side of Vine Street.

"Thought that was you," he says, slightly out of breath. "Doing some retailing, I see. That's good."

Rae gestures across the street. "Did you just come from the Brown Derby?"

"I wish. But I'd have to sell the clothes off my back just to afford one of them Cobb salads." He points out the drugstore on the corner. "No, I'm afraid a grilled cheese at Owl's is more my speed."

He starts trekking west on Hollywood. Rae follows alongside.

"How's the room working out?" David asks. "Must feel odd living alone after group living all those years…"

"I like it."

"No one giving you any trouble, right?"

She looks at him.

"I realize there's a lot of foot traffic going in and out of the south wing. Not exactly Grade-A guests. I don't wanna drag you into all the family drama, but we're aware of it and doing everything we can to turn things around."

Rae nods, knitting her brows. Finally, she just comes out with it. "Flori and Yolanda have been thinking about quitting."

David looks at her, dumbfounded.

"Mr. Gordo's customers have been leaving the rooms a pigpen and they can't take it anymore."

"They're not supposed to clean those rooms," David says. "Red is supposed to supply his own people."

Rae shrugs. "He doesn't. And they have."

David curses under his breath. "I'll talk to them. Thanks for bringing it to my attention." He notices her lingering look of concern. "There's something else. What is it?"

"Yolanda mentioned a strange odor coming out of room eighteen."

"Strange odor?"

"Like… formaldehyde. I've smelled it myself. Reminds me of the disinfectants they used in the infirmary at McDaniel's."

"Can't she just go in and check it out?"

Rae shakes her head. "It's locked from the inside. Someone from Mr. Gordo's group is always in there and refuses to open it. So the ladies just stopped cleaning it. Probably getting awful disgusting."

"We'll look into that, too." He rakes his fingers through his hair and exhales. "Thanks for being our eyes and ears. But do me a favor?"

"Sure."

"Promise me you'll stop referring to him as Mr. Gordo. He's not worthy of the honorific."

She smiles. "Promise." Then, as an afterthought: "Let me know once you get that dirtbag out of there. Maybe I can help fill some rooms."

David stops abruptly on the sidewalk. "What did you just say?"

"Sorry." She covers her mouth. "I was trying to be funny, and I – "

"No, not the dirtbag part. I liked that. The other part. Filling rooms."

"Oh… well, I keep in touch with a lot of my old friends. Most of them, when they get out, they move to the city for work and need places to stay. 'Specially if they can double up in a room."

"How many rooms do you think you could fill?"

"Depends. If they know the hotel will take our kind, you'd get a lot of interest. People who already have a place may wanna move in too."

David nods absently. At the newsstand on Cahuenga, a man is selling drinks out of his cooler. David gets two root beers for them and brown-bags a cheese sandwich to go. "How would you feel if I put you on a commission?" he asks Rae after a gulp of soda. "For every room you fill, you keep twenty percent of the rate."

"Can you afford that?"

"Right now we pay Rudy an 'entertainment' stipend to hustle guests to the hotel. It's money down the drain. So we've – *I've* – decided to cut him off. This would be money well spent."

Rae thumbs the rim of her bottle. "I don't want Rudy to be upset with me."

"He doesn't need to know. It'll just be between you, me, Aaron and Leo. We won't even tell Pop."

She smiles. "Thanks. I'll see what I can do."

They walk in silence down Cahuenga. "Is that weird for me to say?" David says.

"What's that?"

"'Pop.' Y'know, '*Dad*.' I'm not sure what you're comfortable – "

"I just call him Max."

David grins and finishes off his soda.

•   •   •

When they return to Paradise Palms, David crosses the courtyard to Room 6 – Elron's unit. As usual, the drapes are drawn. David gets no answer when he knocks on the door, so he opens it with a key. The ensuing light is like a pickaxe cutting through the inky murk.

"Freeze, motherfucker!" Elron caws. David finds him squatting in a corner, stark naked, aiming his pellet gun at the door.

"Hey Elron," David says, not missing a beat. He pulls the sandwich out of his bag and places it next to a discarded package of Oreos on the bed. "Got you something from that joint you like."

Elron lowers the gun and blinks at David, who tosses him a bedsheet. "Why don't you wrap yourself in that," he suggests.

Elron staggers to his feet and comes over to the bed, shunning the sheet. He flops on the corner and tears into the sack. With his scrawny, exposed body, raggedy hair and splotchy goatee, he looks like a cave troll, emitting grunts of approval as he wolfs down his food.

"When did you last eat anyway?" David asks. He doesn't expect an answer. He knows Elron is in one of his bad spells – for the last two days, he hasn't let the maids in – and probably doesn't remember the last time he had real food. Like his career itself, his existence is either feast or famine. A former teen actor from New York, he initially feasted on a flurry of television gigs for NBC – bit roles on *Kraft Television Theater* and *Philco Television Playhouse*. He was lured to Hollywood in the early '50s by an actress-girlfriend, who moved out here ahead of him to jump-start her career in movies. That's when the famine started.

In a sad irony, his good looks worked against him. In New York, he was prized for his dramatic training, but in L.A., he was just another pretty boy in a city full of them. Agents put him up for all the wrong parts. Frustrated, Elron fell in with proto-beatniks, who turned him onto marijuana and Benzedrine. It wasn't long before he was hooked on the harder stuff. After threatening his girlfriend with a gun – the first of his many blackouts – she dumped him and moved back to New York to teach kindergarten.

For a brief shining moment in 1954, things picked up for Elron. For once, he landed an agent who put him up for parts that played to his edgy, brooding persona. He had a recurring role as a thug on *Dragnet*, and landed a walk-on on *The Lone Ranger*, playing a bank robber who gets shot between the eyes. He nailed an audition for an upcoming movie with James Dean called *Rebel Without a Cause*, so impressing the actor himself that he pulled Elron aside afterwards and said he would lobby for him to play his knife-wielding nemesis Moose alongside another upstart, Dennis Hopper. To celebrate, Elron went out and partied with friends...

only to oversleep his final callback the next morning. The role went to another unknown, Jack Grinnage, who would go on to have a career that spanned over six decades.

Broke and washed-up at twenty-eight – but still young enough to turn his career around – Elron moved into Paradise Palms. He has been here ever since, his days alternating between vampire-like nights in drug-addled darkness and curative spells drying out by the pool. When he really needs to sober up, he disappears into the desert for "spiritual cleanses." At night he throws a sleeping bag down in the sand, gazing up at the Milky Way to reconnect with the cosmos. During the day, he roams abandoned gold mines, looking for shiny flecks of fortune. Sadly, he usually returns to L.A. more frazzled than when he left, like someone who has been up for forty-eight straight hours strung out on peyote and black coffee.

To throw Elron out on the streets at this point would be to kill him. Because the hotel is never at full capacity, the Shapiros have agreed to let him – as well as Dirk and Art – pay whatever rent they can. In three-plus years, he's coughed up twenty-two dollars and fifty cents. It's not that he hasn't tried. When he isn't laboring over his unproduced play, he's been up for occasional commercial spots. And he's never lacking eager girlfriends trying to "fix" him. But even by Elron's own account, he's trapped in a vicious cycle. The only money he makes is from selling plasma and dealing dope – money he promptly spends on more dope to sustain his fix.

On his way out the door, David finds the pill vials Leo snatched from Max's room on Elron's dresser.

"What's the verdict on these?" David asks, inspecting each one as he drops them into his paper bag.

"They're all downers," Elron says between bites. "Some of that shit left me groggy for days... you could bring down an elephant."

David shakes an unlabeled container and realizes it's now empty. "You took these things?"

"How else was I gonna know what they do?"

• • •

Meanwhile, the "interesting" envelope that Leo found in Max's garbage had a return address for the California Division of Highways, Public Works Dept., in

Sacramento. Leo instantly knew what it might be about. He had read in the papers that the state was thinking about running a second freeway through Hollywood. The proposed route that caught Leo's attention was the Whitnall Freeway, which would start somewhere near Los Angeles International Airport, cross over the Hollywood Freeway, burrow under the Hollywood Sign, and let out in the Valley. It was by far the most ambitious of all the expressways and, Leo thought, the most ludicrous. An eight-lane tunnel under the Hollywood Sign? Who would ever go for that? Then again, it was only a few years ago that the Hollywood Freeway – thanks to eminent domain – cleaved right through the tony celebrity enclave of Whitley Heights. Even Rudolph Valentino's historic lair couldn't stave off the insatiable beast of progress.

The letter itself requested a meeting within the next ninety days with the "Owner(s) of the Property at 6735 Selma Ave., Hollywood, Cal." to discuss "Title 7 of Code of Civil Procedure for possible reuse for the public good." The words "eminent domain" never appeared, nor was a specific reuse purpose spelled out, but the intent was clear enough – the state was considering tearing down the hotel for a freeway.

The fact that the letter lay in a garbage heap was further proof that Kitty – either through carelessness or duplicity, it didn't really matter – was not acting in Max's best interests. What other important items or bills she was throwing away? During one of Max's more lucid moments, the boys showed him the letter, copping to fishing it out of his trash. He was surprisingly appreciative. In fact, his eyes lit up with dollar signs at the prospect of compensation for the hotel, and he was peeved at Kitty for tossing it. Lately, he was showing more indifference toward her, if not outright hostility. During his marriage to Marta, he swapped out mistresses like old socks once he got bored with them. David was hopeful a similar pattern was developing here, although he recognized that some of Max's behavior could simply be attributed to the onset of dementia or the fog of drugs. But one thing the patriarch was clear on: He would gladly join David and Leo when they hosted transportation officials at the hotel.

• • •

On the morning of the meeting, the twins get up early and head over to The Easy. It is the first Friday of April – the start of Passover. Though the Shapiros are not overtly religious, they have a longstanding tradition of closing the restaurant on the High Holiday and giving the staff the day off. Today they will have the dining room all to themselves with no distractions.

As Leo pushes together furniture to create a makeshift conference table, David brews a fresh pot in the kitchen and lays out pastries. Their guests are expected at 9 a.m. The clock in The Easy reads 8:53.

"We should ring Pop's room," David says, reentering the dining room. "I don't want him to be late."

"I just did, from the front desk," Leo replies.

"And?"

"The line was off the hook."

"Christ." This was not unusual. Max had a tendency of improperly returning the handset in its cradle after using the phone. Still, David wonders if maybe Kitty purposely dislodged the receiver to avoid calls.

"I'm going to his room," he says, striding to the door.

As he swings it open, two men in business suits block his exit, one of them with his right hand coiled in the knocking position.

"Oh, hello!" says the man. He has a pleasing gap-toothed grin and shiny cheeks. "We're a little early – hope that's okay."

Momentarily flustered, David is quick to show them inside. "Not at all. Please!"

Introductions are made. The friendly man identifies himself as Xavier Cortez, a representative from L.A.'s Metropolitan Transportation Agency. His partner, Garrison Olstead, is an older gentleman whose sloping forehead and beak-like mouth make him look like a turtle. He is from the state's Division of Highways, working with Cortez's outfit. He clutches a large weathered briefcase.

"Are those crullers?" Cortez gushes, tearing into a pastry.

"There's fresh coffee, too," Leo says.

Olstead partakes of neither. Parking his briefcase on the conference table, he unlatches its lid and starts to methodically pull out dog-eared maps and manila folders.

Cortez loudly slurps some coffee. "Let me start by saying, I'm a local kid. Went to Fairfax. Grew up in Hollywood. Know the area quite well. In fact, I know all about family businesses."

"That right?" David says.

"Mm-hmm. I used to help my father with his gardening service. He had a monopoly on all the houses between Sunset and Fountain – all word of mouth."

"That's fantastic. Is he still in business?"

Cortez grimaces. "He passed seven years ago."

"I'm sorry to hear that. He must've been kind of young."

"Never missed a day of work in his life. Then *boom*. Keels over mowing someone's lawn." Cortez reaches for a chocolate muffin and laughs. "Me? I got a black thumb. My brothers took over his business. I went on to college, got an urban planning degree…"

"First in your family?" Leo says.

Cortez beams. "Yes, actually."

"I'm sure your father would be incredibly proud of you."

Cortez looks at both Leo and David. "Brothers, huh? If you don't mind my saying, you guys look the same, but then you don't."

David chuckles. "We get that a lot. We're twins, actually. Fraternal."

"I got the ugly genes," Leo jokes.

"Nah, c'mon," Cortez cackles. "Hey, speaking of dads, you said yours is coming, right?"

"Should be here any minute," David says.

"That's good because, well… him being the owner of this place and all… it's important he be here."

"Unless either of you has power-of-attorney," Olstead drones, snapping shut his briefcase. "Do you?"

The brothers look at each other. "Not technically," Leo says.

"Well, you either do or you don't."

"No," David says flatly. He doesn't like Olstead, and senses some sort of good-cop/bad-cop jive with him and Cortez. He wishes his father would just get here already.

"This is just a feeling-each-other-out kinda meeting anyway," Cortez says casually. "No action will be taken today by either party. You could always report back to your father if he doesn't show."

Cortez sees that Olstead is prepared for his presentation. He proceeds to launch into a longwinded spiel that, to David, sounds suspiciously scripted. "Now, Mr. Olstead and I can dazzle you with our graphs and charts and whatnot about the phenomenon that is the Southern California freeway system. But understand this. We're not just pencil-pushers whose only concern is cars and concrete. We're people too. Which means we're in the people business. Every inch of freeway impacts someone's life. And we have *failed* in our job if you don't feel better about our visit than before we walked in here. Because when we walk out, we want everyone to feel like winners."

"Well," Leo says after a long beat, "I feel like a winner already after a speech like that. May I ask, why are we one of the 'lucky' ones?"

"Excuse me?"

"I've been talking to some of the neighboring businesses. They said no one from either of your departments has contacted them."

"Eminent domain is a selective process," Olstead says. "There is no one size fits all."

"Maybe now would be a good time to show them the plans," Cortez advises his map-wonk partner.

Olstead unfurls various maps of proposed and existing Southern California freeways, arranging them around the table like big square doilies. Then, as a kind of entrée, he places the largest map in the middle – the Hollywood region.

Olstead's bony finger traces a dotted line representing the proposed Whitnall Freeway. Officials, he explains, are trying to determine the best route through Hollywood. One faction favors simply paving over Bronson Avenue, directly below the Hollywood Sign and cheaper to engineer. Another contingent, Olstead continues, would prefer to dog-leg the freeway westward, merging with the Hollywood Freeway for a mile, then tacking south down Highland Avenue. While trickier to engineer, this scenario has several advantages. There are far fewer property owners along Highland, and most of those are businesses, not apartment-dwellers. What's more, Highland is a State Route – SR-170. "Less bureaucracy," Olstead says, the assumption being less interference from city officials. David gleans that Olstead's position as a state guy makes this his preferred route.

Cortez too seems bullish on this plan. He points to the intersection of Hollywood and Highland. "If we proceed with this route, where we're standing right now would be a northbound offramp!" he says gleefully.

Leo sweeps his hand up and down Highland. "And all these other businesses? Why haven't you approached them, again?"

"This is only Phase *One*," Olstead propounds impatiently. "Junctions. Ingresses. Egresses."

"Think of the money distribution like a pyramid," Cortez explains in plainer English. "The initial outlay goes toward buying up key plots along the freeway that will require wider berths. If the project keeps advancing, the state will be paying millions to those along the freeway itself – your bottom-of-the-pyramid folks."

David cocks his head at the men and smirks. "So I guess the sixty-four thousand dollar question is, what kind of compensation is the state prepared to offer those of us at the top of the pyramid?"

Before Cortez can respond, The Easy's swing doors fly open, startling the group. It's Kitty, strutting into the room in full business attire. "Sorry we're a little late. What'd we miss?" Max shuffles in several feet behind her, stooped over and hollow-eyed, a geriatric zombie.

"I'm sorry," Cortez says, "and you are...?"

She puts out her gloved hand for him to shake. "Kitty Kay." She sneaks a deriding look at David, then grabs Max by the crook of his arm and roughly scoots him forward. "Soon to be Kitty Shapiro."

Cortez takes a moment to put two-and-two together. "Oh, well... congratulations."

Kitty leans into Max's ear and shouts, "Say hello, Max. These are the freeway people. Here to talk to us."

David desperately wants to throw her out on her ass but doesn't want to make a scene – it's what she would want. She's playing grown-up. Best to ignore her and focus on his father.

He pulls a chair out from the map-strewn table. "Here, Pop, why don't you have a seat. You want some coffee?"

Max looks up at David with waxy eyes. He seems to not recognize his son. David has never seen him this incoherent, and swaps panicked looks with Leo.

As David guides him into his chair, Max scowls at the large map, as if it's in the way of an impending meal. "Who's is this?" he grumbles. "Why's it here?"

Kitty crouches next to Max. "Don't worry about that, sweetie." As she stands up to address the officials, she undoes her single-button jacket, exposing a tight bullet-bra sweater. "Listen, I don't know what you all were discussing before we came in, but the first thing Max wants to know is – what's your offer?"

Cortez notices Olstead mesmerized by her bust. He answers for them. "Well, we were actually just getting to that when you came in."

"And?"

"We hadn't discussed a figure yet." Cortez looks at Max, who appears to be nodding off. "Perhaps we could restart our presentation and see what your fiancé thinks."

"I can speak for him."

"Actually, you *can't*," David interjects.

Kitty crouches down next to Max again, rubbing his bald head. "Max, tell them I can speak for you…"

Max stirs. "Huh?"

Cortez chuckles nervously. "Look, we don't have to bandy about figures today. This is more of an informational meeting. We'll follow up…"

"Cut the crap," Kitty snaps, "what're you paying?"

Olstead rolls his eyes and audibly sighs. Cortez looks to David and Leo, who helplessly throw up their hands. Left with no choice but to placate this nutty woman, Cortez takes out a pen and pad from his suit pocket and starts to scribble out a figure, talking as he writes. "Sacramento has authorized us to compensate Phase One parties three dollars and eighty-three cents per square foot. Property tax records show this tract to be about fifty-five thousand square feet. Which computes to this amount – rounded up."

Cortez rips the sheet out of its perforation and hands it to Kitty. David and Leo crane their necks over her shoulder.

"Two hundred eleven thousand dollars," David announces as he reads it.

Kitty swallows hard, then says curtly, "It's too low."

David is pretty sure he hears Olstead murmur "for fuck's sake" to himself.

"It's just a guideline," Cortez clarifies.

David presses his finger to his pursed lips. "We *have* made numerous improvements over the years, including a swimming pool. In all fairness, there's a lot that figure doesn't factor in."

"You're right about that," Olstead says sardonically. "Looking around your property before we walked in here, I think it may be a little on the high end."

Did he just insult me? David thinks.

"It's too low!" Kitty repeats, this time in a petulant tone.

"Miss Kitty – " says Cortez.

"Kay. Miss Kay."

"Now that your fiancé is here, I really think we should – "

Max's chin bangs onto the tabletop. He's out cold. Olstead rushes over to slide his pristine map out from underneath Max's prodigious jowls before he drools on it.

Kitty crosses her arms and motions toward Max. "He gave me a figure he thought was fair."

"And what was that?" asks Cortez hesitantly.

"Half a million dollars."

All at once, Cortez, David and Leo let out an exasperated expulsion of air.

Olstead explodes. "Miss Kay, this is not a game show where you get to name your price. It's driven by fair market value. And half a million dollars is way, *way* above market value."

"Well, that's just your opinion then," she replies calmly.

"It's not an opinion – it's based on formulas!" Drabs of white spittle have formed on the corners of his mouth. "Comps. Data. Facts!"

"Tell it to the judge."

"It is absolutely your right to take us to court," Cortez concedes.

"You'll be laughed out with a figure like that, sweetie," Olstead harrumphs.

David and Leo hang back with droll expressions. This meeting hasn't just gone off the rails, it's entered the theater of the absurd. As Kitty and Olstead continue jawing, David walks over to Cortez and whispers, "Can I talk to you for a moment?"

"Uh... sure."

They head into the quiet of the kitchen. Kitty doesn't even notice.

"Please ignore everything she said," David says. "She doesn't represent Max or the family. And if we're gonna do this right, we'll hire a lawyer to negotiate in good faith."

Cortez smirks. "I figured as much." Then, turning serious, "But can I level with you?"

"Sure."

"We've both lived in this city our whole lives. You see what's going on. White flight. People escaping to the 'burbs. We can't build freeways fast enough for them. Like rats leaving a sinking ship, know what I mean?"

"I do."

"But just the same... our offer won't be on the table forever. A project like this can take years to get off the ground, at which point your property could be assessed even lower if the trends continue."

"I understand."

Cortez cringes. "Mmm, I'm not sure you do. See, that's if it even gets off the ground at *all*. All those proposed freeways on that map? We'll be lucky if one in five are ever built. Bonds mature, priorities change, fiscal calendars flip... there's just not enough money to go around."

His foreboding words have the effect of a wave crashing over David.

Cortez pulls out a business card. "Take this. Call me if anything changes." He hands it to David.

"Thanks."

"If it were me, I'd take the money while the going's good."

CHAPTER 15

The shrieks come in staccato fashion, primal and guttural, punching a hole in the placid night. Bolting up in bed, Leo feels his heart thumping in his ears. The sound is blood-curdling. Someone – a woman – is being murdered at the hotel. There can be no other explanation.

But Leo's inner-voice warns him not to do anything rash. The screams appear to be emanating from the southern annex – Red's wing. He knows Hollywood vice has turned a blind eye toward his prostitution ring in the form of kickbacks. David had warned everyone to be suspect of local law enforcement for fear of being framed. Leo decides to consult his twin before calling the cops.

He dials Darlene's place. David has been spending most nights there, going home with her when her shift ends.

"Hello?" The voice on the other end belongs to David, who figures any call in the dead of night must be for him.

"You gotta get over here," Leo says breathlessly. He drags the phone to the window and peeks out onto the courtyard. "A girl – she's being attacked, or killed, or… something awful."

"Wait – what are you…? Where?"

"Hard to tell… I think one of Gordo's rooms."

"Don't call the cops," David says. He is sitting up in Darlene's bed. She rouses and tries to listen in. There's a long pause in their earpiece. "Leo? Leo!"

"The screams… they stopped," Leo finally says. "There's some guy leaving room eighteen. I can see his silhouette. He's shutting the door behind him. Should I go out there?"

"Jesus, Leo, be careful," Darlene shouts into the mouthpiece.

"David, what should I do? He's walking away."

"Stay put," David instructs. "He might have a gun. Try to lock in his description."

"He's walking toward the lobby!"

"That's okay, no one's there at this hour."

"What's he look like?" Darlene says.

"It's dark," Leo says. "I can't even tell what race he is. He's tall – about six-feet."

"Does he have a gun?" David repeats.

"I don't think so. He's holding a briefcase."

"We're coming over."

As David and Darlene hurriedly dress, Darlene surmises the man is a tourist who assaulted one of Gordo's hookers. Sadly, it wouldn't be unusual in that line of trade. David has a sinking premonition it's more complicated than that – something darker and more twisted. Room 18... didn't Rae suspect something peculiar going on in there?

It's a three-minute drive from Darlene's to Paradise Palms. By the time she and David arrive, an ambulance is already parked in the driveway.

In the lobby, two strapping paramedics are crouched next to a person on a sofa. It's hard to get a good look – half a dozen guests, stirred by the screams, have bunched around the victim. David pushes through them. It's a woman, clad in a nightie, bent over at the waist. She's shivering like a small furry mammal, her stringy red hair veiling her face.

She lifts her head to moan in agony, eyelids flittering. *Kitty!* David almost doesn't recognize her without makeup. Her face is bedsheet white. A medic applies some sort of compression under her garment, dampened by so much blood it looks like someone dumped a bucket of dark red paint on her lap.

"Get back!" a paramedic barks, jabbing David's chin. Outside, the whining of sirens announces a second ambulance pulling up.

Dirk, one of the huddled, sidles up to David. "I see you and Darlene are late to the party."

David looks at him. "Her screaming wake you?"

"Only me and half of Hollywood."

"What happened – Gordo go on a rampage, try to slice her up?"

Dirk rolls his eyes at David. "Tell me you're not that naïve."

Two more EMTs crash through the front door with a gurney. As the men ease Kitty onto it, she howls in pain, clutching her abdomen. Darlene approaches the stretcher to comfort her, walking alongside, stroking her hair.

David spots Leo coming through the rear lobby. "Leo!"

Leo looks ill himself, still trying to process the night's events.

"The fuck happened?" asks David.

Leo motions David through the back door.

"Where's Pop?" David frets as they head into the courtyard. "Wasn't Kitty with him? You'd think the screams would've woke him."

"I'm sure he's out like a light. Probably for the best."

As they walk along the pathway, David notices droplets of blood. They stop at Room 18. A robed Rae blocks the room's entrance, arms wrapped around her waist. David finds this odd, but quickly realizes Leo stationed her there.

"Thanks, Rae," Leo says.

Rae and Leo train their leery eyes on David, anticipating his reaction.

He is alone as he pushes open the door. A tsunami of incongruous vapors swirl in the air – turpentine and bleach, piss and shit, formaldehyde and baby powder. The king bed is a cradle of ghostly carnage. David can hear the screams in its thrashed sheets, its mangled white towels caked with blood. The rest of the room resembles the marks of a ritualistic torturer. A bloodied knitting needle and gnarled rubber catheter lie by the door, seemingly dropped in haste. Next to the bed is a food cart – appropriated from the kitchen – holding an assortment of industrial containers and a jug of antifreeze. Here too are instruments of mutilation.

David is only four steps into the room when the nausea overtakes him. He looks for Leo and finds him bent by the door, eyes askance, as if witnessing this house of horrors one more time might do him permanent psychic damage. David squints beyond the bed, toward the dim light of the bathroom. Several masonry jars are lined up along the baseboard, each containing a small gray blob floating in a yellowish solution.

David puts his hand to his mouth and closes his eyes, willing himself not to puke. He fails.

• • •

The following morning unfolds like any other Sunday in the Aaron and Peggy Shapiro kitchen. Peggy ferrying blueberry pancakes from stove to table. Jolene, Billy and Nancy noisily and messily shoveling them into their mouths. And Aaron, draining cups of coffee as he peruses the real estate section in L.A.'s three main dailies, looking for more investments to support his family beyond those he shares with his twin brothers. Unshaven in a black bathrobe with thin colored stripes, the man of the house looks mismatched against the rest of his brood, who are all dressed up in their Sunday best.

He is also blissfully unaware of last night's shitshow at the Palms.

"How come Daddy always gets to stay home in his PJs but we have to put on church clothes?" six-year-old Billy protests as he gnaws on a flapjack, syrup dribbling down his chin.

"Daddy doesn't *believe* in Jesus, remember?" eldest Jolene answers in a sharp tone.

Aaron folds back his newspaper and eyes Peggy, the couple sharing an amused grin. He parks his elbows on the table and gazes at his three children. "Hey, you know how you all like different types of noodles?" he says conspiratorially.

He has their attention, but they can only offer up blank stares.

"Like, Billy likes spaghetti?" he says.

"Yeah!" Billy says triumphantly.

"But Jolene likes linguini?"

The kids smile.

Aaron points at Nancy. "And *you* like... hmmm, I'm trying to remember..."

"Macaroni!" she declares.

"Macaroni!"

"Yeah!"

Aaron leans back. "Well, there you have it. Mommy and Daddy just have different tastes in religions."

The kids look puzzled, not getting the metaphor.

"How come we aren't Jewish?" Billy demands.

"You're Catholic *and* Jewish," Aaron replies. He closes his index finger over his thumb so that they're almost touching. "You're just a teensy bit more Catholic, is all."

Peggy unties her apron and collects the kids' plates. "Alright, everyone. Teeth-brushing time. Let's go!"

As the siblings tumble out of their chairs, Billy whines, "I wanna be a little more Jewish so I can stay home with Daddy..." They disappear down the hall into a bathroom.

"That has to be the worst explanation I've ever heard," Peggy teases when she and Aaron are alone.

"You're right. Next time, I'll use a recreational drug analogy. Daddy into black tar, Mommy into bennies..."

Peggy slaps his arm.

Continuing their morning routine, Aaron heads to the sink to scrub the dishes while Peggy pads to the bedroom in slippers to put on nice shoes and finish her face. Five minutes later, everyone rematerializes in the kitchen, ready to go.

Peggy kisses Aaron. "Meet us for lunch?"

"I'll see you in a couple hours."

Smiling on the front stoop with his coffee, he watches everyone file into Peggy's car – Billy in his corduroy pants, ill-fitting dress shirt and red clip-on bowtie, the girls in matching purple jumpers. Peggy looks stunning as usual in a stylish black pencil dress. Aaron's pretty sure her motivation for attending church is driven by her desire to turn heads in the pews.

No sooner does Aaron return to the sink when there are four loud knocks on the front door. He turns off the faucet and grabs a towel.

"What'd you forget?" he calls out as he heads to the entryway. When there is no answer from the other side, he looks through the peephole – then quickly pulls his head back.

"Can I help you?" Aaron shouts.

"Agent Kyle Betts," comes the sandpaper voice from the other side of the door. "Federal Bureau of Investigation."

Fear flashes over Aaron's face. "I didn't do anything!" he yells reflexively.

A dry snicker. "Mr. Shapiro, I assure you this is not about you. Could you open the door please?"

Aaron's hand trembles above the doorknob as if it's emitting an electrical charge.

"This will only take a moment," comes the agent's beseeching voice.

Aaron slowly grasps the knob and opens the door. Agent Betts flashes his badge. He's got broad shoulders and slicked-back hair with a bristly mustache. He's dressed in a polo shirt and khakis, the kind of unassuming get-up Aaron might see on the links at the Brentwood Country Club, with one big difference – the handgun holstered on his hip.

"Come in," Aaron says. "Please excuse my appearance. I just saw my wife and kids off to church."

"I know, I saw them leave," Betts says as he enters.

Aaron blinks at him.

"So that we could be alone," the agent clarifies.

"You've been following me?"

The agent's brushy whiskers spread out in a smile. "Is there a place where we could sit down?"

Glancing at his firearm again, Aaron motions toward the veranda, where he leads Betts to a patio table by the swimming pool. An inflatable duck drifts aimlessly on its surface.

"Nice view." Betts sinks into a chair, gazing out onto the fertile hillside.

"Yeah. I like to come out here and think. Kids love the pool. We're teaching our youngest to swim."

Agent Betts unfastens the straps of his satchel.

"I'm sorry," Aaron says, fidgeting, "I'm being a terrible host. Can I get you something?"

"Me? Nah, I'm good." He looks up at Aaron. "Why don't you have a seat? You're starting to make *me* nervous, and I'm the one with the gun."

Aaron lets out a little laugh and joins him at the table. Betts pulls out a single eight-by-ten photo and hands it to Aaron. It's a picture of Gordo exiting Paradise Palms. A woman who appears to be Kitty is cropped out of frame. The shot was snapped with a telephoto lens, accounting for its fuzziness.

"Know that guy?" Betts asks.

"That's Vance 'Red' Gordo."

Betts leans over and points to the doorway in the photo. "And that's your family's hotel."

Aaron looks at him. "Is that a statement or a question?" He tosses the photo onto the table. "Look, I'm gonna need a lawyer if you want me to answer any more questions."

"Relax. We're not after anyone in your family. It's him we want."

"Then why don't you just get him?"

Betts tickles his mustache. "Well, we would if we could. We've been casing him for a while. But then he just… disappeared." He shuffles through a stack of documents from his bag. Each page is stamped "FBI - CONFIDENTIAL" in red ink. "We were hoping someone in your family might have an inkling where he'd be."

Aaron catches Red's name and likeness on Betts's report, including old mug shots. "We're not in bed with Gordo."

"But he *does* conduct a business at your hotel."

"And we've told the police about it."

"Useless, huh?"

"They won't even investigate. He's bought 'em off."

Betts nods gravely. "A lot of people think organized crime hides behind fronts of their own making, but you're not the first business that's been hijacked. Case in point...." He produces an image of a men's clothing store called Del Vista Haberdashery – the same place that issued Red's "work order estimates" for the Palms' radiation shields. "People like Gordo... they're a disease. Once they embed themselves, only way to get rid of them is to cut 'em out like a tumor. Otherwise, they spread like cancer."

Intrigued by this trove of Gordo dirt, Aaron sweeps the pages toward himself. "May I?"

Betts scoops them back. "'Fraid not, Mr. Shapiro." He points to the haberdashery. "I only showed you this one 'cause he's running jobs for your hotel through Del Vista. We'd be here all day if I enumerated all the rackets he has a hand in. Right now, that's not why we're looking for him."

Aaron stands up, growing impatient. "Honestly, I don't know what to tell you. It's my father you wanna talk to. It's his hotel and he's known Gordo for years." He walks over to the railing and looks down at his neighbor's house, then turns back to the agent. "Why *are* you coming to me?"

"Max and your brothers... they live full-time at Paradise Palms, correct?"

"Yes."

"We didn't wanna make a scene and spook your employees. Also didn't wanna tip anyone off connected to Gordo. My super figured we'd start with you... away from the Hollywood glare, as it were."

Aaron lights a cigarette, waving his hand through the smoke. "I'd like to help, but *you* know better than I where he roams outside the Palms." He finds it odd that Betts doesn't inquire specifically about Rudy, the only brother who runs with hoods. But he doesn't dare invoke his name.

"May I ask why you're looking for him?" Aaron asks.

Betts tickles his stache again.

"C'mon," Aaron goads, "I let you in here to ruin my quiet Sunday morning... you could tell me that much, huh?"

The agent exhales through his lips, causing his whiskers to flutter. "You heard of Johnny Stampanato?"

Aaron's eyes light up. "Of course. Lana Turner's boyfriend. Just got iced by her fourteen-year-old daughter. It's in all the news."

"At least, that's the story Miss Turner is telling."

"You think Vance Gordo killed Johnny Stampanato?"

"No. But he *is* what we call a 'person of interest.'" Betts jams Gordo's file back into his satchel, his business done here. "Him and Stampanato… they ran in the same circles. Gordo's name came up during a search of Johnny's personal property. Both were linked to Mickey Cohen."

Aaron almost swallows his cigarette. *Did he just say Mickey Cohen?* "The papers said Stampanato was Cohen's bodyguard."

Betts nods. "He also managed Mickey's prostitution and abortion empires. Gordo was what you call a facilitator. Trafficking underage girls across state lines, keeping johns in order, paying off local authorities…" He stands up and heads toward the house, Aaron walking alongside him.

"He's a pimp," Aaron says. "It's the world's worst kept secret. Why didn't you guys bust him when he was still around?"

"It takes forever and a day to build an air-tight case." Betts wags his head ruefully. "Anyone connected to Mickey has the best lawyers money can buy. Even Capone wasn't nailed on any of the real heavy shit – it was for tax evasion."

Betts pulls several business cards from his pocket and hands them to Aaron. "Look, if he comes back around, gimme a call. There's extra ones there for your brothers and father."

"Thank you."

Aaron opens the front door. Betts stops and turns to him. "I guess there is one good thing about Johnny's murder."

"Yeah?"

"Red's gonna be out of your hair now. Mickey obviously has him cooling his jets. Could be for a few weeks, maybe a few months." He shrugs. "Could be forever."

Aaron allows himself to feel a ray of hope… until he remembers they still owe Gordo a small fortune for saving Rudy's ass in Vegas. If Red can't run his prostitution ring in their hotel, how will they ever pay him back? The gangster isn't one to forgive debts, even if he isn't around.

III

SHADOWS OF THE PALMS

CHAPTER 16

Normalcy. It's all David, Leo and Aaron Shapiro crave, when it comes right down to it. Rudy, the brothers have determined, is a lost cause. The kid is wired differently, happiest when cavorting with danger. If he can't live on the razor's edge, he'll probably slip and find the razor anyway. And so the boys alternate between sticks and carrots, taking away his entertainment stipend but bumping up his fixed handyman salary – money he can't misappropriate. "What he does outside of the Palms is his own funeral," as David is prone to saying.

As for Max, his relationship with his sons has evolved into an unspoken understanding. David calls the shots. Leo and Aaron are his first lieutenants. Max is done with hotel management but clinging to his role as Palms patriarch. He still relishes the prestige that comes with being the owner, likes holding court in The Easy. Even if he wanted to make the myriad decisions needed to operate a hostelry on a daily basis, he is incapable of it, his mind slowly turning to mush since Marta's death.

That hasn't stopped him from registering opinions that are unpropitious to the hotel's well-being. But David has found a workaround here too – inertia. Whenever he disagrees with anything the old man requests, he simply "agrees" and never acts on it. Invariably, Max will forget. If he persists, David assures him they have encountered delays and will look into it, repeating this cycle as often as necessary until the directive is cleanly scrubbed from Max's memory bank. Radiation-resistant rooms and a fallout shelter are just some of the dreck David has successfully swept into the bin of Shitty Ideas, many of which originated from Kitty and Gordo, who are now – thank God – indefinitely out of the picture.

One morning in early summer, the Paradise Palms lobby really *does* feel like old times. With Gordo MIA, his merry band of perverts have been vanquished from the south wing. Rudy's sketchy friends have stopped dropping by. And Kitty hasn't been seen since her traumatic, near-death experience in April. Assuming their familiar roles, Darlene and Leo man the check-in counter while Elron and Dirk laze on sofas with other stragglers, including a recently arrived, adorable old Polish couple, Simon and Lena Kaminski, who speak nary a word of English but are quick with a laugh. All eyes are glued to the giant Zenith to watch Art Mankowitz's alter ego – Chubs the Clown – make his television debut on a local children's show called *Hopalong Harry*. He enters the stage tugging a wagon full of deflated colored balloons for the live studio audience.

Dirk – looking sallow and using a walker – teeters over to Elron and rains down five singles onto his lap.

"What's that for?" Leo says from his post, smiling.

Dirk glares at Leo. "I made a bet with Elron: We'd land a man on the moon before Art ever got on TV." Dirk returns to his seat, grumbling. "Clearly God's idea of a sick joke."

Rudy and Aaron have just entered the lobby. Rudy is in manual labor mode – carpenter pants, toolbox, T-shirt smudged with grease. Aaron looks immaculate in a crisp suit and open-collared linen shirt. Standing in the back, both are amused by Art's frazzled appearance, flop-sweat muddying his whiteface as he frantically blows up sausage-shaped balloons and wrestles them into animals for an army of hyper children.

"Poor Art," Darlene clucks, rocking her head.

"Dream gig for the perv," Rudy says to Aaron.

Aaron looks at Rudy, then back at the TV, unsure what he's driving at.

"He has a whole stash of little-boy material." Rudy hoots. "I've seen it under his sink when I was fixing it. The kinda queer shit they peddle in Holland. But I guess whatever floats your boat, right?"

Aaron turns toward the lobby's rear door. "Let's go," he says abruptly, "we got work to do."

The brothers head toward the south wing, now undergoing a facelift. Ever since Red skipped town, David felt that Rooms 13 to 18 were tainted and ordered guests redirected to other units. Then the brothers made the hard decision to shutter The Easy's kitchen for lunch. The money saved by not operating a full-time restaurant should offset the renovations but will hardly make a dent in Rudy's remaining debt – now down to $4,000, according to Gordo before he vanished.

Tackling Room 18 was a whole other matter. The Shapiros never did find out who the abortion "doctor" was who bounced in the dead of night, leaving Kitty to bleed out. David's top priority was to make sure no mention of the black-market clinic ever went public. This wasn't a concern with the hotel's entrenched tenants – they had grown accustomed to bizarre goings-on in return for below-market rates – but it did present a challenge for the half-dozen tourists awakened by Kitty's ghoulish screams and bloody aftermath. David promptly gave them free maps to Hollywood Stars' Homes (street value: twenty-five cents) from a stack they kept behind the check-in counter. Now that they are presumably in the clear, David entrusts Aaron to oversee Rudy's efforts to expunge Room 18 of its past incarnation. Rudy is convinced the work is punitive – a kind of perverse payback by his brothers for the financial hole he put them all in.

Today, Aaron orders Rudy to scrub the carpet with an industrial cleaner while he talks to Max. He finds him on the pool patio, chowing down a breakfast of fried eggs, bacon and toasted rye that Rae prepared for him. He looks alert and well-groomed, his complexion ruddy, back to wearing clothes instead of a bathrobe for most of the day when Kitty was around. Even his signature fedora is back.

"Looking good, Pop," Aaron chirps.

Max looks up from his paper. "You say something, son?"

"I said, you're looking good."

Max shrugs and continues his meal, predictably eschewing introspection.

"Heard from Kitty?" Aaron prods. David has advised his brothers not to mention her, but Aaron can't help fishing.

"Matter of fact, she sent me a letter from Kingman," Max says, referring to the Arizona town where Kitty moved back in with her mother. "Says she's doing better, but her 'plumbing' is shot."

Aaron nods. Sometime during her procedure, Kitty had previously written, the quack had missed her cervix with a knitting needle and pricked an artery, leading to her severe hemorrhaging. She also suffered internal organ damage from untold injected solvents.

"At least she survived," Aaron says. "Probably good she's reunited with her mother. I know they were estranged. Maybe a new beginning for them…"

Just then, Rae comes onto the scene to ask Max if he needs anything else.

"Nothing, dear," Max replies warmly.

Rae smiles, turns to Aaron. "Have you eaten?"

"I did, thanks," he says brusquely. She lingers for a spell but sees that she's interrupted an important conversation. While she has bonded with her other half-brothers, she continues to get an inexplicable cold shoulder from Aaron.

Aaron and Max watch Rae leave, after which Max surprises Aaron with a candid admission. "I miss her," he says wistfully, referring to Kitty.

Aaron takes a seat next to his father. "Yeah, but Pop... look how good you're doing." He appraises his father with a sly grin. "Besides, a player like you? You'll be fighting broads off again in no time."

Max isn't biting. "I need her."

"You're just lonely, Pop. I get it. You're a red-blooded male in need of female companionship. It's human nature to – "

"Goddamn it, stop telling me who or what you think I am. All of you. Who the hell else is gonna take care of this ole bag o' bones?"

"*Us*. Your children. And if we have to get you help, we will."

"You're talking bodily needs." He clutches at his chest. "I'm talking affairs of the heart."

Aaron sees there's no reasoning with his father's dusty, amorous precepts, so he tries shame. "You know that baby was Red's, right? Does it bother you that they'll just end up shacking up again if she comes back here?"

"He's gone," Max grunts with a dismissive wave. "He ain't coming back."

"How do you know?"

"Never mind how I know. I know."

Aaron isn't sure if his father is relying on a hunch or direct communication, but he fears it's the latter. It certainly can't be from the L.A. papers. Every morning since his visit from Agent Betts, Aaron has been poring through the *Times*, *Herald-Express* and *Examiner*, front to back. There *have* been several follow-ups about the Johnny Stompanato murder. Mostly juicy tidbits about Stompanato himself, including the revolving door of bogus storefronts he owned – a pet store, a gift shop, a jewelry boutique, a car lot – to help sustain Mickey Cohen's empire. There was also a quirky anecdote in which Johnny stormed a movie set and threatened Sean Connery with a gun for trying to steal away Lana Turner, only to have the comically unperturbed Welsh actor wrench the weapon out of his hand and get him booted off the set.

A couple of articles, however, hit close to home. It was revealed that Stompanato was under investigation by the FBI under the White Slave Act as a "procurer of prostitutes" – part of a massive L.A. ring that included several pimps now under investigation. He was also confirmed as Mickey's "point person for back-alley abortion parlors." There was never a mention of a Vance "Red" Gordo, but his presence as a facilitator to said crimes hovered between the lines.

Aaron sees that his father has returned to his breakfast and morning paper, a sign that they're done talking. He decides to pop back into Room 18 to see how Rudy is coming along with that cleaner, but is distracted by the sight of David and Francisco leaving Room 3 and heading toward Max. The normally elegant Francisco has a pinched expression and heavy gait, as if carrying the weight of the world on his back.

"Pop," Aaron hears David say, "I'm sorry to interrupt your breakfast, but I'm afraid Francisco's got some bad news…"

• • •

That night, Aaron waits until the last patron files out of The Easy to make his move. Earlier, he had called Peggy to tell her to kiss the children good night for him. "Hotel emergency," he said. And there was – just not one that he could share with her.

After walking through the empty dining room, he pushes through the swing doors of the kitchen, where he finds Franny alone, sweeping the floor. His back to Aaron, he does not notice him enter.

"Heard you and your father are leaving for Cuba," Aaron says.

Franny's shoulders tighten. He spins around to find Aaron standing on the other side of the food prep table. He leans his broom against the wall.

"It's bad," he asserts forlornly. "Castro seized a bunch of weapons from Batista. My dad thinks it's reached a turning point. Says the *ola roja* – red wave – it's coming. We wanna try to get his parents out before it's too late."

"What will happen if you don't?"

"Their bakery will probably be taken over by martial law. The rebels talk of nationalizing all businesses." He slumps onto a stool, speaking in halting measures. "My abuelo… he's not well. He won't be able to take the strain of a revolution. My mother, when she was alive… she has family in Miami. We're hoping – " Franny catches himself and stands up. "I'm sorry, I don't mean to trouble you with all this."

Aaron slinks around to Franny's side of the table. "I wouldn't have asked if I didn't care."

Franny looks at him, bemused. "You've been drinking...?"

"Only... a lot."

They share a nervous laugh.

After a charged silence, Aaron's body edges closer to its target, as if pulled by a magnetic force. "If you and Francisco go, it..." He pauses. "It'll be a big blow to our kitchen."

"You already reduced our hours anyway," Franny says blithely. "I was thinking of getting a job with someone who cares before all this happened."

Aaron reaches out and runs his index finger along the sinewy underside of Franny's left forearm. Franny closes his eyes.

"David's idea," Aaron whispers. "He's a bad boy."

Franny smiles faintly. "Like you?"

Their arms wrap around each other's backsides, waists melding together. "You realize if you go, you may not make it back out," Aaron says hazily.

"It's a risk we have to take."

Their lips lock in a passionate kiss. Aaron thrusts into Franny, sending their entwined, slouching bodies up against the table. He reaches under Franny's shirt and kneads the firm flesh of his pecs as if sculpting clay. His desire for Franny is painful, almost mournful. He can't bear the thought of him leaving. Can't imagine not being able to follow through on their mutual attraction, not when he's finally found the courage within himself to *become* the man he knows he is.

Suddenly, Aaron jerks his head up. Still hovering over Franny, his body goes rigid.

"What was that?" he says breathlessly.

Franny pulls Aaron in close again. "Mmmm?"

"I think someone opened the dining room door."

Franny slips out from under Aaron, less frantic than the situation might call for. "It's just my father. He went out to get suitcases for us. Said he'd be back when I'm done cleaning."

The two men find their feet, each brushing imaginary dirt off themselves and running palms through their mussed-up hair, just as the kitchen door swings open. But their visitor is not Francisco.

Rudy does an exaggerated double-take when he sees his brother and Franny standing like palace guards. He breaks into a wide grin. "'Eeeeey, muchachos!"

He holds up an empty fifth of scotch and scoots past them toward the crockery cupboard. "Just looking for some more hooch." He forages through the cabinet, loudly jostling plates and dishes. "Fran, help me out here, would ya? What ever happened to those bottles I used to stash around here?"

Aaron, now stone-sober, transforms into a complete stranger before Franny's eyes. Franny watches him wordlessly shamble out the kitchen, head down. Seconds later, he hears the cold flap of the dining room door opening and closing.

Rudy looks over his shoulder at Franny, who is staring at the kitchen door.

"Y'know what? Don't sweat it," Rudy says, smirking. "I'll figure it out."

CHAPTER 17

With a daisy-patterned apron draped over his T-shirt and flannel slacks, David scurries around Darlene's kitchen with caffeinated efficiency, flipping eggs, turning sausage links, checking on toast. It's a cramped but homey space, made cheery by yellow-tiled walls and soft sunlight filtering through the jacaranda outside the apartment's second-story window.

David sets out three place settings on a small Formica table – a half-oval abutting the wall. He unplugs the electric coffee maker and pours himself a fresh cup when Darlene's roommate enters the kitchen.

Barbara McAllister works the perfume counter at Bullocks Wilshire, accounting for her heavy make-up and monochromatic work dress over an ample figure. But belying her professional façade is an infectious Irish girl with impish eyes and a mouth like a sailor prone to closing out dance clubs. It is for this reason that she adores David, an early riser who is usually the first one up to brew a pot for the girls on his way to the Palms.

"To what do we owe this occasion?" she ribs him, pouring herself some coffee. "You get laid last night?"

David chuckles and removes his apron. "I wish. I'd be cooking up a feast every morning."

"Darlene still into that kinky shit? Or did you both graduate onto full-blown S&M?"

David arches a brow at her. Having grown up with no sisters, he's still getting used to the sororal relationship between the two roommates, their disarming honesty and propensity to share each other's darkest secrets. He likes Barbara, looks forward to their charged bon mots, appreciates how she brings out the silliness in Darlene, who usually keeps that side of herself in reserve. The roomies titter like schoolgirls when they get going on an inside joke that leaves David cluelessly stone-faced.

Barbara butters a slice of toast. "You fellas still thinking of selling your hotel to those freeway people?"

"Not at this time. Our financial situation is starting to turn around." David knocks on a wooden cutting board as he plates his eggs and sausage. "We think it's better to hold on for the long-term."

"I heard you've returned to 'original management.'" Clearly a nod to Gordo's absence.

"I'm hopeful," he offers, leaving it at that. He sits at the table.

Barbara plucks a sausage out of the pan and leans against the stove. "Well, *I* hope you never sell it. I'd hate to see Darlene shitcanned from her job." She crooks her right elbow on her left palm and shakes a half-eaten link at David. "'Course, she may not be working much longer at the rate things are going," she intimates with a soothsayer squint.

"What does that mean?"

Barbara flashes him a suggestive grin and looks at the doorway, where a yawning Darlene has entered the room. She is wearing one of David's button-down dress shirts and has a serious case of bedhead. She takes a long, satisfying whiff and spots the spread in front of her — then smiles at Barbara. "Thanks, doll... that's so nice."

Barbara grabs another sausage. "Oh, don't thank me. It was loverboy here." She pops the link in her mouth and says through clenched teeth, "Welp, off to sell some smells!" She disappears out the door.

Darlene wraps her sleepy arms around David's neck and collapses in his lap, her wild black mane nuzzling his face. "You're very sweet." She kisses his nose, her eyelids drifting shut.

David takes in her unusually laconic demeanor. "You okay?"

"Yeah, why?"

He parts her hair and searches her face. Any thoughts are quickly banished by her dewy skin and full red lips. "Ah, it's nothing. Barbara was just giving me shit."

Darlene's eyes snap open. Not one to play games — especially with David — she climbs off his lap and heads for the coffee. "I missed my period," she pronounces. She turns to face him, waiting for his reaction. He looks... puzzled.

"Are you sure?" he finally says.

She looks at him cockeyed. "Uh, yeah, it's usually not a pretty picture."

"No, I mean… sure that you're pregnant?"

"Oh, well… no. But I'm like a Swiss watch down there, and it's been a while."

"So you haven't seen a doctor…"

"No yet." She bites her lip and twists her hair. "I wanted to see how you felt about everything first before I did that kind of thing."

He draws a long breath. Talk about a loaded statement. His mind races. Surely, she can't be suggesting aborting the pregnancy, not after what they witnessed with Kitty five months ago. Even if they could afford a competent specialist, there are risks and costs. No, she must be talking about first seeking confirmation from an obstetrician. One step at a time. This would be like Darlene. And a big reason he loves her. She seems to intuitively know how to handle life's curveballs through an adept display of countering emotions – solicitous yet assertive, nurturing yet detached, emotionally clinical… or is it clinically emotional? Anyway, she is his rock. The first woman since his mother to open his eyes to feminine strength, a force so much stronger than the empty posturing of the Shapiro men, himself included. All important points to consider before he utters anything rash. And so he tells her…

"Gimme a minute?" He offers her a reassuring smile. "Just a little fresh air to clear my head."

"I get it."

David heads downstairs and exits the building. He steps over a drunk splayed across the sidewalk and commences a walk around the block. As is his wont, he needs time to analyze the puzzle presented to him, to sort out where all the pieces go so he can connect them together into a future that makes sense.

He starts by accepting his complicity in her presumed pregnancy. They had been playing it pretty fast and loose. He was excited by their bold sex and his willingness to relinquish control, and knew he was tempting fate. He was, after all, the man whom the gods of fate had short-changed. Hadn't he forced himself to be more impulsive – irresponsible? reckless, even? – to see if that might change his fortunes? Going outside his comfort zone was already paying dividends with Darlene. Wasn't he already happier with her than he ever was as a lone wolf, stewing and stressing over his get-a-life status as the family's thankless decision-maker while others had their fun? Based on the immediate past, Darlene *is* the final piece to his future, a middle-finger salute to the gods that have dogged him until now.

And what *of* Darlene? What kind of baggage does she bring that might weigh them down later in life? He knows she had a surprisingly conventional childhood – far different than his own. An only child, she moved around various South Bay communities as her engineer father changed aerospace jobs. He met her folks once on a trip home. Good people. They showed David pictures from Darlene's youth. He was shocked to see a photo of her on the high school cheerleading squad. She was a wholesome-looking brunette then, locking arms with a sturdy yell leader with matinee-idol looks. Preston something-or-other. They were engaged at nineteen right before he was sent off to war. During basic training in Long Beach, he had gotten a heart tattooed on his shoulder with his and her initials. She reciprocated, successfully hiding it from her parents for years.

Preston something-or-other was killed in the Battle of Okinawa in the summer of '45, mere months before Japan's surrender. David felt a pang of envy upon hearing this. The guy was a true patriotic hero compared to his own unfulfilled tour of duty. To memorialize her permanent mourning for her fiancé, Darlene had a tattoo artist cover up their initials with flames engulfing the heart. Later, another artist encased the whole thing in barbed wire. Her heart was closed for business, never to be hurt again. She devoted herself to getting a degree in Hospitality Management and moved to Hollywood, where she answered a want ad for a front-desk job at the Palms. She's been there ever since, as loyal an employee the family has ever had.

By the time David returns to the drunk vagrant, he is unsure what the future will bring or if he's ready for fatherhood – or ever will be. But he is clear-eyed about one thing. Come what may, he can't imagine his life without Darlene in it.

• • •

Leo and Rae stand in the parking lot of the Greyhound station at Vine and Fountain, watching Max clamber aboard a bus bound for Kingman, Arizona. It is late September of '58, and Kitty has spent almost half a year recuperating in her mother's trailer. Now that she's strong enough, she can't take another second living with her. Mom is a vicious drunk with a series of abusive boyfriends who cycle in and out and often hit on Kitty, even when she was on death's door.

Bored by her absence, Max leapt at the chance to play the shining knight when Kitty begged him to accompany her on a bus back to Los Angeles.

As he observes the bus doors *whooshing* close, Leo feels unsettled. He grabs his gut and grimaces.

"Ulcer acting up?" Rae asks him.

He nods. Recently, he was diagnosed with gastrinoma, an appropriately scary word for small tumors on the pancreas, which could be contributing to his peptic ulcers.

After a quick stop across the street to Hollywood Ranch Market for a bottle of milk of magnesia, he hands the keys to his Mercury over to Rae. "Watch your lead foot," he tells her. "All I need is a heart attack on top of everything else."

Rae drives them north to McDaniel's Residentiary without incident. When they pull into its dirt parking lot, Misty the cat darts by, chasing leaves in the hot wind. Glynda and several preteens are sticking homemade pinwheels into the soil along the front walk. They look up and wave at Rae and Leo.

Stepping out of the car, Rae is mobbed by the kids, who pester her with peals of "Did you bring me anything?"

"Boys and girls, where are your manners?" Glynda gently reprimands.

Rae laughs. "It's okay." She reaches into the back seat. "I have bags full of stuff from the five-and-dime."

"You are *too* kind, Rae."

Leo helps Rae carry the bags inside. Several children glide alongside and peer inside, glimpsing snow globes, Silly Putty, Paddle Balls, and an assortment of cheap yet priceless tchotchkes. As Glynda spills the items onto a table in the receiving room, an eight-year-old girl hollers out, "Rae, look how good I've gotten!"

Rae turns around to find the girl wiggling a hula hoop – another Rae gift – around her tiny hips. She gets five rotations in before the giant plastic loop bangs into the doorway and teeters to her feet.

"You've gotten really good, Michelle!" Rae enthuses.

Glynda funnels the kids back out front. "Now y'all know, no hula hooping inside!" She turns to Rae. "You gonna be okay for an hour or so?"

"Of course." Because it's a Saturday, McDaniel's school is not in session, relegating Rae and Glynda's staff to glorified babysitters for a few dozen kids.

Glynda smiles and turns to Leo. "Ready to make some money?"

He chortles. "More like blow some."

The two of them head back to the parking lot, where they climb into Glynda's avocado green Volkswagen Beetle. As she starts it up, it belches black smoke from its tailpipe and loudly pangs, causing Leo to jump. Glynda giggles as she pops the gear into reverse. "Don't worry, sweetie, this ol' girl is as reliable as gravity."

Glynda steers the VW due south, through Val Verde until the town runs out. They enter a wide-open country road traversing the Santa Clarita Valley, a rambling stretch of brownish gold hills, oak trees, and wild poppies, spread out in clumps and patches like orange marmalade.

Across a two-lane bridge is a neat clapboard shack with giant words painted on its slant roof: "Newhall Land Company." Glynda pulls over.

"This is the real estate office I was telling you about," she says.

A young man with slicked-back hair steps out of the office for a smoke. He is decked out in peach-colored western wear with rhinestone-studded pants and cowboy boots. Spotting Leo and Glynda, he initially registers confusion – a look that seems to say, Is this balding nebbish and Afro-centric colored lady a *couple*? Just as quickly, he flashes an unctuous smile and waves at them to come on in. His garishness reminds Leo of Rudy.

"I don't really feel like getting pitched a whole song and dance by this joker," Leo confesses to Glynda. "If you don't mind, maybe we can just drive around a bit so I can get a feel for things before talking to anyone."

"You don't have to twist *my* arm," she says.

The salesman's grin droops into a frown as he sees the Beetle drive off.

As Glynda's VW putters around the burgeoning basin, she delivers an oral history of the area as she's come to know it over the past twenty years. They stop occasionally so Leo can take pictures of street signs and lots for sale to show his brothers. At one point, they drive alongside a 300-foot wide trough with sloped sides. "Interstate 5 – Your Tax Dollars At Work!" exclaims a billboard. "Coming 1962." Leo snaps photos of the sign, excited at the prospect of an eight-lane ribbon of concrete connecting Los Angeles with the entire Santa Clarita Valley.

Leo suggests a quick bite somewhere so he can swig some milk. Glynda drives them to the Saugus Café, a greasy dive with cattle-head décor dating to the horse-and-buggy days. Over lunch, Leo confides information he hasn't even shared with his brothers – he's thinking of pulling out of the hotel business so he can focus exclusively on Shapiro Bros. Properties' operations. Running the Palms is just too stressful, and doctors have advised him to cut back on stress.

"Who would run your books?" Glynda asks.

Leo slurps from a cup of split-pea soup. "I was thinking maybe Rae. I could train her." He pauses. "We like to keep jobs like that in the family... people we can trust."

"Doesn't she run your kitchen?"

Leo blows out his cheeks. "We're closing the kitchen. Guests loved Rae's cooking, but most tourists prefer eating out these days. We also lost two key employees. It just became cost prohibitive..."

"It's the single biggest expense we have at McDaniel's, is that blessed commissary."

Leo smiles crookedly. "Booze, on the other hand... that's where the *real* margins are. We plan to keep the bar open. Kind of bringing the whole thing full circle when it was just a speakeasy."

Glynda expresses more concerns about McDaniel's. The home is receiving only one newcomer for every four or five residents who leave when they turn eighteen. The business won't be able to sustain that kind of attrition rate for long. If they can't hit the state-mandated threshold of at least thirty children, funding will get cut off. Bonding over their liquidity problems, the lunch-mates completely lose track of time until Glynda looks at her watch.

"Oh Lord! We've been gone almost two hours."

Leo grabs the bill. "Let me go pay this."

Back in her car, Glynda cranks the ignition but the engine won't turn over. It appears her trusty VW's battery is dead. She and Leo ask people around the parking lot for a jump. No such luck. They do, however, find a sympathetic gray-haired farmer in a pickup truck. He agrees to give them a lift so Glynda can return in Leo's car with jumper cables.

The pair gamely climb into the cargo bed and rest their backs against the cabin. The drive back is a white-knuckle affair. The truck's shocks are shot, the farmer is a speed demon, and the road is rutted with potholes. Holding onto each other for dear life, the two bounce up and down and laugh with each big ridiculous jarring bump.

• • •

Several days later, at 6:30 p.m., Darlene picks up an outside call at the front desk. Leo is stationed to her left, absorbed in his Shapiro Bros. Properties ledger.

David relaxes on a loveseat, enjoying the late-edition *Herald-Express* with a glass of scotch. On the TV, playing only to Simon and Lena Kaminski in matching *I Love Lucy* shirts, is the low drone of *The Huntley-Brinkley Report*. More obligatory space news. Something about the creation of a new federally-funded agency called NASA, which hopes to put a monkey into orbit sometime next year.

"Are you sure?" Darlene says into the phone. She frowns and glances at David and Leo. "Okay. Thank you, Aaron. I'll let them know." She hangs up.

David and Leo look up at the word "Aaron."

"Your father wasn't there when Aaron went to pick him up at the Greyhound station," Darlene says with concern.

"What does he mean 'wasn't there'?" David asks. "He never took the bus?"

"Kitty was supposed to be with him," Leo adds.

"They *did* take the bus," she clarifies. "Aaron found that out from the driver. But the bus got in early. Right before Aaron arrived."

"Ah, fuck," David snarls, slamming down his drink.

"The driver remembers them getting off it, but that's all he knows."

"Did Aaron check the bathrooms?" Leo asks. "Ask around inside the station?"

Darlene nods gravely.

David massages his scalp to help himself think. "What's Aaron doing now?"

"He's gonna hang out there a little longer, in case they went across the street to Ranch Market to grab food. He's afraid of leaving the parking lot in case he misses them."

David nods – good idea. He slips on his jacket. "Leo, you stay here in case Aaron finds them and calls us back."

"Maybe they took a cab," Leo proposes.

"If they *did* take a cab, they're not coming here."

"No? Where do you think they went?"

David doesn't answer, instead setting off for the two-block walk to Musso and Frank's, where Kitty will find any excuse to induce the old man into emptying his wallet on exorbitant steaks and vodka martinis. Tonight – reunited with Max, hungry after a long bus ride, back in L.A. after a summer in purgatory – seems as good an excuse as any.

When he arrives at the steakhouse, David tells the maître d' he's simply looking for someone and marches into the dining area. Cigarette smoke, thick as San Pedro fog, suffuses the cavernous room, shrouding the faded "hunting party" mural wrapping the walls. Ancient waiters in red bolero jackets push Caesar salad carts and serve up organ meats like lamb kidneys and sweetbread. The red leather booths are fully occupied, a rambunctious mix of dinner dates, Hollywood players and gauche tourists off the boulevard. Max and Kitty are not among them.

David heads into a newly opened second dining room. He spots them at a snug little booth along the back wall. As he gets closer, he sees that his father is working through a Bouillabaisse. Kitty, looking like her old self, has ordered a chicken pot pie *and* a tenderloin. Both look untouched. A bottle of red wine sits between two drained martini glasses. Neither party is dressed up, each still wearing casual clothes from their bus ride.

David approaches the table from the side. "Welcome back," he announces tartly.

The couple is startled by his sudden presence. Max's face quickly softens. "David, m'boy! What're you doing here?"

"We wish you would've called. You had us all worried. Aaron was waiting in the parking—"

"Aaron?"

"Yes. Aaron." He jerks his thumb at Kitty. "He called and talked to *her* before your bus left Arizona. He was gonna pick you up." He turns to Kitty, glowering. "Didn't you give Pop the message?"

"I don't remember that," she says cavalierly. "Maybe he talked to my mother? She's a drunk, y'know."

"No. He talked to you."

Max laughs heartily. "Look, the important thing is you found us." He slides over and merrily pats the seat beside him. "Join us for a drink, help us celebrate!"

David refuses to sit. "What are we celebrating." His tone is flat and chary, sounding more like a statement.

With a simpering grin, Kitty jams her left middle finger toward David's face. For a moment, he thinks she's flipping him off. Then he realizes it's not her middle finger – it's her *ring* finger.

"That's my mother's wedding ring," he sputters, transfixed by her blue-diamond-studded gold band. "Pop, what's she doing with Mom's wedding ring?"

"It's just temporary till I get her a real one," Max says, dunking a chunk of bread into his soupy stew.

"You fuckin' married *Kitty*?" David hisses, pounding his fist on the table.

"Hey!"

"Excuse me!" cries Kitty.

Diners at nearby tables look up from their plates with captivating grins. This is just getting good...

Kitty chides David, "I don't go by Kitty anymore. That was my stage name. I am back to Abigail." She grabs Max's hand and squeezes. "Abigail Shapiro."

"You are *not* a Shapiro," David protests.

"Marriage certificate says I am. And I was hoping we could all make a fresh start since we're all family."

"You went to Vegas..." David's eyes smolder in fury as he figures it out. The city is only an hour or so from Kingman – how convenient. "That's why you had Pop come out to you. You wanted to drag him to Vegas so you could do a quickie marriage behind everyone's backs."

Max laughs again, this time more tensely. "No one's sneaking around on anyone. My life is my life." He rubs Abigail's back. "This woman almost gave *her* life, y'know. *Thirty more seconds*, they said she'd be dead. The least I could do was—"

Abigail interrupts him, preferring a more romantic tenor. "We wanted to do something that would cement our commitment to one another. We were gonna tell everyone tonight."

Her lips start to tremble as she turns on the waterworks. David rolls his eyes in disgust.

"It was completely spur-of-the-moment... the most joyful day of my life." She rests her head on Max's shoulder, clutching at his jowly neck. "We were hoping you'd be happy for us."

David leans into Abigail's ear – almost kissing her – so that only she can hear him. "You know what would've made me happy?" he seethes, practically spitting venom. "Thirty more seconds."

Abigail bursts into sobs as David charges out of the restaurant.

CHAPTER 18

Like a Santa Ana wind blowing in from the desert, the return of Kitty Kay has a combustible effect on the Palms. Within days, a squad car pulls into its turncourt. Two LAPD officers approach the front desk just before Darlene's shift ends at 10 p.m. Seated to her left, Leo huddles with Rae over the books, providing tutelage in hotel management.

"Evening, miss," drawls the first cop to Darlene, displaying his badge. His bald head is offset by a patch of brown neck hair creeping out of his shirt collar. "I'm Detective Hinkle, and this is my partner Sergeant Kulpepper."

Kulpepper nods. Lean and leathery with stress-lines crossing his face like earthquake faults.

"Is there someone in charge here we can talk to?" Hinkle says.

"What is this about?" Leo asks.

"This your place?"

Leo hesitates. "Yes. Yes, my family runs this hotel."

"The Sha*piro* family?" Hinkle spits out the "P" in "Shapiro" as if disgorging a sunflower shell.

Leo turns to Rae. "Call David." She dials Room 3 from the house phone.

"Sir, I'd like to see your guest register," Hinkle says.

Darlene interjects, "We'd like to see your search warrant."

"Of course." Shockingly, the detective pulls out a document that looks like a legitimate "Search & Seizure" warrant, signed on the bottom by a local judge. As Leo looks it over, he nods to Darlene.

"Go 'head," he tells her. "Do what he says."

Darlene pulls out the registry book and drops it onto the desktop with a disdainful thud. The detective puts on reading glasses and opens it to the most recent entries. Two more black-and-whites pull up outside, lights flashing, sirens silent.

"What in God's name…" Leo says.

Three cops burst through the front door. They form a tight semi-circle behind Detective Hinkle, hands on holsters, bug-eyed and nostrils flaring like wild mustangs.

"Would someone please tell us what's going on!" Darlene demands.

By the time David reaches the courtyard, Hinkle's charges are fanning across all four wings in tandems. Leo, Darlene and Rae shadow them. The cops trudge toward specific units jotted down on scraps of paper, the beams from their metal flashlights penetrating the darkness.

"Who's in charge here?" David barks at the passing lawmen.

Hinkle emerges out of the shadows. "Where's Max Shapiro?"

"Max is not here right now. I'm David Shapiro. I run this place."

"We've been given an anonymous tip of multiple violations among some of your guests. This is a procedural investigation in order to secure the safety of the public."

"Well, I don't grant you permission. Fourth Amendment rights. No unreasonable search and seizures."

The courtyard echoes with the rapping of flashlights on guest doors.

"Hey! Don't do that!" David hollers.

"This is a court-issued authorization," Hinkle says, absently twirling his curly strands of neck hair. "Noncompliance constitutes obstruction of justice."

"Come back later when I can get hold of a lawyer."

"No can do. This is a matter of great urgency. Preserving evidence, and all…"

David notices the cops have congregated at Elron's and Art's rooms, waiting for them to answer their doors. He turns back to Hinkle. "Who are you investigating and *what are the charges?*"

"Let's see…" The detective pulls a pad from his shirt pocket and monotonously reads off names and charges. "Mankowitz, Arthur…. Distributing or Possessing Obscene Matter Showing Sexual Conduct by a Minor in violation of California Penal Code Section 3.11.1 and 3.11.2…"

David's jaw drops in disbelief.

"Jakes, Elron…. Possession of Illegal Narcotics, in violation of California and Safety Code 11350…" He flips a page. "Also, Possession of a loaded firearm in a public place, in violation of California Penal Code 25850…"

"He owns a BB gun!"

"Kaminski, Szymon and Kaminski, Lena, agents acting on behalf of a foreign adversary, aiding and abetting Communism, in violation of the Espionage and Sedition Acts…"

David chortles, incredulous. "McCarthyism is dead. Or haven't you heard?"

"Johnson, Tyrone…. Sanders, Steven…" Hinkle squints at his notes. "Unaccompanied minors…"

"Those guests are eighteen. They were discharged from a boarding home and have every right to live here."

"Esteban, Alejandro… Illegal residence in defiance of the Immigration and Nationality Act…"

"Who sicced you on us? Was it Vance Gordo? It was Red, wasn't it?"

Leo comes over to talk to his brother. "They claim they found damning evidence on Art and Elron."

David looks past Leo and sees the habitués being hauled off from Rooms 5 and 6 in handcuffs. "Sonofabitch."

As Hinkle heads over to supervise the arrests, other guests emerge from their rooms. Darlene and Rae respond to their distressed looks with assuaging words.

"We need to call Pop," Leo says to David.

David grits his teeth. "They just left on their honeymoon. Probably in Solvang by now."

"We could call different hotels…"

"And then what? Tell him his wife is complicit in a raid that's wiped out half our guest rolls? Think he'll ever believe that?"

Leo nods pensively, then looks sideways at David. "Do we believe that?"

"This is a message from Gordo. A reminder he still 'owns' us until we pay back the rest of his money. There's no way Kitty doesn't know. Now that she's married to Pop – she and Gordo… together… they're emboldened." He looks at Leo. "How close are we to scrounging up Gordo's four grand?"

"Close… within eight hundred dollars."

David's attention is diverted by two African Americans – Tyrone and Steven – being yanked out of their room by Kulpepper and a junior officer. They are shirtless, scared and confused, looking to their former McDaniel's housemate Rae for help. David is apoplectic. "Jesus *fucking* Christ."

He runs over to intervene. "Leave these gentlemen alone. They didn't *do* anything!" David puts his hand on the young officer's shoulder.

The cop whirls round. "Easy!"

"We're just taking them in for questioning," Kulpepper says.

"Then question them here!" David insists.

Both boys, rangy and tall, dig in their heels, adding to the cops' exertion as they attempt to pull them onto the lawn. David throws himself into the fray, latching onto an officer's arms to pry them loose from Steven.

The cop whips out his baton and delivers a crushing blow to David's face. He crumples to the dead grass, yowling in pain.

• • •

That night, David self-medicates with a bottle of Jack Daniel's on Darlene's bed. Darlene comes out of the bathroom with a newly damp washcloth, applying it to his bloodied and possibly broken nose.

"You were always too much of a pretty boy for me anyway," she teases.

"Fuckin' D-Day," he slurs, well-lubricated.

"What?"

"The detective. He was mocking me as they left. Said today was 'D-Day. Detainment Day.'" He scrunches his face. "Ever notice how every bad word starts with 'D'? Detainment. Destroy-ment. Destruction."

Darlene, indulging him: "Divorce. Disease. Devil."

"*Death*." David's eyes get wide. "Holy shit, you and I – our names – *we're* on that list."

He free-associates back to the hotel. "Place is cursed. Better off just selling the whole damn thing. The money we make off it, we could finally build houses on our lots, my brothers and me and..."

"That's your father's call."

"He said he would consider it."

"When did he say that?"

"When Kitty was in Arizona. He agreed that two hundred grand sounded reasonable." He abruptly sits upright.

"What're you doing?"

David staggers over to his pants, slung over a chair. He fishes around in the pockets.

"I'm calling that freeway guy, Xavier Cortez," he says in a burst of drunken inspiration.

"*Now?*"

David finds Xavier's business card in his wallet. He grins and clutches it as if it's a winning racetrack ticket. "I wanna talk to him before Kitty gets back and has a chance to fuck it all up again. Tell him we'll take his offer!" He laughs goofily. "Him and his stick-up-the-ass partner!"

"He won't even be in his office."

David goes to the nightstand and pulls the receiver off the phone.

Darlene turns her alarm clock toward him. "David, it's past eleven o'clock." He squints hard to focus on it. "Oh yeah. Look at that."

Darlene hangs up the phone. "You can try him in the morning. But first you *need* to talk to Max."

"I don't know where he is. They're somewhere in Solvang."

"What's a Solvang?"

"Some fru-fru Danish tourist trap near Santa Barbara. They're not coming back till...." He furrows his brow – another thought skipping through his cerebral cortex. "Wonder if Kitty would've dragged Pop out of town unless Red ordered her to..."

Darlene stands up, prepared to put an untidy bow on the whole rotten evening. "Let's get some sleep." Her heart breaks for David – slouched on the edge of the bed, staring into space, a broken man with a broken face. "I'm gonna run to the bathroom. You gonna be okay?"

He looks at her with a faltering smile. "Miss you already."

She heads back to the bathroom and quickly showers. After toweling off, she slips into a black negligee hanging on the door and brushes her teeth.

When she returns to her bedroom, David is still in the same stooped position, but this time the phone's handset is pressed to his ear. He's in the middle of a conversation.

"Uh huh. Uh huh..." With his other hand, he repeatedly pounds his fist into his forehead. "No, yeah. Yeah, no. I get it..."

Darlene sinks onto the bed next to him, trying to decipher who he's talking to.

"Yes, you did say that, but you didn't say *when*." He stands up, stabbing the air with his finger. "You never gave me a deadline. See, that's *not fair*. You only said…"

Darlene can hear the other party raising his voice. David grimaces. Abruptly shifts into chastened mode. "I'm sorry. You know I like you, Xavier." He emits a bitter laugh, which unleashes a hiccup. "You're a good man for a bureau-cat," he says, dry-mouthed. "They should employ more men like good men like you."

Darlene closes her eyes.

"If you change your mind…" David stifles another hiccup. "What's that? No, I know it's not up to you. But if the *state* changes their mind…" He nods. "They won't. I get it. But if they *did*…"

He plops down again. "Okay. You too. Sorry to bother you. Good night."

He puts the handset back in its cradle, slowing turning to Darlene with a hangdog expression.

"You looked him up in the phone book," she says, noticing the white pages opened up on her nightstand.

David shrugs. "With a name like his, figured I had a good shot. Turns out there's *two* Xavier Cortezes in Hollywood. First guy I called cursed at me in Spanish for waking him up."

Darlene bursts out in a snort-laugh, and soon he is hiccup-laughing with her, caught in this tragicomedy that only David's cynical gods could deliver.

"So the freeway's dead. So we blew it!" He looks at her and shrugs, eyes watering. "Not the end of the world. We could still unload it on someone, right?"

Their gaiety settles into a sober silence. David runs his fingers along his nostrils to check for blood. Finding none, he curls up on the bed and closes his eyes. Darlene climbs behind and spoons him. He reaches out with his hand and strokes her taut tummy.

"Take it from me," he wheezes. "A hotel is no place to raise a kid anyway." After one final hiccup, he falls asleep in the crook of her belly.

• • •

The next afternoon, Aaron is behind the wheel of his Bel Air, cruising down the Miracle Mile. Leo sits up front, David in the back, nursing a raging headache. It's a far cry from the last time they drove this stretch of Wilshire Boulevard together about a year ago. Back then, rocking tunes filled the open cab as the boys chatted up the glorious future they would inherit with the Palms. Now, the roof is closed, the radio is conspicuously off and everyone is too tense to talk.

It had already been a long, grueling morning. They had spent it at the Hollywood police station, scratching together bail for Art and Elron. The brothers knew about Elron's drug habit but the charges against Art were troubling. While David and Leo speculated the cops may have planted underage pornography in his room, Aaron remembered Rudy's discovery of queer rags under the sink. He didn't *dare* share this intel with Leo and David. Rudy spooked him. He knew things. Knew about Art. Had the goods on Aaron and Franny — or at least suspicions. Instead, Aaron agreed with his brothers that the whole thing was a shakedown.

But now, an even bigger battle awaits them. Once the brothers learned about Max's elopement to "the bloodsucker" — they steadfastly refuse to invoke his wife's reclaimed birth name — they lobbed repeated phone calls to their estate attorney, Robert Spiegelman. Each time, the calls went unanswered. The boys never trusted the trustee, who never took their claims about Kitty and Red jacking Max seriously. David wanted to see the original signature trust with his own eyes. Had it been amended since Max and Kitty's union five days ago? What about the hotel deed? Leo said there were legal shenanigans she and Gordo's lawyers could pull to transfer it to her — a quickclaim, David thinks they call it. If nothing *had* been changed, what was the legal procedure to convert the trust from revocable to irrevocable, preserving Max as the sole trustor, with the boys — and Rae, if they could persuade Max to add her — as beneficiaries?

Thus today's mission: To blindside Spiegelman at his office.

It's located in Beverly Hills' famed Golden Triangle district — a bragging point that looks impressive on a business card. In reality, the office is a squat brick job that begs shame in the shadow of Wilshire Boulevard's gleaming office towers.

Aaron parks his ride out front. David buzzes the intercom next to the opaque door. A lady's scratchy voice asks who it is.

"This is David, Leo and Aaron Shapiro. We'd like to see Robert Spiegelman."

"Spiegelman?" She spews a phlegmy cough.

"Spiegelman. Trustee for our family. We haven't been able to get him on the horn so we thought we'd drop by."

Silence on the other end.

"Ma'am?" Aaron calls out. "If he's busy, we're happy to wait."

"Hold on, dears," she says.

The brothers are let into a dreary lobby with plastic folding chairs, parched potted plants, and a large wall mirror with a crack down the middle. The older lady with the smoker's voice is stationed behind a typewriter. Her white hair is set in curlers, draped in a scarf.

"You're new," David says to her. "What happened to Mr. Spiegelman's old secretary?"

The woman lets out a raspy cackle. "You mean *young* secretary. I'm a temp."

A heavyset man with kind, moist eyes and raging halitosis plods into the lobby. He introduces himself as Chuck Stuber. "Help you fellas?"

"We're looking for Mr. Spiegelman," David replies, stepping back. "What do you do?"

"I'm a personal injury lawyer."

"You guys partners?"

"No no, I barely know the man. We just share an office… and her." He nods toward the secretary. "That's Irene."

"We've met."

Stuber sizes up his three guests, then waddles down the hallway. "Come with me."

David, Aaron and Leo follow.

"When's the last time you spoke to Robert?" Chuck asks.

"Several months ago on the phone," Leo says.

"Maybe June?" David ventures.

"Does he not work here anymore?" asks Leo.

Chuck shrugs. "Tell you the truth, I'm still trying to figure it all out myself."

He leads them into Robert's old office. Clues abound that the lawyer took leave in a hurry. Boxes of shredded documents and stained coffee mugs sit on the desk, but based on the ghostly outlines of certificate frames on the wallpaper, Spiegelman is not coming back. Even his desk chair is gone.

Aaron walks over to an olive file cabinet in the corner. The drawers are all opened and emptied out.

"He took everything," Chuck sighs, standing in the doorway, "including our young secretary, Patty. Ditched his wife and kids for her."

"Swiped all the damn coffee stirrers too!" Irene hollers from down the hall.

Aaron turns to Chuck. "I don't get it. When did this all happen?"

"Four days ago," Stuber says. "Craziest thing. He and Patty just up and left the building with two clients, and I haven't seen them since—"

"Wait a minute," David interjects. "What clients? Were they a man and a woman?"

"Did you get their names?" Leo asks.

"Red-headed broad," Aaron specifies. "She pals around with some greaseball."

Stuber scratches his stubbled chin. "No, there was no woman involved." He looks at Aaron. "The greasy fella, though. He was hard to forget. Loud as all hell. I remember he had a really small mouth."

"And the other guy?"

Chuck shakes his head. "I dunno. Older. Serious. Nice suit. Looked like a lawyer. I think he – "

"Think he what?"

Chuck sidesteps toward the doorway. "I never mingle in Robert's affairs."

David catches a note of fear in Chuck's voice. He clenches his eyes in frustration.

"You don't know *where* he went?" Leo asks. "I mean, he must've said something…"

"I have to get back to work," Stuber says softly. "I'm sorry I can't be of more help." He waits in the hallway for the brothers to leave the office. One by one, they file out, each holding his breath while passing by.

In the lobby, Chuck gets David's phone number and promises to call if he hears anything about Spiegelman's whereabouts. As they turn to leave, Irene directs a question to Chuck. "What about the old man in the car?"

David looks at Irene, then Chuck. "What's she talking about?"

Irene continues, "Mr. Stuber told me when the two gentlemen left here, he saw them get into a swank car with an old man sitting in the passenger seat. Then the car just sat there."

"Why didn't you tell us this?" David asks Stuber.

He shrugs. "Thought it was immaterial."

"Well, you told *her*. What did this guy look like?"

"I couldn't say. I think he was asleep. His head was pressed against the window."

The brothers exchange looks.

"Pop," Leo says gravely.

Veins start to protrude on David's neck.

"Nice to meet you, fellas," Stuber says, scurrying back down the hall.

• • •

The drive back to Hollywood takes on a funereal edge. Aaron attempts to soothe their souls by turning on the radio. Gene Vincent's "Be-Bop-A-Lula" comes on mid-song, but the explosive snares and Vincent's stuttering, slapback vocals have the opposite effect, imbuing the cabin with aberrant fun-house mischief. David, slumped in the passenger seat, slaps the radio off with his left hand.

"When did Pop say they're coming back from their honeymoon?" he asks aloud.

"He didn't," Leo answers glumly from the backseat.

"We gotta get our hands on the latest trust. He and Kit must have a copy. And I know Pop has the original somewhere." He swivels toward Leo. "Did you come across any legal documents when you were fishing around their room?"

"Everything I brought out is what I found."

"Mom kept a copy of the trust in her safe deposit box," Aaron offers. "Pop emptied it out when she died, remember?"

David fists the dash. "We look in their room as soon as we get back. I don't care if we have to rip out the floorboards, we're not leaving till we find it."

• • •

Back at the Palms, the Shapiros' sleuthing in Room 1 is surprisingly anticlimactic. As David and Leo rummage through Max's belongings, Aaron finds an unmarked nine-by-twelve-inch pink envelope deep in the recesses of Kitty's underwear drawer. The envelope is fastened with only the brass clasp. Aaron unhooks it and slides out five bound pages of cream-colored paper.

He turns to Leo and David. "Uh... guys?"

David grabs the document from Aaron. As his brothers peer over his shoulder, the pages ripple in his trembling hands. It is their worst fear realized — an amended trust, dated one day after Max and Kitty's return to Los Angeles as husband-and-wife:

This Trust Agreement is entered into this <u>2nd</u> day of <u>Oct. 1958</u> by and between MAXIMILIAN ISAAC SHAPIRO and ABIGAIL SCHLEBERCOFF SHAPIRO, hereinafter referred to as 'Co-Trustors'..."

David flips to the last page, almost hyperventilating. The document is notarized and executed by Robert Spiegelman. It contains two signatures on the bottom: Abigail's and Max's, the latter in a shaky penmanship that suggests an altered state, likely rendered in the mystery man's car.

David releases the pages and feels the blood rush out of his face. He collapses on Max's bed.

"David?" Aaron says.

David can feel the whole of his being grappling with this seismic shock. The world has been knocked off its axis. The normal laws of the universe no longer apply. Up is down, right is wrong, evil trumps good.

And the meek shall not inherit the earth...

CHAPTER 19

Since coming back from their honeymoon on October 7, 1958, it is clear to all that the marriage of Max and Abigail – née Kitty – Shapiro is one in name only. In the preceding months, Abigail skillfully tapped her theater background to pretend to love Max. Even if he didn't believe it deep down, he knew plenty of widowed or divorced men who married much younger women. Such wives, like Abigail, often kept lovers on the side. But in return for being provided for, they granted their husbands a checklist of benefits. A warm, curvaceous, sweet-smelling body in bed. A reliable date for nights out. Homecooked meals. Emotional and ego-boosting support. Someone to talk at, vent to, laugh with, buy gifts for. A shirt-ironing, errand-running, foot-massaging, car-driving, doctor-scheduling, husband-keep-aliver. True, Abigail didn't check most of those boxes. But the important thing was that now, for the rest of his life, he would never be alone.

Except that he is.

He has been alone since they returned to the cramped confines of Room 1 as a wedded couple. Max noticed the switch in her immediately. Grouching that he snored too loudly, she stopped spending nights in their unit. Though she claims to crash in vacant rooms, Leo sees her leave in her car at night. She is gone most days now too, disappearing for long, mysterious stretches when she isn't buying out the Broadway or treating girlfriends to martini lunches. Where she used to indulge Max's absent-mindedness with an easy laugh, now she is cuttingly cruel, quick to scold him and make him feel ashamed. A terrible cook – Max once observed she's the only person who could "burn water" – Abigail used to at least fetch food for him from The Easy. But the closing of its kitchen put the kibosh on that, and Abigail is never around to order takeout. And forget about pills or doctor's appointments. Max is left to fend for himself now – a shift that has left him more clear-headed but also more depressed and hobbled due to bodily ailments.

In some ways, the turn of events is the best thing that could've happened to the Shapiro family. Max made it clear he would "divorce the bitch" if she didn't start acting all wifey. The boys knew this was as likely as Mother Teresa turning tricks. Instead, they fed into Max's insecurities, bruising his ego and feeding his fantasies of a quickie-divorce or an annulment. Either mechanism could lead to a nullification of the trust if false pretenses could be proved in court. "You always did like the chase, Pop… the hustle," David casually said. "Now that you got a sweet piece of ass, you didn't *really* expect her to hang around an old fart like you, did ya?"

Recently, Max had gotten up in the middle of the night to use the toilet. He slipped and struck his head against his desk. Abigail was not in the room, of course, so she was not there to help him up or hear his cries for help. He was finally able to crawl to the phone and call Rae in her room. The damage: A gash on his forehead and a broken hip.

Fortunately, X-Rays found only a hairline fracture. No surgery would be needed, but Max would be relegated to crutches for several weeks before moving onto a walker and walking boots. For David, Aaron and Leo, this incident was the last straw. The hotel was no place for an old man to live, let alone one with an abusive wife with ulterior motives. They suggested to their father that he move into an assisted living center. After accusing them of trying to stash him away, he agreed to consider it.

Leo and Rae take him to a retirement home called Sylvan Gardens to tour the grounds. Tucked in a scrubby corner of Chatsworth, the building looks onto boulder-laden hills and a cactus garden. Rae pushes Max in a wheelchair down a nature path as Leo saunters alongside.

"Whattaya think, Pop?" Leo says buoyantly. "Could you see yourself here?"

"Why's it so far away?" Max groans. A bandage is splayed across his forehead.

"Hollywood's dead, Pop. The Valley is where it's at." Or, as he doesn't tell him, senior centers in L.A. proper are just too damn expensive. "We own land out here, y'know. Hope to build on it someday… maybe we'll be neighbors."

"I'm gonna be lonely."

"Nah, we'll come visit you every chance we get. With the freeways, it's only a twenty-minute drive."

"What about Abigail?"

"What about her?"

Max is distracted by two ancient ladies sitting on a bench. They regard Max with blank stares and open mouths. "Christ, look at the old hags here," he grumbles as he rolls by. Coming the other way, a woman shuffles by in a walker, shadowed by a female aide with a faint mustache. "I gotta look at these gasbags all day? They're gonna put me in an early grave."

"*Kitty* would've put you in an early grave," Leo quips.

Max looks across the expansive grounds, suddenly concerned about money. "What's this gonna set me back?"

Rae pats Max's shoulder. "You don't need to worry about that. We'll take care of it."

Leo adds, "Rae's experience has come in handy, Pop. She found out you're eligible for low-income status, which means the state will kick in part of the rent."

"Gaming the system, huh?" Max says, squeezing her hand. "Thatta girl."

"She even got you moved up the waiting list."

"Couple months' wait – tops," Rae pledges.

Max holds up his hand for Rae to stop the wheelchair. When she does, he starts to rise out of his seat. Leo rushes over.

"Whoa, Pop... what're you doing?"

Max makes a "gimme" gesture with his hand. Rae unclips Max's crutches from the chair back and hands them to him.

"She's pruning 'em all wrong," he says, slipping into his crutches.

"Who is?" asks Leo.

"Her." Max points to a woman tending to a small flower garden about ten feet off the walkway. She's a younger resident – about mid-sixties – tan and lithe with gray hair cascading out of a straw hat. "She's cutting 'em too high on the stems. Gotta cut them lower to the ground if you want bigger blooms. That's why the others are all stubby."

Max hobbles to the lady to dispense advice, though based on the sparkle in his eyes, it's clear he's tapping the same dormant impulse that once bequeathed daily flowers to Marta as a courting teenager. Leo and Rae shake their heads, marveling.

"You didn't tell him he'll have to share a room," Rae says.

Leo shrugs. "Why mention that now?" He points to the woman. "In the end, he'll probably be sneaking in her room half the time."

"He reminds me of those lovebirds that drop dead without a companion."

Leo turns to look at Rae. "How do you do it, anyway?"

"What?"

"You're so… accepting of him. You must have *some* built-up resentment." Leo jerks his thumb toward the building. "Even today, when we first walked in here, they thought you were his personal nurse. I was… I dunno…"

"Humiliated for me?" she asks, finishing his sentence.

Leo nods.

"It was worse when I was young," she says, her voice tightening. "I was lighter-skinned than a lot of my peers at McDaniel's. Once they found out I was some 'whitey accident,' I was definitely ashamed."

She looks at Max. He is squatting in the garden with his new friend, his shaky hands cupping hers, guiding her shearers to the right spot.

"But as I got older, I realized there were others much worse off than me. Half the kids were abused, molested… sometimes by their own fathers… just vile, terrible stuff." She looks off in the distance, her eyes reddening. "I was far from the only 'accident,' either. So who was I to complain?"

"Has he ever apologized to you?"

"For what? He gave me life."

"For not *being* in your life."

She arches her brow. "Has he ever apologized to *you*?"

"What, for being a shitty father?" He kicks at the dirt. Smiles. "No, I suppose not."

"Glynda once told me – all of us, really – we never get one hundred percent of any one person. Nor should we expect it. You might get ten percent from one parent and none from the other. But you'll make up the other ninety percent from aunts, grandparents, teachers, friends – people who care about you. Doesn't matter how it adds up, everyone is one hundred percent complete one way or another."

"I never looked at it that way," Leo muses.

Max has now taken over pruning duties from the lady, who observes him with gracious patience.

"He could only come up with ten percent, and I've accepted that," Rae says, watching Max. "He did the best he could with what he had. Even a little bit can help get you to a hundred."

• • •

Sometime that same morning – perhaps the night before – Dirk Havenhurst finally passed. Flori had been bringing him coffee, brandy and muffins in the mornings and was the first to find him. She immediately called David at Darlene's.

Presently the couple watch paramedics roll him away on a gurney through a gauntlet of looky-loos in the courtyard. An errant gust lifts the bedsheet to reveal Dirk's face. His brittle skin is the texture of parchment paper, with constellations of red splotches around his cheeks and forehead. No one ever knew his exact age – he had alternately said he was "young enough not to know better" and "older than Father Time" – but the longtime resident had been sick with leukemia for years.

David cracks a smile as the medics tuck the bedsheet back over his face. "He probably did that on purpose, just to give everyone a good shock."

Darlene wags her head. "He was so alone. Wish we could've done more for him."

"We did as much as he would let us. Old crow hated hospitals. This was home for him."

Now it's Darlene's turn to smile. "He once told me he wanted to be cremated and have Bette Davis smoke his ashes."

David chuckles. "Let's have Rae look into what that would cost," he says – a job that used to fall to Leo before his gradual withdrawal. "The cremation part, obviously. Although if Rae wants to reach out to Mrs. Davis herself, she's more than welcome."

"We should have Rae whip up some Shrimp Louies in his honor" comes another voice. David and Darlene turn around to find Rudy hovering behind them with a gaping smile.

Rudy points toward Dirk's room, its door still open. "I suppose you want I should put a new bed in there now, huh?" He hoots. "Guessing most people wouldn't wanna sleep in the same bed as a dead man."

"A little respect, huh?" David snaps.

Rudy frowns. "I see... so you can get in little digs, but I can't?"

The three of them are joined by Aaron, who has just arrived on the scene. "I drove here as soon as I heard," he says, out of breath.

He catches the gurney rounding the corner to the rear lobby door. Where David and Darlene are wistful, Aaron looks tortured. Even in Hollywood, Dirk was a man who never spoke outwardly about his homosexuality – a prisoner of his own secrets. In the end, it got him nowhere other than broke, alone, and reliant on the generosity of others.

David is suddenly suspicious that Rudy seemed to materialize out of nowhere. "You got something to tell me?" he asks him. "Haven't seen you around here much lately."

Rudy throws off a noncommittal shrug. "Just doing my thing. Guy's gotta make a living beyond the chicken scratch you pay me, y'know."

"You running with Gordo? So help me, Rudy, if you're running with Gordo..."

Rudy scoffs at the absurd accusation.

"He's back, isn't he?" David says.

"Hey, all's I hear is rumors."

"Mmm-hmm. What kind of rumors?"

"Well... actually, I got a message from him... through intermediaries."

"Uh huh."

"He said our debt is past due."

Aaron is outraged. "Don't you mean *your* debt?" David tries to shush Aaron, but he continues. "Is that why he unleashed the cops on us?"

"Where exactly did you hear this rumor?" David asks.

"Snig and Felix. I run into them now and then at the track."

David smirks, knowing his kid brother is up to something. "Well, it just so happens we have his final four thousand on hand."

Rudy brightens. "You guys... got it?"

"We didn't just 'get it.' We *earned* it. Every legitimate penny." He turns to acknowledge Aaron and Darlene. "Me, Aaron, Darlene, Leo, Rae. Everyone worked their asses off to cut costs, fill rooms, find savings... anything to get out from under that grease sandwich once and for all."

"Wow."

David grants Rudy a beat for an expression of gratitude. It never comes.

"No one knew where to find him since he skipped town," Aaron explains to Rudy.

"Oh, Red never skipped," Rudy gloats, suddenly knowledgeable about the gangster's whereabouts. "He was always in L.A."

"What the fuck?" David says. "Either you know where he is or you don't. Quit playing games."

"I know where he is."

•   •   •

That evening, Aaron uses Dirk's death as a pretext to inform Peggy he'll be coming home late. Something about setting up a last-minute memorial at a local tavern Dirk frequented. In reality, Aaron is doing no such thing. His destination tonight is the Crown Jewel in Pershing Square. It will be his first visit to a gay bar.

In typical meticulous fashion, he did his homework about where to go, gleaning intel from *One* magazine, underground guides, and his own drive-bys. Recently, he overheard a couple of dreamy men on the pool patio rapping about the House of Ivy and the Windup, two notorious queer bars in Hollywood. But he quickly ruled out any place within a five-mile radius. Pershing Square seems promising, with a variety of choices. On one end of the spectrum are bars like Maxwell's, appealing to a more flamboyant, out-of-the-closet crowd. The Crown Jewel falls on the other end – refined and classy, with a coat-and-tie dress code that appeals to the discreet gentleman. A gentleman like Aaron.

He spots the downtown club by its iconic neon crown above the entry. After adjusting to the dark interior, he finds it much like any other bar save for its all-male clientele. Soft jazz plays in the background, competing with the lively din of cocktail chatter. Parties of well-tailored men hobnob at tables in the main room. The marble bar finds paired-off patrons and nervy singles, who sit erect over colorful concoctions. Aaron walks the length of the bar, his radar on high alert for anyone looking up at him. No one does. He settles along the back wall and orders a Rob Roy from an elegant server.

The drink helps alleviate his anxiety, which is less about meeting men and more about police stings. LAPD's vice squad is the most vigilant in the country, employing a secret weapon other cities lack – out-of-work actors. From Malibu to downtown, these handsome hunks have been prowling gay bars for decades, entrapping unsuspecting customers. A subtle pass, a suggestive comment, an inadvertent touch – it doesn't take much for these badge-carrying thespians to charge someone with lewd and lascivious conduct – "vag lewd" in police parlance – and arrest offenders on the spot. Aaron had heard they have quotas to fill, with the decoys competing to see how many "fruits in a basket" each could pluck.

A beefcake of a man notices Aaron hanging out. "You waiting for the little boys' room?" he asks Aaron in a quiet, swishy voice.

"Oh… no," Aaron says, noticing the red-neon men's room sign behind them. "Be my guest."

"I would love to," the man purrs with a bawdy head shimmy.

Aaron's "cop" sensor sends distress flares. His suitor seems to be playing a caricature of a queen and could easily be an undercover cop. If Aaron were to simply acknowledge him with a laugh or a teasing comeback, it could be perceived as flirtation – an instant vag lewd charge that would land him in the Glass House jail. He would be stamped a pervert, a sexual deviant, or as the American Psychiatric Association recently termed it, a human pathogen of a mental disease. A hard-ass judge could assign him to a mental institution, where he could be subjected to shock therapy or castration. In the best of circumstances, he would walk away with only a fine, poor prospects for future jobs, and the dissolution of his family – a life in ruins from one innocent exchange with a man he had no interest in in the first place.

Aaron drains his drink and moves away from the interloper. If merely conversing could be considered risky behavior, what were his chances of meeting anyone at all? In a pique of panic, he decides he's not ready to play such a high-stakes game and makes a play for the exit.

Still, pushing his way through the throng, he instinctively scopes out the array of men along the bar. Near the door, he notices a new face. A single man is settling into the last empty bar stool. He has a bookish face and a handsome aquiline nose, with darting eyes peering through tortoise-shell glasses. His self-conscious manner reminds Aaron of himself.

Without thinking, he leans into the stranger. "First time?" he asks with a crooked grin.

The man is startled by Aaron's directness, but relaxes once they lock eyes. "That obvious, huh?" he chuckles.

Aaron puts out his hand. "My name's Raymond. Buy you a drink?"

• • •

Just outside Gordo's scrapyard – where he first laid eyes on mismatched neon signs for Paradise Palms – David sits in the passenger seat of Rudy's Hudson Hornet. In his lap is a sealed manila envelope. This will be his first hand-off of cash after previous payments were deducted from Red's "business" profits on the hotel grounds. His shirt is damp with perspiration.

Rudy watches him from the driver's side. "You nervous?"

"A little." David stares at the imposing corrugated wall and razor wire that separate the street from Gordo's yard. "I just don't wanna get screwed out here in the sticks, is all."

"These guys have their own code. It's not in his interests to screw you."

David turns a cynical gaze toward Rudy. He was, of course, thinking of him, too.

The brothers hear the squeaking of the driveway gate opening. Snig and Felix are first to exit the premises, followed by Gordo and his pit bull Sally. As he lumbers toward their car, the brute looks heavier than the last time David saw him just before Stompanato's murder in April. His V-shaped face is now soft and doughy, and his snug white tank top betrays man-boobs and a bulbous gut.

Red, scowling into the sun, reaches into the back pocket of his trousers. David swallows hard, feeling the steady drumbeat of his heart. Gordo proceeds to whip out a harmless flap of yellow carbon paper. His boots crunch on gravel by the side of the road as he comes around to David's open window.

"By the book, the way you like it," Red mocks, flashing his rodent grin. He hands him the yellow-papered receipt.

David inspects it. Printed across the top are red letters reading "J&M Scrap Metal. Pacoima, Cal." In messy scrawl appear the words "For items rendered," with a little happy face as an extra flourish. $4,000 appears in the total. David wants to make sure every hotel expenditure is traceable in the event of an audit or sale of the hotel. The receipt represents a "transaction" – one he can explain away by saying it was related to the hotel's signage.

David hands the envelope to Gordo, who doesn't bother to double-check the cash. "This makes us a hundred percent free and clear," David says.

"One hundred and *ten*," Red winks.

David slips the receipt into his pocket and starts to roll up his window. Red shoves his hand in and blocks it from closing.

"I feel like we got off on the wrong foot, superstar," Red says through the crack. "Y'know, I was telling your kid brother here, us crazy kikes… we're practically family!"

David looks at Rudy – *come now?*

"Red's grandfather was a legend in Chicago," Rudy explains. "Leonard Elbowitz."

David shakes his head impatiently. "I don't know who that is." He points through the windshield. "Let's go, Rudy, we're done here."

"Elbows," Gordo clarifies.

David blinks away his shock. Elbows was well-known in the Shapiro household. The boys grew up hearing about Max's father-figure mentor, the gangster who ran the flower shop where he worked. Everything Pop knew about business, broads, life, and the importance of a well-appointed hat, he absorbed from the bon vivant at a young age. He claimed the worst day of his life was when the poor bastard got swiss-cheesed by a rival gang's gunfire. All these years later, David never even knew his full name.

But what of it? Was Red's familial link to Elbows supposed to make David sympathize with him? If it were true, it might clarify why Max seems strangely loyal to Gordo – and by extension, defensive of Kitty – yet it would not explain why the prick seems intent on fucking over the family.

"I know your old man don't say much, but you should ask him about our connection someday," Gordo says cryptically. "You might find it very en-luminating."

David refuses to get sucked into Red's mind games. "You got what you wanted." He turns to Rudy and issues a loud directive: "Let's *blow*, Rudy. Now!"

Rudy looks at Gordo, then shoots David a sheepish look. Leaving the keys in the ignition, he opens his door and steps out of the car.

David is confused. "Rudy…?"

Gordo crosses in front of the Hornet, joining Rudy, Snig and Felix by the open driver's side door.

"You go on without him," Red commands. "He's got business with Red…"

David sighs. "Rudy, get in the car."

"It's okay, bruthuh," Rudy replies. "I'll get my wheels later."

"Actually, it's *not* okay," Red barks, stepping forward, "what you done to him." He leans in the cab and jabs a finger in David's face. "Ever since you took away the kid's slush fund, he's been stone broke. Now you got him doing nigger work? Slaving away for you bozos, paying him a pittance? That ain't right. He's better than that."

David holds his ground. "What're you, his fucking agent?"

"No – his employer. He don't work for you no more."

David feels the acute sting of betrayal. Mouth agape, he looks at Rudy, who refuses to meet his gaze.

Red drapes his porkchop of a forearm around Rudy's chest. "A real crackerjack, this one. *You* never appreciated his skills. So he came to someone who would." His arm is like a vise, squeezing Rudy's diaphragm. "I was happy to take him on."

Rudy writhes out from under Red's hold and takes a step back.

"So if you're putting him to work," David says, "why didn't you just have *him* pay down the eleven grand?"

Gordo, offended: "What – and punish him even more?" He sneers. "Besides, a lot more fun to watch you squirm like a little bitch."

Rudy and David lock eyes. David searches for signs of remorse. A spark of shame. A gesture of reconciliation. But all he sees is the familiar craven hopelessness he's always associated with his runt brother. It is clear to him now that Rudy is the one who sold out the Palms loyalists, providing intel to Gordo that led to the LAPD bust. What other deals has he cooked up with Red against the family?

"You gave me no choice..." Rudy says feebly.

David is done expending words of disappointment and stern looks of reproach. They're lost on Rudy anyway. He slides behind the wheel and cranks the ignition. The Hornet fires up as he delivers a parting salvo to his brother. "I want nothing to do with your world. And from now on, stay the fuck out of ours."

He punches the gas, nearly running over Gordo's dog. Rudy watches him disappear down the road. David doesn't bother to look in the rearview mirror.

IV

TROUBLE IN PARADISE

CHAPTER 20

It takes several tries for David's wingtip shoe to break the glass – so tightly wrapped in a towel, his foot can't find it – but on the fourth stomp, he finally succeeds in consummating the ceremony.

"Mazel Tov!" come the cheers from the wedding party, mixed with strains of relieved laughter.

David and Darlene smile broadly at each other and lean in for a long kiss. He looks elegantly handsome in a simple black tuxedo. She is exquisite in a creamy V-Neck taffeta gown, with dark heels, black lace gloves and black under-lace lining her hem – touches only Darlene could pull off. At twelve weeks pregnant, she is still not showing.

The young rabbi spins the newlyweds toward their guests. He does the same for Best Man Leo and Maid of Honor Barbara, who wipes away tears. Once all four are lined up shoulder to shoulder, a professional photographer with a Kodak Brownie – its flash larger than the camera itself – snaps the money shot. The party is framed by an ivy-lattice chuppah set up on Aaron's redwood deck. Wispy clouds of orange and purple announce the onset of dusk, another of the picture-perfect backdrops that always seem to grace this residence.

Amid tears and shouts of joy, the fifty guests rise from their white folding chairs and applaud as David and Darlene stride down a red carpet. Darlene's parents – a sturdy, delightful pair – step into the aisle to kiss their daughter as she passes. The newlyweds disappear through the sliding glass door into Aaron's house.

The reception is an inside/outside affair. Guests flow between the living room and deck, where a quartet of hep white guys billing themselves as the Fat Cats plays jazz covers. Celebrants are treated to a massive spread of cold cuts from Greenblatt's Deli. A hired bartender shakes up cocktails for those preferring something other than bottles of champagne, beer and wine.

Peggy whipsaws through the living room with nervous energy, thanklessly piloting the party through endless land mines – the bartender not bringing enough ice, children tracking in mud, a short in the Christmas tree lights, the needs of picky guests – that could explode into chaos at any moment. And she must do it all with a smile frozen on her face, to show how effortless and fun hosting the wedding of your brother-in-law truly is!

Parked on a sofa in the living room, a convivial Abigail fills Max's glass to the rim with champagne. She is slathered in a tight blue dress that barely contains her ample cleavage and shows off miles of husky leg. Sipping from his drink, Max looks logy, eyelids growing heavy, his rumpled suit bunched up at the knees to accommodate his Frankenstein's monster-sized rehabilitation boots, which rest on an ottoman. At least his fedora looks like a million bucks.

About two hours into the reception, Leo instructs the Fat Cats to take a break. Standing in front of the stage, he raps on his beer glass with a fork. Peggy knows this is her cue to shoo guests outside and send David and Darlene to the forefront. Once everyone has quietly gathered around, Leo launches into a toast – one he seems to have well-rehearsed.

"Well, what can I say? Without getting into the down and dirty details, it's been a tough year at the Palms," he says in a loud voice. "In fact, the last several years have been... challenging... with one big but pleasant surprise along the way!"

This last part is meant to elicit knowing, gentle chuckles but is met by stolid silence. Leo catches Rae in the back, bowing her head. He clears his throat.

"It's no secret Mom held the place together. When she finally lost her battle with cancer, it was up to all of us to step up. But you know something? Through it all, there was one employee – our longest-tenured – who shined a light in the darkest of times."

He finds Darlene, standing up front with David, beaming back at him.

"I sat alongside her at the front desk almost every day for a year. During that time, I really got to know her – probably better than David does."

This gets yuks. Leo turns to David: "Don't worry, brother, you did good."

"Whose baby is that anyway?" someone joshes from the back. Darlene and David turn around with good-natured grins – just a drunk uncle from her side of the family.

Leo grows serious. "In fact, if how she is as a person is any indication, Darlene is going to be the best wife… mother… daughter-… and sister-in-law anybody could ever ask for. Makes perfect sense that she's part of the family now, because she always *was* family." Leo raises his glass to a chorus of swooning "ooohhhs." Darlene skips forward and kisses Leo on the cheek. Blushing, he says, "Just don't go tattooing the baby, huh?"

He turns to the groom.

"As for my twin brother, all I can say is… you may be older than me, but I *look* older than you. So you should respect me as you would your elders and indulge my rambling, especially when I'm four beers in." He turns to the guests. "Did you know, I don't think we've ever had one real argument our entire lives? I don't mean disagreements, but *arguments*." Looking back at David: "That must be some kind of sibling record."

"Never too late to start!" David jests.

"Ah, shut up!" Leo retorts.

"You shut up!"

Darlene playfully smacks David to let Leo continue.

"All kidding aside," Leo says, "I just wanted you to know how appreciative I am of you. All my life, you've looked after me." His voice catches in his throat. "Ah, shit, look at me, I said I wouldn't cry." He dabs his eyes with his sleeve. The guests are moved to their own silent tears.

Leo concludes, "Frankly, we don't thank you enough for everything you've done. For Pop. For me. For *all* of us brothers" – a not-so-veiled reference to Rudy, who is conspicuously absent. "You're more than just our big brother. You're our leader. And I love you." He and the guests raise glasses. "Here's to a bountiful future for you two" – his eyes drift to Darlene's midsection – "and to many 'small' returns."

David and Darlene embrace Leo in an emotional group hug.

As they pull apart, Leo lingers by the stage, waiting for a successor to come up and make the next toast. He expects it will be Aaron, standing off to the side. But Aaron is like a statue – face hardened and stoic as he props young Nancy in his arms like a shield.

Just as the pause becomes noticeably uncomfortable, an eager Barbara pushes her way forward. But before Darlene's roomie can get to the stage, Max staggers to his feet, forcing her to stop out of deference. He hobbles stiff-legged to the stage, boots knocking loudly on the wood.

"Pop…?" Leo whispers, laying a steadying hand on his shoulders.

Max brushes him away, stumbling momentarily from the motion of his arm. Darlene clutches David in a death-grip. The Shapiro patriarch is clearly drunk, and the guests lean forward in nervous anticipation.

Max looks up to the night sky. He grins. Turns to David, glassy-eyed. "I know your mother is looking down right now. Smiling…."

David nods stiffly.

"As a parent," Max informs the assembled, "you just want your kids to be happy. And uh…" A lapse as he loses his train of thought. He sees Darlene biting her lip. "We think the world of Darlene, of course. I'm sorry Rudy isn't here to join us. I wanted him to be here, but… you know how it goes. When you get to be an old fogey like me, your kids start treating you like a child. Heh." Squinting toward the back, his eyes bring into focus Rae. "There she is! Rae, come on up here. C'mon!"

Rae – the only Black guest – waves him off with a horrified look.

"That's my daughter, Rae, for those of you who don't know. I couldn't be prouder of her. Look at 'er. Ain't she beautiful? I'd say she got my intelligence, too, but that would be an insult to her."

Rae disappears inside the house.

"Leo mentioned tough times," Max prattles. "I seen a lot of 'em over the years. The thing about Rae is, she's not like others like her. By that, what I mean is – "

David practically pounces on his father, smothering him in a bear hug to put an end to the nightmare. "Thank you, Pop. I love you!"

"I wasn't through!" Max protests as Leo and Darlene escort him away.

"Thank you all for blessing us with your presence!" David shouts to his guests. "And an extra-big cheer to Aaron and Peggy, for their generosity in opening their beautiful home up to us. Now let's blow the lid off this joint!" He waves over the Fat Cats, who break into a spirited version of Thelonious Monk's "Well You Needn't."

Back inside the house, Peggy drops the Happy Homemaker façade, strikes up a cigarette, and pours herself a healthy portion of white wine. She is visibly seething as she stalks into the kitchen.

Seeking sanctuary herself, Rae also heads into the kitchen, not realizing Peggy is present. "Oh – hi," she stammers, seeing an aproned Peggy at the sink, vigorously scrubbing plates and glasses in sudsy water. "Can I help?"

Peggy turns and glowers at her. Rae doesn't wait for an answer, slipping on a pair of rubber gloves.

"What do you think you're doing?" Peggy finally says.

"Thought you could use a hand."

"No, I don't mean this. I mean, what are you *doing here?*"

Rae cocks her head. "Excuse me?"

"Take those off. Those are my gloves. I didn't say you could put those on."

Rae, shocked by Peggy's offensive behavior, doesn't budge.

"Fine," Peggy hisses. "If you're not gonna take 'em off, *you* do the goddamn dishes." She tosses her apron on the counter, then grabs her wine and leaves the kitchen.

• • •

Later that evening, Max is once again ensconced on the sofa, his legs stretched out on the ottoman. He is joined by Billy, who mopes to his grandfather that his sisters are doing "girlie stuff, playing dress-up and wedding with all the other girls." Max invites him to use his legs as a "table" to play with the new Disney Space Ship Set he got him for Chanukah – an early arrival on this second week of December of '58.

Billy spreads out his rockets and astronauts on Grandpa Max's legs, accompanying his make-believe with explosion sound effects. His play has a soothing effect on Max, who rests his head against the sofa cushion and dozes with a faint smile.

David flops down next to him to take advantage of his liquored-up, unguarded state. "Hey, Pop, I keep forgetting," he says with faux-absent-mindedness. "Elbows was Red's grandfather, right?"

"What of it?" Max slurs, eyes still shut.

There it is – the affirmation David was looking for. He keeps probing. "Did Elbow's descendants – y'know, Red's parents – did they have any kind of financial stake in the Palms?"

"Of course! They lent me the money to open the goddamn place."

David looks stricken. Gordo wasn't bluffing. His family's tentacles *did* wrap around Max. "I thought you took out a loan from the bank…"

"What *bank?*" Max opens his eyes and looks at David like he's an idiot. "It was the Depression. Banks weren't loaning out money! Certainly not to a pipsqueak flower-store manager like me." He drops his head back on the cushion and closes his eyes. "Where else would I find the cash?"

David feels betrayed. All these years he and Marta perpetuated the myth that they acquired Paradise Palms in auction through honest hard work! Why had they kept the secret from their kids? To protect them? How much deeper did the partnership go? What other debts were owed the Gordo clan?

Before David can ask more questions, Billy performs a noisy "splashdown" on his grandpa's stomach with a parachuting space capsule. Max drifts off with a loud snort.

David gets up to fix himself a drink. He finds Leo mixing a Kahlua and milk.

Leo points to Max and Billy. "I should have the photographer get a picture of that, huh?"

"Sure," David says distantly.

Leo throws an arm around David, conspiratorial. "Listen, I've been waiting for the right time to tell you this. It's about Pop."

Now what, David thinks. "Is this gonna ruin my wedding night?"

"Actually, it may be the best gift you could ever ask for. Because it might guarantee that you, me... we all get the hotel."

David grins, grabbing Leo by the shoulders. "Pop's gonna ditch the bitch?"

Leo nods. "He wants me to track down Aunt Rochelle's lawyer – the one who handled her divorces – and set up a meeting."

David's smile fades. "Did he just tell you this? 'Cause if he did, he's drunk, and he – "

"Stone-cold sober. Rae was with me. He told us when we took him back to Sylvan Gardens to fill out the applications. He wants a clean break when he moves out."

David's mirth returns. "He's moving into that place, eh?"

"January one."

"God*damn* it, four-eyes, why didn't you tell me any of this earlier tonight?"

"I didn't want to upstage the nuptials. And we could never get a private moment."

David gets his brother in a headlock and musses his thinning pate, expressing his giddiness in mock rage. "You sonofabitch," he laughs.

He releases Leo and immediately notices Abigail plopping down next to Max. The heft of her hips jars him awake, causing his legs to jerk. Billy's space world tumbles to the carpet. The kid leaves.

"How's the mooch handling all of this?" David asks.

"Don't know, don't care."

"She *does* know, right?"

"Oh yeah, all of it."

Abigail thrusts another flute of champagne into Max's shaky hand. David wonders why she's still being so lovey-dovey to the old man tonight, then figures it's for show.

"Drink up!" Abigail implores, physically grabbing Max's forearm and guiding the glass to his mouth. He makes a sour face like a baby, refusing to part his lips. Sparkling wine dribbles down his chin.

David springs across the room. "Whoa, whoa… easy!" He removes the glass from Max's hand, placing it on the coffee table. "Pop, you don't have to drink that!" He turns to Abigail, trying to keep it light. "I think he's reached his age-mandated quota."

Undeterred, Abigail grabs the drink again. "It's his son's wedding. Let him celebrate."

David takes the glass from her. "He's past the point of celebration," he says testily. "This is annihilation."

Abigail tosses her hair back with a flick of her wrist. "Remember what you told me after *we* got married? You said you wished I was *dead*."

David sees guests starting to look their way.

"*Dead!*" she cries, pointing an accusatory finger. Darlene swoops in to defuse the situation.

"Oh, hey, Abigail. Everything okay? Can I get you anything?"

David rises and wraps his arms around Darlene – a signal to Abigail. If she wants to tangle with him, she'll to have to go through his lady now.

"Just peachy, Darlene," Abigail replies, switching to a coquettish cadence. "You look amaaaazing." She notices the rock on Darlene's finger. "Love your ring."

"Thank you. Love yours."

"Oh, thank you." Abigail holds her wedding ring out for Darlene to fawn over.

Darlene studies it. "Is that the one that used to belong to Marta, or…?" Unlike the blue-diamond band she used to wear, this one features an interlacing vine with rose diamonds.

"Hmm? Oh, *that* old thing?" Abigail laughs with a casual cruelty meant for David. "It was time for an upgrade. I sold it for something newer and better."

Seeing his silent, enraged reaction, Abigail whispers into David's ear as she gets up to leave: "Daddy never even noticed."

• • •

As the clock ticks past twelve, the party starts to wind down. The band and bartender pack their gear and the kids and their cousins are in their pajamas. David finds Aaron having a smoke on the patio, casting a faraway gaze to the somnolent houses as a heavy mist rolls in.

"You coming in?"

Aaron turns around, forcing a grin. "In a minute."

"Thanks again for hosting us. It was perfect. Not to mention, you saved me a fucking fortune!"

"Please. You covered the catering and band, the rest was Peggy's and my present to you. Truly our pleasure."

David tilts his head. "You guys have a fight or something?"

"No. Why?"

"I don't know. She just seemed kind of…"

"She was just a little stressed. Wanting everything to go right. You know how she is."

"I thought maybe it was because we were marrying in sin."

Aaron emits a hollow laugh. "Hey, she's thrilled you're having a baby. We all are. My kids are over the moon. Jolene is already talking about babysitting."

David smiles.

"Hey, uh, about the toasts…" Aaron says. "You know how I am about public speaking…"

David coolly waves him off – don't worry about it.

Aaron suddenly bows his head as Rae walks up to her brothers. She leans in and kisses David on the cheek.

"I just said goodbye to Darlene, and wanted to say congratulations again," she says. "Leo and I are leaving…"

"He's not driving, right?"

"No," she assures him.

Aaron stubs out his cigarette. "I should go inside and see if Peggy needs help cleaning up," he says awkwardly, leaving the other two.

As David watches him go, he says to Rae, "I don't know. They've both been 'off' tonight. Maybe having the wedding here was a mistake. It was just too much…"

"Nah, I don't think that was it," she says. "At least, not all of it."

"What do you mean?"

"I shouldn't have come."

"What? Don't be crazy."

"I just made everyone uncomfortable." Her lips curl in bitterness.

"Know what? Fuck 'em. You're family – "

"Stop!" Rae exclaims. "I can't take one more person telling me I'm 'family.' You all didn't even know I existed until eleven months ago. It's an empty word. We just have the same dad. That's all we have in common."

Her outburst stuns David, but he's not naïve either. He too was humiliated by Pop using Rae as a self-serving prop during his toast. He understands that any compensatory behavior from her half-brothers or "now-I-see-the-light" displays from their father – even if genuine – could never entirely wash away her bad hand. He had thought of his own situation in relation to hers. Although he knocked up his girlfriend, their baby will grow up in a loving, conventional home with married parents. Rae wasn't even a love child – there was no love involved – but the product of a mistake during a tryst between an entitled white man and his Black help. Who the hell was David to sing "kumbaya" to her?

"I'm sorry," she says.

"No, Rae… I am."

They lean against the railing and watch the remaining guests through the glass doors – Darlene and her parents, Max and Abigail, aunts, uncles, couples, all socializing under the warm glow of midnight.

"I guess what we're *trying* to say," David ventures, "when we say you're family is… you and us, we're in this together. We value you. We care about you." He looks at her. "We love you. Straight up."

Rae waves her hand in front of her misty eyes, then shoves him in the chest. "You're just a drunk idiot."

"Sorry, kiddo, but you're stuck with this idiot."

They hug each other in a long embrace. David whispers, "Aaron's world is different from the rest of us. Give him time, he'll come around."

She pulls back with a dubious smile. The mist has turned into a drizzle. She bounds off to find Leo, with David ducking behind her.

As the final guests prepare to leave, Peggy has already gone off to sleep in one of the kids' beds. David and Darlene, who will crash in Aaron's guest room, open the front door to see off Max and Abigail.

"Be careful out there," Darlene tells Abigail, who, curiously, hasn't touched a drink all night. "Looks like the rain is starting to pick up."

Abigail helps an unsteady Max navigate the stairs while David holds an umbrella over him. He and Abigail guide him into his Cadillac. After shutting the passenger door, Abigail avoids any awkward farewells with David by scooting around to the driver's side with her jacket over her head. David watches the Caddy drive off.

At the front door, Leo hands the keys of his Mercury over to Rae. The twins share a slap-happy embrace, exchanging sloppy brotherly sentiments.

"Where're you parked?" David asks.

It's been a long night for Leo. "I... can't remember."

Everyone laughs.

"Just down the street," Rae says. "We'll be fine."

David and Darlene watch them splash down the hill toward Leo's car.

• • •

Rae tentatively guides the Mercury down Tigertail Road, commencing the mile-and-a-half descent toward Sunset Boulevard. Complicating the wet conditions, the street is steep and narrow, with blind curves and few streetlights. Leo trusts her enough to doze off in the passenger seat. Nonetheless she puts the radio on to calm her nerves.

Halfway down the hill, a dark figure darts in front of her high beams, causing Rae to gasp and pump the brakes. She checks her mirrors – it happened so quickly, she can't be sure if it was an animal or a person. Could it simply have been an illusion created by the windshield wipers? She eases the car back into drive mode.

Rounding a bend, she lowers the radio's volume. She hears the long and sustained blare of a broken car horn through the squeak of the wipers. The source reveals itself in the form of a Cadillac crushed against a wooden utility pole, its smashed-in hood hissing steam.

"Ohmigod!" She slams the brakes twenty feet from the accident. Leo snaps awake. Gapes at the horrific scene through the windshield.

Rae and Leo rush the Caddy. The pole is fixed on a cliff – the only thing that stopped the car from plunging down the mountainside. But based on its brutal impact with the pole, it may not matter.

"That's Pop's car!" Leo clamors. The driver's side of the fogged-over windshield has a bullseye crack daubed with blood. Leo cups his hands against the pane but it's too cloudy to see in. "We gotta get them out!"

Leo and Rae attempt to pry open the car doors. They're jammed shut.

"Fuck!" Leo screams.

"We need something to break the windows!" Rae shouts.

As she continues yanking the door handles, Leo pulls a tire jack out of the Mercury. Shutting its trunk, he's distracted by a shadowy woman flopping barefooted down the street – perhaps someone coming to help. It's only when she crosses under a street lamp that he realizes it's Abigail.

Her hair is matted over her face and eye makeup streaks down her cheeks. Her wet blue dress droops heavily around her bosom. But in the revealing light, she doesn't appear to have a single scratch on her. And her head – which presumably struck the driver's-side windshield – bears no signs of a bloody gash.

Leo is confused. "How did you get out of the car?" he yells.

She looks at him with haunted eyes.

Leo sees he's wasting precious time and hurries back to the Cadillac. Rae has managed to get the warped passenger door open a crack. She is startled to see Abigail coming up behind Leo – it must've been *her* who flashed past the Mercury's headlights.

Leo peers through the door. The passenger seat is empty. He spins around and cries to Abigail, "Where is he? What'd you do with him?"

Abigail crouches down in the rain. She covers her eyes with her fists, opens her mouth wide and wails to the heavens – wretched, halting sobs.

There's a shattering sound. Rae has smashed in the driver's window with the jack. She and Leo swat away shards of glass and are shocked by what they find: Max – in the driver's seat, slumped over the wheel, his chest crushed between the dashboard and the seatback. Blood coats his head from its impact with the windshield.

"No!" Leo reaches through the window frame and clutches his father, his anguished cries blending in with the squall of the horn. "*Nooooo!*"

CHAPTER 21

"Is there anything more depressing than spending Christmas Eve with people on the precipice of death?"

David poses the rhetorical question to Leo as they walk through the Intensive Care Unit of UCLA Medical Center. Since their most dire patients can't enjoy holiday cheer outside, the ICU staff has tried to recreate it inside. Colored bulbs line the dreary walls, and each of the sixteen beds' wraparound curtains – including Max's, last one on the right – is adorned with cardboard Santa heads and reindeer antlers. Even more depressing for David is the fact that he and Darlene had to postpone their honeymoon to Hawaii. When they'll be able to reschedule is anybody's guess. It all depends on Pop.

Pushing back the drapes, the twins pull up chairs next to Max's supine body. They immediately fall into routines. David rubs his dad's legs and Leo massages his arms to help with circulation. He has been in a nonresponsive comatose state since his "accident" two weeks ago. His skin is chalky white, and even with a humming ventilator in his mouth, his face seems permanently fixed in a pissed-off scowl that seems befitting of Max Shapiro. Maybe it's better this way, Leo had quipped one night. If he were conscious, he would spit out the ventilator and rip out the feeding tube in his arm, though he might be okay with the catheter.

Doctors have warned the family that he is at a critical juncture. The prognosis for patients who remain in comas after fourteen days becomes increasingly poor with each passing week. Oh sure, there are always miracles, but Max has three strikes against him. Poor health, his age, and the fact that his coma was caused by a head injury.

A neurosurgeon actually diagnosed *two* blows to his head – the dash and windshield in quick succession – causing his brain to rattle inside his skull and tearing vital nerve fibers. "Like the plastic triangle inside a Magic 8-Ball," he crudely explained. If the swelling in his brain persists much longer, the diminished blood flow means it won't get enough oxygen. Next stage: Human vegetable. Or death.

Even if Max were to recover, he will never be the same. The longer he's unconscious, the greater the likelihood he'll need to relearn how to walk, talk, feed himself and go to the bathroom. David remembers the grueling therapy sessions Rudy went through – and *he* was at the height of his youthful years.

If that weren't enough, a hospital administrator had recently asked the boys if their father had an advanced medical directive. The trust that they copied from Abigail's dresser drawer contained no such language, and Max and his kids had never brought the issue up. "There is none," David told the woman. "My brothers and I will make that call."

"Well, I'm sorry, but that's not your call to make," she said coolly. "We'll need to talk to his wife about these matters. Maybe you can all arrive at a decision together."

Presently, David and Leo welcome Aaron into their father's quarters. He places two brown bags containing their dinner on the bed, then shuts the drape for privacy. He sits next to Max's recumbent body opposite David and Leo.

The brothers dig into the sacks, pulling out Styrofoam soup cups and sandwiches. David lifts the white bread off his sandwich and finds a flap of gray deli meat caked in mayonnaise. A wilted piece of lettuce clings to it like mold.

"What's in this thing?"

Aaron chomps into his sandwich, shrugs. "Some sort of mystery meat."

"Don't you know?" Leo says. "Hospitals inject their cafeteria food with salmonella to make sure you never leave."

David samples the soup and drops his spoon in disgust. "Like piss-water. Jesus Christ, how do you mess up chicken noodle soup?"

Leo eyes his soup. "May I?"

"Please." David hands it to Leo. He swivels in his chair and pulls a folder out of his briefcase on the floor.

"What do you got there?" Aaron asks between bites.

Leo responds, "A pre-emptive statement from the parasite's lawyer. Says they'll fight any criminal or civil claims made by us against her. It was hand-delivered to David."

David spreads the sheets on Max's blanket – each page filled with confusing legalese.

Aaron snorts. "She hired a legal eagle, huh? One of Gordo's men?"

"Worse," David says. "One of Mickey's."

"Max Solomon," Leo sighs. "His name comes up in all the rags as his go-to defense attorney. Handled Bugsy Siegel too."

"Leo and I think he must be the 'serious-looking lawyer' who showed up at Spiegelman's with Gordo. *He's* the one who changed the trust, got Pop to sign. And Spiegelman's on his payroll."

Aaron stops chewing as the enormity of what they're up against sinks in. He glimpses the embossed gold letterhead on fine linen paper. "So we hire our own lawyer and go after her anyway. Fight fire with fire."

"No, we're screwed," David mutters. He nods toward their father. "As long as Sleeping Beauty here never wakes up to refute her claims, we don't stand a chance."

"But this was a calculated ploy on her part. Gordo too. This was attempted murder!"

"*We* know that," Leo says, "but it's what happens in the courtroom that counts. David's right. We don't have a winnable case."

Aaron looks away and clenches his jaw. David considers another way to cut through his brother's myopia.

"Look," he says to Aaron, "let's do a simulation. You argue our side, and I'll shoot it down like I'm this Solomon hotshot. You'll see they have an answer for everything."

David looks to Leo for his opinion. Leo shrugs. "Why not?"

"Go 'head," David prods Aaron. "Give it your best shot."

Leo clears his throat and adopts a deep baritone. "Hear Ye, Hear Ye, this court is called to session…"

"Stop," Aaron grumps. "This is stupid."

"You wanna prove our case? Prove it."

Aaron throws down. "Alright. He knew he couldn't drive because of his hip. He was wearing heavy boots on both feet. Then he's found behind the steering wheel? Doesn't make sense."

David wags his head. "According to the defendant, Max thought *she* was drunk. He told her he was okay to drive them home."

"That's bullshit. He was incoherent. And we all saw her drive off."

"He threatened her. Told her to switch places after they pulled away from the house. She was scared. She did what he said."

Aaron scoffs. "Scared of a feeble old man?"

"With known ties to mobsters stretching back decades, and who could make her disappear if he wanted to."

Leo looks at David.

"What?" David says to him.

"She set him up," Aaron counters. "She got him plastered on purpose at the party. We were all witness to that."

"She never coerced her husband into getting hammered. She simply supported his desire to celebrate his son's wedding, as any wife would."

"*You* saw her force a drink on him – "

"She was helping him… he has trembling hands."

Aaron flies out of his seat in indignation. "Look. She got him drunk. She switched places with him. Right before that big curve. But she never got back in the car. Her plan was to have him lose control and drive it over a cliff, and make it seem like she bailed out. His foot was found pressed on the gas. The boot was too heavy for him to lift his foot off, and there were no skid marks. Plus, the doors were jammed. *Proof* she wasn't in the passenger seat at the time of the accident. *Proof* she sent him off on a death sentence. Why? So she could take control of his assets. Greed – pure and simple."

Aaron crosses his arms in triumph. Even David manages a smile.

The brothers are interrupted by a Nurse Tania sweeping back the curtain. She's a petite young thing with a Santa hat who blows in like a Force-10 gale, checking the patient chart, adjusting his ventilator, fluffing his pillows.

"You boys almost done here?" she asks in a distinct Southern voice. "Visiting hours are over."

"Where's your yuletide spirit?" Leo kids.

"Yeah," Aaron adds, sitting back down, "you can come visit *us* anytime." He immediately starts to blush, his lame pretense of hetero-guy humor fizzling like flat soda.

Tania answers their comments with a sideways smile and ducks out. The brothers look down at their comatose father, then at each other.

"Court back in session?" Leo asks.

"I call on Rae Lynn," Aaron says, now fully engaged in this exercise. "She saw Kitty – "

"Objection – speculation," says Leo.

"Overruled," says David.

"Rae saw Kitty on the street just seconds before," Aaron maintains, "running *away* from the accident, leaving Max to die."

"We don't know what she saw. It was dark and rainy, and the defendant was wearing a dark dress." David glances at the statement. "And the defendant attests she wasn't running away. She was trying to seek help after the crash."

"She *did* eventually come back to the car," Leo points out.

"Only after Rae had spotted her," Aaron disputes. "She had no choice at that point but to play the hysterical wife."

David reads from Solomon's statement: "'The defendant is the victim here. The real criminal is Maximilian Shapiro, who records will show was well over the legal alcohol limit set by the state of California, and under different circumstances, could just as easily be up for manslaughter charges.'"

The defense lawyer's counter-claim casts a pall over the group. David looks at Aaron. "Still think we have a case?"

Aaron's shoulders slump. "What gets me is, Pop was on the verge of divorcing her..."

"Hearsay... not admissible..." Leo says.

"Can it, Leo. This is just us talking now. She knew that. And whatever she knows, Gordo knows. The threat of a divorce exposing her fraud? That was all the motive they needed to lock us out. Now there's no way for us to challenge the validity of the trust."

David, agreeing: "If Pop goes, Mickey, Gordo, Kit... they'll own our asses." He clasps his hands behind his neck. "They were planning this coup forever, always one step ahead of us, playing the long game. Didn't matter how they got there. They were gonna get there."

"And so here we are," Aaron says grimly. "One artificial breath away from disaster."

The brothers study their father's face. The scowl is still present, as if to announce he's tired of all this pointless yammering.

"We can't change what happened," David intones. "The only thing that matters now is where do we go from here?"

•   •   •

Rudy holds a bowling ball up to his nose. He takes three meditative breaths and strides forward, his steps lopsided but steady, eyes locked on the painted floor arrows. As he releases the ball, his thumb ejects from the hole with a satisfying pop. The ball thuds on the wood and tornadoes down the lane, hooking into the pocket at the last second for a glorious pin-spinning strike.

Candy — Red's "PR" girl — squeals into Rudy's arms before stepping up to take her turn.

"You're carrying our sagging asses," says Snig, manning the score sheet. "Keep it up."

Rudy's teammate marks him down for a third strike in a row. In the adjacent lane, Red, Abigail and Felix make up the opposing squad. The sextet is enjoying a friendly match at the Sunset Bowling Center — a 52-lane alley in the shell of the old Warner Bros. Hollywood studio.

Rudy slides into a plastic chair and chugs his beer. He watches Gordo miss a seven-pin spare. The thug turns around and shrugs, his lips tightening in mischief as his right foot curls behind his left leg and slyly kicks the ball-return. The bottom latch drops open, exposing the machine's spinning rotor. Felix dutifully scrambles over to snap the partition back into place.

Gordo grabs a beer and plunks down next to Rudy. Together they watch Candy heave a ball down the lane with two hands. She tries to guide its leisurely, serpentine trajectory with her voluminous hips, wiggling them left and right. Red leans into Rudy.

"Can't bowl worth a damn, but that ass-shake can start an earthquake."

Halfway down the lane, the ball dips into the gutter. Candy couldn't care less, spinning around with a little jig and an "oh well" grin at Rudy.

Red jabs Rudy. "You like her?"

"She's alright."

"She likes you, superstar. Plenty more where that come from."

Snig turns around from the scorekeeper table. "Hey, Rudy. Beer us, would ya?"

"Get it yourself!" Red jaws at him. "We're having a deep conversation here!"

Snig grunts and gets up to take his turn.

Gordo slaps Rudy's shoulder. "Seen your pop lately?"

"Yeah. Three days ago."

"You should go every day. You came from his loins, you gotta respect that."

Abigail overhears them discussing her husband as she prepares to roll her second ball.

"It's not so easy," Rudy grouses. "They have limited visiting hours and I gotta schedule my visits around David's."

Abigail returns to the seating area, downing the rest of her vodka tonic. "Vance, you're up," she says tartly.

"Skip our turns for now." Red smacks her butt. "Abby, why don't you go hunt down that server, get us all some more refreshments."

She does as she's told and walks up the steps into the crowded, cavernous alley.

"Listen," Red goes on, "what your brother is doing to you is disgraceful. Treating you like dog shit, playing the bigshot. He has more respect for that nigger girl than he does you."

"Hey, c'mon… she's my half-sister. I like her."

"Sure, what's not to like? Kid seems alright, good head on her shoulders. But she just popped up out of the blue and aced you out of the family. Abby tells me she was at your brother's wedding. And where were you?"

"Disinvited."

"Damn right. He respects her more than you?" Red lets out a harsh breath. "That's a slap in the face. What're you gonna do about it?"

Rudy lights up a cigarette. "Ain't I already doing it?"

Red smirks. "Yeah, I guess you are."

He tilts his beer forward and the two clink bottles.

"Listen, you wanna really stick it to him, I need you to do me a favor," Red continues. "See, ever since that new prick of a police chief took over, they've been coming down hard on people like us just trying to eke out a living. What worked in the past don't work no more. That's why Mickey's got us diversifying."

Rudy parks his elbows on his knees, listlessly bobbing his head.

"I need you to move some canisters out of the yard and into the hotel. Maybe into that storage area behind the rooms."

"The utility closet?"

"Sure."

"What kind of canisters?"

"You know… for inhalants."

"Like laughing gas?"

"Only better. Butane gas. All them Hollywood Young Turks are doing it. They say it makes you see God." Red rocks back and laughs.

Rudy cringes. "I don't know. Bringing drugs into the Palms. You yourself said Chief Parker's cracking down on – "

"No, see, that's the beauty. They can't get us on nothin'. Butane's not a drug. It's a gas." He points to the blue-glass lighter in Rudy's hand. "It's used in fuckin' lighter fluid."

Rudy blows a plume of smoke and tilts the lighter in his hands, watching the liquid seesaw back and forth.

"These pinko actors, they burn money," Gordo crows. "They don't know what to do with it. They've been forking over a hundred dollars a tank."

Rudy's eyes light up.

"That got your attention, huh? There's ten percent in it for you for each tank you move. But I need *you* to store 'em. I can't be showing my face around your place. Your brother, the feds, the fuzz – everyone wants a piece of ol' Red!"

Felix turns around from the scorer's table. "Hey Red, you goin' or what?"

Red fists Rudy in the chest, then mocks Felix and Snig at the scorer's table, their burly flesh spilling over their chairs. "Fucking turds," he hums to Rudy. "Look like something a giant shit out, don't they?"

Rudy, still mesmerized by the liquid in his lighter: "Tanks are probably heavy. I'm not sure I can lift them myself."

"The turds are gonna help you. They got the van and everything. It's a done deal."

He stands up and lifts his ball from the carousel. Jamming his fingers in the holes, he turns to face Rudy. "Hey. Don't be such a worrywart. Pretty soon, this will all be over." He lines up at the top of the lane, addressing the youngest Shapiro one last time over his shoulder. "Won't have to go sneakin' around no more. We can finally claim what's ours."

Rudy responds with a circumspect stare, watching Red fling the ball like a shot put. It sails almost halfway down the lane before it crashes onto the floorboards and shatters the pins with such force, one of them catapults outside the reach of the mechanical sweeper. When the dust clears, one wobbling pin – a stubborn seven-pin – remains standing.

Red trudges the length of the lane, picks up the wayward pin, and flings it against the seven-pin for a "spare" – killing two problems at once.

Swaggering back up the lane, he is showered with razzing and sarcastic applause by other bowlers.

CHAPTER 22

As Max teeters in a suspended state between life and death, Rae dozes next to his hospital bed. A half-finished bottle of Dr. Pepper rests at the base of her chair. Flipped over in her lap is a sleep-inducing hardback borrowed from the library – *Business Fundamentals*. Coincidentally, today she is dressed like a young professional, a ploy to avoid a repeat of her embarrassment at Sylvan Gardens, where she was mistaken for Max's personal aide.

Rae snaps awake with a start. A male visitor has entered the ICU. Though she can't see him through the drape partition, she recognizes his unmistakable tinny voice.

"We know where we're going," says Red. "Last bed in the corner."

"Thank you, nurse," comes another voice – Abigail's.

Rae shoots out of her chair, collecting her book and purse. She doesn't want them to see her, doesn't want the awkward exchange of pleasantries with two very unpleasant people. Red has only treated her with disrespect since he met her, and Kitty or Abigail or whatever she's calling herself these days is a shameless gold-digger who tried to kill Max and is out to destroy the family. The only problem is – she's trapped. Since Max is the farthest patient from the door, she can't sneak out without being seen.

Red can be heard pestering Abigail, their voices getting closer. "What'd you buy more flowers for anyways? He won't even know you brung 'em."

"I haven't been by much. Don't want the nurses thinking I don't care."

Rae, on the verge of panic, finds a break in the curtain near the headboard of Max's bed. She slides through the crack and squats next to a radiator behind the drape. She can't imagine the pair visiting Max for very long. If she can just wait them out, everything should be fine.

Gordo whips the curtain back from the foot of Max's bed, then shuts it after he and Abigail enter. Mrs. Shapiro is holding a vase of artificial flowers that still has the price tag on it from the gift shop downstairs. "Hi sweetheart," she says aloud. "I got you these."

She places the vase on Max's nightstand, next to other flowers and Get Well cards. Max looks the same as before – still scowling and chalky, a bit more gaunt. Abigail flumps on the bed but refrains from kissing him.

"How's the service around here?" Red yells, as if that will make Max hear him. "They treating you right?"

"You're looking good," Abigail says.

"Yeah, you better not be giving them nurses a hard time!"

Abigail, more quietly: "We're gonna make sure you get the best treatment. Vance knows the best doctors."

"Yeah," Red concurs. "We're gonna get you out of here."

Abigail studies her husband's face. The tangle of plastic tubes connecting his nose and mouth to the ventilator make him look like an amphibious underwater creature. "You think he hears us?" she asks Red. "They say people who wake up from comas often remember people talking to them."

"Yeah? Well, too bad he ain't never waking up, so we'll never know."

"He looks angry."

"You would too if you had them things jammed in your kisser."

Abigail runs her hand along the ventilator hose. "Wonder what would happen if this just stopped working…" she muses.

Red guides her hand away from the ventilator. "Ho ho, hey…" His voice drops to a trebly whisper. "They see wifey leave the hospital and all of a sudden *this* thing mali-functions? You don't think that looks a little fishy?"

"I was just wondering, is all."

"No, baby, you gotta do it through the IV drip." Red walks over to the intravenous bag, padding it with his gorilla hands. "You add formaldehyde to the saline, gradual-like. It kills the blood cells, eats away the tissues and such. The Mick did it with that Feinberg fella who double-crossed him. Slipped him into a coma. But you gotta get a doc on your team. That's why we gotta get him to Adventist."

Gordo leans into Max, raising his voice again. "You hear that, Max? We're gonna get you the VIP treatment – your own room and doctor. No more bullpens with all the other riff-raff!" He laughs and reaches for the chair that Rae had sat in. As he scoots it closer, its legs knock over the Dr. Pepper bottle, spilling the remaining soda on the floor.

"Jesus, be careful!" Abigail scolds. She throws a towel over the sticky mess.

Red fingers his unibrow. "What the hell was that doin' there?" He picks up the bottle. Faint lipstick stains are visible on its mouth, and the glass is still cold. His little beady eyes dance around Max's quarters.

On the other side of the curtain, Rae silently pounds her forehead in self-abasement. What a *fool* for not picking up her bottle!

She hears a muffled gripe from Abigail: "His kids will never go for the move."

"Ain't up to them," Red assures her. "It's up to you."

Rae keeps her eyes shut, concentrating on their conspiring.

"Can I help you?" comes a woman's voice, loud and clear.

Rae's eyes pop open. It's Nurse Tania, standing in front of her.

"N-nuh, I... I was just getting some air..."

"Who y'all visiting?" the nurse asks officiously.

The shade around Max's bed suddenly flies open, revealing Abigail and Gordo, staring Rae down. "She's with us, miss," Red sneers, eyes fixed on Rae. "Ain't that right, Rae?"

Tania studies Rae a beat, then, satisfied with Gordo's answer, moves on.

Rae doesn't hesitate, quickly hurrying toward the ICU exit. When she reaches the hallway, she becomes disoriented – the halls all look the same. Is the elevator to the left or right? She turns right. Gordo is on her heels.

"Hey, where you going?" he bleats after her. "Didn't you wanna see your daddy?"

Rae blurs past hospital personnel in the hallway. The mad patter of Red's feet gets louder. She spots the elevator twenty yards ahead – too late, no time for that. She sees an orderly heading into the ladies' room to her right and scuttles behind her.

Rae enters a stall and quietly exhales several times. She hears the door opening and closing, the comforting, mindless gossip of female hospital workers as they stream in and out – followed by stretches of stressful silence.

Finally, after fifteen minutes, Rae peeks her head out of the stall. The restroom is empty. She edges into the hallway. Gordo is nowhere to be found.

Rae heads to the elevator. She hits the "down" button, glancing over her shoulder as she awaits the car. It arrives with a *ding*. She gets in and presses "L"

— three flights down. As the doors start to shut, she closes her eyes and exhales again. She is alone.

"Going down?" Red's fist punches through the crack, forcing the partition back open. He is suddenly in the elevator with her, blocking her exit, the closing doors entombing them inside.

Rae lunges for the "Door Open" button but Red rebuffs her with a forearm sweep. She flails backwards, her purse tumbling to the floor, belching out lipstick, a hairbrush, an apple and a small container of cottage cheese. He turns to the bank of buttons and flips the switch marked "Emergency Stop." The elevator comes to a grinding halt.

Rae turns her back to Gordo and crouches in the corner, pawing the car's cold metal walls. "I didn't hear anything back there!" she cries.

Red doesn't reply, but she can hear the air whistling through his nostrils.

"Even if I did, I wouldn't say nothing to no one. I'm not that stupid."

"No, see, that's the problem," he finally says. "You're actually pretty smart. And that's what makes you dangerous."

Rae hears the distinct click of a gun hammer. She peeks over her left arm. Red's corpulent frame closes in behind her, so close she can smell his stale breath. With a shocking jolt, she feels the shaft of his gun jam her from behind, between her upper thighs.

"Please don't!" she begs, wincing.

Red whispers into her ear, "If you say one word of it to David, the cops, even a fucking priest… I'll stick my rod in you so fucking hard, it'll split your cooter in two." He yanks his gun deeper into her crotch. As Rae starts to scream, he puts his other hand over her mouth, sheathing her like a fur coat. "Then when I'm done with you, I'll blow your fucking brains out. Chop you into tiny pieces. Feed your remains to my dog. She loves dark meat."

Gordo backs away. Rae collapses on the floor, curled up and crying. Red slips the gun back in his waistband and closes his jacket over it. He starts to place the spilled contents back in Rae's purse. As he picks up the cottage cheese container, he pauses, juggling it in his hand. A sick grin plays across his face.

He whirls around and flings it toward Rae. She shrieks. It explodes inches above her head, white cottage cheese splattering the walls like curdled confetti.

"Take a good look at that," Red exhorts. "That's your brains."

He turns around and disengages the "Stop" switch. The car lurches back into operation with a groaning whine, descending to the lobby.

Gordo straightens his shirt and smooths his hair. "On your feet," he voices to the door, holding out her purse. Rae scrambles to her feet and grabs her belongings.

As the doors open, Red struts out into the lobby with a tuneless whistle. Rae remains frozen in the elevator, coagulated milk tangled in her hair and splayed across her racked face, only emerging once the doors threaten to close her back in.

• • •

Peggy Shapiro, dressed in a nightie, violently rubs avocado-green cold cream into her cheeks and forehead in the bathroom mirror. Her reflection glares back. Once again, she finds herself preparing for bed before Aaron comes home from "social business." Lately, he's been trying to close a real estate deal with younger Armenian guys who like to conduct business over drinks. And of course, there's always some drama with Paradise Palms renovations that keep him after-hours.

But Peggy isn't buying it anymore. She had smelled a rat – or more specifically, men's cologne on the collars of shirts he had thrown in the hamper. She had rationalized to the point of denial that her husband wasn't a swish. The cologne probably came from the Armenians – weren't they always spraying on the strong stuff? – and she had found no unusual calls on their phone bills.

On the other hand, Aaron had taken to hiding his wallet when he got home instead of leaving it on his dresser. And what was with the sharp new threads? It was as if his style aesthetic had changed overnight. He was always a clothes hound – friends dubbed them America's Best-Dressed Couple – but lately he had gone on a buying spree of bold print shirts, expensive camelhair jackets and two-tone oxfords, none of which he wore out of the house, only to return late at night in a whole new ensemble. One morning, he had left with black chukka boots with black socks; when he came home, he was wearing penny loafers with no socks.

Hanging over all of this are Aaron's mood changes. He could become snippy on a dime and doesn't like to be interrogated about his whereabouts. Of course, Peggy is prone to bilious behavior herself, but she blames Aaron's late-night ways for this, the way he's abandoned her to deal with the kids' homework and squabbling and bedtime drama – isn't discipline the job of the *man* of the house?

"Mommy?" Littlest Nancy appears in her parents' bedroom doorway. "I feel stuffy and my head is achy."

Peggy throws on a bathrobe and comes out of the adjoining bathroom. She kneels to feel Nancy's forehead. She feels hot. *Great*, she thinks. Let's throw a sick kid into the mix.

"Sweetie, I think you have a fever. Let's go to the kitchen and get you some orange juice and an ice pack."

Nancy slinks away from her mother.

"What is it?" Peggy asks.

"Your face scares me."

Peggy laughs to keep from crying. "It's my anti-wrinkle mask. Don't worry, it's still Mommy underneath."

As they wander down the hallway, Jolene joins them from her bedroom.

"What are you doing up?" Peggy shout-whispers. "It's after midnight!"

"Nancy got into my bed and woke me up. Now I can't get back to sleep." She tilts her head. "Are you guys getting a snack?"

Five minutes later, Jolene and Nancy are lapping up bowls of Rice Krispies at the kitchen table. Peggy rests her head in her hands, gaping at them with a distant look.

"Mom?" the ever-attentive Jolene asks. "You okay? You're daydreaming."

"Hmmm?" she says, shaking herself. "Just tired, honeybear."

As the girls continue eating, Peggy reaches out with her hands. "C'mon," she instructs. "Pray with me."

The girls look at each other. "Now?" Jolene asks. "We just prayed before bed."

"Yeah," Nancy whines, "and it's not suppertime."

"Do as Mommy says!" Peggy snaps.

The girls give exaggerated sighs and close their eyes, linking hands with their mother and each other.

"What are we praying for?" Jolene asks.

"We're praying for Daddy," Peggy says in a hushed tone.

"Is he sick?" Nancy asks, worry in her voice. "I hope I didn't make him sick."

"Shhh." Then: "Maybe. Let's just ask God to show him the way."

As they pray under the dim glow of the kitchen light, the headlights from Aaron's Bel Air flash across the front window.

"Daddy!" Nancy shouts. She runs to the door to greet him, Jolene following behind.

Traipsing into the house, Aaron is surprised to find the two girls up at this hour. "Uh oh," he says to Peggy. "Who's sick?" His normally meticulous coif is mussed up and the top two buttons of his shirt are undone. As he hangs his keys on a hook by the door, Peggy starts to sniff his shirt collar. He backs up and laughs.

"What are you, a Saint Bernard? What is this?"

The alcohol is apparent. Less so is the scent of another man.

"Seriously," he says, getting annoyed. "Stop it."

Peggy glowers at him, then grabs the keys to his car. She marches down the driveway and opens the driver's side.

"What's going on?" Aaron shouts from the doorway.

"We were praying for you, Daddy," Nancy cheerfully replies.

Aaron spins around in a fury. His blazing eyes and flared nostrils scare Nancy. She ducks behind Jolene.

"Peggy, goddamn it!" Aaron runs to the Bel Air, where he finds his green-faced wife flipping visors, fishing into the glove box and running her hand under the seats. Whatever she's looking for, she doesn't find it. She comes around the hood and confronts him.

"Give me your wallet," she commands. "I wanna see what you have in there."

"Have you lost your mind?"

"Your wallet, Aaron. Give it to me!"

He puts his hands on his hips. "I don't need to stand for this. If you think I'm out screwing some girl – "

"I never said a *girl* – " she says icily, unable to get herself to complete the accusation.

Aaron's mouth drops open. He looks over his shoulder at his daughters in the doorway, tears streaming down their faces. He doesn't think they heard their mother – if they did, they wouldn't understand the implications anyway – but their trauma is his own, and he feels it like a punch in the gut, rousing him to strengthen his resolve.

"You're off your Tofranil, aren't you?" he says, referring to a new antidepressant on the market.

"Don't turn this back on me!"

"The doctors told you, you gotta take that stuff daily."

"What are you hiding, Aaron?"

Aaron reaches into his pocket and whips out his wallet, angrily rifling through the thing. He flings out business cards, receipts, banknotes, his license – all spilling onto the shiny white hood of his car.

"Here!" He slams his empty wallet on the hood. "You happy? There's my life. It's all there. Wanna strip search me too?"

Peggy takes a step back. His denial – his *offense* – is very persuasive. She glances at the scattered scraps on the hood, bowing her head in shame.

She looks up to apologize to Aaron, but he's already at the front door, scooping up his sobbing girls to take them inside.

· · ·

The next morning – over the hill in Studio City – a decidedly more idyllic domestic scene is playing out as David and Darlene schlep moving boxes from the trunk of his Impala into a tidy two-bedroom ranch house. Darlene's belly is starting to show, and David is careful to make sure she doesn't overexert herself. An outdoor table with four chairs is set up on the front lawn, a housewarming gift from Leo.

As they stow another load inside, Rae suddenly materializes at the white-picket gate in the front yard. David, coming back to the car, stops in his tracks.

"What is it?" he says, alarmed by her foreboding expression.

"We need to talk." Her voice is tight and trembling.

"Something happen this morning?"

She sees Darlene appear in the doorway behind David. "Yesterday. But I was thinking about it all night…"

"Rae?" Darlene calls out. "Why don't you come in?"

Rae drops her head.

David can feel Darlene's concern projected on his back, but he knows if he turns around, he'll have to involve her in whatever emergency is unfolding. Is he being protective of his pregnant wife, or patriarchal and secretive like his father? Either way, his intuition tells him to exclude her.

He opens up the gate. "Let's go for a walk," he says to Rae. The siblings disappear down the tree-lined sidewalk.

CHAPTER 23

The placard in front of The Easy's locked doors reads "Closed" – a fixture since Max's car accident. The brothers reassure guests that the bar's shuttering is only temporary. But David can't imagine it or the restaurant ever opening again. He just doesn't have it in him anymore to try to make it work amidst shifting trends, the loss of key personnel, and the uncertainty in all their lives.

Since its closure five weeks ago, David has noticed a palpable change at Paradise Palms. Something has been lost. Where lively patrons used to spill out of The Easy with drinks in hand, the lobby is now a wasteland. Where Max's alte kaker friends used to join him in The Easy's booths, now they have no reason to come around at all. Though he'd never admit it to Rudy's face, David even misses the gimp's carousing pals, who used to drop small fortunes on booze and appetizers.

It's not just the suspension of food and drink services that has contributed to the gloomy atmosphere. Of the hotel's three tenants, Dirk has died, Art is now incarcerated, and Elron has become even more of a recluse. The Easy used to be Elron's lifeline, a place where he could get a decent meal on the house and socialize and *get out of himself*. Now he spends most days holed up in Room 6, shunning the maids and all visitors.

After a brief surge during the holiday season, only six units are rented out as of mid-January 1959. Besides the losses of Dirk and Art, the LAPD bust last fall dissuaded Rae's friends from staying at the hotel for fear of being railroaded like Tyrone and Steven. Rae also vacated, moving into a Pico-Union flat where she could have access to her own kitchen. Meanwhile, David and Leo left Room 3 – David into his Studio City digs, Leo into another hotel, The Valley View Suites. There he can prepare meals that adhere to his strict diet, soak in the common hot tub, and simply take better care of himself away from the stress point that is the Palms.

It's fitting that both David and Leo fled for the Valley, mirroring the migration of so many Angelenos in the late '50s. During David's lifetime, he has witnessed several major studios relocate "over the hill" – Disney, NBC, Warner Bros., and soon enough, Columbia Pictures, furthering Hollywood's slide into neglect and irrelevance. Hospitality businesses now shun Hollywood for Burbank to serve the needs of the entertainment industry. Suburban subdivisions continued to proliferate, providing homes for thousands of defense, aerospace and manufacturing workers. Alas, no one blinked when plans for the Whitnall Freeway through Hollywood were scuttled, but the whole town is abuzz over the much-anticipated opening of the San Diego Freeway, billed as the "Gateway to the San Fernando Valley!"

Tonight David swings by the desolate lobby at 9:45 p.m. to get ready to drive Darlene home. After kissing her at the front desk, he excuses himself to "go check inventory." Once the boys decided to make the restaurant-bar's closure permanent, Leo ran the numbers and figured they could net at least two grand selling off the booths, the bar, the jukebox and kitchen appliances to a resale restaurant supply shop.

David pulls out his key chain and lets himself into The Easy. As he flicks on the overhead lights, one of them pops and goes out – scaring the bejesus out of him. No one has set foot in here in weeks. Roving through the dusty booths, he half-expects the ghosts of guests past to toast him. He smiles when he sees the small booth by the door – Dirk's domain. He can see him sitting there with his Bloody Mary and *Variety*, busting somebody's balls or rhapsodizing over Rae's Shrimp Louie. But mostly, he finds the lifelessness unnerving. He swings through the kitchen doors.

Unlike the dining room – thanks to a back door accessible from the courtyard – the kitchen still hosts human life forms from time to time. Flori and Yolanda use the sink to store mops and buckets. They also take their lunches in here, storing food and soda pop in the refrigerator and snacks in the pantry. Once, a stoned Elron busted the lock on the back door and raided their stash. Flori found him passed out on the floor the next morning, a trail of Oreo cookie crumbs leading from the cupboards to his snoring body. David hired a locksmith to change the lock out with one befitting Fort Knox.

To the right of the sink is the heavy wooden door to the basement. David crosses over to it and turns the knob. It opens with an old-lady groan. He pulls an overhead chain and the fluorescent lights flicker on with a buzz. The basement's thick must pierces his olfactories like smelling salts. He descends two steps on the stairwell and gently shuts the door behind him. He runs his fingers along the base of the door, checking its clearance. About a half-inch of kitchen light seeps through. He makes a mental note to cover that with masking tape.

Batting away cobwebs, he continues down the stairs until he reaches the concrete floor. His eyes find two rectangular vents located eight feet apart on the east-facing upper wall. Ambient street light from McCadden Place streams through their screens. These will need to be covered too. Perhaps cardboard flats and industrial tape. In between the screens – running along the ceiling – is the old "ventilation" pipe installed during Prohibition, used to transport beer through a hose from trucks parked on McCadden. He'll need to remove its rat-proof steel mesh that Julio installed twenty-some years ago.

David ambles to the middle of the basement. He sinks his hands into his pockets and stills his body, allowing himself to absorb the room's energy. How strange is life. From age four to ten, this place ignited his imagination in innumerable ways. Julio's watchful eye notwithstanding, it was David's private quarters – a sanctuary where he could conquer his fears, hide from the world and, with his makeshift office desk, play grown-up. In the expansive, complicated universe that would come to define his life, this served as his Big Bang.

But now there is no more role-playing. The cynic he's become sees this room for what it is, not what it could be – a dingy, leaky shithole with rank air. If it fires his imagination at all anymore, it's as a setting for his most savage thoughts. What if this room wasn't an incubator for life, but a final resting spot, a snuffing void, a *reverse* Big Bang? Hell, if this room truly imprinted a young David Shapiro, what could be more apt than to reclaim its empowering possibilities as an adult? Big questions all for the gods of fate to ponder.

• • •

The next morning, David rises early and drives to UCLA to see Max in ICU. When he was leaving the house, Darlene asked him if he wanted company. Max's condition was deteriorating and it was accepted that he might not be long for this mortal coil.

"I feel like I need some alone time with Pop," he said. "Maybe even talk to him. I'd feel self-conscious if someone else was there."

Darlene totally understood. She always did, bless her heart.

As he makes his way down the hospital's third-floor hallway, David has a chance encounter with a disheveled, bearded doctor making his morning rounds – Dr. Alex "Tark" Tarkanian, head of neurology.

"I wish we had better news on your father," Tark says, patting David's shoulder.

David sighs. "We knew what he was up against. You've done everything you can."

"And we'd *like* to continue to."

David looks at him quizzically.

"I'm sure you know your, er… stepmother – Abigail – she wants to move him to Hollywood Adventist."

David knows this, of course, from Rae. "No," he says, feigning surprise. "I did not know that."

Tark scowls. "Really? I would've thought she'd discuss it with you and your brothers."

"It's possible my brothers know and were gonna tell me today."

"*Today*? Well, she's planning on arranging it *tomorrow*."

David blinks – he hadn't realized he would have to act this fast.

"I think it's a terrible idea, to be candid with you. Your father is in an extremely precarious state. We just did a tracheotomy on him and I'm really worried about his ICP…"

"ICP?"

"Intracranial pressure. The swelling in his brain. We need to cut into his skull to relieve some pressure… try to keep oxygen flowing in there. It's a very delicate, urgent procedure. If you transfer him to another hospital at this point, it's just going to delay things. The trauma of moving him alone would put his life in jeopardy."

The doctor searches David's face for signs of shared concern. But David doesn't give him what he wants. In fact, his reaction is quite the opposite.

"Mrs. Shapiro has the utmost faith in Adventist," David says woodenly. "I stand behind any decision she makes."

Tark gives a patronizing chortle. "C'mon. Nothing against Adventist, but they're minor-league compared to us. In fact, some of their surgeons are under investigation right now by the California Medical Board. I'm sure you saw the – "

"I appreciate your concern, doc, but it's a risk we're willing to take."

Tark won't give it up. "May I ask why? Your father has insurance, but if money is a concern, we're always willing to work with our patients' families."

David responds with a stiff smile and starts to move away from the doctor.

"If you don't mind my asking," Tark says as David turns, "does that… gentleman she comes in with have anything to do with this?"

David's facial muscles tighten. "Dr. Tark, I am not in the habit of sharing intimate details about my family…"

"Now wait… who said 'intimate'?"

"You're implying he's my stepmother's boyfriend."

"I said no such thing."

"I'd like to spend some quality time with my father now. Thank you for everything you've done here. But I must respect his wife's wishes. It's how he'd have wanted it." David whips out his hand to shake. "I'm sorry it didn't work out."

Tark limply shakes his hand, and David heads toward ICU.

Max's knitted brow is fixed in place when David finds him in bed. Tubes are now jammed into his trachea, and his shaved head looks like a cue ball – marked up with a felt pen to indicate where Tark wants to operate – just two more indignities to piss off the old man. David wraps the drapes tightly around them and pulls up a chair. He leans his forearms onto Max's body so that he's almost genuflecting before him. Peering at his father's shriveled husk, his eyes are moist and vulnerable.

"Look at you, you stubborn old putz," David mutters. "Marta's up there, and all you can do is keep her waiting…" His mind flashes to a joke Max was fond of telling at social gatherings…

"I have two weaknesses in my life," it went. "One is a pretty girl. The other?" Pregnant pause. "*Any* girl."

David never found the joke all that funny, but he recognized its element of truth. From an early age, he bore witness to his father's infidelities. Marta's response was to focus even more on the pursuits she could control – raising her boys right, the business of the hotel, throwing herself into women's charities.

Weeks before his mother died, David asked her why she stayed with Pop after the way he treated her. "He's a romantic, your father," she said wearily. "It's his nature. He can't help himself. It's why I fell in love with him." Her response disappointed him. What she saw as unconditional acceptance, he interpreted as weakness. Then again, David mused, he had never been in love himself, so who was he to pass judgment on his mother? Now he realizes he was the one who looked at it all wrong.

He taps his father's bony arm. "Hey, Darlene is eighteen weeks pregnant. And get this. If it's a boy, she thinks we should name him after you. 'Course, Jewish law being what it is, we can only do that if you're deceased. So don't hold on *too* long…"

As David chuckles, a gurgling sound emits from Max's trachea plug. He waits to see if it gets worse, but it clears after several seconds.

David grits his teeth, wags his head back and forth. "Should be Kitty lying here – not you. We warned you she was bad news." He lowers his voice to a croaky whisper. "She tried to kill you, Pop. What do you think of that? I just thought you should hear the words. Me to you. And now she and Gordo plan to finish you off. But I'm not gonna let that happen. You'll go out on your own terms…"

David's flinty eyes narrow in determination. "Remember you said the world was crooked and I run too straight? No more, boy… I'm gonna prove you wrong. Maybe even make you proud." He puts his finger over his lips. "No one else knows. Not even Leo. Just you."

He sinks back in his chair with a satisfied grin, studying Max's face as if trying to glean some sort of approval. But the longer he looks at his wispy father, the more his bravado starts to wilt. Within minutes, he's fighting back tears of self-loathing.

"I'm sorry, Pop. Here I am, playing the bigshot. It never should've come to this. I failed you. I should've stepped in sooner. Done more. You were right. I was never a scrapper like you. I didn't have the stomach. By the time I realized it, it was too late…"

David bows his head on his father's arm, his words wet with muffled sobs. "Just give me this one last chance. I promise I won't fail you again."

CHAPTER 24

David fucking Shapiro is back, a goddamn man of action. It starts at home with a phone call to the Department of Water and Power, whom he chews out in front of Darlene to demand why the electricity has been shut off to their house. Turns out the utility company purposely killed the power – the previous owner was often delinquent – without realizing new owners had moved in. This being Sunday, supervisors won't be in the office until tomorrow to resolve the issue. When Darlene suggests they overnight at the Palms, David shrugs her off. Hadn't her parents been wanting to see their expectant daughter?

"Maybe spend the night down there…?" he suggests casually.

She frowns. "Where would *you* go? They only have that twin bed."

"I could just crash at Leo's. Or the Palms. I could drive down tomorrow morning and we could take your folks to lunch."

She contorts her face. Two separate sleeping quarters and two cars? Sounds complicated…

"We could hit the Pike," David chirps. He knows his girl is a sucker for the seedy amusement park on the Long Beach boardwalk, a quick hop from her parents in Seal Beach. It's where she and Preston something-or-other got their heart tattoos. She loves its undercurrent of tangible danger – the anachronistic freak show, the shooting gallery with real rifles, the rickety roller coaster where drunken sailors occasionally get thrown off – all put to the happy smells of fried corndogs, diesel fumes and freshly roasted peanuts.

"It's a date," she says finally.

David replies with a smile reserved for his own cleverness. For he was never on the phone with the utility company. He had cut the power himself. After returning from the hospital, he had climbed the roof while Darlene was in the shower and neatly unscrewed the power lines connecting to the weatherhead, making sure to spare the phone cable.

After calling her parents to announce her impending visit, Darlene throws together an overnight bag. She and David make plans for him to swing down by 11 a.m. tomorrow to take Mr. and Mrs. Flanagan to lunch, after which the two of them will make a day of it at the Pike. David sees her off with a kiss, and watches her Ford Fairlane motor toward Ventura Boulevard.

With Darlene out of the way, the rest of his day is clear. Time for more action.

Hopping in his car, he dashes up to Stearns & Sons contractors' supply in North Hollywood. He purchases an extra-long, heavy-duty rubber hose, an assortment of clamps, industrial-grade tape, coiled 20-foot rope, a shovel, collapsible boxes, slip-joint pliers, needle-nose cutters, a flashlight and three plastic trash cans, stacked inside one another to fit into his Impala.

From there, he drives toward Paradise Palms. But rather than turn into its driveway, he parks several blocks away on De Longpre Avenue. He exits the car and walks over to the junky rental car place on Highland and Fountain, where, under a fake name, he drives away with a '49 Ford Woody Wagon for eight bucks and one hundred dollars cash deposit. He parks it on the street next to his Impala, then hoofs it to the hotel.

It's late afternoon when he arrives through the front door. Rae is working the front desk alone – Darlene having Sundays off anyway. The lobby is empty.

"Doing some killer business, I see," David says facetiously.

Rae smirks. "You missed the family of six that was just in here."

"Oh! Are they staying?"

"No, the dad was just asking directions to the footprints at the 'Chinaman Theater.'"

David guffaws, trying not to oversell it.

As he and Rae go over hotel matters, she tells him about her desire to enroll in college courses in the fall with an eye toward a business degree. Leo is going to help her. David jokes he hopes she's a fair boss when the day comes that he works for her. He ends their conversation by announcing his intention to crash at the hotel tonight, given the power outage at his house, then joining Darlene and her family in the morning. Can Rae fill in for Darlene's shift tomorrow? She says of course.

Next David strolls up to the boulevard and picks up Chow Dun for himself from Don the Beachcomber. Night falls on his way back to the Palms. By the time he lets himself into Room 3, he's starving. In the course of his adrenaline-fueled day, he had forgotten to eat lunch and had only coffee and a bagel during his early morning hospital visit.

He perches on the sill to observe the courtyard. In the solemn silence of the room, the magnitude of what he's about to do starts to hit him. He decides his nerves are too shot to eat. He dumps the Chow Dun in the trash can out by the pool.

At 10:05 p.m., David re-emerges from the room. He checks out his surroundings – careful to avoid any unnecessary chit-chat with guests – before entering the lobby's back entrance. Rae has gone home for the night and the front door is locked to all except guests.

David leaves the hotel property through the secured gate along McCadden Place. From there, he walks the several blocks to De Longpre, where he transfers all the items he bought from his Impala into the wagon. He drives the wagon back to McCadden, parking it on the west shoulder where it abuts the hotel. With its dirt sidewalks and narrow width, the street is ostensibly a glorified alley that sees little traffic.

Stepping out of the car to set up his contraptions from the hardware store, David can feel his spirit detaching from his body – or at least, tries to convince himself that's what is happening. Real or perceived, it has the effect of instilling him with the clinical fearlessness he needs as he starts to execute his plan.

$$\bullet \quad \bullet \quad \bullet$$

At 11:23 p.m., the most important element of David's scheme materializes – Kitty – finally returning to the hotel after a night out. Back in a darkened Room 3, he watches her cross his window. She is wearing her favorite sailor dress with red heels and a red clutch. He can tell by her sluggish gait that she's tipsy. She disappears from his view as she lets herself into Room 1.

So as not to be too obvious, he waits twenty minutes before calling her room. She picks up on the third ring.

"Hello?" She sounds fatigued and annoyed.

"Abigail? It's David." He can't remember calling her by her real name before.

She doesn't respond. He can hear her labored breathing on the other end, no doubt wary of his late-night solicitation.

"Listen, uh, I'll make this quick because I don't wanna wake Darlene. I heard from Dr. Tark you're moving my father to Hollywood Adventist…?"

She exhales noisily. "Yes I am. I'm not happy with his treatment at UCLA. His condition has gotten worse, and I want him closer to home."

"Uh huh."

"So don't bother trying to talk me out of it, my mind is made up."

"Well, listen… far be it from me to fight you on it. It's your right as his wife."

"You're damn right."

"Speaking of Pop, I'm assuming you don't want the vodka he left for you. So after I throw it all away, don't come screaming to me – "

"What vodka?"

"The Smirnoff. The *case* of Smirnoff." The hook is set. Now it's time to ever-so-carefully reel it in. "There's a no-alcohol policy at Sylvan Gardens. God willing, if he recovers, doctors said he should never drink again."

More silence.

"C'mon, he told me he was gonna tell you about it." David ponders for a moment, changing tack. "Unless he changed his mind… He did talk about leaving it to Rudy…"

"No, he told me about it. Where is it again?"

David smiles. "In the basement."

"The basement? Of the Palms?"

"Yeah, through the kitchen. He left me and my brothers the wine and wanted you to have the vodka. Frankly, I wasn't even gonna tell you. But I never break a promise to Pop, and like I said, he was gonna tell you anyway…" He stops, realizing he's rambling.

"A case is too *heavy* for me," she gripes. "I'm liable to get a hernia. I'll get Rudy to pick it up some time."

"No, see – you need to get it *yourself*."

"Why?"

"There's no time for Rudy to get over here" – *Calm down, Shapiro* – "y'know, over to the Palms. If you want it, it has to be done right now."

"I've already changed for bed. What's the rush?"

"I'm swinging by there in half an hour to close up the place for the night. If you go now, you should find the back door to the kitchen still unlocked."

Kitty lets out a languid yawn. "I'll do it in the morning."

"You'll do it *now!*" he insists, then bites his fist. "First thing tomorrow, movers are loading up all the restaurant gear to take to auction. It's gonna be chaos. They're boxing up appliances from the basement too. The vodka is the *last thing in there.*"

"But it's too heavy! Can't you get it when you get here and bring it to me?"

David pulls the handset away and sucks his teeth. He gets back on the line and adopts a calm, fatalistic stance. "You know what? Don't worry about it. I'll give it to the movers as a tip. They'll actually really appreciate – "

"Oh sweet Jesus, *fine.* Where do I go again?"

He reiterates his instructions one last time before hanging up. Then he bolts outside, through the back door of the kitchen before Kitty has a chance to leave her room. He is strangely giddy. *This is really happening.*

The kitchen is dark, so he turns on a counter light to create some illumination for Kitty. He ducks behind the food prep station at the far end of the room. Like a panther, he waits.

Within minutes she jiggles open the kitchen door and shuffles in, wearing a red silk kimono and pink slippers with little fuzzy pom-pom tassels. She goes to the cellar door. David staged it so it's slightly ajar, and thoughtfully left the light on downstairs.

She hesitates. David hears her noisy breaths, the lack of footsteps on the wooden landing. Now what? He can't see anything and is afraid to peer around the corner. Maybe her sixth sense is kicking in, like a mouse smelling a trap. Maybe she simply finds the cellar creepy at this bewitching hour. Should he just leap up and shove her down the stairs?

And then – the creaking of wood. She is definitely going down the steps. She is *in the basement.* He considers waiting until she's all the way in – give her time to root around for the case of non-existent vodka. But given her trepidation, she is just as likely to bail out, sensing something amiss.

David springs to his feet and rushes the basement door, slamming it shut. With quaking hands, he locks the deadbolt from the outside.

"Hey – hello?!" He can hear her muffled voice from down below, more confused than scared. "David?"

He runs a strip of industrial tape along the bottom crack of the door, then backs away, staring at the knob. No time to think. *Only action!*

David turns off the counter light, plunging the kitchen into darkness. He slips out the back door and locks it behind him, then exits the McCadden gate. His rented station wagon is cast in shadows, the nearest streetlight two hundred feet away.

The apparatus is already in place. At the rear of the vehicle, David had set up the three trash cans to obscure the hatch and muffler. Clamped to the tailpipe is a thick hose. It snakes through thick oleander bushes alongside the hotel before disappearing into the basement's ventilation pipe.

David slides into the driver's seat, keeping the headlights off. He feels like he should utter "I'm sorry," but he's not sure to whom. Words hold no meaning anymore. He's in an ethics-free zone, a bizarre feral state – kill or be killed, as returning war vets described it – a lone-wolf whiz-kid warrior instead of a rejected fighter pilot from Sad Sack.

He turns the ignition. The 350-horsepower engine growls to life.

He's not sure how long it will take for Kitty to asphyxiate on the carbon monoxide. Each idling minute increases the odds of a patrol car cruising by. He had read that people who commit suicide in their garages pass out within forty-five minutes and die within sixty. The basement is the size of a single-car garage – maybe 380 square feet.

Grabbing his flashlight, David exits the vehicle and walks over to the bushes. He drops to his knees, parts the branches, and shines the light on the two ventilation screens between the hose conduit. They remain tightly covered with taped-up cardboard. How *badly* he wants to peel back a corner – just a quick peek into the cellar to see the sheer panic on Kitty's face. The vents are too high off the ground for her to pop off the cardboard and the door is made of thick wood. The only way she lives is if someone hears her. But wait – *can* someone hear her?

Pressing his head to the cardboard, David can barely make out her tremulous cries for help and bursts of invective toward him. Her voice sounds almost atmospheric, as if originating from space or some other dimension, impossible to pinpoint.

David gets back in the car and looks at the clock on the dash: 12:01 a.m. She's been in there for four minutes but it feels like four hours.

Suddenly, there's a loud rapping on his window. David nearly shits himself.

He snaps his neck to the left. It's a hooker – a Black skanky woman. Or a man dressed as a woman. He or she has thin wrinkled lips slathered in orange lipstick and motions for David to roll down his window. He lowers it a crack.

"Yeah?" he says curtly.

"What's your pleasure, John Boy?" Definitely a man.

"I'm not – I'm just waiting for a friend."

The prostitute cocks his head and cackles, revealing a mouth full of missing teeth. "You don't have to play coy with me, sweetie. I'm no cop."

David reaches into his wallet and pulls out a twenty-dollar bill. He waves it in front of his propositioner. "I appreciate the offer. But not tonight. I'll give you this if you promise to leave this block for the night."

The hooker juts out his hip and adjusts his blond wig. "Honey, this *is* my block."

David pulls out another twenty. "Now it's mine. Please leave."

The man snatches the forty bucks and slips it into his brassiere, disappearing into the night.

If there was anything good about their interaction, it was that the dude didn't suspect any foul play. But the incident rattles David, and once his mind races, he can't make it stop. What is he doing in the car to begin with? Why go through all the trouble of a fake name at the rental car company and then staying in the car itself like a sitting duck? Better to just *leave* the scene until she's dead. Of course, if the cops stumble on an idling car, his fingerprints are all over the damn thing. And the tools in the back seat – why did he leave them in the car? The hose still has the price tag on it. They'll see it was bought at Stearns & Sons. The cashier will remember him. The connection will be obvious.

Fuuuuuuck!

He exits the wagon and paces back and forth on the other side of the street. Maybe he should just go down there and murder her. But with what? And could he even pull that off? She's a big, feisty girl – a tigress. The whole point of doing it this way was it would be clean – no blood to clean up, no physical contact, no scratches or other telltale signs of struggle on his face.

He checks his watch. She could be dead within forty-five minutes. Then all his niggling will be for naught as he disposes of the evidence. If he could just hold on a little while longer...

12:10 a.m.: Another pedestrian. An older man walking his poodle, coming down from Hollywood Boulevard. David hides under the canopy of a tree. Who the fuck walks their dog at this hour?

12:13 a.m.: The dog-walker is now coming back the other way. He stops at the station wagon. Stares at the driver's window, seems to be curious why the engine is running with no one in it. Will he notice something fishy about the trash cans covering the tail pipe? This is not good.

12:14 a.m.: The poodle trots back to his owner from the front grille of the car. He must've been taking a dump and the man was simply waiting for him to finish. They continue onward.

12:23 a.m.: David hears sirens in the distance, the whir of a helicopter overhead. It's a police chopper, faintly lit in the overcast sky. Is it circling him, or just passing through? Fucking poodle guy. If the chopper blasts a spotlight, he's dead.

12:25 a.m.: The helicopter was simply passing through, like the occasional passing car. *You can't expect the whole city to shut down for you. Relax, it's all going to be fine.*

12:30 a.m.: Joyriders in a convertible cruise down McCadden blasting music. One of the greasers shouts expletives and shatters a bottle against the front fence of a bungalow. David swallows hard, waiting for a light to switch on in the house. He imagines the owner calling the cops, asking them to investigate.

12:31 a.m.: The light never flicks on.

12:32 a.m.: David can't take it anymore. He has to know what's going on in that basement. Even more, he fears he's overplaying his hand, ignoring omens, leaving himself exposed. A classic Rudy move. David is not Rudy.

He jogs back to the cellar vents and folds back a corner of cardboard – just enough to peek in. Kitty is still alive but there are signs of resignation. She is seated on the floor, head bowed, arms over her knees, as if trying to inhale whatever tiny pocket of oxygen is left within the confines of her enfolded body. The fight is no longer in her.

David suspects she is at least ten or fifteen minutes away from unconsciousness. Death will take even longer. He's tempted fate long enough.

He runs back to the car, kills the engine, and stacks the trash cans. From the tail pipe, he unclamps the hose and flings it into the bushes. He can clean everything up later. Right now, he needs to get in the basement and finish the job. She'll be too incapacitated to fight back.

Get in the basement? It's teeming with deadly CO fumes. David rips the cardboard off the vent screens and waves his hand as if to shovel fresh air into the room. How long before enough oxygen flows in for him to safely enter?

Wait a minute, wouldn't that revive her as well?

Don't think – do, motherfucker!

David peels off his cotton shirt – leaving only his undershirt – and marches back inside to the basement door. He opens it. Hovering at the top of the stairway, he stares into the abyss of his makeshift crypt, his shirt balled up against his nose.

Kitty is still hunched over in the center of the room. She weakly lifts her head and sees David thudding down the steps. She tries to scream. David's forearm clamps over her and constricts her windpipe from behind. Gurgling and gagging, slippers flying, her legs kick out from under her. Her grabby fingers lunge backwards for his face. David takes a deep breath and drops his shirt, allowing for a two-armed chokehold. Her spasms continue for thirty seconds. He feels her getting limp under his arms.

Then, all at once, her body transmogrifies into dead weight, collapsing on the cold concrete floor.

David continues pressing on her neck… continues until he himself is out of breath. At last he pitches forward, heaving and coughing.

He staggers up the staircase. Takes a huge gulp of air in the doorway. Regards her lifeless body. He's struck by how oddly graceful she looks – arms above her head, knee pressed out from her hip, toes pointed downward – as if she died in the middle of a pirouette. Her open glassy eyes and parted lips tell a different story, one of horror and shock and suffering.

David rests on his haunches, panting, trying to gather himself. He'll need to let the cellar air out before dragging her up the stairs. He takes advantage of this downtime by heading outside to dispose of any traces of his malfeasance. Popping the wagon's hatch, he returns the hose, cardboard covers, and trash cans to the wagon's hold, leaving room for Kitty's body. By this point, it seems safe enough to head back in.

Back in the cellar, he unrolls a six-by-eight-foot patch of old carpeting left over from the room renovations. David has always been squeamish; he must psych himself up for the next step, hoping to avoid a repeat of the botched abortion aftermath in Room 18 when he retched all over the floor. He tells himself that none of this is real. It's all pretend, like a movie. But his body knows otherwise. One more glance at Kitty's expression of frozen terror is enough to set off his gag reflex.

He swiftly rolls her inside like a spider spinning a cocoon. As a final touch, he heavily cinches both ends of the roll with tape.

David lugs her carpeted corpse to the top of the stairwell – grunting with each back-breaking step. He dumps the roll on the kitchen floor, then, sweaty and lightheaded, unlatches the back door in order to drag her out. This really should be a two-person job. Yet despite the hiccups and momentary freak-outs, everything is proceeding on course. He reassures himself the hardest part is done. Most importantly, he's the only one who will ever know what happened to Abigail Schlebercoff – a pact with himself that he will take to his grave.

There's just one problem. Outside, someone is loudly pounding on the kitchen door. Before a dumbfounded David can even sputter a reply, the door flies open.

V

DEBTS OF RECKONING

CHAPTER 25

Elron Jakes skitters around the kitchen like a pinball, poking his head into empty cupboards for elusive midnight munchies.

"I'm starving, Dave," he announces. "I need sustenance to sustain me."

David, standing over Kitty's carpeted coffin, has only one objective – to get Elron out of the kitchen as soon as possible. The kid is so high, he may not even notice anything afoul. "The kitchen is closed," David states calmly.

"I saw a light on."

"You need to go back to your room."

Elron doesn't hear him through the slamming of cabinet doors. "I found some takeout in the trash – perfectly good Chow Dun – but there were fucking ants on it."

"Go back to your room and I'll find you something."

Taking a step back, Elron focuses his dilated eyes on David, then looks to the floor. "What's that?" he asks, pointing between David's legs. So much for not noticing.

"Hmm?"

"That. Whatcha doing with that?"

David nonchalantly looks down at the roll, as if forgetting it was there. "Oh, this? Just getting rid of some junk."

"Is that… a carpet?" He giggles. "Looks lumpy."

"Yeah. It's old."

Elron is strangely fascinated by its amorphous shape in the way druggies fixate on one thing and instill it with warmed-over significance. "Can I have it?"

David, growing irritated: "What would you want with an old carpet, Elron?"

"I wanna put a rug in my bathroom. My feet get cold on the tile."

"It's a *carpet* – not a throw rug." David subtly guides his twitchy tenant to the back door. "I'll order you a rug for your bathroom, how's that?"

At the door, Elron peeks around David. "I'll help you carry it out," he insists, hunching down to pick up one end.

David blocks him. "No. I'm leaving it in here for the night. Veterans group is gonna swing by tomorrow and pick it up."

Elron straightens up, scratching his matted hair. "Thought you said you're getting rid of it…"

"I am – to them." David pushes Elron out the door. "Listen, I'm closing up for the night."

Elron stops. "Food…?"

"It's – in room three. Let me go digging around and I'll bring it to your room." He escorts Elron into the courtyard.

"Beer?"

"You don't need beer. You need sleep!"

Elron laughs. "Nah, I've been awake for two days!"

It's obvious to David he's on some kind of uppers – greenies, maybe coke – so he's somewhat relieved when Elron pulls out the remains of a joint. Maybe that'll bring him down.

Elron takes a long toke and extends it to David. "Want a hit?" he asks with a pinched honk.

David tweaks his head no. Elron moseys over to a lounge chair by the pool.

"What're you doing?" David hisses. *This will not do.*

Elron stretches his arms over his head and looks up at the night sky. "What? Can't I just kick it with Mary Jane and enjoy the cosmos?"

David's in a bind. He doesn't want to make a big deal about everything. Even in his wasted state – or rather, *because* of it – Elron could grow suspicious or paranoid by David's behavior.

Elron slumps in his chair and closes his eyes, settling in for the trip.

"Cool, you just rest," David says. "I'll be right back."

He bustles back through the kitchen door, shutting it behind him, then steps around the carpet roll. He still has quick, unfinished business before dragging Kitty out.

Descending the basement stairs, he finds his shirt that he had dropped on the floor. As he straightens it out, he notices a slight tear in the fabric – Kitty must've caught a fingernail on it when she was trying to gouge his face. He shoves the shirt in a burlap bag pulled off a shelf.

Next, he scours the floor for Kitty's slippers, kicked off during the struggle. One of them sailed all the way to the far wall, under the vents; the other came to a rest just under the shelving. As he goes to retrieve them, he hears the kitchen door creaking open.

"Davey?" It's Elron again, calling out. "Food?"

Goddamn junkie, David bristles. *Just pass out already!*

He almost makes the mistake of hollering out to Elron in his flustered state. Instead he quickly snags the slippers and jams them in the bag, then bounds up the stairs – swirling around to make sure nothing is left behind. All good. On the top step, he rips the tape off the door bottom, turns off the light, and proceeds through the doorway into the kitchen...

Which is where he finds Elron – staggering backward, jaw agape, arms flailing against pots and pans on the counter and sending them crashing to the floor.

"H-h-holy shit!" he warbles.

Elron has uncoiled the tape from one end of the carpet roll.

"Hooollly shiiiiit!" he repeats, bouncing on his feet, unhinged.

David notices a pair of pedicured red toes peeking through the open end.

"Who is that?" Elron asks.

David bows his head. He wants to run his usual risk-assessment but doesn't have the luxury of time. He sticks with fast facts. Fact: Elron knows he killed someone. Fact: He is not going to kill Elron. Fact: He just exposed himself, so if he's not going to kill Elron, he needs to scare, cajole or blackmail him into keeping quiet – perhaps a combination of all three.

"Listen," David says evenly, refastening the exposed carpet end, "you said you wanted to give me a hand with this? Now's your chance."

Elron backs up to the door. "No can-do, man. I ain't no fucking killer." He points a trembling finger at the carpet. "They already got me on drug charges – this would lock me up for life."

"About those charges... who bailed you out of the slammer when they busted you?"

"You did."

"Uh huh. And who got you off the charges due to a technicality?"

"My lawyer."

David frowns. "Who *hired* that lawyer for you?"

"Look, man, I know I owe you, but this is…" He tugs on his goatee. "Fuck, who *is* that, anyway? Your mistress of something?"

David kneels at the other end of carpet. "Elron, if you help me with this, I'll let you stay at Paradise Palms rent-free for the rest of your life. How's that sound?" He would've let him anyway – as long as his family owned it, at least – but verbalizing it does sound enticing.

After a charged beat, Elron grudgingly hoists up the other end, giving himself a pep talk. "I don't know what's in here," he rationalizes, his voice straining under the weight. "Just helping him move a lumpy rug for some veterans."

Elron backs out of the kitchen doorway, followed by David, who, still clutching the burlap bag, locks the door behind them. He then swings to the lead position, guiding Elron through the McCadden gate to the station wagon, where the men slide the carpet-casket into the back. David places the bag with his shirt and Kitty's slippers in last.

As David shuts the hatch, Elron starts to skip away, waggling his hands as if they've become contaminated.

"Where're you going?" David calls after him.

Elron turns around. "I did what you asked, man."

David motions to the passenger side. "Hop in."

"No!"

David sighs. "Elron, don't make me play hardball with you. You know I could waltz into your room right now and have the DA haul your scrawny ass to jail."

"So could I – with *you*."

"Well then… looks like we both need each other."

CHAPTER 26

It's a little before 4 a.m. when David's rental car enters the township of 29 Palms, a scorched patch of high desert near Joshua Tree populated by hermits, yahoos, and jarheads from the local Marine Corps base. It's also the gateway for hundreds of abandoned mines – gold, silver and mineral – dating back to the 1870s. It was always David's intention to dump Kitty's corpse in the desert. He had thought about doing it somewhere on the fringes of Antelope Valley, an hour north of Hollywood. But then he remembered that Elron knew all sorts of abandoned mines near 29 Palms, site of his mescaline-fueled sojourns and get-rich-quick flights of fancy. Having Elron as his guide now seems well worth the extra hour drive. Maybe his involvement was some sort of assist by the gods of fate.

But then, there are drawbacks to having a junkie along, too. He had already made David lose focus in the kitchen, when he left the back door unlocked after presuming Elron passed out by the pool. And now, just when he needs to be as focused as a heat-seeking missile, David expends precious energy trying to contain Elron, who has spent most of their journey convinced they're being followed. When a highway patrol cruised behind them in Beaumont, the kid almost leapt out of the car with David clocking sixty-five. David pulled off the highway to let the cop pass, then gave Elron loose change to buy Oreo cookies from a vending machine at a closed gas station.

The break mellowed Elron out. Briefly. Now he's suffering withdrawals. Sweating profusely from hot flashes – "like being pricked with a thousand needles dipped in hot oil!" he cries – he disrobes in the front seat and lowers the windows to let in face-stinging frigid air.

A chattering David curses under his breath. He had one overriding condition for his crime – No Partners. And yet here he was involving someone he didn't trust, who wasn't even his own blood. Not that he would *ever* implicate Leo and

Aaron, let alone tell them. Sure, they wanted to kill the bitch – and that sonofabitch Gordo, too – but it was just idle talk. Therein, David realizes, lies the fundamental difference between himself and his brothers. It's one thing to identify life's intractable problems; it another to do something about them. David's always been the leader, and that suits him just fine. In some ways, he sees himself more as a father than a brother to his siblings, filling the void left by Max's emotional detachment.

Darlene is another matter. He trusts his wife, but he has only known her intimately for a year. Would she stand by him – "for better, for worse" – if she found out her husband was a stone-cold killer? Beneath her cool, princess-of-darkness veneer is the heart of a saint with an inviolable moral code. She would forgive him. But she would probably leave him. How could she raise a family with a husband who was capable of such impulsive, heinous acts? Who was this man she married, and what would stop him from one day doing harm to her and their child?

And what of Rae? She was, after all, the one who tipped David off to Kitty's and Red's ploy to kill Max by transferring him to a crooked hospital where Red held sway. She will probably, in time, suspect David killed Kitty – then might blame herself for it. He would hate to burden her conscience like that. She has come so far since he's known her, and this could really set her back. Or would it? He had rarely met anyone as poised and resilient as Rae. Maybe she'll see it as karmic payback. Or maybe, hoping to keep her college dreams alive and her upward trajectory unsoiled, she'll want nothing to do with David ever again.

By the time they arrive at the cutoff for "Rio Muerto Mine," David can barely feel his numb fingers on the wheel while Elron sits comfortably in his skivvies.

"You sure this is it?" David asks, headlights illuminating a dusty lane snaking up a hillside. "These roads all look the same. I don't wanna drive a half-hour and it turns out it's the wrong one."

Elron doesn't answer, slipping back into his clothes.

"Elron?"

Elron turns to David with a pained look. "Who was she?"

Ever since Elron stumbled on the stiff, David has been avoiding his queries. But after helping David transport it 150 miles – and arranging where to dump it – he's earned the right to know.

"Kitty," he says grimly. "Kitty Kay. Abigail."

Elron's mouth forms a perfect "O." "Your stepmom?"

David cringes. "Please – that sounds ridiculous."

"Why did you – "

"It was an accident," David lies. "We got into a bit of a heated argument in the kitchen. It was about important medical decisions involving my father, if you need to know."

"That poor ol' cuss..."

"Anyway, you know how she is. Hot-tempered and shit. Drunk as usual. She slipped and fell backwards on the stairs. Must've broken her neck."

Elron blows out his cheeks.

"The problem is, no one would ever believe me if I told them what happened. They'd say I pushed her. I have a baby on the way, and it seemed riskier to come forward with my story instead of just... well..."

"Making her disappear."

"Exactly."

Elron points through the windshield. "This way. It's perfect."

They drive in silence as the road climbs a rutted grade. The moonlit landscape is desolate but otherworldly beautiful. Rolling past their open windows are the outlines of fuzzy hollas, jagged yuccas, and the occasional Joshua Tree, its limbs reaching majestically for the heavens. Elron's mood seems to be stabilizing, his mind more focused on the task at hand. When the wagon's beams flash on a faded wooden marker – Rio Muerto Mine – Elron calls for David to make a quick maneuver.

"You *don't* wanna dump her in a place hikers can access. You need a 'slot.'" He gestures to the right. "This way to slots."

David off-roads toward an outcropping of volcanic rocks. After a minute, he notices the steering becoming spongy. He realizes he's driving on sand and hits the brakes.

"What's up?" Elron says.

"If we get stuck out here, we're screwed!" David pops the transmission into reverse.

"I come out with my truck all the time – it's fine."

"Maybe you haven't noticed, but we're in a station wagon."

David guns the gas.

"Don't gun it!" Elron cautions.

Sure enough, the wagon's whirring rear tires spin fruitlessly in the soft terrain.

"Fuck!" David fumes.

He grabs a flashlight and the duo exits the vehicle. The rear tires are buried halfway in sand. The front tires are still exposed. David shines the light on his watch: 4:43 a.m. The sun will be rising soon, and he promised Darlene he'd join her in Seal Beach by eleven.

He closes his eyes. Fact: Disposing of the body under the cloak of darkness is Priority Number One. If they're still futzing with the car with a cadaver in it come daybreak, they might be seen. Forget the car and his lunch date for now – those are Priorities Two and Three.

David opens the hatch and grabs the rope, looping it around his shoulder. He starts to slide Kitty's carpet-casket out. "Help me with this."

Elron slaps his brow. "We're carrying her?"

"Do we have a choice?"

"It's a half-mile to the rocks... and we gotta go uphill!"

"You look like you could use the exercise – let's go."

Lifting the roll onto their shoulders, they traipse through the moonlit sand and up an incline. When they reach the rocks, Elron lowers his end and takes the flashlight from David.

"There," he wheezes, pointing out a flat boulder. "There's a drop there that no one would ever go down unless they had a death wish."

They scramble up the boulder and lay the carpet on its surface. David takes the light from Elron and looks for the hole.

"I don't see anything."

Elron coaxes his beam between two smaller boulders. In between them is an elongated, narrow opening with tapered ends, its outline resembling an eight-foot-long garden slug. David blasts his light into the gaping maw, a chasm of darkness so deep, the beam doesn't even penetrate to the bottom.

"How did you ever find this thing?"

Elron smirks, pleased that David approves.

David rakes his hair. "Well, it's deep enough... but is it is wide enough? Seems tight."

"Oh hell yes."

David isn't so sure, but what choice do they have at this point? Looking down at the roll, his stomach churns. After removing Kitty from the carpet, they'll need to strip off her kimono, lest she get stuck in the hole.

He untapes the carpet and cinches the rope around her bare ankles. Her skin is ice-cold to the touch. Even in the night, he can see reddish-purple discoloration on her feet.

"Help get her out of this thing," David says soberly. They squat down and unspool her from the carpet. Rigor mortis is setting in. She rolls onto the flat boulder like a mannequin, coming to a stop belly-up, her expression still locked in abject horror. Elron cranes his neck and heaves. When he turns around, he sees that David has already stripped off her clothes with his cutter.

Grasping the end of the rope, David crosses over to the "gateway" boulders. He drags Kitty's body over the flat rock. Her stiff limbs contort into inhuman positions, like a doll with her arms and legs screwed on wrong. Elron is so unsettled by the sight, he forgets to assist.

Once her body is positioned next to the twin boulders, David stops pulling. All that's left is to dangle her through the crevice from her ankles. At that point he'll simply let go of the rope and watch her plunge into the gorge.

"Little help?" he hollers.

Elron scoots over to David, and together they pull on the rope until Kitty's head slides over the slat. Gravity suddenly takes over, yanking her entire body downward.

"Let 'er go!" David announces.

The two release the rope, but her shoulders block her body from sliding through. David reaches down and pivots them ninety degrees. This succeeds in dislodging her... but her ample bust creates another logjam. David will need considerable force this time – hands won't do. Buttressing himself against the rock, his feet press on her back to jam her through. Nothing doing.

Elron scratches his head. "Damn. She's bigger than I thought."

"*Stay* here." David starts to clamber down the same pathway they took up.

"Where you going?"

David bolts back to his car and pulls out his 42-inch scoop shovel – initially purchased to bury his victim. By the time he returns, the eastern sky is dawning a faint blue, blanketing over the stars. Shovel in hand, he forces the metal blade between the stratum and Kitty's body, giving a good jiggle to loosen her. When that doesn't work, he wedges it into her flesh, jamming his foot on the shovel's step for added force. This is equally ineffective – the blade merely slices into her brittle skin.

"It's getting light out, man," Elron warbles.

In a panicked frenzy, David jabs the blade into her broad back like a bayonet, cutting through flesh, striking her scapula and rib cage. Blood pools out on his shoes and pants. As her body starts to give way, he jumps up and down on the pulpy red mess that is her torso like a boy throwing a temper tantrum. She slides through up to her hourglass hips, which form another blockade. David resumes the process – ramming, slicing, jumping, stomping – until her bottom half at last wrenches through the slot.

Three seconds later, he hears the dull thud of her carcass striking bottom.

• • •

Miraculously, David manages to get the station wagon back on the road by 6 a.m. After abetting him in the messy work of body disposal, the shovel again proved its worth when Elron suggested they stick its blade under one of the tires for traction. For the other tire, David made a ramp out of a slab of basalt rock. With the car in reverse, David pumped the gas pedal – the car lurching backward over the objects – and didn't stop until two hundred yards later when they were safely on solid ground.

As he blazes through Morongo Valley on Highway 187, David makes the first of three stops on the way back to L.A. – a port-a-potty at an idle construction site. David envisions its slushy shit-pit as the perfect spot to dump his bloodied garb. He wishes he had packed a change of clothes, but who could have predicted a splattering bloodfest? Having already removed his outer shirt when Kitty ripped it, he is now forced to dispose of his shoes, socks, pants and T-shirt, leaving him outfitted only in boxer briefs and the shirt off Elron's back, which hangs extra long on the shorter David. For his part, Elron is merely naked from the waist up. David's logic was that it's less odd for strangers to see a shirtless man in shoes and trousers than a man wearing only underwear (covering himself in Elron's shirt was merely to retain *some* thread of dignity). Thus it is the shirtless skinny one who gets out of the car to dump David's clothing – as well as Kitty's slippers – into the cesspool.

Five minutes later, cruising down an alley behind a row of shuttered shops, David parks alongside a trash bin. Here Elron dumps the carpeting that contained Kitty's corpse, along with all the tools, trashcans and supplies that were still in the car. The wagon is now completely devoid of anything other than the (remaining) clothes on their backs. To address that issue, David has resolved he will stop by his house first to shower and change before dropping Elron at the hotel. After that, he'll fetch his Impala and should be able to just make it to Darlene's parents' place by eleven.

Their last stop is a Texaco in Cabazon. As a pimply teenager places the gas nozzle in the tank, Elron heads to the vending machines to purchase Oreos, chips, and hot coffee for their breakfast. When he returns to the vehicle, the attendant makes small talk with him.

"Ain't never seen you out here with a partner before," he yaps, eyeing Elron's driver friend who appears to be pantless.

Elron opens the passenger door. "Oh, this here's my pal David," he says casually. "He knows a lot about the mines out here."

"Any luck this time?"

"'Fraid not, but you know I'll be back trying!"

The attendant nods and places the nozzle back. He comes around the driver's side and says to David, "That'll be three-ninety-two, sir."

David hands him four dollars. "Keep the change," he says tersely, avoiding eye contact.

The kid lingers at his window, giving him and Elron the once-over.

As David drives off, he glances in his rearview mirror. The attendant is standing in the middle of the driveway, watching them leave.

"You friends with that guy?" David asks Elron.

"Nah, he just recognized me from my trips out here."

"What the *fuck* were you thinking, saying my name?"

"What?"

"He suspected something…"

Elron cackles. "Yeah, that we're a couple of fags!"

As David stews in his seat, Elron gazes out the window, his mind wandering. After a minute, he reconsiders his position. "You don't think he thinks something else, do you?"

David shoots him a look that could burn through steel.

Elron begins to unravel. "Fuck, man, we're gonna pay for what we did!"

"Don't start…"

"I'm a lover, not a killer, David. I'm an artist. I have a sensitive soul."

David rolls his eyes. "Says the man who waves guns at people."

"That's not me. That's the dope talking. You know that."

David sees this as a teaching moment. "You need to lay off all that junk from now on. Not just for your health, but, you know…"

"Know what?"

"You already dodged one bullet. We don't wanna give the cops any excuse to bust you again. From now on, I want your hotel room to be as clean as a nun's underwear." David looks at Elron. "We go down that rabbit hole, God *knows* where it leads. Am I making myself clear?"

It is not clear if David is making himself clear. Elron has worked himself into a lather, and David can tell he's jonesing to take the edge off. What is clear to David is that the very qualities that make Elron an addict are the same that make him unsuitable for the rigors of life. No wonder he's such a failure. As long as he keeps escaping into drugs, he'll never own up to his own reality.

The problem will come if it spills into David's life. Elron is weak. The type to crack under pressure. David needs him to be strong, clear-eyed, able to compartmentalize. He's beginning to wonder if he made a huge mistake involving him once he found out about Kitty. Could there have been another way?

Seriously, would anyone have noticed if Elron were to disappear too?

David forces himself to banish the thought. Surveying the horizon, sun cresting over the mountains, he turns his mind to a more pressing issue. Today is the day Red was going to help Kitty move Max from UCLA Medical Center to Hollywood Adventist Hospital. Such a move can't happen unless Kitty is there to sign off on it.

Very soon now – if he hasn't already – Gordo will be wondering where she is.

CHAPTER 27

On a small bluff across from Silver Lake Reservoir sits a sleek, Richard Neutra-designed home. Its generous bay window opens onto the water, especially attractive in the gloaming hour. Its owner – the bookish man Aaron met at the Crown Jewel nightclub – shambles over to the pane with a glass of rosé wine to watch the onset of dusk over the rippling lake. He is barefoot and wearing blue jeans with an open button shirt. Ten seconds later, Aaron appears next to him. He is dressed to the nines as usual, also clutching a glass of rosé. He discreetly pats the man on his buttocks, and together they take in the view.

Later that night, Aaron emerges from the man's house. He hops into his convertible a block away. Settling behind the wheel, he inhales the satisfying sagebrush air as he turns the key.

"Turn it off" comes the tinny voice behind him.

Aaron nearly jumps out of his skin as he finds Red Gordo's visage in the rearview mirror. He does as he's told, but doesn't appreciate his beautiful upholstery being desecrated by this sweaty goon. "What the hell is this?" he demands.

Red drapes his pork-loin forearms over the front seat. "I'll tell you if you tell me," he teases, his little lips forming into a heart.

"I don't follow."

"Oh, I think you do."

Aaron scoffs. "You can't prove a damn thing. I meet with businessmen all the time – home, office. Part of my job in land speculation."

Red extracts an Agfa Optima camera from his jacket. "Then it's a good thing we got some of them meetings on film. So we don't have to speculate..."

Aaron sighs loudly and bangs his head against the steering wheel ring. "What do you want?"

"I just wanna know what happened to my baby doll."

"Kitty?"

"I call her Abby."

Aaron turns to Gordo. "How the *fuck* am I supposed to know what she does with her time?"

Red purses his mouth and solemnly bobs his head, a gesture that makes it clear he doesn't believe Aaron.

"Why, can't you find her?" Aaron asks with feigned concern.

"We were supposed to meet earlier today." Red twirls the straps of his camera. "She never showed up… won't answer her phone. Something ain't adding up."

"I don't know where she is. I swear it." Aaron pauses. "Have you asked David? He runs the hotel."

"He's been gone all day. But I figure better to ask you anyway."

"Why me?"

"'Cause I ain't got nothing on him like I got something on you. Comprehende?" Red leans over and pinches Aaron's right cheek, making loud smooching noises. Aaron throws up his elbow to ward him off.

Gordo chortles and lets himself out. He leans on the jamb of the passenger door. "You better hope nothing happened to her. You got twenty-four hours, pretty boy. You find her. And you tell me…" He holds up the camera. "Or I'll ruin you."

He knuckles the car door, then swaggers off whistling around the corner.

• • •

David, Leo and Rae are convened around Max's bed when Aaron pushes aside the curtain with a surprise visit. All are pleased to see him. Of the three oldest brothers, Aaron has spent the least amount of time by his father's side, owing to his family, business commitments, and disinclination to wallow in Pop's hopeless prognosis. Everyone has his own way of grieving, and the brothers don't begrudge him his.

After ten minutes of hushed chatter with his siblings, Aaron pulls David aside. "Can I talk to you for a minute?"

"Sure," David says. "What gives?"

Leo and Rae swivel their heads toward the pair.

"Alone," Aaron says.

David takes them down to the commissary, adding he could use something to eat anyway. Grabbing a tray, he orders a roast beef sandwich, chips, and a bowl of lime Jell-O. Aaron gets a cup of coffee. As they sit down, Aaron lights a cigarette, exuding nervous energy.

A busboy swings by their table. "Uh, there's no smoking in here, sir."

Aaron extinguishes his cigarette.

"Everything okay?" David asks.

Aaron drums his fingers on the table. "I just had something really weird happen last night. Gordo tracked me down at a business associate's office and asked me where Kitty was."

David stops chewing. "Huh." He swallows. "What'd you tell him?"

"What could I tell him? Told him I have no idea." Aaron stops drumming. "Do you?"

"No. How would I know?"

"Exactly." Aaron swings one leg over the other, swiveling his body in his chair. "Thing is, he made threats that if we didn't find her – "

"What kind of threats?"

"Uh… he didn't say. But I think he suspects – y'know, given all the family drama – that we…"

David waves Aaron off. "Fuck Gordo. He's got nothing on us. We got nothing to be worried about."

Aaron is taken aback by David's cavalier response. "Just the same, don't you find it strange she'd suddenly disappear?"

David glances over his shoulder and leans in. "Let me tell you something. Scumbags like Kitty… you never know what they're up to. Maybe she had a falling out with Red and is avoiding him. Maybe she's on the run. Maybe she's lying in a ditch somewhere." He leans back, takes another bite from his sandwich. "Am I happy she's not around? Yeah, I guess I am. But that's not my concern. All I care about right now is Pop."

Aaron concentrates on his brother's face as if trying to solve a riddle. "You'd tell me if you knew something, right?"

David throws off a crocodile smile and tosses the rest of his sandwich on the plate. "This shit tastes like sweaty socks." He stands up and grabs his tray. "You coming back up?"

Aaron stays seated. "Nah, I'm good. Too depressing."

"Suit yourself."

As he leaves the commissary, David experiences a suffocating sensation, like his body is encased in a tight iron sheath through which nothing can penetrate. It disturbs him whenever this happens. He feels he's becoming as dead as… her… and has to mentally remind himself to feel, to act, to emote in the presence of others. Perhaps this detachment is his body's answer to self-preservation. Still, was he too blasé with his brother?

Back on the third floor, David sees Dr. Tark conferring with a nurse. Not wanting to interact with the neurosurgeon, he spins around, but it's too late.

"Mr. Shapiro!" Tark trots up to David. "I assume your stepmother is keeping your father here for the time being…?"

David nods stiffly. "Yes, she had a change of heart."

"I think that's the right call."

David forces himself to smile and slips past the doc into ICU.

Back at Max's bed, Leo asks, "Where's Aaron? Is he alright?"

"Ah, you know Aaron," David says, leaving it at that.

Leo nods and turns his attention back to Max. Rae, on the other hand, continues staring at David. In his hyperaware state, he swears he can feel her gaze penetrating his armored soul like an X-Ray.

•   •   •

That afternoon, Aaron lies in wait outside J&M Scrap Metal. He had been trying to track down Rudy all day but his kid brother is an elusive target. Besides careening all over town running jobs for Red, Rudy changes up cars like others do breakfast cereals. And forget trying to reach him on the phone. Aaron wasn't even sure where Rudy was living these days – he might even be homeless, crashing at different chicks' pads.

Around seven o'clock, Aaron catches a profile of Rudy's pompadour in a beat-up Rambler exiting the junkyard. Aaron starts his car and follows safely behind. Just past Sepulveda Boulevard, Rudy turns into the driveway of a divey restaurant called the Safari Room. Aaron hooks a U-Turn and parks on the street. He watches Rudy leave his car and limp into a phone booth by the entrance.

Aaron stealthily approaches the booth, where Rudy is hunched over the phone. He can hear him talking to a bookie, relaying bets from a scrap of paper for Jai Alai matches in Tijuana. Aaron waits for him to finish, then rushes forward, blocking Rudy in the narrow fold of the door.

"You sold me out to Gordo," he says acidly.

"Aaron!" Rudy is shocked to see him — figures he just stepped out of the Safari Room. "You drinking alone tonight, bruthuh?"

"Sold *me* out, sold *yourself* out, sold out the whole fucking *family*."

Rudy muscles his way out of the booth, shoving Aaron back. "Whoa, whoa… we gonna get into this? Because you all shut *me* out. You gave me no choice."

"You had a choice." Aaron jabs his fingers in Rudy's chest. "You chose a known gangster over the family. You were too fucking lazy to go straight so you kept chasing the easy money."

Rudy gets up in Aaron's grill. "What would you know about being 'straight.'"

Aaron shakes his head in disgust. "So that's your revenge? You go and tell Gordo your brother's a fruitcake? What, so you can shatter my life, so that my wife and children — *your fucking nieces and nephew* — will want nothing to do with me?"

Rudy, tapdancing: "Hey, I never said nothing…"

"I don't believe you. Lying is like breathing to you. It's what you do."

"C'mon, don't be like that…"

"Tell me to my face you didn't tell Red about my 'deviant' lifestyle."

Rudy averts Aaron's steely gaze and throws off a smart-alecky grin.

Aaron has his answer. "I always gave you the benefit of the doubt. But David's right — you're irredeemable." His eyes are red-rimmed, his voice cracking. "We don't want you back. You're not worthy of this family." He turns and plods back toward his car as if wading through mud.

Rudy reaches out. "Aaron, c'mon…"

Aaron stops, as if reconsidering. Instead, he checks his watch and turns around.

"I got one hour left to find out what happened to Kitty or else Gordo will 'out' me to Peggy," he tells Rudy. "But I'm not gonna give him — or you — the pleasure of owning my humiliation."

He gets in his car and leaves.

• • •

As he motors toward home, Aaron lets the tears roll freely off his cheeks, which are battered by the cold night air. He knows the route from here on out will only bring more pain. He prepares himself for its inevitable denouement.

Driving up Tigertail Road, he coasts to a stop in front of his utopian Brentwood aerie. Everywhere he looks is a twinkling firmament – blue stars in the late January sky, white and tawny lights of the urban glow, and, through the living room window, blinking rainbow-colored bulbs on the still-thriving Christmas tree. Steady flames from the gas fireplace bathe the tree in an amber glow.

His eyes shift over to the kitchen pane. Peggy, in the cactus-print apron he bought her in Acapulco, is getting ready to put dinner on the table. He can see her buzzing about with her usual manic energy, swilling from a glass of wine each time she returns from the dining room.

Back at the living room, he spots the children and his throat instantly clenches. Jolene is picking up a gameboard from under the tree. Billy and Nancy, both in their PJs, peek over her shoulder with joyous faces. Of course – it's the Chinese Checkers game he got Jolene for Christmas. He smiles. Peggy had warned him not to buy it, complaining that the marbles would immediately go missing. It proved to be a big hit with the siblings – one of the few games they all play together, just as he and his brothers did when they were kids.

Aaron slides over to the passenger side and pulls a notepad and pencil out of the glove box. Angling his pad toward its dim light, he writes the message he had been composing in his head. When he's finished, he neatly folds the paper in half and scrawls "Peggy" on the back.

Wiping away tears, he exits his car with the note and trudges to the front stoop. He coils his fist to knock but can't bring himself to do it. Instead he drops the note in the mailbox by the door and scrambles back to his car.

Five minutes later, he's at the bottom of the hill, calling home from a phone booth in Brentwood Village. Peggy answers on the third ring.

"Yes... Hello?" she says in her frazzled way.

"It's me," Aaron says. "I'll be staying at the Best Western if you need to reach me." He pauses. "I hope you do."

"What – what do you mean?"

"Check the mailbox." He can barely pinch out the remaining words. "I love you." He hangs up.

Back at the house, Peggy had finally succeeded in getting all three kids to sit at the kitchen table. And now this. This cryptic phone call from Aaron. And some mysterioso letter. She removes her apron in disgust. *Now* what's he up to?

She opens the front door — looking around to make sure Aaron isn't there — and pulls the note out of the mailbox. Desiring to be away from the children as she reads it, she lowers herself on the coffee table in front of the tree, its cheery lights dancing over the page as she opens it:

My dearest Peg,

Sometimes the stories we tell ourselves are enough to convince us they must be true. But I have learned that there is no running away from our inner-truths.

I love you and the children more than life itself. It is for this reason I cannot keep living in the fictional world I created. Words cannot express how sorry I am to have deceived you all these years. I am, as you rightly suspected, a fraud. But we will get through this together, and I do hope…

She is barely halfway through his letter when she crumples it into a tight ball and lets out a rageful scream. She cannot — *will not* — read another word. She cannot — *will not* — let this letter infect her house. She cannot — *will not* — allow him to destroy her family.

Stomping over to the fireplace, she boots away the Chinese Checkers board in her path. Hailstones of marbles ricochet off the walls as she spits her husband's name in a torrent of curses. Jolene looks on stoically while Billy and Nancy shriek for Mommy, who wings the balled-up note into the fire and watches it incinerate into black ash.

CHAPTER 28

Strolling through the courtyard of Paradise Palms, Rae is particularly attuned to the reactions of her companion. Glynda has taken the day off to visit and Rae wants to make a good impression. Before her former house mother's arrival, she spiffed up the lobby with Yolanda, then took it upon herself to clean the pool and sweep the walkways. But her efforts are akin to putting lipstick on a pig. Like the gravitational pull between Earth and the moon, the Palms and Hollywood are inexorably linked in a force of mutual descension.

Nonetheless, Glynda *is* impressed by Rae's ability to transition into the real world and make something of herself. "You've got an old soul," she told Rae more than once. Rae used to consider it an insult, as if Glynda were making fun of her stodginess compared to her housemates. It was only when she got older that she realized it was a compliment. At nineteen, this old soul now has her own apartment, a driver's license, a cheap used car, plans for college, and gainful employment – not great-paying, but at least one that provides learning and supervisory opportunities.

As if on cue, Rae is approached by Flori, pushing her cleaning cart past Rae and Glynda.

"Sorry to bother, Miss Lynn," she says. "But the electricity is out in sixteen and seventeen now."

Rae lets out a frustrated cluck. "Thank you, Flori." She turns to Glynda. "We've had problems with that entire annex ever since the revamp. I've closed it off to guests for the time being."

"Didn't you say that's the youngest fella's job – Rudy? – to fix those things?"

"Used to be. Not anymore. David fired him." Rae notices a pool of mud between flaccid birds of paradise along the pathway. She picks up a broken metal sprinkler head. "Things have been in disarray since Max's accident. Seems like nobody's around, everybody squabbling… distracted…" She slips the valve into her pocket.

"I hope they're paying you manager money. 'Cause that's what you're doing — you're *managing* this place, Rae."

"It's okay. They're always hurting for money, and I like the increased responsibility."

"Honey, don't go playing the martyr. They're taking you for granted. I'll call Leo right now and tell him to send someone over here and fix the electricity."

Rae smiles. "You'll do no such thing." She steps off the walkway and turns the corner of the south wing. "I'm gonna go check the breakers."

After unlocking the door, Rae and Glynda enter the utility closet behind Rooms 13 through 18. Rae pulls on a light chain. The dirt-floor corridor contains a maze of insulated wires, ducts and pipes. The breaker panel is by the door, but their attention is diverted by the unexpected presence of dozens of butane tanks lined up from one end of the shaft to the other.

Rae sucks in air. "Whoa…"

She and Glynda approach the first set of metal white cylinders. Each has a "100 LBS." label and a red-diamond "Flammable" insignia.

"What in God's name…" Glynda says. "What could you possibly need with all these?"

Rae does a visual guesstimate and counts about forty tanks. "Rudy…"

"What?"

"I didn't know about any of this. Rudy must be coming in after-hours and storing them here."

"Sweetie, he is bad news. You need to tell him to *vamoose* these out of here."

Rae nods absently, overwhelmed by the task ahead of her. David is going to blow his stack. She wonders if she should even tell him, or try to handle the situation herself.

Glynda nudges her. "Hey, you remember that fire at McDaniel's when you were about eight years old?"

"Of course. Burnt down half the barn. I was scared to go to sleep that night."

"Yeah, well, it *could've* jumped to the main house if the volunteer fire department hadn't been driving by, but for the grace of God." Glynda raps her knuckles on the side of a tank. "It was caused by one of these bad boys. We'd been storing them as fuel for portable heaters."

"I thought the fire was from Clayton tossing a cigarette in the trash."

"That's what we told you kids to keep the story simple. No, dear, he and a friend got the bright idea to take hits off a butane tank. They let the gas out and sucked a hose." She winces, the morbid event still entrenched in her memory. "Clayton got high, wasn't thinking straight. Struck a match to light a cigarette. Next thing he knows, there was a big fireball… that's how he got those third-degree burns."

Rae shudders and returns to the breaker panel. She opens the cover and checks all the switches.

"Everything good here. Nothing tripped."

"You probably got a short somewhere," Glynda suggests. "Like you said, things going to pot around here. Lots of deferred maintenance."

"It's like their hearts aren't in it anymore."

"I know it ain't for Leo. He's done with the hotel business. Told me he wants to start building on their lots." She looks at Rae. "Did you know he bought a parcel near McDaniel's?"

"I didn't."

"Quarter-acre prime, right off a main boulevard. Future site of some freeway off-ramp. He's thinking of putting in a gas station or something." She laughs. "Can you imagine Leo pumping ethyl in one of them hats and a cute little name tag? Not with those baby-soft hands! Although he *promised* I could manage it if McDaniel's ever goes under, which – let's face it – is just a matter of time…"

Rae tries to gauge her mentor's thoughts. Even in the murky light, she can see her laugh lines crinkling, her eyes radiating warmth.

"Leo's been spending a lot of time up there lately, huh?" Rae asks.

"He's a good man. A kind man. Very smart." Glynda chuckles. "And just enough of a fool to make me laugh."

"I'm sure he appreciates a strong woman like you."

Glynda looks at her. "We're… friends," she says obliquely. "Good friends appreciate good friends."

• • •

A spray of sparks shoots out of the open hood of a beat-up '54 Plymouth Belvedere, the head of a coveralled welder buried deep inside the engine block. Taking a break to crink his back, the man lifts his goggles and rubs his nose with a greasy glove. It's Rudy – modifying another car at J&M Scrap Metal for drug runs to Mexico. His checklist to conceal contraband includes a false back behind the glove box, hidden partitions in the seat cushions, a secret nook in the back bumper, and now, a hollow metal compartment against the firewall.

Rudy flips his goggles back down and resumes welding. If he could just finish this job today, he'll be done with this junker, at which point Red said he'd slip him forty bucks. Then again, he promised that on the *last* car Rudy retrofitted and only floated him twenty – the rest payable when he finished the Belvedere. Snig had warned Rudy that Red's a "floater." Always delivering just enough money to keep you working but promising the rest only when you finish the next assignment. Complicating things is the fact that Rudy is still paying down racetrack loans Red gave him that predate the Riviera Casino fiasco, causing Rudy to lose track of the money Gordo owes *him*. Maybe that was the point.

Rudy feels a tug on his coveralls. He lifts his head out of the hood. It's Felix. "Boss-man wants to see you."

Rudy feels a pit in his stomach as he dawdles toward Red's makeshift office. He can sense the greasers looking up from their welding and riveting and oil changing to witness his summons. All his life, Rudy wanted to be The Man who answers to no one but himself. He could never escape David's long shadow when he worked for the family. He dreaded being called in to see him, taken to task for his latest fuck-up, then observing the pucker of disappointment on his face. Working for Gordo was supposed to change all that. And yet, here he is again, awaiting further judgment from someone of a superior rank. When would the cycle end?

Rudy hobbles into an abandoned parking lot attendant kiosk – Gordo's office. The goon is on the phone, kicked back in a chair with his feet on his desk. Rudy moves a clump of tire irons off a seat cushion while Sally lazily one-eyes him from the floor before drifting back to sleep.

"Tell the Mick we got another run in two days," Red squawks into the phone. "Five kilos. I'll call you when it's in." The caller is trying his patience. "I told you what I told you. I gotta go, I got a customer." He hangs up.

Turning to Rudy, he gets right to it. "How many tanks did you move this week?"

"Two," Rudy says quietly. "But a few guys expressed an interest."

"I got an interest in fucking Kim Novak, don't mean it's gonna happen."

More classic Gordo. It was *he* who presented Rudy with a plan to store butane tanks at the Palms, to tap into the moneyed kids to whom Rudy had access. But the craze to inhale the noxious gas never quite took off with the fickle set. Rudy guessed some of that had to do with a high-profile death that made the papers and scared kids off. Some teenager, reportedly a second-cousin-once-removed or some shit to Desi Arnaz. Had a tank in his bedroom. He was found slumped against the wall with a hose in his mouth. Morgue called it "Sudden Sniffing Death." Now, instead of blaming a changing market, Red was blaming Rudy.

"What's it gonna take to facilitate more action?" Red asks him.

"Well, I think if enough time passes, it should pick up again."

"We don't got time. I'm in hock for those tanks. If we can't move 'em all by the end of the month, Red's in the red." He stands up and hovers over Rudy, his monobrow crimping into a giant furry "V." "I ain't gonna dip into my other rackets to make up for yours."

Rudy massages his scar. "I guess I'll just have to – "

"Try harder? Good!" Gordo moves over to the window and closes the blinds. "What about Abby?"

"Still trying to get to the bottom of it."

"What does that mean, 'Get to the bottom of it'?"

Rudy tries to spin a response but Red leaves him frustratingly tongue-tied. The truth is, he hasn't gotten to the bottom of anything because he doesn't know where else to look. He had already ransacked Abigail and Max's room at the Palms. Nothing seemed amiss, no clues pointing toward her whereabouts.

"You dead weight?" Gordo says.

"Excuse me?"

"What the fuck I got you on payroll for if you're just dead weight?" Gordo's wet lips coalesce into their familiar heart shape. "Lemme give you a clue. How 'bout you start with the man with a motive. David. Find out where he was that night she disappeared."

"I really don't think..." He looks up at Red's menacing smile. "I mean, I just don't know if he's capable."

"All men are capable of anything if they're pushed hard enough. Could be he hired someone..."

Rudy glances at his watch, trying a different tack. "It's been forty-eight hours now. Maybe we should open up a missing persons file with the cops first. They could start an investigation."

Gordo lets out a hollow cackle. "Maybe you should swap brains with your old man." He palms Rudy's cranium like a basketball. "His may be mush, but it's gotta be smarter than the one you got rattling around this coconut."

• • •

At eleven o'clock that night, Rudy parks his latest hot rod on Selma Avenue, two blocks from Paradise Palms. He finds the public mailbox behind the Crossroads of the World mall, inserts a sealed white envelope, and steps away. He pauses, turning back to make sure the letter slipped through the slot. Satisfied, he continues walking toward the hotel.

He enters through the McCadden Place side gate using a key – one of dozens on a master ring that he kept after David banished him from working at the Palms. He is clad in all black to better blend into the night.

Stepping into Room 1 – his follow-up visit to Abigail's and Max's unit – he digs through drawers and re-checks the medicine cabinet. Still nothing concrete that would hint toward her whereabouts or foul play.

Moving outside, he strides past the doors of every unit of the hotel. A languid pall hangs in the air. Most rooms are empty, and those that are occupied have their drapes drawn. Only one room betrays stirrings of activity – Room 6. Rudy notices the curtain undulating after he walks past. He guesses Elron's on one of his benders and has been watching him. He makes a mental note to talk to him.

Rudy turns toward the back door of the kitchen. As he pulls out his key ring, the door suddenly opens. Out steps Rae, slipping on a jacket. Both are surprised to see each other. Rudy quickly defuses any awkwardness with his flattering charm.

"Ladies and gentlemen… the hardest-working Shapiro in the hospitality biz!"

Rae offers him a placating smile. "Just stalling for time until my roommate picks me up when she gets off waitressing."

"Uh oh – the ladies are gonna paint the town red!" Rudy emits a mirthful hoot. "Y'know, I miss our wild joyrides since you moved out of this dump." He tilts his head. "Still living in the Western Arms building?"

"Yup."

"I should come by with my new wheels, take you out for a spin."

Rae buttons her jacket with an equivocal nod. She looks past Rudy, toward the south wing. "Those tanks behind those rooms… You can't leave them in there, y'know."

Rudy looks behind him, and it occurs to him she thinks he just came from the utility closet. "Oh, right. No, I know. They're donations for the Boys Club. Y'know, underprivileged kids camps. I've been bugging them to send a driver over to pick them up."

Rae, not buying it: "Just the same. They're highly flammable." She gives him a playful knock on the shoulder to soften her directive. "Don't want you getting in trouble or nothing."

Rudy play-jabs her back. "So you're kinda running things now that Pop's in the hospital and Darlene's got a muffin in the oven, huh?" He sizes her up with a proud grin, genuinely impressed. "Very cool."

Rae turns toward the McCadden gate. "Gotta go. My ride's here."

"Yeah, I'm gonna split, too. G'night!" He watches her leave.

When the coast is clear again, he opens the kitchen door and turns on the light. A cursory check yields nothing out of the ordinary. The cabinets are bare save for snacks for the maids.

He continues to the basement door. He's not expecting anything peculiar down there but wants to be thorough for Gordo. He unbolts the door, flicks on the overheads, and steps onto the landing.

Descending the stairs, he's struck by déjà vu. The last time Rudy was in here was when his brothers made the decision to close The Easy. It was a night like this one. He came in after-hours to make off with all the wine his parents had been storing since the end of Prohibition. Though the shelves are now mostly empty, the cellar's heavy air remains, as if something unseen is still present.

Rudy steps into the center of the room, right about where Abigail took her final breath. He visually combs the walls, the vents, the shelving. Scopes his flashlight into the crevice under the wooden staircase, finding only spider webs. He returns to the middle of the room and angles his head sideways to the floor. In the dusty two-inch gap between the bottom shelf and the concrete, he makes out dead insects and something else – is that a golf ball? He hits it with his beam. It's a fuzzy pink orb. He reaches in with his thumb and index finger and plucks it out.

Holding the ball in his hand, Rudy can see frayed pink threads. Clearly a decorative thing. Must've gotten detached from an article of clothing. He's struck by another feeling of familiarity. He's seen this pom-pom before. He pictures Abigail in his mind's eye. Sees her lounging by the pool in her robe and slippers. The robe is easy to conjure up – a red kimono with a thigh-high slit that leaves just enough to the imagination. The slippers are hot pink, with two little tassels in the front, fuzzy and roundish – like pom-poms. *Holy shit.*

Rudy pockets the pom-pom. He locks up the basement and kitchen, then makes a beeline for Room 6. He politely knocks on the door. Once again, the shade ripples.

"Hey, Elron, I know you're in there, buddy," Rudy says amiably. "Let me in and maybe we could get some chow and talk."

He hears the door click open. Elron looks like death warmed over, eyes sunken deep in their sockets, cheekbones protruding. He keeps the chain on the door, refusing to open it more than a crack.

"Whattaya want?" he asks lazily. Clearly on some kind of downers.

"Can I come in?"

Elron glances around his drug-infested room, turns back to Rudy with a slow-motion wave. "Be gone."

Rudy chuckles. "Sure, man. Hey, uh, I was wondering if you could help me out. See, Red's looking for Abigail – y'know, Kitty – but no one's seen hide or hair of her."

Elron's face goes blank. "Whattaya asking me for?"

"Well, I know you're up all hours. Maybe you saw her walk by your room one night, or remember anything unusual…"

"Unusual?" Elron twists the whiskers of his goatee. "Whattaya asking me for?"

Rudy sees he's having a hard time penetrating his fog. He switches to a more direct mode. "Did you see my brother David here three nights ago?"

Elron blinks several times. "He never came in here," he says defensively.

"Oh… so he *was* here. Did he stay in room three?"

"I'm not your brother's keeper." Elron starts to shut the door, but Rudy blocks it with his shoe.

"You clean, Elron?"

"C'mon, man…"

"Hey, *I* don't care. But we can't have another drug bust here. We run a clean joint. Isn't that what David always says?" He cranes his neck to peer into the unit. "Would hate to see that happen to you again. Next time, you might not get so lucky."

Elron sighs heavily. Different brother, same threat.

Rudy removes his foot from the doorway and digs into his pocket. "If you do see Kitty, tell her I found part of her slipper." His thumb strokes the pom-pom in his palm, like someone petting a pink mouse. Elron's eyes nearly bug out of his head. "I'm sure she's missing it. I'll hold onto it for safe keeping."

Rudy slips it back into his pocket and winks before strolling off into the night.

CHAPTER 29

The phone call comes immediately, its jangly trill jarring David and Darlene as they read in bed. David instinctively thinks of his mom's old saw – "no good can come from a call after midnight." He looks at the clock: 11:34 p.m. Close enough.

"I'll take it in the other room in case you wanna sleep," he says to his wife, vaulting out of the covers. He shuts the bedroom door behind him and races to the living room phone.

"Hello?" he says quietly.

"They know," comes Elron's trembling voice on the other end. "They fucking *know*. It's over!"

David's face turns ashen. "Calm down. Take a deep breath. Who knows?"

"I told you I'm not cut out for this. I'm an artist. A sensitive soul. I rescue spiders from my shower drain – "

"Elron, *focus*. What happened?"

"Rudy. He found her slipper."

David's jaw slacks open and he nearly drops the receiver. He glances down the hallway. "That's *impossible*."

"Well, he did. Or a part of it… some little ball. Fuck, I don't know."

"Tell me you didn't say anything to Rudy."

"Oh God oh God oh God oh – "

"Tell me!"

"I didn't say nothing. But he threatened me. Just like you did." Elron is in full-on meltdown mode. "Gordo's gonna get me and string me up by my short-hairs and make me talk I know it I know it I know it…"

"He won't find you! We'll get you into a new room where you can hide out."

"A lot of good that'll do!"

David hears the bedroom door squeak open. "I'll move you out of the Palms," he whispers hoarsely.

Elron has been reduced to heaving sobs laced with anger. "I thought you liked me. But you *used* me, man. I'm just a tool to you. A patsy. You killed her and you dragged me into this and now you're gonna hang me out to dry, you *motherfuck—*"

David hangs up the handset like it's a hot potato and backs away from the phone. Darlene is standing in the living room.

"Who was that?" she asks.

David swallows hard, trying to slow down his breathing. "Fuckin' Elron. He's having one of his freak-outs. Sometimes you gotta just knock some sense into him." He waggles his head. "I keep pushing him to get help, but it never sticks, y'know?"

"You seem upset."

"Yeah, I don't appreciate him calling us in the middle of the night."

"No, I mean, like... there's something wrong."

"I just *told* you, he's a paranoid pain-in-the-ass. What the fuck more do you want from me?"

He storms past her and grabs his car keys from the kitchen counter.

"Wait – where are you going?"

He slams the front door and drives off.

• • •

David cracks the windows of his Impala and flies down Ventura Boulevard. He's hoping the night air will blow out all the bad thoughts swirling in his head and provide him with a clear directive. He feels bad shutting Darlene out. There will be consequences later. But he is not prepared to tell her the truth and introduce a new crisis – his marriage – when the existing one is already more than he can handle.

His mind revisits the "what if" he briefly entertained while driving back from the desert. What if he killed Elron? Elron himself admitted he was weak. He will no doubt crack under pressure from Gordo, who will come looking for David next. If Elron went away, everything else would too. David would be left with just one living witness – himself – which was his plan all along. But for the same reason he can't confess to Darlene, he can't fathom taking the poor schlub's life. He tells himself he *is* still human after all, not a monster. Right?

He finds his car almost steering itself to Leo's pad at the Valley View Suites. He could really use his brother's counsel. He would have to spill the beans, although he could fudge it as he did for Elron – saying Kitty fell down the stairs and he simply panicked, leaving out the stone-cold killer part. Leo would be too smart to believe his cock-and-bull story, but he would swear to secrecy. He would tell David exactly what he thinks *they* should do, providing a collective ego that David could only get from a womb-mate.

But Leo was also increasingly frail. In addition to stressing about their father, his gastrinoma had flared up again, contributing to more painful ulcers. He recently had an overnight stay at Cedars of Lebanon Hospital that he hid from family members for fear of worrying them. David only found out about it through Glynda. Did David really want to lay all this at Leo's feet too?

He switches directions, heading toward the Pico-Union neighborhood to see Rae. It was obvious to him at his father's bedside – the day Aaron was falling apart – that she knows David is involved in Kitty's disappearance. Rae's entire life has been built on secrets, and she can sniff them out. Besides, what did she expect when she told David about overhearing Red and Kitty plotting to kill Max? It was almost as if she were *daring* him to take action, especially when she showed up at his house. Suddenly, it makes all the sense in the world that she would be the one to whom he confides in his manic search for a way out of this mess.

He pulls up to the Western Arms at Western near Olympic. It's a four-story brick apartment building, its name paraded in cursive neon atop the roof. David presses the security button for her unit. No one answers. He tries again and again, not realizing she's out for the night with her roommate. After two minutes, he gives up. Clearly another sign – this is his burden to bear and bear alone.

Aimlessly driving back home, he can feel the governor of detachment cinching more tightly around him.

• • •

Red Gordo inspects the pink pom-pom in his calloused palm, then clamps his fingers tightly over it. Mashing his rodent teeth, he shoves the furry token into his pocket. Rudy notices his face turning various shades of red, the veins on his temples popping out. He looks like he might combust at any moment.

"Tell me again exactly what this Elron character said about your brother," he says to Rudy. It's the next day, and the two are back in the J&M office kiosk. Red stands before Rudy, who leans against his boss's small desk.

"Just... that he was there that night. The night Abby vanished."

"Uh huh. And then what?"

"He didn't say." Rudy wants to move the emphasis off his brother. "I think it was just a coincidence David was there. I mean, he often comes by the Palms to – "

"You trying to tell me Elron acted alone?"

"No. I mean – I dunno. Yeah." Rudy forces a sardonic hoot. "This guy... he shot up our lobby with a gun once. He's capable of *extreme* violence, especially when he's high."

"What reason would he have to off my Abby?"

Rudy makes an exaggerated shrug.

"Lemme get this straight. We got some bozo who don't value human life, but who also got no reason to off my Abby." Red crosses his arms and pinches his lips, a brainstorm brewing. "Know what he sounds like to me? A hit man for someone who *did* have a reason."

"Again, I don't think David had *anything* to do with this..."

"I guess we'll find out."

Red reaches around Rudy and yanks open the top drawer of the desk. Inside is a .38 caliber handgun. He pulls it from the drawer, slams it on the tabletop, then takes a step back, flashing his choppers.

"What's that for?" Rudy asks.

"You and me are gonna go see this Elron fella in his room. That's your piece." Red pulls a pistol from the back of his pants and waves it. "This here's mine." He lodges it back in his waistband.

"What're you gonna do to him?"

"We," he corrects.

Rudy swallows hard. "What are *we* gonna do to him?"

"Just a friendly conversation-like. Maybe ask if he knows how part of her slipper ended up in the basement. See who he got his orders from. Maybe talk to that person too." He rubs his palms together as if savoring the showdown.

"If neither man wants to talk, you and me will move onto more 'facilitory' measures."

Rudy swipes the gun from the desktop and aims it directly at Red's chest with two shaky hands.

"Leave my fucking brother out of this!" he shrills.

Sally lifts her head from Red's feet and growls at Rudy, intuiting a threat. Red doesn't flinch. "Little kids shouldn't play with matches. Liable to get burnt."

"I'll shoot you straight through the heart if I have to. Don't make me have to!"

Gordo pumps the air. "*That's* the kinda fire I was waiting to see from you instead of all this moping around. Hot *dog!*"

Rudy's face twists in confusion. He looks at his gun as if somebody else stuck it in his hands.

Gordo's voice takes on a hushed, compassionate quality. "Hey. He's your big brother. You got a soft spot for him. I get it. But remember where it got you. He treats you like dirt. Cuts you out of the family. Puts the colored broad over you. Then bad-mouths you to the world. He don't deserve you, superstar."

He sweeps his arm across the window, to his underworld wonderland and the worker-bees servicing it – a motley gang of drug-runners, bet-fixers, grifters and sex-traffickers. "Here, you got a home. A future. You're part of *our* family now." Then, really pouring it on: "I had big plans for you. I was hoping maybe I could be the big brother you never had, y'know?"

Rudy's facial muscles – tensed in psychic pain – begin to slacken. Suddenly, he exhales loudly, dropping his arms in relief. He places his gun back on the desk.

A hollow smile creeps across Red's face. "Ain't you a gullible piece of shit."

While he was stalling, Gordo's hand picked up a tire iron from a chair. He whips it forward and cracks it across Rudy's face, shattering his left cheekbone. Rudy staggers back in shock. The skin has folded off his cheek, exposing slabby tissue. He spits out blood and teeth. Fumbles for the other gun. Manages to aim it at Red.

As he pulls the trigger, it emits a harmless *tink*. It was never loaded.

"If you ain't over him by now, you ain't never gonna be," Red says, shaking his head. "I liked you, Rudy, but I can't have traitors working for Red."

Gordo pummels Rudy's skull with repeated blows from the iron. Rudy emits horrified squeals before slumping to the floor unconscious. An agitated Sally barks and whimpers. The blows continue to rain down, blood squirting up onto Red's face with each squishy thwack of bone.

Snig and Felix, drawn by the commotion, race to the doorway of the kiosk. They look down at the creeping reservoir of blood beneath Rudy's lifeless body.

Gordo flings the bloodstained tire iron onto the desk. "Get this cripple outta here and clean this place up. Dump him in one of 'em drums for now." He grabs his car keys and pushes past them. "I got business to take care of."

CHAPTER 30

Gordo torpedoes through the front door of Paradise Palms, flexing his .38 Special. "What room is Elron in?" he booms to Darlene and Rae, the only ones in the lobby. The girls screech and duck behind the front counter. "I'll go through each and every one if I fucking have to!"

"Call the police," Darlene whispers to Rae. She gets on the phone from behind the counter and starts to dial from her knees.

"Peek-a-boo!" Red croons, coming around the desk. He snags the clutch of room keys off the wall, then points to Darlene. "Don't get too cozy. Your husband is next." Darlene clenches her eyes. She hears him exit through the back door to the courtyard.

As Rae connects with the Hollywood police department, Darlene calls David from the other desk phone. Both women reach their parties at the same time, engaging in spirited conversations that occasionally overlap.

Rae: "I'd like to report an armed intruder."

Darlene: "Red just came in with a gun. He's looking for Elron then he's coming for you."

Rae: "Paradise Palms hotel. 6735 Selma Avenue."

Darlene: "We're safe for now."

Rae: "Yes, we know him. Vance Gordo."

Darlene: "No, *don't* come down here whatever you do. You need to get out of the house *now!*"

Rae cups the mouthpiece, addresses Darlene: "Don't have him to go his brothers' either. Gordo will look for him there."

Darlene: "Don't go to Leo's or Aaron's."

Rae, to the police: "Please hurry. People's lives are in immediate danger!"

Darlene: "How should I know? David, what the hell is going on?"

Rae, to Darlene: "Tell him to go to McDaniel's. I'll drive us there."

Darlene, to Rae: "What? Why?"

Rae, to the police: "Why do you need my name?" To Darlene: "I dunno, it's far away and Red doesn't know about it. It should be safe."

Darlene, to David: "Meet us at McDaniel's. We're closing up."

Rae, to Darlene: "I'll call Leo, you call Aaron." To the police: "Look, just get here! We'll be waiting."

The girls hang up their respective phones, then rush to the courtyard. Red is on a rampage, flinging open doors in a clockwise manner as he hunts for his targeted tenant. Terrified guests spill onto the grass, including one woman wearing only a bath towel. Most rooms are empty.

By the time he hits the north wing, Gordo has blazed through eighteen units. Unlocking Room 6, he finds he can't open the door all the way — the chain lock is secured. Red drives his size-14 right boot into the wood. It budges but doesn't break. After several more whacks, the chain snaps and the door splinters open.

Red barges in — then recoils from a sweetly sour stench.

"Ah Jee-zus Christ!" he yowls, plugging his nose.

Rae and Darlene cloister at the doorway, cupping their hands over their mouths. Elron is on the floor, slumped against the bed frame in soiled underwear. A heroin needle dangles out of his left forearm, strapped by a rubber hose. Half a line of cocaine flecks a spiral notebook by his hips.

Police sirens keen in the distance. Gordo stammers backwards, glances at Rae and Darlene, then continues out the door without a word. He's gone by the time the cops invade the courtyard and come across the dead junkie in Room 6.

· · ·

Glynda and a teen kitchen aide carry dinner leftovers into the library at McDaniel's Residentiary. The small, converted classroom is festooned with inspirational motifs — Black leader profiles, photos from educational field trips, and shelves of books donated by Black celebrities, scholars, and alumni.

At the center of the room, two tables have been pushed together with place settings for five. Glynda and her assistant place steaming heaps of roasted turkey, collard greens and white rice on the tabletop. Rae, Darlene, Leo and Aaron are gathered around the spread, their bodies squeezed into small chairs. As good as the food looks, no one feels much like eating.

Glynda regards the one empty chair. "When did you all expect David again?"

"He's never been here before, so he probably just got lost," says Darlene, who looks worried sick. David is not the type to get lost, and besides, Aaron found the place with no problems.

As Glynda directs her helper to wait for David in the parking lot, Leo makes small talk with Aaron, uncharacteristically disheveled in a wrinkled suit and five o'clock shadow. "Revisiting your bachelor days?" Leo jabs.

"Actually, yes," Aaron responds stoically. "Peggy and I had a falling out. I'm staying at a hotel on Bundy for a few days until things blow over."

Other than Rudy, no living family member knows about Aaron's secret life. Sure, the brothers knew there were fissures in his picture-perfect marriage, but an actual separation comes as a news flash to Leo.

"Oh geez, Aaron, I'm so sorry," he says. "Why didn't you tell us?"

"I didn't wanna make big deal…"

"Well, what're you wasting your money for? Come stay with me. I got a pull-out bed in the living room, a full kitchen…"

"I wanted some place close to the kids, but thanks." Aaron turns away from Leo, dishing out rice in an effort to avoid further discussion.

At last, David is guided into the library by the assistant. She and Glynda leave the room to give the Shapiros privacy. David's face is unyielding, his gait rigid, almost robotic. Always the one in control – especially in regard to family matters – he now seems almost like a caricature of someone in control.

"Evening, everyone," he says impassively, wedging his body into the empty chair. A long silence ensues as everyone waits for David to fill the family in on what sparked Red's rage. But no explanation is forthcoming. His aura of control, of course, is that of a man trapped in an impenetrable fortress.

Exasperated by David's bizarre behavior, Darlene seizes the gauntlet. "Elron is dead," she says flatly.

Leo and Aaron gasp, hearing this for the first time. David slowly turns and stares at her.

"Did Red get him?" Leo asks.

"When?" says Aaron.

"The paramedics arrived earlier today," Darlene laments. "Overdose of cocaine and heroin. They said he 'expired' sometime last night."

"Where's his body now?" Leo asks.

"They're holding it at the morgue, waiting burial instructions," Rae says, glancing at David. "He didn't have any family that we know of, so…"

"Have them call me," Leo tells her.

There's a respectful lull in the conversation, as if to give Elron's passing its proper due. Yet there remains an elephant in the room – two elephants, really: The timing of Elron's overdose, and the stated targets of Red's wrath.

"Gordo was looking for Elron," Darlene informs David. "Why was he looking for Elron?"

"And he was looking for you," Aaron adds. "David, what the fuck?"

All eyes are now trained on the alpha Shapiro. He can no longer ignore their inquiries. And then it hits him. A confession – inasmuch as he was contemplating it – is now unnecessary. With Elron's death, there is a clear path forward, a way to let everyone in. It's right there on their faces. Rather than be the man with all the answers, all he needs to do is project their confusion back on them.

His response to Darlene and Aaron is unequivocal: "I have no idea."

Darlene gives him a ponderous look that signals her skepticism.

"He was coming after you and Elron with a gun!" Aaron exclaims. "Obviously something triggered him or we wouldn't all be up here in the boondocks hiding you out and figuring out what to do."

David nods gravely. He has cobbled together a vague outline in his head, but he can't deliver it in this tiny chair. He feels pinned down, the eyes of his loved ones burning into him like laser beams. He stands up and grabs a plate, dishing himself some grub.

"Four days ago, the electricity went out in our house. Darlene went to her folks' place. I overnighted at the Palms. By sheer coincidence, that was the last time Gordo saw Kitty. She's been missing ever since."

"Did *you* see her?" Aaron asks.

"Who, Kitty? What would I want with her? No, I ordered dinner from Don's and retired to my room for the night." David takes a bite of the turkey, pausing to savor it. "You guys should try this. The gravy is really flavorful."

David continues directing his gaze at his plate. "Elron saw her," he offers, rearranging his rice. "He was on a midnight-munchie run, sifting through trash cans. Kitty was lounging by the pool, smoking or drinking or something."

"How do you know?" Darlene says.

"He told me the next morning. Before I met up with you."

"You saw Elron before noon?" Aaron snorts. "That's a first."

"He was still up from the night before." David walks over to a pitcher of water and pours himself a glass. "I only remember because he said Kitty was acting weird, like she wanted to leave Red… but she was scared. Said he was abusive toward her, raped her, had affairs. Maybe she just… had enough."

David peeks at his audience. Furrowed brows all around, except for Leo, who has been strangely quiet and looks like he has something to get off his chest.

"But she's married to *Pop*," Aaron says. "Why would she leave town when her husband's on his death bed? It doesn't make sense."

"Exactly," David says, as if to prove his point, which is that there is none – or perhaps many.

Aaron scratches his head. "Well, regardless… he's convinced you have something to do with her missing."

"Of course he would! Given our history with Kitty… abusing Pop, making a play for the Palms… he doesn't trust us. Once she went missing, he immediately thought I was behind it."

"Then why's he after Elron too?"

David shrugs. "Maybe one of his stooges saw them talking by the pool and told Red. And now he suspects the poor sap had something to do with her disappearance."

"So, wait – *Elron* had something to do with it, or *you* had something to do with it?"

"Exactly."

He's lost the room. Worse, he has spun such a thick web of obfuscation, even he's not sure he can find a way out of it. Fortunately, Leo provides one for him.

"She's not dead," Leo declares, to the shock of everybody. "Gordo's playing us. He wants money. That's his angle."

"How do you know?" David asks, intrigued.

"He called me right before I came up here since he knows I handle money matters. Rudy must've tipped him off where I live now… or maybe he just knew, like he knows everything."

"You gonna tell us what he said?" Darlene prods.

"He said 'Abby' was missing. And he holds David responsible. But if we pay him – get this – fifty thousand dollars, he'll leave us alone for good… and spare David his life."

Aaron lets out a trenchant laugh. "The sack on that guy…"

"We go to the cops, obviously," Darlene states.

"No," David cautions. "We can't prove anything and he'd just deny he said it."

"Kitty's still alive," Leo reiterates. "He's probably telling her to hide out. I think she and Red cooked this whole thing up to make it seem like David or Elron or *someone* associated with us killed her. So he's blackmailing us, hoping we'll pay him off."

Darlene pounces on the flaw in Leo's argument. "In order to blackmail someone, you need compromising evidence."

"He claims he has it — a tassel from Kitty's slipper that was found in the basement."

David's face goes white. He turns his back to pour himself more water.

"I don't know what he thinks it proves," Leo smirks, "but I don't think you can build a case based on a part of someone's shoe and nothing else."

"What do you mean, 'a tassel'?" Darlene asks, fixated on that detail.

Rae throws out a question before Leo can respond. "So theoretically, what happens if you pay Gordo and then Abigail 'comes back from the dead' and re-enters our lives?"

"Yeah," Aaron says drolly, "is it a money-back guarantee?"

Leo throws up his hands. "It's a moot point since we don't have the money. Besides, if she really *is* missing, David didn't kill her. So even if we got our hands on fifty grand, why would we pay that slimeball?"

"Because it could get him off our backs for good," David attests.

He reflexively runs his hand over his mouth, as if double-checking that the words did in fact leave his lips. Based on the jaw-dropping reactions of Darlene and Aaron, they must have.

"Why in God's name would we even entertain that?" Aaron asks.

"You're not the one whose life is being threatened!" David huffs. Privately, he sees Gordo's *Get Out of Jail Free* card as his ticket to mollify his guilt and stave off an investigation by Gordo's men. Outwardly, he packages his concerns around the safety of his family — although there is that too.

"I'm not saying we should do it," he continues, "only that… Darlene and I are starting a family. I can't always be looking over my shoulder, waiting and wondering when this monster is gonna strike. It's not fair to Darlene…" Then, beseeching his brothers: "How much longer are we gonna let him terrorize us? I mean, if he's offering us a way out…"

David's voice trails off. He can feel himself shrinking the longer he speaks. David fucking Shapiro — keeper of the family flame, anti-crooked crusader for clean business practices — is suddenly Gordo's bitch? He can't even bring himself to look at Darlene. Not that it matters. She's more interested in her previous unanswered question.

"This tassel…" she probes Leo, "… it was part of Abigail's slipper?"

David breaks. "Y'know what? Fuck it! Fuck the whole goddamn thing!"

He tears out of the library and disappears down the hall.

• • •

After David's histrionic departure, the remaining four eat a quiet, fraught dinner. The conversation is of the surface-level variety, and the only time David is mentioned is in the context of how much stress he must be under knowing he's in Gordo's crosshairs. Darlene picks at her plate, disengaged from the others, until finally she says to Leo, "I'd like to go. Can you drive me home?"

Leo dabs his mouth with a napkin. "Sure."

The two of them thank Glynda in the receiving room before proceeding out the front door. David is in the parking lot, pacing like a caged animal under a waxing gibbous moon.

As Leo fetches the Mercury, Darlene walks up to her husband. "I'm catching a ride with Leo. You have a place to stay?"

David turns to her. "I talked to Glynda. She said there's a decent motel a couple miles from here."

Darlene's bites her lip. "I just want you to be safe."

"I'm gonna line up a bodyguard tomorrow. Glynda knows a McDaniel's graduate who could be perfect. Although he once guarded Nat King Cole, so he might be a little out of my league." He forces a chuckle, trying to ease the tension. "If we can agree on a figure, I could be back home tomorrow, baby."

He reaches out to grab her hand. She pulls away.

"My apologies back there," he says with a heavy sigh. "I was a real jackass. I'm scared too, is all."

"Why didn't you tell me those things Elron said about Abigail? You never mentioned one thing about it when you saw me that morning."

"I didn't think it was important at the time. I have lots of conversations with tenants."

"Well, this one's dead. And the timing of it all just..." She studies his face, a ghostly hue in the moonlight, his eyes hollowed-out orbs. "Do you think Elron's life was less important than yours?"

"What kind of question is that?" His voice quakes with indignation. "I did more for that guy than anybody!"

"But you didn't answer my question. Do you think Elron's life was less important than your own?"

"No!"

"So... even drug addicts with no families – "

"Every human life is just as important as another."

A long pause. "Even Abigail's."

"Of course!"

"I'm glad to hear you say that," she says frostily. She lingers for a beat as if still searching for the window to his soul. Finally, she frowns and walks toward Leo.

• • •

The motel – the Roundup Room – is on the outskirts of Castaic, an unincorporated hamlet with a popular recreational creek. Rae herself had played in its waters during McDaniel's summer field trips. To make sure he finds the lodging, Rae drives slowly enough for David to follow in his Impala.

She pulls into the motel's gravel parking lot and exits her car. David pulls up alongside her, kills the engine – and stays put. Rae tries to read his face through the warped streaks of light on his window. She makes a motion for him to roll it down. Still no movement.

Finally, she raps on the glass. He lowers it, looking queasy, as if he just swallowed a batch of bad oysters.

"Everything okay?" she asks.

"No. Yeah. Fine." Merely uttering each syllable is a herculean task.

"David... I know you're hurting."

He evinces a pained smile.

"And... you don't have to say anything" – she pauses to steel herself – "but I'm pretty sure you killed her."

Like a drowning man coming up for air, David gasps loudly and closes his eyes, his torso convulsing in short, sharp breaths. She reaches through the window frame and grabs his hand.

"I think Leo knows too," she says, eyes rimming with tears. "That's why he was trying to take some heat off you."

He clutches her hand and bows his head against the steering column.

"I wanna help you. And I think I know a way to get Red the money he's demanding. It's kind of 'out there,' and I don't know if it would work…"

"What is it?" he croaks.

She hesitates. "I don't want the idea coming from me. And if you tell anybody it did, I'll deny it to my grave." She pauses. "Hey."

He raises his wrecked face and looks at her.

"I'm not getting involved in any way," she says ardently.

"Tell me whatever you're comfortable with. I'll take care of the rest. I'm in so deep now, there's no turning back."

Another car pulls into the parking lot. Rae waits for the driver to get out and enter the motel office. The gap allows David to pull himself together.

"Rudy's been storing butane tanks for Red in the south-wing storage," Rae says in a sotto voce. "Must be three dozen tanks in there."

David slowly nods, the dawn of realization cresting on his face.

"I'm only telling you this because it's a safety concern," she says.

"I understand," he says throatily. "Thanks for bringing it to my attention."

CHAPTER 31

They thought it was World War III.

That was the description in the *Los Angeles Times* given by residents on McCadden Place, who awoke at one in the morning to a furious firestorm across the street. Other eyewitnesses reported a percussion of booming noises, like cannons shot off in the dead of night. The explosions were heard as far west as Beverly Hills, as far east as Los Feliz. Each thunderous clap was accompanied by an orange-red fireball lighting up the sky, blooming into mushroom heads. With the daily specter of nuclear war and monthly air-raid drills, Angelenos had been on edge since World War II – first the Japs, now the Ruskies – the city's Pacific Rim location making it a vulnerable target. But to everyone's great relief, Armageddon had *not* rained down on Hollywood. Just a hotel.

By the time Fire Stations 6 and 27 arrived on the scene, most of the butane tanks had already ignited. The south wing, lobby, and restaurant/bar of Paradise Palms – all under the same roof – were engulfed in flames. The inferno raged for two hours, punctuated by loud gaseous pops, as if a fiery wraith were devouring the hotel from the pits of hell and randomly pausing to belch. Walls began to crumble. Just as the firemen's hoses were dousing the final spot fires, the weakened southern roof finally gave way, dropping onto the charred belly of the beast like a lid closing over a coffin.

Fortunately, there were no casualties, the southern quarter having been shuttered due to electrical problems. And while the blaze also scorched the roof of the west wing, no one was harmed here either. Concern about electrical issues in three of the four wings led to David's decision to relocate all the guests to the northern units. In an amazing "coincidence," the transference of guests to the rooms farthest from the fire occurred soon after David and Rae spoke at the Roundup Room – mere days before the conflagration.

David got the call from Rae at four in the morning. It was, of course, all choreographed ahead of time. To add a layer of verisimilitude, David pretended to be in a deep sleep and let Darlene answer the phone. The Palms is gone, Rae told her. She got the news from a lodger in Room 4 — a friend from McDaniel's who immediately called Rae from a phone booth upon evacuating.

After a flurry of phone calls, David, Darlene, Aaron, Leo and Rae all descended on the hotel at daybreak to see the smoldering wreckage for themselves. To David's surprise, Darlene dropped to her knees and wept. As he comforted her, David himself felt nothing, save for a vague sense of relief. He had utterly and completely surrendered to his worst impulses, as he had always inwardly threatened to do. Maybe now the gods would finally grant him absolution, and the real David Shapiro could once again rise from the ashes.

A thought struck Leo, who turned to his stupefied party. "Anyone know how to reach Rudy?" he asked.

· · ·

Several hours later, Ian Thigpen roves the charred remains with a clipboard and a camera. A bow-legged, mirthless old-timer counting down the days to his pension, the investigator from the Shapiros' fire insurance company is nonetheless an ace at his job. He is shadowed by Leo, who, after consulting with David, agreed to stick around to meet with officials while the others went home to make calls and get some rest.

Ian and Leo crunch over the still-simmering rubble, in and out of skeletal spires that used to be walls and doorways. From the street, it had reminded Leo of photos of Dresden after the war. Now that he's touring the damage up close, he's thinking more Pompeii. Broken, blackened toilets, blown over by the cannister explosions, resemble boulders hurled from a volcano. Serpentine copper pipes and grotesquely warped dining booths look like they were sculpted by molten lava.

Ian picks up a melted fragment from a butane tank, turning it over in his gloved hand.

"This was a white-hot fire," he shares. "Probably over twenty-five hundred degrees. Enough to melt all this metal." He chucks the shard back on a pile of smoking debris. "Any idea what all these butane tanks were doing here? Because right now, we're looking at a pretty clear-cut case of arson."

Leo was prepared for the investigator's preliminary finding. Without confessing his role in Abigail's disappearance, David did confide in Leo about his outrageous scheme to cash out on their fire policy to pay off Gordo. Leo harbored doubts. He knew it would be risky and didn't think paying Red fifty G's would necessarily end his feud with the Shapiros. It was a big, ballsy swing. But Leo was willing to go to bat for his brother – anything to help keep him alive... or out of prison, since he wouldn't be surprised if Kit's vanishing led to David's doorstep.

"I know it strains believability," Leo tells the agent, "but my brothers and I had no idea these tanks were here."

"You're right, that does strain believability."

"We've been victimized by a member of Mickey Cohen's gang. The FBI knows about it. They're looking into his facilitator. He's been using our hotel to run his operations and store contraband – including these tanks – often without our knowledge. We intend to prove our case."

Ian furnishes a patronizing grin. "I've heard all sorts of stories in my thirty-eight years with Liberty Mutual, and I can tell you this is the first time I've heard something like this." He pauses to take photos of burnt-out tank shells. "I'm not saying you might not be right. And maybe this is your Mrs. O'Leary's cow. But you're gonna need a really good lawyer to prove it, and the investigation could drag on for months."

"With all due respect," Leo avers, "we'll take our chances."

• • •

Across town, Rae is walking back from the corner deli with sandwiches and cream sodas for her roommate and herself. As she approaches the entrance to the Western Arms, she hears a woman's mocking voice calling out. "Hey hey Rae Rae!"

Rae squints up at the second-floor fire escape. It's Kenzie, the ditzy white girl prone to painting her nails on the steel grating.

Rae returns a polite grin and opens the door to the building.

"Rae Rae, I'm talking to you!"

Rae steps back and looks at her. "What is it, Kenzie?"

"I got a letter in my mailbox but it's addressed to you. I keep forgetting to give it to you." She pauses. "Hold a sec."

Kenzie disappears into her open window and returns to the landing with a sealed white envelope. She leans over the railing of the fire escape. "Catch!"

The letter plummets ungracefully to the sidewalk like a falling palm frond. Rae picks it up. The envelope is postmarked January 19, 1959 with no return address. The addressee is written in lumpish capital letters, the sender apparently unfamiliar with Rae's unit number:

RAE LYNN C/O WESTERN ARMS APTS.
1057 S. WESTERN AVE.
LOS ANGELES, CAL.

"Is that from a *secret admirer*?" Kenzie teases.

Rae ducks inside the entryway. She carefully runs her finger along the seal to open it. The letter is a single sheet – more blunt penmanship visible through the fibers. She unfolds it with the delicacy of an origamist, apprehensive of what she will find.

• • •

Rae pulls up to David's house a half-hour later. As she walks through the front gate, envelope in hand, an imposing young Black man in a dark suit stands guard on the front porch.

"How are you, Rae?" he asks, his stoic mask dissipating.

"I've been better, Edgar," she professes. "But good to see you."

"Good to see you too!"

Edgar's been conditioned not to pry into his clients' affairs – even if it involves an old friend – and turns around to unlock the front door to let her inside.

David and Darlene are waiting for her in the kitchen. Rae had called ahead of time with potentially devastating news regarding Rudy. Anticipating the worst, David is slouched over the kitchen table, unshaven and haggard from the previous long night, tilting nips of whisky into his coffee.

Darlene pours Rae a mug from the counter. "Coffee?"

"Please," Rae says. She joins David at the table. He slides the bottle of whisky to her, but she refrains.

"Did you guys ever reach Rudy?" Rae asks.

"No," Darlene says, handing Rae her coffee and sitting down.

"Darlene called an old girlfriend of his but they had fallen out of touch," David elaborates. "I was gonna swing by the hospital to see the last time he visited Pop."

Rae places the open envelope on the table, the letter sticking out. "This was addressed to me but didn't have my apartment number. I only got it today. It was postmarked five days ago." She sighs heavily. "The last time *I* saw Rudy was six days ago — at the hotel."

The letter freaks David out. He recognizes his brother's blocky writing and reacts as if the thing is radioactive, sliding his chair back.

Seeing her husband's trauma, Darlene unfolds the letter and reads it aloud:

"'Rae. I trust you to deliver this letter to the family more than anybody. If you can't find me it does not mean I'm hiding out or nothing, it means something happened to me. It means" — she stops to look at Rae and David and swallows hard — "I was killed by Red.'"

David grabs the bottle back and drinks directly from it.

"Dear God," Darlene utters, closing her eyes before resuming. "'Just thought you should know so the cops can look into the SOB. David and Aaron know the place.'"

She folds the sheet and slips it back into the envelope. "He signed it 'Rudy Shapiro.' He underlined the last name three times."

"Fucker's mocking me by doing that," David grumbles.

"*What?*"

"This whole thing is a set-up."

"Oh Jesus... How can you be so sure?"

"He's aligned himself with Gordo, honey. He wants me to show up at that desolate junkyard looking for him so they can ambush me and knock me off."

Darlene isn't sure David truly believes this or if he simply can't reconcile himself to Rudy's probable death. Truthfully, David doesn't know either.

Rae jumps in to support Darlene's case, reiterating passages from the letter. "He says we should *call the cops*... He's coming right out and saying they should *investigate Red's place* — the scrapyard." She looks at David. "There's no reason for you or Edgar to go there and put yourselves in danger."

Darlene grabs David's arm. "Rae's right, sweetie. It sounds like Red turned on him and he wrote this letter when he felt his life was in danger."

"He wrote it to me – not you," Rae points out. "He would never use me to frame you."

David looks at her. She's right. Rudy had too much respect for Rae. There was no family baggage there, no bitterness or hidden agendas, and so he knew he could trust her to carry out his message.

David rises from his chair and reaches into his wallet, pulling out a business card.

"What're you doing?" Darlene asks.

He goes to the phone on the kitchen wall and starts to dial the number on the card. "Calling that FBI agent – Betts. The guy who met with Aaron."

"Shouldn't your first call be the LAPD? Chief Parker's been on the warpath against the mob."

"Betts has been looking to bust Gordo on something that could stick."

"That's fine, but I think you're skipping a step here."

David hangs up the phone and slumps back in his chair. Reaching for the whisky, he and Rae steal knowing glances. He can't tell Darlene the real reason he doesn't want to involve the cops. He's afraid. Afraid that Red will not go quietly into the night. Afraid the hood will trot out Mickey Cohen's shark lawyers and turn the tables on David – lawyers who will work with LAPD dicks or hire their own to find the *real culprit* behind Kitty's disappearance. They'll talk to a homeowner on McCadden who remembers a station wagon idling all night. They'll figure out where it was rented, get a warrant to search the car. They'll track down that drag-queen hooker – "this is *my* block," he'd said. Someone on the road to the desert will have recognized David. That nosy gas attendant who Elron stupidly spewed David's name to. David was pantless and the kid thought they were lovers – of course he'd remember him. They'll dig up witnesses at the Palms, people who heard Kitty's screams, too scared to come out of their rooms but who later saw David and Elron lugging a lumpy rolled-up carpet to the side gate. He would have no alibi either; even his own wife knew he was overnighting at the Palms the night Kitty was last seen alive. The number of ways his case could unravel went well beyond a stray pom-pom from a slipper – they were limitless.

Just when it looks like his ship is sunk, David finds Rae stepping in to right it.

"Maybe we *should* reach out to Agent Betts first," she suggests to Darlene. "He did say to call him if there was anything they could pin on Red to get him behind bars." She looks at David, then back at Darlene. "If murder doesn't qualify, what else would?"

CHAPTER 32

Red Gordo strikes up his second cigarette on the front porch of an unassuming ranch house in Brentwood. His taut canary yellow suit looks like it may burst at the seams trying to contain his anthropoid frame. He alternately crosses and uncrosses his legs, trying to get comfortable on the wrought-iron chair – an impossible task. He's always nervous sitting out here, wondering what sort of feedback awaits him inside as he makes his money drop. Will he be lavished with praise? Excoriated for incompetence? Or a head-spinning combination of both?

Finally, the door creaks open. A diminutive Filipino man-servant named Amado recognizes Red and offers him a pleasant grin. "Mr. Cohen will see you now," he says with a lilting accent.

Red clears some phlegm and snuffs out his cigarette in a clay ashcan. "Thank you, Amado."

He steps through the portal and hands his jacket to the man-servant, then walks into the sunken living room. Its muted beige colors are offset by an explosion of floral patterns to the point of gaudiness. Matching fabrics on the curtains and sofas display red roses crisscrossed by a tangled vine, as if the stalk's creeping tendrils are about to choke out the blooms, an apt metaphor for the city's most feared crime kingpin.

In the middle of the room sits Mickey Cohen. His roly-poly, five-foot-four frame melds into a La-Z-Boy chair. He is draped in a barber's bib, getting a shave, his left hand clutching a rolled-up newspaper. A bald groomer with the look of a sad clown hunches over Mickey's left cheek, scything smooth swaths through the shaving cream with a straight-edge razor.

Cohen cocks open an eye and sees Gordo enter the room. "Hiya, Red."

Gordo nods. "Mr. Cohen." From his back pocket he extracts a sealed envelope overstuffed with a wad of bills. He ritualistically places it on the fireplace mantle.

He moves to the foot of the makeshift barber chair, staying in the gangster's line of vision. He knows from experience not to sit. He is never to sit. Their meetings don't last more than five or ten minutes. Moreover, Mickey prefers to see people standing upright with no hats or jackets – less room to hide things. His paranoia isn't unfounded. Fired at some dozen times in his life, the Mick was once targeted in this very house. Nine years ago, someone from Jack Dragna's outfit blew up his bedroom with thirty sticks of dynamite, leaving a crater twenty feet wide and six feet deep. Cohen wasn't home, but ever since, he feels safer in the living room.

Mickey unfurls a copy of the *Los Angeles Examiner*, smacking his manicured fingers on a small headline that reads "Hollywood Hotel Fire Investigation Continues."

"I'm sure you know about this...?" He hands the paper to Gordo.

Red tries to hide his shock from Mickey, but it's clear from his face this is the first time he's hearing about the fire.

"Isn't that the Shapiro place? What's the story there?"

"The oldest brother – he's the one that won't play ball," Red says, gnashing his teeth. "I'm on him like herpes."

Mickey cackles, his rubbery jowls puffing out like a beach ball. "Oh yeah? You and what army?" His eyes drift shut as the barber towels off excess foam and moves onto the other side of his face. "Times are changing, Red. You heard about this blowhard Bobby Kennedy? Chief counsel to John Kennedy, that horndog senator from Massachusetts they say is gonna be the next president. If he does, he's gonna make his kid brother his Attorney General. Two snot-nosed rich kids trying to make their daddy proud..."

"Washington's a long ways away from here."

"Not anymore. You know what that turncoat Parker did? He gave this Bobby every shred of evidence he could dig up on me. Now I'm being called before a senate committee next month. Me... Hoffa... Giancana... Marcello... they're gonna televise the whole goddamn thing, make a spectacle out of it." He opens his eyes and points to the paper in Gordo's hands. "It's all right there, page two. They're gonna try to get us to rat each other out, bust up the syndicate..."

Gordo flips to page two and sees another headline: "Capitol Hill Subpoenas Mob Bosses." He doesn't much read the fishwraps, reverting to lame platitudes when confronted with inconvenient information.

"Ain't never gonna work," he declares, handing the paper back.

"Then on top of it," Cohen rails, "you got the feds muscling in. You've seen the hard-on they got for us. They're triangulating… the FBI, the LAPD, all these cocksucker politicians." He rocks his fat head back and forth.

"So what's the answer?"

"Guess I just gotta help out some more old ladies," he chuckles. There's a desperation in Cohen's gallows humor, in his stab at past glory. Red has heard the story a million times. The little old lady who got shafted by an electronics shopkeeper repairing her radio – she couldn't afford it, so the man foreclosed on her home – and the Mick getting permission from L.A.'s police chief and mayor to beat the bastard within inches of his life. Then the Mick being heralded in the paper as a "Patron Saint." An illustrator superimposed his face over Snow White's – the gangster with a heart of gold flanked by his equally angelic gangland dwarfs. But that was ten years ago, and such cozy relationships don't exist anymore. The Patron Saint is now Public Nuisance No. 1.

His work done, the groomer lays a hot towel over Mickey's face. Out of nowhere, Amado materializes with Red's jacket, a sign for him to leave. Red follows Mickey's lackey to the front door.

"Hey Red," Cohen calls out, lifting the towel from his mouth. "Whatever happens, just remember to tell 'em you're pleading the fifth."

Red stops, furrowing his unibrow. "The fifth?"

Cohen smirks at his ignorance. "Legalese for no squawking."

"Of course, boss."

After Amado sees him out and shuts the door, Gordo stops on the front porch, closes his eyes and exhales through his sphincter lips. He lumbers down the street to a black Lincoln Continental, where his driver – a young sycophant named Eli – races around to the passenger side and lets him in.

"Where to, boss?" Eli asks.

Red considers heading to Paradise Palms – or, what's left of it. He looked like a horse's ass for not hearing about it before Mickey did. He hadn't been to the Hollywood area for days and only read racing forms, but ignorance is never a good look. Worse, he has a sinking feeling David torched the place with the butane tanks, putting Red on the hook for thousands of dollars.

He abruptly punches the windshield, causing a spiderweb crack. He looks down at his bloodied right knuckle, then, improbably, starts to snicker. "He's a dead man," he simpers. "Dead as all fuck."

Eli turns his gaze to the steering wheel.

Red reaches into the glove box and removes his .38. "Take me to the yard," he orders Eli. "I wanna pick up the turds and end this thing, once and for all."

The Continental screams up Sepulveda Pass to Pacoima. Two blocks from J&M Scrap, Red has Eli slow down. Just the usual precautionary measure, making sure there are no suspicious parked vehicles that may signal an undercover cop.

As they pull into the driveway, Snig opens the security gate. The Lincoln drives through, at which point Snig closes the gate and relocks it. Eli parks the car in front of the kiosk.

Gordo steps out, securing the gun in his waistband. Twenty feet away, Felix tinkers with the bumper of a car that's being tweaked for drug smuggling. Red whistles to get his attention. Felix lifts his head laconically, regarding Red with detached indifference.

"Get over here, I got a job for you," Red hollers. He notices Felix has leashed Sally to the bumper. The dog looks at Red and whines. "Whatcha got my baby on a leash for? We got company?"

Felix turns to look at the junkyard's entrance. Red follows his gaze. Snig is in the process of moving a tractor-trailer in front of the gate, blocking the entire width of the entryway. The truck's air brakes squeal to a stop, its diesel engine still running.

Red marches toward Snig. "What the fuck you doin'?"

Snig jumps out of the cab and immediately puts his hands in the air, as if to surrender. "Sorry, chief, just following instructions."

"*I* give the instructions. Who told you to block the entrance?"

Snig motions with his head behind Red. "They did."

Gordo whirls around. A phalanx of police officers stream out from behind rusted-out vehicles and piles of scrap metal. They approach Red in a V-formation, guns drawn.

"Hands in the air where we can see them!" screams a detective over the roaring truck engine.

Gordo breaks into his little gopher grin, hands glued to his sides. He glances to his right – if he's quick on the draw, he can train his gun on Snig and take him hostage. But Snig is one step ahead of him. Like a scared crab, he scuttles ten feet away behind stacks of oil barrels.

"Hands up or we *will* shoot!" the detective repeats.

The troops start to fan out, encircling Red in the shape of a noose. The standoff grows more tense. Other cops begin to yell at Gordo in fevered pitches, trigger-happy fingers at the ready.

Red stands his ground. In his periphery, he detects movement from behind the oil drums. A man dressed in a polo shirt and khakis, with slicked-back hair and a walrus mustache.

"Agent Kyle Betts, FBI," he shouts, flashing his badge. "This is a joint raid. Party's over, Red."

Red swivels his head toward the agent. The cops seize on the distraction by gang-rushing him, shoving his face in the dirt. The detective stomps on his neck while others cuff his wrists. Red puts up no resistance. An officer gets on his walkie and alerts units. Sally strains against the leash, barking herself hoarse.

"You're under arrest for the murder of Rudolph Shapiro," the detective bleats in Red's ear. He punches his jaw as an exclamation point.

Agent Betts turns to Snig, who has scurried back out from the drums. "Move this thing, would ya?" he says, referring to the truck. "And reopen the gate."

Snig hops back in the cab. The tractor-trailer rumbles forward and clears the driveway. Outside the yard, three black-and-whites screech up to the gate. Snig steps out of the truck and opens it.

Gordo is now on his feet, flanked by two officers leading him on a perp-walk toward the waiting vehicles. Agent Betts follows behind. Red stares daggers at Snig as he shambles past, licking his bloodied lips.

"They came with search warrants," Snig pleads. "They were looking for his body."

Red spits out blood. "So you yapped…"

"They gave me and Felix immunity if we promised to cooperate. You should too. Our days are over, Red."

Gordo yells over his shoulder as he steps onto the street: "Snake-in-the-grass stoolies…. I'll have you iced, you fuckin' turds!"

Red is placed in the backseat of a squad car. Agent Betts comes around to the door. "LAPD will be taking you downtown. After they're done with you, I got a few questions for you myself."

Red scoffs.

"You have anything you wanna say at this time?"

The mobster turns to Betts, his lips curtaining into a one-tooth grin. "Sorry, G-Man... I'm pleadening the fifth."

Betts scowls at his malapropism but understands. He nods once and shuts the door, then stands and watches the police drive Gordo away, as if he must witness his shackled departure with his own eyes to truly believe it. Once it turns the corner, Betts turns and walks the three blocks to his used Olds.

He drives straight to Aaron's house to personally deliver the news about Rudy's murder and Gordo's arrest. But no one answers the bell. He doesn't realize Aaron has moved out, and Peggy and the kids are at the country club. He drives back down the hill and calls David from a pay phone. No one answers his house either. He finally just dials UCLA Medical Center. He knows the brothers frequently visit their father – maybe he'll get lucky and find one of them there.

•   •   •

David is slumped in a chair next to Max's bed, head lolling backward, drool dribbling out of his open mouth. He is zonked to the point of oblivion. It's as if the exhaustive events of the last week have left him as comatose as his father. And so he is heedless to the piercing trill of the patient's heart monitor, which has just started beeping.

It is only when Nurse Tania comes racing in that his eyes snap open and he realizes that Max Shapiro has expired.

CHAPTER 33

"Let us talk about fathers and sons," the rabbi eulogizes.

He is the same portly rabbi with the triangular beard and hexagon glasses who presided over Marta's funeral. Today, in a chapel at the same Mt. Sinai Hollywood Hills cemetery, he stands in front of not one Solomon poplar casket, but two – Max's and Rudy's.

The rabbi glances down at index cards. "For Rudolph Benjamin Shapiro was not just cut from the same cloth as Maximilian Isaac Shapiro. He was his father's most cherished son. The baby Shapiro. Marta's favorite. And no wonder. Rudy possessed many of the same qualities that made Max so endearing. Each shared a love of the good life – an appreciation of fine spirits, the thrill of a friendly wager…" A pregnant pause. "The company of the fairer sex..."

Gentle laughter ripples through the forty-plus attendees. The first row is occupied by immediate family – David, Leo, Aaron, Rae, Darlene and Rochelle, all with black ribbons on their garments. When the tittering lasts longer than David thinks it should, he turns around to locate the source of it – Rudy's pals, manning the back rows.

"They were unapologetic romantics," says the rabbi, "each willing to spend his last nickel on a friend instead of on himself."

Leo leans into David and deadpans, "Some would call that irresponsible."

David smirks.

The rabbi eyeballs David and Leo. "At times, Rudy tried Max's patience – as he did his brothers'. But you couldn't stay mad at Rudy forever. Rudy had a big heart. And people who lead by their hearts and not their heads – like children or sheep straying from the flock – are the ones most in need of a shepherd."

Knowing nods from the assembled, a few sniffles.

"What d'you think," David whispers to Leo, in reference to notes he gave the rabbi, "did I lay it on too thick?"

"No, it's perfect 'cause it's true."

"Max understood that about his youngest son," the rabbi resumes. "Theirs was a covenant that mirrored that of God and Abraham. God had instructed Abraham to serve Him, as the son serves the father. And in return, God would protect him, as the father protects the son. But the father grew old, no longer in a position to protect his progeny. We will never fully understand the ways in which God works. But it was God's will that when Maximilian was on his death bed, Rudolph was to follow."

A somber silence. Aaron looks over his shoulder and finds Peggy, alone in the third row in a stunning black number. Her eyes brim with tears.

"Max may be gone from the earthly realm, but what a legacy he leaves." The rabbi's roving eyes alight on the front row. "Three sons – David, Leon and Aaron – and…" His eyes rest on Rae, then drift over her. "Three gorgeous grandchildren – Jolene, Billy and Nancy, with a fourth on the way! And of course, his loving older sister, Rochelle."

David feels his cheeks burn with anger. He had gone over the talking points with the rabbi ad infinitum. Rae was a member of the family and was to be acknowledged as such, just as there was to be no mention of Abigail Schlebercoff.

The rabbi continues his thread. "Max's legacy also included the Paradise Palms hotel. It employed countless people, provided for his family, sheltered the destitute, and served the greater Hollywood community for decades – making the world a better place and thus fulfilling the second covenant between God and Abraham. Who ever thought a street urchin from the slums of Chicago would amount to anything?" The rabbi whips off his glasses for effect. "*Marta* did. Now they're finally joined together again… this time for all eternity, with God's help – *Be-ez-rat Ha-shem*." He pauses. "Amen."

The gallery responds "Amen."

The rest of the funeral proceeds with the usual customs – the separation of the family, the procession to the gravesite, a final Psalm prayer. Max's interment abuts Marta's burial site. Rudy is placed next to Max. The brothers are handed shovels to lay the symbolic first piles of earth on the caskets. They do so deliberately and wordlessly.

As the guests file to their cars to attend the reception, David spots a man standing on the roadway, observing the proceedings from a distance. He has slicked-back hair and a mustache. Aaron walks ahead of David and shakes the man's hand. David follows.

"David, this is Agent Betts," Aaron says, introducing the two.

David smiles. "I figured that must be you. You didn't look like one of Rudy's friends and you're too young to be one of Pop's."

"I'm really sorry about your losses," Betts intones to the brothers. "I just came to pay my respects."

"We appreciate that," says Aaron.

"Thank you for working with the LAPD to finally nab Gordo," says David.

Betts grimaces. "Just working our way up the chain to Mickey." He puts a hand on David's shoulder. "Hey, uh, can I get a word with you?"

David looks at Aaron, shrugs. "Sure."

The agent takes them to a secluded walkway behind a grove of cypress trees. "I have it on good authority what your brother's last words were from one of Red's associates – the one they call Snig. Thought you might be curious since it concerns you."

David's jaw goes rigid. "Look, we didn't get along for most of our lives. So everything he says, you have to – "

"Oh no… no, this is positive."

David eyes him warily but lets him go on.

"Snig said Red had a hit on you. Rudy stood up to him. He said 'Leave my brother out of this,' or something to that effect. Actually tried to shoot him. Snig heard and saw the whole thing."

Betts notices David now seems to be staring *through* him, not at him, as if Betts is not even there.

"Anyway," Betts says, bowing his head, "that's when Gordo, uh…." He pats David's arm – "You take care of yourself" – and leaves. David keeps staring into space.

• • •

The funeral reception is held at Sportsmen's Lodge, a pastoral Valley resort with wooden bridges and man-made streams popular with the Hollywood set. The Shapiros have rented a small banquet hall with windows opening onto a small pond with gliding swans. Guests help themselves to food out of silver serving trays and to wine, beer and sodas from a beverage cart. Several mourners congregate around collages of Max and Rudy, set up on twin easels.

Leo breaks away from a group to refill his plate. He sidles up to David. "You see the stains on this tablecloth?" he carps, pointing to numerous grease spots.

"The halibut was fishy," David gripes. "Tasted old. I had 'em take it back." He glares at Rudy's chums loading up on beers. "Most people are here for the booze anyway. Kinda like The Easy."

Leo looks at David for a long beat. "You miss it?"

"What, running a restaurant?"

"The whole thing. The Palms."

David's brain does not have the capacity for nostalgia. Not now. He is still replaying Betts's chilling comment that Rudy died for David. "It served its purpose," he replies limply. "It was time for a change."

Across the room, Peggy is saying her goodbyes to a small party that includes Aaron. She catches sight of David and Leo and gives them a terse wave. Aaron goes in for a kiss, but she dodges his lips, brushing past him. Aaron watches her waltz through the exit. He heads to the beverage cart, snags a bottle of white wine on ice, and joins his brothers.

"Was it something we said?" Leo cracks.

"She has to go get the kids from her mother's." Aaron's eyes linger on the exit. "I don't think we'll be getting back together."

David and Leo look at him with surprise. Aaron himself seems taken aback, as if he is only now realizing it.

"I'd like to stick together for the kids, but Peggy won't hear of it," he sighs. "What we have is deeper than your normal marital discord." His eyebrows slope inward. "Frankly, she's disgusted by me."

"Oh come on… it can't be *that* bad," Leo says.

"She says I'm living in sin." He bends back the bottle for a fortifying slug of wine, looks at David. "Remember in the hospital when I said Gordo made threats against me unless we told him Kitty's whereabouts? He had been following me. Claimed to have photos of me with certain… men I knew."

Aaron pauses to assess his brothers' reactions. Their faces give nothing away.

"*Rudy* tipped him off," he continues. "Somewhere our brother's yukking it up right now. But you know what? Something good came out of it. It forced me to stop living a lie." He takes another drink. "Anyway, if I'm taking a vow of honesty, you might as well know about it…"

There's a long gap before David says quietly, "We're here for you, brother."

"Anything we can do," adds Leo. "You want us to talk to Peggy? There's gotta be some way she'd take you back. People stay married for all sorts of reasons. It doesn't always have to be out of love."

"Oh, I *love* her," Aaron maintains. "And I want to stay married. But the only way she said she'd take me back is if I got into… conversion therapy." He shivers at the phrase. "I told her I'd rather keep living in sin than living a lie."

Aaron and his bottle saunter off.

David once again feels like he's been kicked in the teeth. Poor goddamn Aaron. *Gordo made threats against me unless we told him Kitty's whereabouts.* David had a plan – an air-tight, best-laid plan – all worked out in his head. Now it was putrefying like maggots burrowing into his psyche.

• • •

With the reception winding down, Aaron cruises the hallway outside the banquet hall, admiring its photographs of John Wayne, Bette Davis and Humphrey Bogart fishing in the lodge's lakes. The bottle in his hand is almost empty. From the far-end of the hall, Rae has just left the ladies' room. Aaron is standing between her and the reception – an encounter is inevitable. He turns toward her and squares his shoulders.

"That was bullshit that the rabbi didn't mention you today," he steams. "That was his choice, not ours."

Rae shrugs. "I have no expectations."

"Well, in light of that, you're in luck… because I'm in a confessional mood this evening." He flashes a devil-may-care grin. "I've been a real shit toward you."

"No…"

"Yes. And I just wanted you to know it had nothing to do with you, and everything to do with me. Self-loathing works in mysterious ways." His smile vanishes as he taps into a strain of deep sincerity buried beneath strata of cynicism. "Truth is, I've always thought the world of you, Rae. I really have. I wish I had your quiet strength, and maybe I've just been a little jealous. Okay, a lot jealous. You're like a palm tree… you bend but don't break." He toasts her with his bottle. "A real Paradise Palm, as it were."

She rolls her eyes and grins.

Aaron, summoning more saccharine: "Y'know, Marta always wanted a daughter. She told me that once. I think that's why she doted on Rudy so much. She knew he'd be the last one and she treated him like a little kewpie doll." His eyes moisten. "She would've liked you. You're more like her than Pop, isn't that something? In fact, you and me are more alike than any of my brothers…"

"Outcasts, huh?" She eyes a path around Aaron.

"No no, that's not at all what I mean," he says. He leans into her with a conspiratorial grin. "They're *common*. But we've got *style*." He puts his finger to his lips. "Shhh. We don't wanna insult their bad taste."

Rae saves Aaron from himself by snatching his bottle and gulping the last of the wine. Aaron staggers back, happy as a clam.

"You and I should go clothes shopping," she suggests, wiping her lips. "I hear you get your suits in Beverly Hills."

Aaron's eyes light up. "There's some wonderful discount stores south of Wilshire that are fun to rummage around in. Probably within your budget."

"I'd like that." She smiles earnestly and shoves the empty bottle back in Aaron's hands.

Back in the banquet hall, David and Leo see off the remaining guests, including their Aunt Rochelle and her doormat fourth husband, Uncle Philip.

"It was a beautiful sermon, if a little long," Rochelle says, a bit pickled, which means she's feisty. "Why was there no mention of Abigail?"

Philip tries to guide her out the door but she begs off.

"Why hasn't anyone found her yet? She was your father's wife, y'know. Now she's a widow and doesn't even know it."

"She left *Pop*, Aunt Rochelle," David emphasizes.

"You need to find her and you need to tell her her husband is *dead*."

"What if she doesn't want to be found?"

"Hire a private detective. Like that Mike Hammer on TV."

"That's a fictional show created by Mickey Spillane, Aunt Rochelle," Leo says.

"I don't mean *him*, but someone like him. He's always finding missing persons."

Aaron runs into Rochelle as he comes back into the room. He tells his aunt he loves her and David and Leo do the same, the group bonding one last time over the terrible double tragedy that has befallen the family. Once she and Philip are scooted out, Aaron slings his arms around his brothers and draws them in.

"Let's blow this place. It depresses me," he says.

"And go where?" Leo asks.

"Where else?"

• • •

It is only once they're on the road that the boys really let down their guard in a way they never could at the funeral. Coasting down the Hollywood Freeway in the open-air Bel Air – David behind the wheel, Leo in the passenger seat, an inebriated Aaron in the back – they engage in verbal jousting, one-upping each other with outrageous yarns involving Max or Rudy laced with liberal doses of hyperbole. By the time the car exits Highland Avenue, they are laughing through doleful tears.

Pulling up to the Paradise Palms site, the good cheer evaporates, as if someone just popped a helium balloon. The first thing they notice is the neon hotel sign. Portions of the sheet metal have melted in ways that would make Salvador Dali beam. Behind a temporary chain-link fence – hastily put up by the fire department – lie the crumbling charred husks that used to be the front-half of the hotel. Without ambient lighting, there is now only an unsettling dark void that stretches the entire block. Two hookers swagger past the Bel Air, sniffing out the boys' intentions like wild cheetahs tracking game before moving on.

Aaron, cradling another wine bottle, grabs a flashlight from his car and the trio slips through a hole in the fence. As they meander through the spectral remains, Aaron says to David, "I sure as hell hope we cash out on this..."

"We will," David states unconvincingly.

"And if we don't?"

David doesn't answer. He commandeers Aaron's flashlight, his attention diverted by a giant hole in the ground. He squints into the murky crater and finds the former basement. Thanks to the principle of rising heat, the subterranean room is surprisingly well-preserved. He has an unexpected urge to leap in there and root around, as if doing so could provide clues to the man who committed murder within its walls. When Aaron and Leo join him at its rim, David pivots and walks away.

The brothers cross the old courtyard and swimming pool – now a sludgy pit of ash, burnt timber and fire-retardant chemicals – toward the remaining wings. Vandals have spray-painted the walls and bashed in a few windows.

"Animals," Aaron spits.

David comes at it from a different place. Good riddance, he thinks. Good riddance to this place and the hellhole that Hollywood has become.

Nonetheless, the boys forage through the rooms, picking through ephemera, a midnight scavenger hunt to preserve memories. They end their survey in Room 1 – still locked and one of the few units untouched by trespassers. Aaron gleefully kicks in the window and hops inside to open the door. David and Leo walk in.

Abigail had started changing the décor in anticipation of Max's move to Sylvan Gardens but mementos linger. There on the wet bar, his box of Havana cigars. Over here on the bookcase, the red boxing gloves from Max Baer. Though other family photos were taken down, one still remains: the eight-by-ten of Max leaning in the doorway of his floral shop at the Hollywood Hotel with tykes David, Leo and Aaron. Laying eyes on it, David gets a lump in his throat. He unhooks the frame from the wall as a keepsake. Meanwhile, Aaron and Leo have discovered their dad's collection of fedoras – still neatly stacked the way he liked it. Each helps himself to his favorite hat.

The brothers leave the room newly crowned.

CHAPTER 34

David kneels on the carpet in his living room, adjusting the rabbit ears of his brand-new RCA color television set. When he gets it to its optimal position, the static fades and reveals genial Buffalo Bob and his freckle-faced marionette, Howdy Doody, entertaining a nationwide audience of wide-eyed kiddies since 1947. Slouching against the coffee table to monitor the picture, David looks older than his thirty-six years. Twenty months have elapsed since the dual funeral. His wavy black hair is flecked with gray, his square jaw starting to sag. His physique, once taut and muscular, has grown soft around the middle, and instead of nice threads, he's slumming it in sweatpants and a frayed T-shirt.

A giggling, cooing sound draws his attention. M.J., wearing only a diaper, is bouncing up and down in his playpen, his chubby little arms flailing with delight at the sight of Howdy Doody. David smiles. He crawls over and wiggles his fingers at his fifteen-month-old son through the slats of his pen.

"You like that in 'living color,' huh?" he chirps. "Yeah, I do too!"

David turns up the volume for M.J., then settles back against the coffee table, letting the show's dream-like ditties and puppetry wash over him. He finds its childlike merriment soothing, a balm for his frayed adult circuitry. Besides, every time he flips on the news, something bad is happening. Just last month, the Soviets padded their insurmountable lead in the Space Race. Sputnik 5 became the first rocket to launch living creatures into orbit and return them safely back to Earth. Canine cosmonauts Belka and Strelka were more popular than Lassie.

By all outward appearances – on the heels of the fire and his family members' deaths – David has "won." In March of '59, Vance "Red" Gordo was found guilty of murder in the first-degree. As part of a plea bargain, Snig and Felix became informants. It was revealed that the recycled 55-gallon oil barrels on Gordo's property were harboring drugs and contraband. And, most dramatically: Rudy. He was found in not one – but two – of the drums. The apprentices testified that when Red told them to stuff Rudy's cadaver in a barrel, he didn't account for their 33-inch height. So they used a hacksaw to sever his body above his pelvis. The two halves were found in separate barrels along the back of the property. The goons were awaiting Red's instructions as to where to bury the drums but the raid happened before they could roll them off the lot.

A month later, in a second trial, Gordo was found guilty of eleven federal crimes. He was condemned to Alcatraz Federal Penitentiary – the same bleak "Rock" where Mickey Cohen would soon end up – bringing his total sentence to life plus forty. During the discovery process, it was proven that Gordo was storing illegal, non-safety-certified butane tanks on Paradise Palms property. Rae was called as a witness, confirming that she had, on her own, instructed Rudy to move the tanks off the property. Snig and Felix – who continued cooperating with Betts to counter their mile-long rap sheets – corroborated Rae's story. They had helped Rudy move the tanks into the hotel's storage. Even if they wanted to, Red's associates couldn't move them out – not without Red's say-so – and he wasn't saying so. To do otherwise would be to invite death.

Thus, David's gambit ultimately worked. A fire marshal surmised that an electrical problem sparked the tanks. Even more important, Mutual Liberty was now aware of Gordo's complicity. The insurance company ruled, somewhat stingily, that their arson investigation was "inconclusive." Defaulting to the terms of the agreement, they deemed the business a total loss. The settlement money was used to pay off the Shapiros' bank to satisfy outstanding loans, leaving $127,000 for the family. Abigail never materialized in probate court to claim a share, so, as Max's legitimate heirs, David, Leo and Aaron were awarded equal amounts. Each then disbursed ten percent of their portions to Rae and two percent to Aunt Rochelle. As a final fuck-you, Gordo never did see a penny of the $50,000 he was trying to extort from the brothers Shapiro.

For David, the biggest triumph came on June 18, 1959. Maximilian Jonathan Shapiro entered this world a bruiser at ten pounds, two ounces. Everyone agreed he had his mother's eyes and his father's mulish temperament. Other than a brief spell of post-partum depression, Darlene took to motherhood like a duck to water. Every afternoon, she and other new moms would push their carriages around their Studio City neighborhood – parks, shops, restaurants and a movie theater all within easy walking distance.

It took David a little longer to warm up to fatherhood. He felt he didn't deserve his blessed wife and child, and could feel the constant, steady thrum of guilt in the back of his head like a heartbeat. Darlene found him distant and detached much of the time, misreading his self-flagellation for disinterest. David would rally in these moments. Once again, he found himself playing a role, that of a loving father and husband. Once again, it was exhausting work to wear a façade that masked who he really was inside. It was bad enough that he took another's life, though he could *almost* explain that away knowing Kitty and Gordo were intending to take Pop's. What was unforgivable were the things that came after that – the chain-reactions to David's actions. Elron's fatal overdose. Rudy's murder. The dissolution of Aaron's family. What was the point of this great life if it meant living a great lie and harboring great regrets? He had not avoided prison after all; he was simply living it in his own body – a body eaten alive from the inside out by those cursed maggots, aging him two years to everyone else's one.

Presently, Darlene enters the living room to check on M.J., a sexy mom in a sleeveless top and capri pants. Her hair is now styled in a cute bob, her jet-black mane traded in for her natural chestnut brown pushed up by a headband. She crinkles her nose at David.

"Don't you smell that?"

He pries his eyes away from the TV and gawks at her. "What?"

"This stinkbug," she says, lifting M.J. out of his playpen. She peeks into his diaper and pulls her face away. "Ooooof. How long has *this* been sitting in here?"

Darlene and M.J. disappear down the hallway, leaving David to mainline more *Howdy Doody*. Thanks to repeated daily viewings delivered straight into his living room, Howdy's friends – Flub-A-Dub, Sandra the Witch, Chief Thunderthud and Mayor Phineas T. Bluster – almost feel like his own friends. And so he is devastated to learn from host Buffalo Bob that today – *this very show* – will be the last *Howdy Doody* show ever.

"Howdy, Clarabelle, Mr. Clown and I – the whole gang – would like to thank you boys and girls of all ages for watching this show all these thirteen years," Bob croons to the camera and his studio audience. "Kids, you've been wonderful. Perhaps someday we'll come your way and you'll hear us again say 'Howdy Do.'"

David leans into the TV, locking his hands on the walnut cabinet. One by one, Howdy's cast of characters come up to Buffalo Bob to bid farewell, set to the twinkling strains of a sad music-box song. "There's no more show, it's time to go. Goodbye from us to you," says Howdy.

With only a minute left in the program, Buffalo Bob brings up his final guest – Clarabell the Clown, noisily bleating his toy horn. Apparently, he has a surprise. Thanks to some interpretative honking, Clarabell, who hasn't uttered a word in thirteen years, reveals that he can *talk*.

"Golly, I don't believe it!" Bob effuses. "Let's hear you say something!"

The band strikes up a drum roll. The camera pushes into the clown's blinking face, staring directly at the lens. David hovers inches from the monitor, *riveted*.

The drums and zoom-in abruptly stop. David holds his breath. Clarabell's quivering lips part. Out come two immortal words.

"Goodbye, kids," he says in a thin and trembling voice.

As the screen fades to black, children in the studio audience can be heard weeping.

David collapses in front of the screen. An idiophone version of "Auld Lang Syne" plays over the scrolling end-credits, an epitaph to the end of innocence. David bursts into tears and howls – deep guttural cries like a mortally wounded animal – and fetals up in front of the television.

Darlene races into the living room. The sight of her uncontrollably sobbing husband alarms her. He appears to be having a nervous breakdown. "David?" she bays. "David!"

But nothing can penetrate his wailing. The emotional dam has burst open, and David is powerless to stop its flood of honest tears.

CHAPTER 35

The roadside neon sign blinks the colors of a candy cane to passing hungry motorists. "Paradise Café – C'mon In!" it beckons in a jaunty red scrawl, with a white arrow pointing toward the entrance.

Unlike the bastardized "Paradise Palms" sign, this one was custom-made to fit the exact look the boys and Rae had in mind. Gone are the days of carrying their father's water – or Red Gordo's. This idea was one-hundred percent theirs. Pooling their insurance money, the siblings paid all-cash to design, build and open the restaurant. With Rae running the kitchen – in between taking classes at Valley College – Glynda happily accepted the role of day-to-day manager after McDaniel's announced it would be closing on December 31, 1962. Their other big hire was a general manager with extensive restaurant experience to oversee the entire operation. No more winging it, as with The Easy.

Word quickly caught on when Paradise opened its doors two months ago. This was good, honest cooking at a fair price. And the location couldn't be beat. It sat on the same quarter-acre plot Leo had acquired four years ago for a song – near the Valencia Boulevard exit off a newly-opened stretch of I-5.

The dining room's capacity is small, accommodating only thirty-two, including eight seats at the counter. But to-go orders make up half of total sales. Contractors working on the freeway swing through three times a day. Fathers on their way home from work "down under" – Los Angeles – pick up dinner for their wives and two-point-five children waiting in their sparkling new Phase I Valencia homes. House specialties include standard diner fare plus Rae's Famous Shrimp Louie Salad and a rotating menu of delicious desserts. A local weekly dubbed it the best "home-cooking" in the Santa Clarita Valley next to Saugus Café.

Today Glynda is ringing up a hard-hatted construction worker, inviting him to come again. Rae and her line cooks – all McDaniel's alumni – are visible in the kitchen behind her. It's the drowsy hours between lunch and dinner. The only three customers are the Shapiro boys. While Aaron and Leo have polished off lemon merengue pie, David's slice remains untouched.

Aaron is absorbed in the morning edition of the *Los Angeles Times*, dated January 5, 1963. Tilting back his coffee cup, David notices a blue-star sapphire ring adorning Aaron's pinky finger. He's never seen that before.

"Mariner 2 is officially dead," Aaron pronounces. "It stopped transmitting two days ago."

Leo is busy unfurling two tract maps across the table. "I heard it got within twenty-one thousand miles of Venus."

"Whoop-de-doo," David sneers. "The Russians passed by Venus almost two years ago. They're kicking our ass at everything. They'll probably be on the moon by '65."

Aaron folds back the paper with an impish grin. "Hey, how do you know when the moon has had enough to eat?"

David considers this. "When it's full."

"No fair, you heard that one!"

"No I didn't, it's an obvious pun. And a pretty lame one at that."

Leo, jumping in: "So are we just gonna bust each other's balls all day, or are we gonna make a decision on these lots?"

"Can't we do both?" Aaron asks.

"Remind us again what you're proposing," David says, vigorously rubbing his temples as if to spark the neurons in his brain.

"Our lots in the Valley have doubled in value in ten years," Leo explains, "but as Aaron says, the Valley's oversaturated. I say we sell high…" He points to a quadrant on the map. "Unload our four lots in Canoga Park… use that money as down payment to build nearby…"

He places a Santa Clarita Valley tract map over the San Fernando Valley one. "When they subdivided Valencia, all they cared about were homeowners. What about renters? Where're you gonna house the busboys, the gardeners, the domestics, the drywallers – all the blue-collar folks you need to build a planned community?" He points to two rectangular lots, answering his own question. "Here. I think there's enough room for two fourplexes. But I want you guys to check it out, let me know if you think I'm out of my mind or not."

Aaron gives a crooked smile. "While we're at it, they're gonna need a good hotel around here at some point, especially if they put in that amusement park they've been buzzing about."

"Ha ha," Leo says drolly.

"I'm *out* of the hospitality business," insists David with an emphatic wave, his muddled mind incapable of distinguishing nuance.

As Leo rolls up the maps, he looks at his brothers, asking the question they all ask each other from time to time. "Been by there lately?"

"Darlene has," David says. "There's a sign there that says 'Future site of mini-mall.'"

Aaron scowls. "What's a '*mini*-mall'?"

"You mean like Minnie Mouse?" Leo asks. "Like a shopping mall selling Disney shit?"

David, shaking his head: "No no – 'mini.' M-I-N-I. Short for miniature, I guess. Like mini-golf."

Aaron and Leo exchange bemused expressions.

"Who's gonna pay to see a scale-size replica of a shopping mall unless it was part of a miniatures museum or something?" Aaron puzzles.

"It'll never take," Leo concludes, and that is that.

The brothers gather their belongings and head over to the counter to grab toothpicks. Glistening from the hot stove, Rae emerges from the kitchen to pour herself a tall glass of cold seltzer water.

Glynda leaves the register and cups her hand on David's cheek. "A little stork told me you may have new company in the house again…"

David looks at Leo, who flushes, then back at Glynda. "I'm afraid it's true."

Glynda laughs. "How far along?"

"Four months."

"Well, God bless. If you need some looking-after when the baby comes, I'm just a hop, skip and a jump away… You know I love the little bundles."

"Thank you." Then, addressing the whole group: "Actually, we're looking to put our house on the market. Move down to the Long Beach area, where we – "

"Wait, what?" Leo says.

"Yeah, when did you decide this?" Aaron asks.

David shrugs. "Darlene wants to be closer to her parents."

"Well, with two young 'uns, that might not be a bad idea," Glynda offers.

Rae cocks her head, confused. "Didn't you tell me you were thinking of moving to... Phoenix, was it?"

David grimaces. He can feel his siblings' hard, questioning stares. "Still in the cards, but..." He pauses. "Maybe after Long Beach, depending on how that goes... I don't know." And it's true. David doesn't know. All he knows is he needs to get the fuck out of L.A., and maybe California, and maybe even farther away yet, and is looking for any excuse to do it.

"What the hell is in Phoenix?" Leo clacks. "It's like a hundred fifty-eight degrees in the summer."

"Cheaper to raise a family there," David proffers.

"But what would you *do* there – buy a dude ranch?"

"Have you ever been on a horse in your life?" Aaron asks.

"I can see it now," Leo jeers, "David 'Rawhide' Shapiro, legendary Jewish rustler." Aaron punches Leo in the shoulder, the two of them collapsing in fits of amusement.

Rae, covering her mouth, also starts to giggle. David stares at them, unblinking.

"What're you sassing about?" Glynda says to Leo. "Don't you all have some lots to look at?"

"Yes," Leo says, wiping tears from his eyes.

"Then get the hell out of my restaurant!"

Leo playfully salutes Glynda, and he and the boys pivot toward the exit.

Once outside, they crunch through the gravel parking lot toward Aaron's Bel Air, which they all rode in to get here. The afternoon sun is sandblast-hot, the cloudless sky a brilliant shade of blue. Leo and Aaron are just about to the car when they realize David is not with them. Turning around, they find him hanging back by the restaurant's entrance.

"What gives?" Aaron shouts out.

David looks lost, almost panicked, like someone who misplaced his car keys. But he can't begin to explain to his brothers what it is that's missing.

"You know what... you guys go without me," he finally says. "You don't need me."

"Are you sure?" Leo says.

David nods. "I trust your judgment." He shifts his feet restlessly.

"Well, where're you gonna be?"

"I'll be here. In the dining room." He forces a grin. "Maybe I'll polish off that pie." Even though his smile pushes out his cheeks, there is no flicker in his eyes, not even a squint in the harsh sunlight. They have simply become small black marbles – rigid, glassy, lifeless.

Aaron and Leo look at each other with mild concern.

Leo turns back to David – "We'll let you know what we think" – but his words fall on deaf ears. David has already turned his back on them, passing through the doors of Paradise.

About the Author

Paul Haddad is a Los Angeles Times Bestselling Author and multiple-Emmy nominated television writer/producer. *Paradise Palms: Red Menace Mob*, his third novel, was inspired by dark family secrets that coincided with his obsession with old Hollywood. Also the author of several nonfiction books about L.A., he can found at www.paulhaddadbooks.com and on Twitter: @la_dorkout.

Note from the Author

Word-of-mouth is crucial for any author to succeed. If you enjoyed *Paradise Palms*, please leave a review online—anywhere you are able. Even if it's just a sentence or two. It would make all the difference and would be very much appreciated.

Thanks!
Paul Haddad

Thank you so much for checking out one of our **Noir Fiction** novels. If you enjoy the experience, please check out our recommended title for your next great read!

Twist of Fate – A Jack West Novel by Deanna King

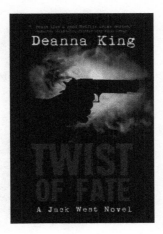

"...reads like a good *Netflix* crime series." –**Samantha Calimbahin,** *Panther City Media Group*